The year is 1862.
The South is winning.
And in the long
valleys of Virginia,
men and women together
taste the majesty and
bitterness of war...

In a beautiful blend of fact and fiction,

CONFEDERATES

offers a picture at once dramatic and ironic of
the poor white soldiers who formed the heart
of the Confederate Army, and of the women
who loved them. Set in 1862, at the floodtide
of Southern hopes, it reaches its stirring cli-
max at Antietam. Thomas Keneally evokes
the cruel conflicts of the war, its victories and
tragedies, with a breathtaking grandeur that
will grip the reader from the first page to the
last.

Confederates

THOMAS KENEALLY

BERKLEY BOOKS, NEW YORK

This Berkley book contains the complete
text of the original hardcover edition.
It has been completely reset in a type face
designed for easy reading, and was printed
from new film.

CONFEDERATES

A Berkley Book / published by arrangement with
Harper & Row

PRINTING HISTORY
Harper & Row edition / September 1980
Berkley edition / December 1981

ISBN: 0-425-05057-2

A BERKLEY BOOK ® TM 757,375
Berkley Books are published by Berkley Publishing Corporation,
200 Madison Avenue, New York, New York 10016.
PRINTED IN THE UNITED STATES OF AMERICA

Prologue

IN THE SECOND year of the war, Mrs. Ephephtha Bumpass saw her husband Usaph unexpectedly one cold March night. This happened way over in the great Valley of Virginia on a night of bitter frost. Usaph had come knocking on the door of the Bumpass family farm near the fine town of Strasburg and, when the door opened, he was the last person she expected to see.

At the time, she was sitting at the kitchen hearth with the old slave Lisa and the fourteen-year-old boy of a neighbor called Travis. Mr. Travis had lent her the boy to do chores for her and to keep her company. Ephie Bumpass had been married some sixteen months up to that point and had lived all those sixteen months on this highland farm in the shadow of Massanutten Mountain. But Bumpass had met and wooed her in a very different country from this. She'd been raised down in the Carolinas, in the torpid swamps round the mouth of the Combahee River. Her father had been a drum fisherman there and it was all the world she knew till Usaph brought her up here to Virginia.

On that March night in the second year of the war, before Usaph got to the door and knocked on it, Ephie had been finding the sight of the Travis boy there by the fire distressing. It reminded her of what Travis, neighbor to the Bumpasses, had said to her when he assigned her the boy. "I'll send my boy to chop the wood an' keep you company. For whatever else you need you can call on me." Saying it he'd touched her wrist in a way you couldn't misunderstand. "You are a rose, Mrs. Bumpass. You are a red rose up here in this valley of lilies. Are you perhaps one of them Creoles or some such?"

Travis's hints weren't any comfort to her. She knew men wanted her, men always had, bargemen and fishermen and parties of gentry her daddy used to take out drum fishing in his boat. Usaph's *own* uncle, overseer on the Kearsage place

1

down in the Carolinas, while sickening for his death, had
desired and had her—in spite of the state of his health—before
she ever met Usaph. That fact and others stung her soul like
a tumor. It would be hard to say where she got the idea that
to be wanted was to be the bearer of a disease. Her daddy had
sometimes taken river wives who all talked as if to be desired
was the best and only fate a woman could wish. Up to that
night in the second year of the war, the only man who had
ever wanted her without making her feel accursed was Usaph
Bumpass. The war she saw as a case of God making her pay
for the sweetness and redemption that came to her in Usaph's
presence—as simple as that. There wasn't anything in her life
history to put that idea in her head either, the idea about having
to pay. She was just born with it.

And so she sat by the fire of the Bumpass family farm which
she'd only known these sixteen months since she'd wed Bumpass, and all she had to sit with was deaf old Lisa and the boy,
and out in a corner of a nearby meadow Usaph's father, Mr.
Noah Bumpass, dead a year, slept under the frosted earth. And
her womb, as on each quiet evening, wept for Bumpass.

When Usaph Bumpass knocked on the door that night it
sounded such a flat neighborly knocking that she didn't expect
anything of it, and so sent the fourteen-year-old to answer it.
There was Bumpass standing in the doorway. He wore a waterproof blanket over his shoulders, and his long musket hit
sharply against the door jamb. Both his hair and his skin looked
like the smoke of all the fires he'd sat at these past few months
had changed them for good.

She couldn't believe this gift that had turned up on her
doorstep. Old Lisa, who still had a clear head at that stage,
recognized the boy she'd known from babyhood and began to
laugh and praise God in a withered voice. "Why, I jest knew
the Lord would give these poor ole bones one sight more of
the boy," she sang. And in the doorway Usaph and Ephie
crushed each other and chewed at each other's lips for a full
minute. The fourteen-year-old thought it was a fine thing to
watch.

"Well," Ephie said in the end, with snatches of breath.
"Well . . . how come you here, Usaph?" She ran a finger down
the fraying edge of his jacket and over the coarse-stitched blue
patches on his collar.

"It's cos of Winchester, Ephie."

"Winchester?"

"Winchester's gone, Ephie."

"Winchester?" she repeated. It was but a morning's ride north of Strasburg.

"When we left this morning," said Usaph, "there was people weeping in the streets. But there ain't no avoiding it. Them Yankees are over to Berryville and they're over the Ridge as well."

Ephie looked about the kitchen as if the enemy could be expected to turn up here at any moment.

"No, no," Usaph said, laughing at her. "Them Lincoln boys has a need to rest at night, same as us mortals."

Jackson's army, he told her, was settled down for the night some three or four miles up the road, in the cold meadows astride the Valley turnpike. Usaph had just gone up and had a talk to his officer, a pleasant dentist called Guess, and had explained how his wife was on her own at Strasburg, no male slave to help her out, no Bumpass senior, only a sick old slave woman. He'd said he wanted to help her put the horse in the dray and to set her traveling southwards towards his Aunt Sarrie Muswell's in Bath County.

So Guess had let him go, but said he had to take a reliable man with him. That was pretty wise of Guess. A husband might decide to stay with his wife and ride with her all the way south. But the husband's friend would say, no you can't do that, you must get back to camp.

"Why," said Usaph, remembering, "I fetched my friend Mr. Gus Ramseur along with me." He pointed out into the dark by the woodpile.

"Good evening, Mrs. Bumpass," called Gus in his half-Dutchy accent. She saw Gus's quiet grin, and his greeting steamed up into the cold air. She could tell he was a gentleman and a scholar, like Usaph said in his letters.

"Why, come in, Mr. Ramseur. Usaph's told me a heap about your cleverness."

Gus entered the kitchen, walking dainty as a dancer past the couple in the doorway. And now Usaph came in properly, setting his musket against the butter churn so that the door could be closed and the perilous night kept out.

Ephie surveyed Gus Ramseur, who even in his dirty clothes and his stained state moved and stood like a man who was used to working indoors. Orderly little steps. Ephie thought he was a fine friend for her spouse, the sort of friend Usaph deserved.

The old slave still sat with her mouth agape, grinning, her hand up palm-outwards to touch either of the soldiers. Gus Ramseur nodded towards her. She made one of those strange black noises no white could ever fully understand.

"I met ole Travis in town," Usaph told Ephie. "There's a big crowd at Main and Bank, discussing all the rumors—and Travis is among 'em. They goddam quizzed Gus and me, I can tell you that much. Ain't it so, Gus? They quizzed us?"

"You got profane in that-there army, my love," said Ephie. But then she laughed.

"Travis says he ain't leaving Strasburg no matter if the armies of Hell arrive. He says he'll mind our hogs and the milch cow—and he will, he'll do it for the memory of my daddy. . . ."

"Mind the hogs, Usaph? I bin minding the hogs like they was Christian souls. . . ."

"I ain't complaining of your care for my pigs, darlin' Ephie. But I mean to put you on the road for Aunt Sarrie's and you're to tell her that as she loved her brother and as she loves me her nephew, she's to care for you. . . ."

"This-here house?" Ephie said, still standing, still held by Usaph. She put out her hand and touched the hot stonework of the house. "This-here house?" she asked again in a voice he could only pity.

For Ephie had a crazy idea of the Bumpass house. It was nothing more than a white frame farm dwelling of the kind you find every two hundred paces up and down the Valley. But it was more of a house than she ever expected to own, and now a harsh God was asking her to pay it up too.

"You can come back to it in the proper season," Usaph whispered.

"Cain't they be held, Usaph? Cain't they . . . ?"

"Oh, Ephie. Banks . . . he has hisself some five divisions of goddam New Yorkers and other similar trash jest up there in Martinsburg."

"Martinsburg?" she asked again, the way she'd asked *Winchester?* earlier. She'd gone to market in both towns. How could there be five divisions of New Yorkers in a place she'd gone to market? "What will them slum-boys do to my kitchen?" she asked.

Usaph and Gus Ramseur looked at each other. Then Usaph

decided it was best not to answer that. "You jest be sure you pack all your clothes, Ephie Bumpass," he told her with a false, jovial gruffness. "Both the winter and the summer style, gal, for I wish you to stun the goddam gentry down there in Bath."

"I'll take the boy, Usaph," Gus Ramseur suddenly called, thoughtful, scratching his tangled blond head. "We'll put the horse in the shafts."

Usaph went a kind of red beneath his smoked face. "Obliged, Gus. I'll jest help Mrs. Bumpass out with her oddments."

Somehow Gus found the task of harnessing the horse to the dray hard enough to keep himself and the boy out in the freezing barn for a good hour. Ephie and Usaph left Lisa sleeping by the fire—too deaf to know the journey that was ahead. Upstairs Ephie made little complaining noises at the buttons that were stiff. She seemed to have forgotten the immediate threat of Yankeedom. She was undressed and trembling in the cold sheets while Usaph, his shivering buttocks facing her, sponged himself with a rag dipped in a pitcher of water. "I don't have no camp lice," he said, turning to her, spreading his arms innocently. "Only them filthy Irishmen in the 5th Virginia has got body lice. It takes an Irishman to pick up lice in the winter."

"I wouldn't fuss me if you did have lice," she told him. "But my, your hair is so lank."

Then, uttering little grateful whimpers, he descended on her.

After the hour they had was gone, she went about in her chemise, throwing clothes and little pieces of china and shawls and sheets into a chest. He watched her from the bed. The room seemed no longer cold.

"What say you, Usaph?" she asked all at once, looking resolute. "Do we burn the furniture?"

"What, Ephie?"

"I asked you will one of them Union generals with his sword and his damn fleas lie in our marriage bed?"

He thought a while. Sure, the prospect Ephie had raised was a painful one. The urge was there to burn the thing, to burn the house for that matter. But he'd been born in this same bed in '38. This was his parents' marriage bed. You couldn't burn something like that.

It came to him therefore that they should leave quickly now, before any more questions of the same species arose. "If you don't get off to Aunt Sarrie's, General Banks might jest take it in his head to lie in this here same bed with you."

"And like Judith in the Bible, I would slice his ole head off while his hands were so busy."

Usaph was up now and dressing quickly. "Gus and me . . . we'll see you on your road."

This made her stand stock still and her eyes filled up. "Hurry there, Ephie," he said, slapping her hip. So at three in the morning, when you could just about hear the earth creaking under the hand of the frost, Ephie drove a dray away from the back door of the Bumpass farm. Her cargo was clothes, crockery, bacon, flour, coffee, soap, a shotgun, and that one senile and shivering black slave called Lisa. Travis had agreed to let his son travel with Ephie all the way to Millboro Springs, where Aunt Sarrie would be known and could be fetched. As payment for that service, Travis would retain two of the Bumpasses' hogs.

Usaph and Gus traveled with Ephie a few miles down the road, Usaph riding at Ephie's side, Gus in the back at Lisa's side atop the goods and the luggage. Usaph had not taken the reins and Gus thought that was sensible of him. It was Ephie who had to make the journey.

Around four by his watch, Gus called, "We told Captain Guess, Usaph, we'd be back near breakfast time."

The words struck Ephie like a sentence. A little *ugh* sound came out of her and turned to vapor in the cold air. Usaph began some fast talking.

"Now you call in on the Rotes at Tom's Brook when you reach there, d'you hear. Missus Rote was a great friend of my mammy's and always fed me up tight as the bark on a tree, and she'll give you a breakfast, Ephie, you won't soon be fit to forget."

Gus had gotten out of the dray and bowed to all the company and started out northwards. Travis's boy watched Bumpass and Ephie knead each other again and cling together. And then Usaph jumped down too.

"That was good," said Gus later. "You got her away from Strasburg in good time."

It was to turn out that before St. Patrick's Day Federal cavalry would be camped all over Travis's and the empty Bumpass farm, and U.S. General Shields would enter town in a formal way, with bands and infantry and all the rest, just a week after Ephie had packed up. By the time a Union band was playing at the Strasburg crossroads where the Valley pike met the road from over the Blue Ridge, Ephie was nearly at Aunt Sarrie's place.

But it was not an easy journey. Lisa got an awesome fever and, before *that* broke, took a fit she'd not get better from, not for the rest of her life.

BOOK ONE

— 1 —

FOUR MONTHS LATER, on a morning in early July 1862, the young General Tom Jackson woke in a dusty bedroom in a rundown plantation house in Henrico County, Virginia. The house belonged to a Mr. Thomas and was pretty typical of the sort of house slaveholders of middling wealth kept here in the Virginian lowlands.

Although the night had been humid, the General felt fresh this morning. Until the war began he'd filled in his time with hypochondria. In those days—when he was a sedentary professor at the Virginia Military Institute—he'd believed he needed eight hours' sleep at least every night if he wanted to live to be fifty. Last night he'd had six, and that was the most he'd had in one lump for the last month.

He found his watch on the commode beside the bed. "Five minutes' luxury," he muttered to himself. For it wasn't much past dawn and the mists and miasmas that rose from the James River and from the swamps of these malarial lowlands pressed hard up against the window. Some fleshy miasmas were rising up in the General too; for maybe ten seconds his blood hammered away for Anna Morrison Jackson, his *esposa*, his wife. Well, he was used to making hammering blood simmer down and he did it now.

This was the Thomases' marriage bed he lay in, for Mr. and Mrs. Thomas had given it up for him. The Thomases were

9

obese, flat-faced people, likely to start drinking at breakfast-
time, exactly the sort of people abolitionists pointed to when
they wanted to argue about the bad effects slavery had on
slaveholders. The General wondered with a little distaste
whether the Thomases still had some passion for each other
and performed the marriage act here.

As he turned on his side the bed quaked and dust fell from
the hangings. He sneezed.

Most mornings he demanded a situation report on waking.
He didn't feel any particular need for one this morning. For
Lincoln's great Union army that had come ravening up the
Peninsula towards Richmond this second summer of the war
between the States had had all heart and sense pounded out of
it. Hoping to take the Rebel capital and end the whole business,
it had been outflanked every day for a week and was lucky not
to have been eaten whole. It kept now to the low peninsula
round Harrison's Landing, it bivouacked in clouds of mosquitoes. It was depressed, it was reflective, it was happy to
keep to its place.

Tom Jackson knew, therefore, that nothing had happened
while he slept. As surely as the Federals could not advance
because of the deficiencies of their souls, the rebel Confederates could not get any closer to Harrison's Landing because
of all the Union gunboats in the James. Tom Jackson had no
need today to holler, straight off on waking, for his sharp
young aides, Mr. Pendleton and Mr. Kyd Douglas.

But it was the very idea that the situation was fixed and
could go stale, that nothing had happened overnight, that nothing much could happen today, that made Tom Jackson decide
that he'd had enough of luxury in the Thomases' moldy bed.
He rang a bell which stood by the table. His body-servant, Jim
Lewis, who slept on a palliasse in the hallway, had been up
an hour already. He'd rolled up his bedding and gone out into
the mists to wash himself at the pump by the kitchen door.
Jim Lewis was husky, not very tall, his hair beginning to grey.
He was good with the needle and his coat looked better than
the coats of most officers in Tom Jackson's two divisions. He
didn't belong to General Jackson, he was on loan to him from
one of the General's friends in Lexington in Rockbridge
County. He'd always been an indoor slave. He had the delicate
hands many house slaves had, hands used to holding the best
of china and old hallmarked silverware. He thought the General
was just about the cleverest man living. You never knew when

you got up in the morning whether you'd find him in his room, whether he wouldn't have crept past your bed at one o'clock in the morning and crossed the Blue Ridge to confuse them Union generals, taking a division or two with him, leaving a message for you to follow on with a change of linen.

Once the General, who could get very solemn, had asked Jim if he'd heard all this newspaper talk about abolition and asked him further to say without prejudice if he'd rather be free. Jim's instinct made him say no—if he'd been a flogged field-hand his instinct would likewise have made him say no, that he was happy as a pig in mud under Massa. But then Jim thought further and found it was the truth. If he was free, would he be servant to a man whose name was known to every pretty kitchen and house-slave in every county in the Commonwealth of Virginia?

The ringing of the bell this morning told Jim the General hadn't skipped out last night. Jim went in carrying a big pitcher, a basin, a clean laundered towel. While he fetched a clean shirt and drawers from the General's traveling bag, the General stood by the window, his nightgown dropped to the floor, thoughtfully sponging the upper half of his body. He could see by now some of the tents of his staff in the plantation park and, in a field beyond, a few fires where his headquarters' regiment cooked its breakfast. The boys over there breakfasted well this morning off Union delicacies taken in the last ten days. There was likely good bacon and ample coffee, and if they were making corn pone, it would be of well-ground Yankee flour and delicious, the sad thing being Confederate cornflour was often riddled with husks. Yet despite what fine breakfasts they might be eating, this place wasn't a healthy one for those boys down there. All night the mists would be working in through their pores, and now a fiercely humid sun would keep those poisonous vapors simmering in them.

"No good for us, Jim," the General muttered. "No good for us mountain folks here."

Jim, who was getting on so well with the Thomases' cook, a large homely woman built on the same mold as her masters, just the same knew when to agree. "I s'pect that's right, Gen'ral. I've bin shiverin' and sneezin' all the night long."

G'bye, Missee Cook, he thought. Next week they'd stay at some other gentleman's house, north, south, east or west— Jim didn't know, even the General's generals didn't know. There he could fall in love with some other grandee's cook.

He fell in love easily but didn't often do much about it. Women were always saying to him, "Lord, Jim, what a talker you is!"

The mist was lifting quickly now and the General could see young Sandie Pendleton shaving in front of his tent, peering into a mirror held by a servant. He could see too the riflemen of the headquarters' regiment, lean boys, hanging their damp blankets to dry over Mr. Thomas's rail fences. Not the right place, he thought again, either for health or general strategy.

"Tell Captain Pendleton to come now," he ordered Jim. He could see that in any case Sandie was shaving fast, expecting to be called upstairs. He was a very deft boy with a razor. While Jim sped downstairs, Sandie finished the left side of his face, drenched it in water, dried himself, got his grey coat on and buttoned it to the neck. In the same time General Tom Jackson had shirted, underdrawered, trousered and booted himself. In the General's command only the quick were assured of any standing.

Sandie was one of the quicker. He came from the town where Jackson had spent all his married life teaching, the town of Lexington. Tom Jackson had therefore known Sandie since Sandie was a child. The boy had shown an early quickness by graduating Bachelor of Arts from Washington College in Lexington at the age of seventeen and by winning the college medal as well. When the war began, he'd been studying for his Master's at the University of Virginia. It was exactly the sort of background Tom Jackson respected.

Sandie came through the General's open bedroom door.

"Where's Mr. Boteler staying?" the General asked him. Boteler was a Congressman and another of the General's friends.

"A mile up the road. People called the Morrises."

"Have you eaten breakfast?"

"I haven't, sir."

"So, we'll both do without it."

The General was already loping downstairs. Sandie opened the window, stuck out his head, yelled, "Horse!" in the direction of his tent and followed the General. At the front steps the General's small dumpy horse Old Sorrel stood being patted by an ostler. Everyone liked Old Sorrel. He wasn't handsome, his coat was faded chestnut, he lacked style, his eyes were soft as a doe's. Altogether he looked—had you wanted to ride him to Richmond—as if he would have pegged out about the Charles City crossroads. In fact he never went lame, he had carried the General up and down the Valley at a crazy pace, across and back over the Blue Ridge and on a wild-paced march across Virginia. The General liked him for his easy gait and could sleep by the hour on his back.

The ostler was English and was telling Old Sorrel, "Old Sorrel's a lively boy, Old Sorrel is." By the time he noticed the General, the General was in the saddle, extricating the reins from his hand. Sandie's horse had also been brought to the steps and Sandie got away a few seconds after his commander.

Sandie wondered why the General was galloping Old Sorrel on a morning when gallops didn't seem to be necessary. It must be that Tom Jackson was answering some secret urgency, most likely one of those black crazy urgencies that were more inside his bowels than in the outside world.

Sandie was a length behind the General when they tore out of the Thomases' front gate on to the Charles River road to Richmond. This is what it is to live, Sandie thought, with a man who sees his job as being to whip history into shape.

— 2 —

THEY TIED UP their horses in woods three miles south of the Thomases', There was the General himself and Sandie, and Mr. Boteler of the Confederate Congress in Richmond. And as well as these three, a tough, scrawny, crotchety little man called General Popeye Ewell. At the Morris House Tom Jackson and Sandie had found Mr. Boteler and Popeye just sitting down to breakfast in the front parlor. Popeye ate only cereal and drank only hot water and talked all the time about his tortured guts, so it wasn't much of a hardship for him to be snatched away from the table. Mr. Boteler liked a Christian breakfast, though—eggs and ham, cakes and gravy. Dragged away from it, he said to Sandie: "Those other two don't have an alimentary canal nor a goddam stomach. They're monsters."

Sandie said, "That's so, Mr. Boteler."

Ahead of the place they had now left their horses, and right at the edge of the forest, some Alabamans were standing picket duty, facing out across a wide wild field in the distant likelihood of a Union movement. To the left, in a further fringe of oak forest, some Georgians were supposed to be doing the same, though you couldn't see them for the foliage.

The Alabamans looked to Sandie as if they were taking their business with proper seriousness, even the ones who were hunkered or brewing coffee. The open ground ahead was a bowl of sunlight now. There were butterflies amongst the lupins out there. But here under the branches there were mosquitoes, and flies as fat as blackberries.

General Jackson ignored the boys in the picket line. Popeye Ewell, who was the sort of man who always had something to say but pushed it out the corner of his mouth as if it were an imposition, called out: "Keep them pupils primed, boys. That meadow you see there is a meadow of Virginia!"

"Wa-ha-ha!" a few of the Alabamans cried.

Sandie Pendleton found a child lieutenant standing by a sycamore, field-glasses in his hands. "Where are they?" he asked the boy.

"See that fence across the meadow? Follow it to the right. Then . . . notice it starts to rise and goes up a hill? Well, there are cottonwoods up there and if you hide among them you can see a line of forest. They're in that forest, the Union pickets, facing the cottonwoods. You can see the Union camp beyond. And the James."

Sandie thanked the boy. Already Tom Jackson and the others were stepping out into the open ground. The meadow was overgrown with blackberry bushes and you could tell which branches the pickets had been harvesting. Maybe these Alabamans would come out of their cover today and crop some blackberries themselves, trading the long chance of a bullet against the assured sugar and succulence of the blackberries. Anyhow, the two generals and Mr. Boteler and Sandie made crouching progress amongst the blackberries and across the meadow. It was low, boggy ground, and Sandie, as General Jackson had already done that morning, disliked it and thanked God he was from Lexington. There were likely more copperheads and water-moccasins in these mean few acres than in the whole of Rockbridge County.

Mr. Boteler's lower left leg slipped from under him and he landed on his knee in bog water. "Hell and damn!" he said, but he looked up smiling at Sandie. He was a tough, genial little man, about forty-five years, and he was a West Virginian like the General. He was one of the opposition in the Confederate Congress, what they called a Whig Unionist, as Jackson was himself, a moderate, a man who wished this whole mess had never got started. He had a lot of power exactly because he fetched from the same part of the state as the General. It was a wonderful thing for a politician to have a successful general from his own constituency. Boteler, who had once been an operator in the U.S.Congress and was now an operator in the Government in Richmond, knew just how wonderful it was.

A politician of less flexibility than Mr. Boteler might have objected to the price the General was demanding today. How many Congressmen would be willing to creep forward past the pickets and spy on the Yankee hosts from behind fences and cottonwoods? Well, Boteler was willing, and it was just as well. General Jackson thought nothing of bringing any civilian out here to witness the state of the Yankee camp and soul. Jefferson Davis himself better beware—he might find himself out here one morning next week.

They kept low behind the fence and followed it uphill. Soon they could stand full height amongst the cottonwoods and tall undergrowth. How tall was the summit of the hill? A hundred and fifty feet maybe. Two hundred. But in that flat land it was like a peak in Darien. Boteler and General Ewell put their binoculars to their eyes. Sandie handed General Jackson his.

Quoting the young Alabaman, Sandie briefed them where to look. There was little need for his instructions, even with the naked eye you could see the Federal camp on the James. Tents and wagons floated in a haze that still clung to the flats round Harrison's Landing. But with the binoculars you could see more. You could see first the blue-coated pickets in the wood three hundred yards away. If they knew there were two Confederate generals and a Congressman on this knoll they would send out a cavalry squadron to bag them. But they didn't do much that was adventurous any more, not after last week. Jackson knew exactly the feelings of the boys over there. Brave enough, they wondered if the Rebs weren't braver still and they began to wonder too about their generals, even about their beloved McClellan. Jackson could read their doubts as he gazed at them through the lenses.

Beyond the pickets and their line of forest some batteries were placed behind fences and earth embankments, and beyond that stretched the vast Union bivouac itself. The Yankees had been bottled up there for some days now and it looked like a well-arranged encampment. There seemed to be the beginnings of pathways amongst the tents. But not all the Union army enjoyed the luxury of canvas. Along with fifty-two pieces of artillery, thousands of stands of sidearms, much beef, pork, flour, coffee and molasses, the Federals had as well lost a few tents last week.

Yet it was a town, that camp. As big as Richmond. A hundred thousand men lived there, however uncertainly. You could see somewhere in the center a great military band playing songs of home, and hymns and tunes to ginger up doubtful souls. You could see ships of the U.S. Navy in the deep-water reaches of the James two miles away.

The General spoke to Mr. Boteler. "I'd like you to just take note of the location of the artillery parks, Mr. Boteler. Not up forward, as if they ever mean to turn their guns on us. They're down by the landings. Plain as day, it's intended they should be ready to be taken on board ship. The great Mac has his bags packed and he's already decided to leave all defense to those gunboats out there."

"I believe you're right," said Mr. Boteler, letting his binoculars fall and hitching his thumbs, farmer-wise, in their straps.

The General's voice became both low and fierce. "Well in that case, do you agree we're losing time here?"

"Oh?"

"Well, we happen to be repeating the old mistake we made last year after Manassas. They are being given a free gift, namely, time to recover. And what are we doing here, apart from catching malaria? There are ten thousand of us already sick with pneumonia and dysentery, and the hospitals in Richmond haven't even got round to treating last week's wounded yet. There are alternative things to do besides standing in these miasmas getting ill. I wanted to talk to you about it."

The General leaned against a tree. He'd always been gangling and a leaner. Popeye Ewell here remembered the day, he himself then a young professor of the Academy, that Tom Jackson had come to West Point, a lean and very handsome boy. Somehow he'd got a place in the Academy even though he hadn't had good schooling. It was rumored that he'd got there through political influence, his uncle Cummins Jackson being the drinking crony of a Western Virginia Congressman. Anyhow, Ewell had been attracted to Tom Jackson's raw talent and helped him with his mathematics. Jackson had been a serious boy who'd had too much death in his family—a mother, a father, his brother. He did everything as if time was limited. Generally he was right on that score.

"I don't mean to tell you, Boteler, anything a private soldier couldn't tell you," said Tom Jackson. "McClellan's whipped as a cur. He'll go home. It'll take him some time to get there. He'll sulk for reinforcements. It'll take him time to get them. Even then . . . well, he'd have to reorganize. And he's not quick at that sort of job. Richmond *is* safe now. What we have to do is move north, into Maryland, if possible into Pennsylvania, to outflank Washington. Put Abe Lincoln in a panic." He sneezed moistly. "I want you to go to Mr. Davis and tell him what I've told you."

"You say that as if it were a simple thing. . . ."

"It's the only thing," said Tom Jackson. "A big move north. The final battle. Maybe in Maryland, as I say. Maybe in Pennsylvania. Either will serve."

Boteler closed one eye and made a dubious squeaking noise with his lips. "What's the use of me going to Mr. Davis? He'd only refer me back to General Lee. Why don't you talk direct to Lee?"

"I've done so."

"Well . . . ?"

Tom Jackson chewed at his narrow lips.

"He said nothing. I know he's got reasons for his silence."

Boteler decided to be funny. "Well, at least you're not trying to rebel against your superior general."

Jackson didn't think that was funny. He thought a while. Boteler coughed; the joke had fallen flat.

The General said: "He can't give me a definite answer because of influences in Richmond. I'm sure the matter's been mentioned by him there. Now it's time to add our voice."

Boteler spat. "It's clean contrary to current thinking," he said. "I mean, it's contrary to ideas of caution."

Sandie coughed and General Ewell called, "Look at that there!"

Out of the Federal camp a ball of white and red silk had risen. It yawed a little in the hot air and came straight for them on a light wind off the James. They knew who it was—Professor Thaddeus Lowe, McClellan's balloonist, flying to observe the Rebels. Very soon the balloon seemed to Boteler to be overhead, and he grinned and pretended to be trying to withdraw his head into his shoulders.

General Jackson ignored the professor's exotic craft.

"You have to let him see," he said, the *him* being President Jefferson Davis of the Confederate States of America, "that Lincoln is more anxious about losing Washington than we are about losing Richmond. And with some reason."

"Maryland?" Mr. Boteler asked. He laughed. "That's a grand strategy," he said.

Behind them the Alabamans had begun firing at and cat-calling the professor.

"We ought to go now," said General Ewell, since firing by one set of pickets would set the other side going. He thought how ridiculous it would be if Stonewall Jackson was lost to the Confederacy because a few Alabamans shot at an eccentric Yankee aeronaut.

But when they were halfway across the field, returning towards their own picket lines, the General was distracted by the plumpness of the blackberries on shoulder-high bushes all round. He was a true country boy. Fruit always attracted him and often he would just sit on a fence sucking a lemon.

He began to pluck the berries and so did Sandie. Boteler waited, shaking his head a little. If he had to ride back to Richmond this afternoon, the last thing he wanted was a bellyful of berries.

General Jackson ate the fruit heartily, but Ewell, with his weak stomach, picked just a few and ate them slowly. He suffered from ulcers and, as did two-thirds of his command, from camp diarrhea. To the left the Alabamans were firing at Professor Lowe's colorful balloon, which was drifting north-west, and to distract them a picket line of Yankees advanced towards the meadow fence and began firing lazy volleys up open corridors amongst the blackberries. Mr. Boteler crouched and Ewell gave up the blackberry-culling and mapped out their best path. He saw that up to the right the woods reached a spot almost level with the place where he and Jackson, the aide and Mr. Boteler stood. In that wing of woods General Robert Toombs's Georgians should be. If the firing didn't get too intense, that was the way to go, into the elbow where the Alabaman and Georgian picket lines met.

With a mash of berries in his mouth, Stonewall let a sly grin creep over his lean jaws. It broadened when a minié ball slapped a leaf some three feet from his ear.

"Some nervous boy from goddam Massachusetts," Ewell

swore. But he was worried for the General and also for himself.

"Tell me, Sandie," said the General, holding a fat berry between forefinger and thumb, "if you knew you were going to be shot and had a choice . . ."

It was an eternal question of discussion. Generals and privates thought about it. With some the consideration became morbid. Others suspected that if they talked about the wound they wanted least, it would stay away from them through some sort of sympathetic magic.

Sandie thought and said: "I just don't want one of those silly wounds, General. You know, the kind that shouldn't kill a man, but you bleed to death."

This wasn't quite the truth. Such deaths made him angry, but the deaths he really feared were wounds from artillery, and especially to be dismembered.

"If I'm shot," Ewell muttered, "I want it to be where I've been wounded already—in the clothing. Otherwise I don't want it to be in the face or joints, not with Monsieur Minié's famous expanding bullet. But I think the face would be the worst." He wondered if some Union boy wasn't at that moment sighting on his head.

"I suppose," Sandie said, picking two particularly nice blackberries and handing them to the General, "you're at a distance from the damage if you get it in other parts of the body. You can inspect a wound there. But you can't inspect a wound in the face."

"Nor one in the back," said Tom Jackson, gorging the berries. He was like that—even at full-scale dinners he often ate just the one thing in big amounts. Sometimes it was strawberries, sometimes it was bread. Hostesses hated him for it.

Flap, flap! went two bullets, ripping leaves from a bush a few paces off.

"The wound I'd hate," said Boteler, grinning but not at ease, "would be to lose my constituency." He knew there was no electoral chance of that. For he was the General's Congressman and neither of them ever lost.

Anyhow, they laughed and the General asked them if they'd had enough blackberries, as if picking fruit had been someone else's idea.

"The Yankees may have moved up sharpshooters," Ewell growled. "Keep low, that's what I suggest. Use the shrubbery."

"We'll visit the Georgians, Sandie," Jackson said, his old gray forage cap low over his eyes.

They said goodbye to each other on the edge of the woods.
Jackson let Popeye Ewell escort the Congressman back to his
horse, then he himself took Sandie off to say hello to the
Georgians, as if this was a routine day; and as if the country's
finest young general had not whispered the word *Maryland* to
one of the country's best political operators..

— 3 —

IN A FIELD near the Thomases' plantation house, the men whose
breakfast fires the General had seen through the mist that morning were now considering lunch. In Usaph Bumpass's mess
they still had half a captured ham left and if they were ordered
to march tomorrow they didn't want to have to lug ham all
over hilly Virginia with them.

They had two slow-burning fires going, the men of Usaph
Bumpass's mess.

On one of the fires, fueled by kindling bought from Mr.
Thomas—for the General forbade them to steal Mr. Thomas's
rail fences—young Ash Judd was frying ham in the mess's
skillet, and on the other, ancient Bolly Quintard baked flourbread. Bolly's dough had been shaped round the ramrod of his
Springfield rifle, like a fleece on a distaff, into the form of a
loaf of bread. As he turned the mixture on its hot steel rod,
in hands made big and harsh by a lifetime of pushing pit saws
and wielding axes, he sang "Oh Lord, Gals One Friday" in his
old tenor voice.

Usaph Bumpass didn't like that noise, but he and the others
tolerated it because they needed Bolly's skillet. Bumpass's
young friend Ash Judd had once owned one which he shared
with Usaph and the others. He'd been carrying it on the march
out of the Valley in a way that was getting to be common in
this army, its handle down the barrel of his rifle, its pan sticking
out of the mouth like a great black sunflower. It was very
likely that Ashabel had been asleep as he walked, a skill a man

had to pick up if the pace wasn't going to kill him. And one of "them horsemen," passing along, must have lifted it without effort out of the rifle barrel of weary Ashabel Judd.

There'd been four men dependent on that skillet. First, there was Bumpass himself and Ash Judd. Bumpass and Judd were both farmers of middling wealth. Then there was the schoolmaster Danny Blalock and the music teacher Gus Ramseur.

Bumpass was secretly proud of sharing a skillet with two educated men like Blalock and Ramseur. So he sought some of the better men in the regiment and said that if anyone would give him and Ramseur and Blalock and Ash Judd half-rights in a skillet, he guaranteed in return that the person who did would get equal shares in any delicacies the four of them managed to buy or forage or find. The only people interested were old Bolly Quintard and his Irish friend Joseph Murphy. Bolly and Murphy knew what a temporary possession a skillet was and that they might need future favors from the others and so thought that the terms were fair.

While the regiment was in bivouac, the skillet was shared. On the march you didn't get a chance to cook anyhow. Not in Tom Jackson's twenty-miles-a-day, eat-from-the-orchards, sleep-where-you-drop foot-cavalry.

Ole Bolly stood out amongst the men about him because of his air of worldly evil and his age. Now, for example, the schoolteacher Blalock and the music man Ramseur were each 24 years of age, Usaph was 23, young Ash Judd was barely twenty. Joe Murphy didn't know how old he was but guessed he was maybe thirty. Bolly, however, was old as any three of them put together.

Sometimes, to put on side, he said he was seventy, but it was likely he was only about 65. He had lived a hard, profane life in the lumber business on the far side of the Shenandoah Valley near Brock's Gap. There was a 22-year-old girl back at Quintard's Mill who was his seventh wife, for he had had seven, all of whom he had loved and heartily impregnated. He would say proudly that the first six all died fair and square, he hadn't encouraged any of them to do so. One had perished of the flux, another had had her skull bust by an overturning wagon, two died giving birth, another of what Bolly called "spotted mountain fever" and a sixth of snake-bite. This seventh wife had been brought in from Loudon County, way up at the mouth of the Shenandoah, because nearly all the pretty faces round Quintard's Mill had been kin if not offspring of Bolly's.

We're poor people, Bolly would say, but not so poor we have to start begetting off each other. Although he had a few slaves he found the free labor of begotten children cheaper.

His friends in Guess's Company teased him about what his young wife might be doing while he was off campaigning, but Bolly had a lot of pride in himself as a lover; he believed that once she had had the taste of him, no woman could do with anything less. Therefore look to your own women, you race of slackroots.

Usaph was not easy about all this teasing over women. Ephie Bumpass was a lovely woman—a girl in fact—living lonely on a farm. Usaph didn't need reminding about what might just happen. Even his Aunt Sarrie might not be able to keep guard against such a thing happening.

It irked Usaph that Ash and Joe Murphy didn't seem to talk about anything except willing widows or ripe girls from farms. It irked Usaph that Bolly, an old man, talked with such ease about his wife, who must have been more or less the same age as Ephie, and about how she wouldn't stray.

As well as for his age and many wives, Bolly was also renowned for having an umbrella he had brought everywhere with him since December 1861, when he first appeared out of Brock's Gap and presented himself to Brigadier-General Garnett in Winchester. It was the umbrella by which men remembered him rather than his age. Somehow he was so tough, you forgot that he was older than your own grandfather.

While they waited for Ash Judd to cook the ham and Bolly to brown the bread, the others moved around the meadows or lolled near a pear tree against Thomas's plantation fence and uttered rumors, mockeries, profanities, prophecies, observations.

"Look at that gloss of sweat on his face there," Joseph Murphy invited everyone.

Across the corner of the field, striped with shadow and sunlight from a paling fence, Gus Ramseur, the music teacher, was sweating out his pneumonia. This midsummer's day he lay on two rubberized sheets and beneath two more. His sodden yellow hair spilled all over his hat, which had been pummelled into the shape of a pillow. Usaph heated bricks he'd borrowed from the Thomases' garden on Ash Judd's fire and put them in rotation between Gus's blankets. He also dosed Gus with frequent mouthfuls of a whisky called *How Come You So* that he had bought from a sutler on the Gaines' Mill side of the Chickahominy a week ago.

"But he looks fine," said Usaph, inspecting the slick of sweat on Gus's face. "That looks as it should look."

"And the shrivel-gut you got in that jar?" asked Bolly.

"It's better'n what you get from the surgeon," said Usaph. "That there morphia stuff ain't good for the soul."

"There's no doubt the man himself is better right here," said Joseph Murphy, who had been away in Richmond at the Chimborazo Hospital suffering from the flux. They had kicked him out of his ward to make way for the wounded of White Oak Swamp and Frayser's Farm and Malvern Hill. "Oh yeh, even if he could get inside Chimborazo, he's maybe still better here. I mean, you should see that Richmond. They got the goddamn wounded all the way down Grace Street from the depot. No such nice situation as a friend slipping hot bricks in under your blankets! There ain't no question of more'n one. The lips on some of them wounds on them boys is like hardwood bark now and still they wait in the streets, and the private citizens of Richmond is all the time bringing more in by dray and wagon. They never made in any goddam Christian country blankets enough for them boys who are still coming in with wounds and the die-sen-try. And half the surgeons drunk and half the nurses sluts. Going through the pockets of the very corpses, looking for cash and trinkets. . . ."

"You must have been right at home in the that there Chimborazo then, Joe," called Ashabel Judd. "With them thieves for brothers and them sluts for company."

Murphy stared back at Judd a while, which made Judd's high laughter thinner still, squeakier.

"Why," the Irishman went on at last—he'd rather tell his traveler's tales than punish Judd, "they led a Yankee lieutenant of cavalry through the streets one day, a prisoner. He had goddam kid gauntlets and chicken guts all over his collar." (Chicken guts, it happened, was gold braid.) "They let him keep his goddam sabre and it was like all the world's best goddam cutlery. And his boots still had a goddam gloss under the dust. He was so young it was like his mother had just dropped him fully uniformed and he went straight to Gaines' Mill for to get himself captured. And there was this poor Reb, thin as a goddam ghost in a bad year, calling to him: 'Lord, you look such a grand feller with your grand braid and your

lovely kid gloves and your boots with a good gloss on 'em
. . . why, and I bet your bowels is oh so regular. . . .'"

That made them all laugh. Good bowels were beyond price
in this gathering. Most of these boys suffered with chronic
diarrhea. Since last winter they had all had dysentery of some
severity or other. It was what they were given to eat that was
the cause. On the Charlottesville march they'd lived off little
green apples and unripe corn. When they got flour they fried
up fritters in bacon fat; a recipe mortally hard on any man's
bowels. If they captured U.S. commissary wagons—as when
at Middletown on the Valley pike last May they surrounded
General Banks's wagons—it made matters worse. They wolfed
captured delicacies very quick. They dreaded having luggage
to carry on the march, so diets of little pellet apples and im-
mature corn gave way to sudden orgies of ham, fish paste,
jellies and bacon, and the sudden violent feast was as hard on
the belly as green apples ever were.

In the Army of Northern Virginia, the man whose bowels
were *regular* was considered so rare and blessed that his friends
might bring guests from other regiments to shake hands with
him.

"One thing they did do for me at that Chimborazo though,"
Joe Murphy went on; "they give me the scratch to stop the
smallpox."

"Inoculation?" said Danny Blalock. He had looked up from
a browning edition of *De Bow's Review* he'd borrowed from
Captain Guess. The article he'd been reading was headed "Will
the British Government Recognize the Confederacy This
Year?" "Inoculation, Joe?" he repeated.

Joe pulled up the sleeve of the new shirt the Southern Soldiers' Comfort Society had given him in Chimborazo. There
was a dime-sized scab on his upper arm.

Old Bolly Quintard's eyes fixed at the idea of a little scab
protecting you all your days against smallpox. He was an old
man from the mountains mixing amongst citified diseases for
the first time in his life. Germans and Irishmen from Richmond
were all round him, and then there were the New Orleans
regiments in Ewell's division who didn't even speak English
and had all sorts of bayou-swamp illnesses about them. So
Bolly was interested in protection against diseases.

"Will they ever come round here, doing that for us'ns?" he
asked.

"Maybe," said Joe. "God knows when."

"I'd dearly love a sovereign shield against the smallpox."

Young Ashabel Judd said, "There ain't been no smallpox in this army."

"But smallpox comes," Bolly told him. "There ain't many valleys it don't find once a generation, and do you think it won't find this-here great army?"

Danny Blalock read a sentence about the pernicious kingdom of Britain which would hold off acknowledging the Confederate States as long as it could. Then he looked up and said, "Joe could inoculate you, Bolly, easy as wink."

"That's right," said Joe. "I seen it done; I make a little cut in your arm, I knock off a portion of my scab and mash it round in your cut, Bolly."

"You're mocking me, Joe Murphy. Damn you, Murphy, I'll give you scab!"

"But it's the truth, Bolly," Danny Blalock announced. Everyone believed Danny. He was their encyclopaedia, he knew he was, he liked the stature, he therefore never told tall tales. Any ignorant farmer from the mountains could tell tall tales. "That scab there is his protection against smallpox. If he gives you a scab, you're protected too."

"Let him give *you* some of his scab then," Bolly challenged him.

"I'm not the one that's worried about smallpox."

Bolly took thought. He blew heavily into his beard which was still a little red at the roots. Danny had gone back to his article on diplomacy so calmly that Bolly had to believe him.

"You're willing, Joe?" he asked the Irishman, just to give himself time to decide.

"I told you that already, Bolly."

"Let it be a clean knife then," said Bolly.

Still reading, Danny Blalock heard the small grunts of discomfort as Joe Murphy knocked off part of his scab and as the boy Ashabel left his cooking a second to cut a small slot for it in Bolly's stringy upper arm. Even while Ashabel plied the knife, Bolly hung on tight to the ramrod and its loaf.

"The Southern Presidents who led the United States in its fledgling years," Danny Blalock read in *De Bow's*, "Washington, Jefferson, Madison, always recognized the *de facto* government of a particular country as a matter of course. The United States, when it was still a fresh and pure entity, recognized the revolutionary government of France before any other nation had done so. But the British have always had a different policy. Albion is, in any case, jealous of the success of its former colony the United States. Therefore they will let the Confederacy bludgeon the United States for a little while longer before they step in to recognize the infant Confederacy.

"The belief long-cherished in the South that need of Southern cotton will force the British to recognize the government at Richmond has proven a little illusory. . . ."

"You're enjoying it," Bolly accused Joe Murphy, who was leaning over Bolly with a knife and a fragment of smallpox scab on its point.

"Don't be ridiculous. I'm the gentlest sort of feller."

"Certainly," Danny Blalock read on, "textile mills and textile workers in cities such as Manchester are suffering. But British governments are accustomed to living with the suffering of their citizens. It would take some sudden and spectacular coup by the South to ensure British recognition. Such a coup would be to enter Maryland and outflank Washington. Or to capture Harrisburg, Pennsylvania, and descend on Baltimore from the north by way of the Northern Central railroad (See Map) and then on Washington itself! In fact, it is certain that by the time Harrisburg fell, the British government would want to talk with respect to the government in Richmond. If Washington could be conclusively threatened, the British would bring force to bear on the North to end the war."

Danny thought it was easy for an editorialist to say "(See Map)." These editorial writers didn't have to do any of the walking or wear through six pairs of boots as he had on Virginia's roads.

He heard Ash Judd applauding but uttering that laugh again, that strange undeveloped titter. It always began for him in a trembling of the jaw long before it was a sound anyone could hear. When Bolly heard it this time he suspected he'd been made a mock of, that his humiliation had been planned by these young boys, excepting Gus Ramseur, of course, who was too fevered for plotting.

Bolly was pleased to notice after a moment that all the others were as mystified by Judd's laughter as he was.

"You goddam ant, Ash. What is it tickling you?"

"Well, Joe told me," said Ash, his fine teeth shining in the sun, "he got his scab off a nice gal in a Foushee Street bawdy house. She had lots of scabs, according to Joe, that nice gal."

Bolly stood up. He looked tike a prophet or something and the sparks of red at the roots of his beard seemed to threaten to set the whole mass of hair afire. "This scab's one of them scabs, Joe? A scab from a bawdy house?"

"No. He's lying to you. It's a scab from Chimborazo, a proper hospital scab, I wouldn't take no other . . ."

"If you done me this damage . . . !"

"Listen, ole man," Murphy roared at Bolly. "I tell you it's a scab from a surgeon."

"It's a scab from a nurse," Ash Judd persisted, finding it hard to sound convincing, though, because of his laughter. "From a nurse who does some work on the side in a Foushee Street bawdy house."

Both the Irishman and Bolly glowered at Judd's handsome but childish face. Ash Judd had joined Jackson's army last Easter at Newmarket, and in that time the beard he had let grow had amounted to nothing more than a stubble. Ash Judd could barely read or write, there was an air about him of something missing; he certainly didn't understand the cause as Danny Blalock did, yet he'd lived through the Valley campaign and rarely straggled. And this though his hair wouldn't grow properly on him, and though his mouth sometimes gaped or his nose ran.

"You goddam eunuch!" said Murphy. He did not want trouble provoked between himself and Bolly. He wasn't sure that Bolly couldn't whip him; Bolly had once whipped a young man from the 21st Virginia. A 65-year-old lumber man who had had seven wives and could keep up in the war of the young must be a tough and crafty being. Now if Joe was whipped by him, there would be the shame. There'd be shame either way. "There goes Joe Murphy. He likes whupping ole men." Or even worse, "There goes Joe Murphy. He gets whupped by ole men."

Ash Judd, having made the trouble, now saved it from taking root. "Look at that there!" he said, pointing down the road from Charles City. You couldn't see far down roads in this country, the swampy oak forests pressed hard up against the edges of the thoroughfares. So the some one hundred or more men who had now halted by Thomas's plantation gate *must* have come down the Charles City Road, yet they were there by the gates so suddenly they might just as well have been dropped like manna out of the sky.

Everyone was silent, taking in these new people, and even Usaph Bumpass turned away from Gus Ramseur for the first time in two hours and studied them. They were men who looked displaced. Some of them had indoor complexions, as if they'd clerked in shops till just last week. More than half of them had gray jackets—some commissary officer must have got a shipment and handed them out. Yet in Jackson's corps there were hardly any of those mythical Confederacy-gray coats and most men lived in the homespun of their forefathers, in jackets stained to a butternut color with a dye made up of copperas and walnut hulls. The newspapers called it the war between the blue and the gray. Well, it was the war between the blue and the butternut.

So even the regulation coats they wore made the boys at the gate something like outsiders. Another strange aspect to them was that they wore gray forage caps. They were therefore fresh soldiers, for veterans wore slouch hats which could be used as umbrellas in foul weather, as parasols in midsummer, as pillows at night.

Usaph noticed the others around him getting to this conclusion and their faces going taut and their eyes beginning to squint. It was natural enough that veterans should feel that way about new soldiers, as if they wanted to ask: "Why weren't you here last month to save us some of our suffering?"

"Your ham's burning there, Ash," Usaph muttered. And the boy, still looking at the men at the gate, took the skillet off and laid it on the ground.

Usaph went on watching the pure hate growing in Ashabel's face and in Joseph Murphy's. Those fellers at Thomas's newel posts had had months more of sweet-talking girls, of eating off plates, of listening to the fiddle by the fire than Ashabel and Murphy had. Now Ashabel and Murphy would like to make the visitors at the gate expiate all that.

Usaph Bumpass found himself laughing at them. "Why are you looking at them all mean-eyed like that, Ash? They ain't the hosts of the Amelekites."

"No, Amelekites they may not be," Ash admitted. "But they're scabs. They're latecomers and poor comers and—and poor hands!"

Joe Murphy whispered, looking at Bolly: "Don't go talking scabs again."

All at once there was a movement to the center of the field in which Usaph Bumpass and the others stood. The colonel had arrived from somewhere and men were drawing in close towards him. Because maybe he would say: "All right, boys, for all your good works and meritorious service, you can have the reward of going down to the gate and crucifying those gentlemen."

The colonel's name was Lafcadio Wheat. He was a lawyer from Clarksburg, way over in the mountains. He stood quite tall, black curls spilling out under his hat, the line of his mouth lost amongst rich black whiskers. He was about 33 years old and had a wit about him. No one had ever seen him laugh, however—he would have made a good judge or a carnival comic.

"Dear boys and brothers of the Shenandoah Volunteers," Colonel Wheat began now, for that was his standard starter for speeches. "You might remember that last April 16 the Confederate Congress happened to pass a conscription law. Or has all this backing and forwarding across the Blue Ridge knocked your memory of April clear off its perch? No? Damn good, I say. Well, it's taken a little time for the conscripts called up under that law to reach us, but the day when they see us and we see them has come, bygad, and that's conscripts there by ine gate."

It was said Wheat had studied law in Philadelphia, that he had a bushel of Latin and enough Greek to know a little of Homer and that crowd. But he'd always talked in a drawling backwoods way, and Usaph thought it was just to get the boys in and cause them to elect him colonel, as they had done some two months back.

Now Usaph didn't particularly object to Lafcadio Wheat's election, for Wheat was a brave man. For instance, on a stewing lowland afternoon the week before, beneath Malvern Hill, when the regiment had been told to lie down on marshy ground in the rear of the Rockbridge artillery and to wait in the event of the guns being rushed, Wheat did the thing all ideal colonels were said to do according to the newspapers of Richmond. He walked amongst the companies of men, who'd been ordered to lie flat on the quaggy ground like sheafs of mown grass, and he joked. And he spoke in his homely mountain way.

Occasionally a feller would say to him, "Colonel, the scourge of the di-harree is on your humble servant."

"Well," the colonel might say, "I suggest my humble servant gets his tail back in that screen of hawthorn and drops his drawers while the dropping is good."

Although there were swamp oaks growing round about, the Federals would have needed no more than binoculars to have spotted Wheat prancing round. It was known the Yankee sharpshooters on the brow of Malvern Hill used Whitworth rifles, long and lovely in their own right and set up with one of the dazzling items of this modern age, telescopic sights. Now, by the talk that went round, a Yankee with a telescopic Whitworth rifle could study the distant man he was about to strike, the way you'd study the daguerreotype of your wife or brother. If he was a Yankee of religious leanings, he might even pray for the soul he was about to send screaming out to judgment, before actually blowing the beneficiary's throat or temples away. Though some sniper might have prayed for Wheat, he didn't succeed in harming any part of his impressive upper body.

In the Thomases' meadow, Wheat went on village-pumping it without shame. "Now I can tell you boys have some feelings of vengefulness about this whole business of conscripts, so we may jest as well draw off all the poison from your glands and say everything that's on your minds. Now some of those boys at the gate are no cowards. No. Some of 'em arc Union-sympathy fellers from over to the South Branch of the Potomac. Well, I swear by my granddaddy's pecker, and that's no small oath, that them Yankee boys are going to settle in and make the best goddam Confederates in North Virginia."

"Granddaddy's pecker?" Usaph asked Ash Judd, scarcely believing. He didn't think it was right of a man to pledge away bits of his grandfather's body to a clutch of ungodly soldiers.

"Yeh, yeh," said Ash, who had never known his own grandfather and so wasn't shocked. "He's some colonel, this Wheat!"

Usaph bent and pulled the blankets closer round Gus Ramseur's golden beard. Gus was a man of *real* talents and worth saving. He spoke of the pianoforte, and would have been in the band if he hadn't considered band music vulgar. Yet he'd played mountain music on his fiddle. He loved those old songs even though he was more or less a foreigner. "Where're your parents from, Gus?" they asked when he first joined them.

"Lorraine."

"Lorraine who?"

For Usaph's money, Gus Ramseur was the true remarkable man of the Shenandoah Volunteers and he must not die of fever in a lowland meadow.

"Let me tell you more about them boys at the gate," Colonel Wheat persisted, "for I want to have it all out with you before you meet them. Some of them is substitutes. Some wealthy boy's got drafted and rather than join us himself, he advertised in the papers or hunted round the taverns or left his name at the cat house to hire a stand-in."

There was the standard laughter, and all the more laughter because Colonel Wheat would not join in it.

"Now down in this palmy section of tidewater Virginny, down here in Henrico and Hanover and Louisa Counties and all that . . ." There were catcalls, for Shenandoah people loved to hear the lowlanders mocked. ". . . where most well-to-do gentlemen own more niggers than freckles on Aunt Libby's ass, a wealthy boy could pay $500 for a substitute. Up in the poor mountains from which we stem, a substitute might fetch no more than $200 or $300. Even so, when did you last see $300 in the one pile?"

"U.S. or Confederate Treasury?" someone called. Everyone laughed again and Colonel Wheat stared, as if angered at the interlocutor.

"Now," he continued at last in a voice that was secretive— if you can be secretive with some hundreds of men, "there is another aspect to them Yankee-leaning or shirking or dollar-stuffed boys at the gate. And that is that they represent a necessity. In plain terms, we have need of them. Therefore, I am telling you and you best heed it. You can use a sharp tongue on them and for today you can *exchange* with them your old equipment for their new. But in spite of all and every perversity you might associate with them boys, you are not to harm them bodily nor, after this first day, humiliate them. Look on them, gentlemen. Let your eyes see them for what they are. New blood, new blood! Lord be praised!"

Favoring the cut on his arm, and having left his loaf of bread to cool on a flat stone, old Bolly Quintard, in view of his age, felt he could raise a subtle point with his colonel. "Colonel Wheat, sir, sure as hell we're going to have to change our name. With them people we're no longer volunteers."

Deliberately, the colonel made his eyes bulge like a mad parrot's. "What, Bolly? Yield up a name you earned yourself jest for a clutch of latecomers. They're going to be volunteers. You gentlemen're going to volunteer them!"

Wheat turned away now and waved his hat towards whomsoever commanded the men at the gate. The conscripts advanced under the direction of two newcomer officers. They were both typical of certain species of Confederate officer. One was a man in his forties, something of a shuffler, Usaph noticed, not a trained officer. Probably an upland lawyer or professor who had decided he could no longer tolerate following the conflict through newsprint and wanted bodily to assist in imposing the Confederates' Christian will on the North. Having volunteered and bought his uniform, he'd been given the drab task of bringing conscripts cross-country. He looked as footsore as you'd expect. The other officer was a tall boy of no more than eighteen. The son of what you'c   1 a good mountain family, gangling but sure of himself, clever-looking yet something of a hick. He would have volunteered as soon as the school year ended at whatever college he'd been at. Probably Washington College in Lexington, or the University of Virginia at Charlottesville. Usaph watched him and thought, what would I give to be a learned man myself, a college boy like that.

He was not to know it, but the boy—whose name was Lucius Taber—had failed his Bachelor exams at Washington College, having not studied since last February, as he saw the history of Athenian democracy and the syntax of Horace and Socrates as irrelevant to this high perilous year in which Virginia found itself. He'd had two friends at Washington College. Their fathers, like his own, insisted they stay there until the end of the academic year. These boys therefore pledged not to study anything, and Lucius formed with them a secret body called The Immutables. The Immutables agreed to avoid study; to shun the company of other college boys and to seek that of the senior cadets from the Virginia Military Institute which stood near by on the hill above the gracious town of Lexington; to get used to taking whisky in quantities, a gift they were sure every Confederate officer should possess; and when asked to answer questions about the Age of Pericles, to reply with an explanation of Stonewall Jackson's Valley command or of the manner in which Yankeedom had destroyed the great American constitution.

After the examinations, the president of Washington College informed the fathers of The Immutables that it was no use keeping them there while the conflict lasted. It was hoped that would not be beyond late autumn, since by then Confederate success must have caused a peace settlement.

Now Lucius considered himself a traveler. In his fifteenth summer he'd been up the Ohio to Cincinnati. But he'd never been down into coastal Virginia before and the fact that he traveled with conscripts hardly touched his joy as a tourist.

Colonel Wheat's adjutant, Major Dignam, met the newcomers at the entrance to the meadow. The scraggy-looking lawyerly man saluted him and handed him a list of the conscripts. All through the ceremony the veterans kept silent, except for Gus Ramseur who called out, "I regret I'm not trained for it"—replying to an officer in his fever who had ordered him to play in a string orchestra of which all the instruments were made of whisky barrels cut in two and covered with drum parchment.

In near silence, the adjutant, Major Dignam, a lanky Methodist preacher from Mount Meridian, appointed twenty of the conscripts to one company, fifteen to another, 25 to the center company which had suffered surprising losses late on the afternoon of Gaines' Mill, and divided the last twenty between companies D and E. Listening, Bolly Quintard thought, the salt has lost its savour. The tainting of the Shenandoah Volunteers is completed. Yet like the others he wanted the new boys to be turned loose in the paddock, so that they could be punished for all the griefs and inequities he had suffered as a soldier of the Confederacy.

The new boys were not fools and could see what lay ahead. When they got the order to fall out they did not want to obey it, but remained in clutches of two or three near the gate to the meadow. Major Dignam loudly called the new captain and young Lucius Taber away to meet the other officers of the regiment, who were living near the general's staff in three captured tents heavily marked—like so much else of the equipment with which the war was being fought—with the enemy's initials, U.S.

The lawyer's name was Hanks. He protested to the adjutant. "I have to see to the comfort of my men."

"There's no seeing to it today. Tomorrow morning, Captain Hanks, is the time you take up your stewardship anew. Until then they have their new comrades."

"You're speaking, sir, from a knowledge of precedent?"

"I'm speaking from a knowledge of reality, Captain Hanks."

"I depend on precedent . . . I am a lawyer, sir. . . ."

"Well, maybe what I speak of can't yet be fully described as precedent, but if we help it along it might be precedent by sundown."

"What is your calling, sir?" asked Hanks. Saying it, he leaned back in a sort of county courtroom stance.

"The word of God is my vocation, Captain Hanks. And heaven my destination. I am a Methodist preacher."

"You are a preacher and countenance the theft that will now commence to be done to the newcomers?"

"Theft, theft, theft, sir?" groaned the adjutant. He smiled as if in pain. "The men about here have not had the touch of woman's hand, nor the ease of feather beds nor adequate corn-bread nor any nicety of linen or toilet since we went out after General Milroy last Christmas. They have lacked all, even Bibles, which I must fetch for them off the corpses on the battlefield, being as how the Bible Society in New York has decided to deprive us of Bibles, as if we were not, sir, fit for the word. No sirree, captain, there will be no theft. There will be adjustments. Come now, both of you."

Still the scrawny little man looked at his hundred conscripts, and his hundred conscripts looked at him.

"Come," Major Dignam insisted.

They couldn't disobey him. Lucius Taber in any case stepped out readily, being an Immutable. Conscripts deserved no defense from him. Lawyer Hanks went more slowly, not sure that the rule of law in that meadow would survive his going. As they went, Major Dignam pointed out to them items of interest of the Thomas plantation and indicated where the guns and teams of Poague's battery were ranged, pointing southwards towards the swamps and oak thickets.

— 4 —

THERE WERE, THAT LUNCHTIME, 73 volunteers in Guess's B-for-brag company of the Shenandoah Volunteers. Of these no more than fifty could walk, for there were eight lame, nursing stone bruises on their feet, three with great swollen carbuncles on their arms or legs, a half dozen with malaria, shivering away in a nest of blankets, five with dysentery so bad they could not rise even for this chance at loot, and two or three with pneumonia and other fevers. Those in that company who *could* move moved now on their fifteen conscripts, all except Usaph Bumpass, who, though mobile, stayed just the same with Gus Ramseur. Sure, he looked at the conscripts with some feeling of malice. Yet he did not trust the malice, it sat un-comfortably in him, there was something not true to Usaph

Bumpass about it. He would have liked to be able to go up to
the new boys and take anything he wanted from their haversacks. Bolly and Murphy and Judd were having no trouble
doing it, and neither was Danny Blalock, even though he was
an educated man. Maybe Usaph would have looked them over
for a pair of new brogans if he'd needed them, but he got
himself a good pair off a corpse after the Shenandoah Volunteers moved up in support of Maxey Gregg's South Carolinans on Boatswain's Swamp the week before. He now felt
fine-shod in the shoes of a poor dead Sandlapper. Now there
might be fish-paste or molasses in the conscripts' haversacks.
Well, he had fish-paste in his, captured Maine fish confection.
And tons of captured molasses filled the wagons behind the
staff tent, and a man could go according to his fancy and draw
off a pint.

He saw large bullet-headed Murphy unbutton a conscript's
jacket, and take from inside it a small Bible. Inside the Bible
he found a daguerreotype of a plump girl in a white blouse.
"Look here then, lads!" called Murphy. "Look what this-here
feller carries in the Word of the Lord!"

Bolly inspected the daguerreotype and got a real evil grin
on his face and asked the boy, "You bring the sword of the
Lord to this damsel, son?"

The boy said nothing. He was very much a boy and, Usaph
guessed, would always remember how he hadn't said anything
to rebuff the veterans when they chose to be sneery about his
betrothed.

"And sure, you must really bounce round in her, sonny,"
Murphy said. "A tiny whippet of a boy like you?"

"A gnat in a barrel of molasses," said young Judd. His chin
was all a-tremble at his wit, and he looked round to inspect the
hooting faces of Bolly and Murphy.

Danny Blalock might have been the most to blame. He'd
been a schoolmaster and must have seen children savage each
other in the schoolyard and got to detest those methods. Yet
although he didn't laugh, he stood by, surveying, the way old
Doctor Mollison, the bug-hunter Usaph used to see working
with jar and net along the cliffs north of Strasburg, might watch
a duck consume a June bug. As far as Usaph was concerned,
the women even of conscripts should have been sacred. For
that was the Southern way. The more they made jokes about
the conscript's plump girl the more like the slum-boys of the
North they became. And it was known what Yankees were

when it came to the commerce of the flesh. The men in A Company had passed round a letter they took off a slum-boy from New York whose body had been found east of Gaines' Mill last week. It was from this boy's girl in the alleys of Manhattan and it promised the boy in straight-out terms carnal pleasures he would never now enjoy. No Southern woman wrote to her feller like that; such writing was even beyond the measure of a crude Irishman like Joseph Murphy.

Throughout the meadow there were like scenes. The veterans went through the conscripts' haversacks and took coffee, real coffee which you could still get in western Virginia, mainly through the courtesy of Cincinnati businessmen who smuggled it across the Ohio. The conscripts' haversacks yielded as well cigars and chewing tobacco; even neat Danny Blalock who didn't chaw or smoke took tobacco out of a haversack.

The conscripts resisted a second here or there, but it was no fair contest. Their spirits had already been worked on. All the way across Virginia from Staunton, they'd been mocked as latecomers. And here they were facing the men whose name the Southern press, the *Mobile Advertiser* equally with the *Richmond Enquirer*, extolled. If only those newspaper scribes, Usaph often thought, knew how much of an accident it is that any of us are here; if they knew how mean average we are, as given to skulking and straggling as any other brigade if we were given a whisker of a chance. We ain't princes, us Stonewall Brigade boys, Usaph thought, scratching himself on the ribs where, beneath his shirt, the lice were active. But the conscripts there find us awesome and let us demean them.

Looking out across the meadow, Usaph saw Ash Judd taking a man's watch, Bolly Quintard grossly feeding still on the plump girl's picture, and Murphy lifting socks out of some poor boy's sack, inspecting them against the sunlight and choosing to keep them. He saw too a neat little Irishman, veteran of Guess's Company, stopping in front of a young conscript, raising his hand to the boy's cheek, taking him gently by the elbow and leading him away to a fence corner.

There was a gangling conscript, a hollow-cheeked sort of boy, maybe 25 years of age, standing off on his own. No one had bothered him. His jacket was open and his haversack sat on the ground at his feet, its flap undone for the convenience of looters. But up to now it remained untouched. It might have been they were all a little shamed by the way he'd laid himself open to theft. And you couldn't be sure of humbling a man like him in too convincing a manner. He had neat black hair, dark eyes and a narrow head, and the eyes gleamed as he looked full on people like Bolly making fools of others and maybe even of themselves.

Bumpass watched him, saw him shift his stance a little, like a man that's been waiting a long time for a train. He seemed to take some sort of interest in Joe Murphy, who had gone back to baiting the boy with the picture, saying such things as: "Does she know you're there, boy? Or is it a flea sting she thinks she's getting?" Tears ran murky through the dust on the boy's face.

The gangling young man said all at once: "Come now. Leave that boy alone. Your jokes are getting gas and repeating on themselves."

Bolly and Murphy and Judd and the others just looked at him. Their sufferings on campaign had given them certain moral rights, no one south of the Potomac should have doubted that. As far as they were concerned, this thin creature had therefore blasphemed them.

It didn't seem to worry the thin creature. He kept showing this clear-eyed indifference to them. "I've got a clean vest. I've got coffee. Don't you gentlemen want it? Or do you intend to spend the summer standing there letting your low jokes chase their own asses?"

Bolly stalked up to him.

"And who are you to speak out, you sowson, you whoreson bastard?" asked Bolly, falling back on the cuss-words his father had favored during the presidency of Thomas Jefferson.

The conscript looked Bolly fair in the eye.

"My name is Decatur Cate . . ."

Ash Judd said, "Your daddy have the stutters?"

He laughed shrilly then, but Bolly stared at him for detracting from the event. The duty of the unmanning of this Decatur Cate. "And I take it you're here substitutin' for a rich boy from beyond the River?"

Cate gave a tight throaty laugh.

"You take it wrong. I am a mere conscript. If I had stayed in my native Pennsylvania and finished reading for the Bar the way my pa commanded me, I would have now been in McClellan's army with maybe a better class of people."

The man's sass was dazzling. There was no punishment you could hand out to a man like this, short of hanging him from one of Mr. Thomas's plantation oaks.

Danny Blalock said in a high-toned way: "In McClellan's army. Under a bad general."

"A bad general but a good cause," said thin Mr. Cate. "Whereas down here it's all good generals and bad causes."

"I promise you, sir," said teacher Blalock gallantly, just like something out of a novel, "if you say one word more in that vein of yours, I shall kill you here by knife or rifle and state to my colonel in defence that I but killed a viper."

"Well goddam me!" said Decatur Cate, kicking the earth with the toe of his shoe.

Most of the conscripts had had their pants taken by now and were struggling, blushing, into the foul and tattered britches of their persecutors, and feeling the first bites of the greyback lice that infested the clothing of veterans. Yet Cate was kicking the earth with a slight smile on his face.

"I would not touch your coffee, sir," Danny Blalock yelled. "I would not touch any delicacy you might have. I would be defiled in touching anything of yours."

"It would be nice," said Cate, still pretending to be interested in the ground, "if the rest of your friends felt that way."

"By Christ," Murphy called, "*I'll* take his coffee and anything else. I'll strip the bastard. I'm not particular like yourself, Danny."

So they moved up and stripped Cate of his shirt and jacket and emptied his haversack. The boy they had forgotten picked up his daguerreotype and moved by stealth across to a bunch of his fellows who'd been through the process.

Ole Bolly was watching this bunch. "Oh Jesus, Usaph," he said. "They shouldn't have done this to us.

"This strikes at the only thing we can halfway call our own. Pride it strikes at, Usaph. It strikes at our sweet pride."

Ashabel Judd was holding a letter he'd taken from Cate's jacket. His lips moved as he read the addressee's name. Then he whistled.

"Hey there, Usaph," he called. "This-here letter's for you."

— 5 —

USAPH'S FACE BURNED. He left Gus Ramseur and took the letter from Ashabel Judd. Ashabel's eyes were fixed, innocent. Yet Usaph felt shamed to get his letter by way of a stranger. It wasn't just that the man was a conscript, but what was his wife doing, giving her precious handwriting into the care of a man who loved the Union?

Usaph saw his Ephephtha's wide letters on the outside of the sheet of paper and then, assured that the letter was hers, shoved it into his jacket. Turning back to Gus, he felt already halfway a wronged husband. Later, at a private time, without Irishmen and evil elders like Bolly looking on, he'd get that conscript aside and ask him what the hell he was doing, acting as Ephie's postman.

After eating a wedge of Bolly's ramrod loaf, Usaph pretended to wander off to the regimental sinks. These had been dug behind a fringe of live oaks by Thomas's slave huts. The sinks were a private place, because most men rarely used them, making their droppings wherever the urge took them. The Surgeon-General was always writing decrees that soldiers would be punished for squatting and excreting at random, but most of them, poor hill farmers, or laborers of the flat lands of the Carolinas, had been doing just that since babyhood. To them, crapping where the urge took you was all part of those direct and honest country ways those Yankees would try to convert you from, if you gave them the chance.

Usaph leaned on a fence by Thomas's slave quarters. There weren't many slaves round, mostly older people and little pot-bellied children. Most of the strong slaves were off on rental to the government, working on the fortifications round Richmond. Usaph didn't feel crowded by black eyes therefore. In a clumsy rush he pulled the letter not only open, but very nearly apart.

Dearest husban Usaph [he read], I take my pen in han
to rite to you. My pen is rude. My ink is pail, my love of
you will never fale my sweetest husban Usaph. My sole
cries for you, yore my turtle dove in the crevers of the rock
darlin Usaph. An my arms cry out and my lips say sweet
Jesus . . .

Usaph pressed his thigh against the fence of the Thomas
slave quarters, hoping that the dumb wood would turn to feminine flesh, Ephie's flesh. When she said arms and lips she
meant her sweet body. A Valley woman, unlike a slum Yankee,
didn't go in for immodest particulars. But the pink skin of her
groin would have wept as she wrote. And what consolation did
she have? No more than he did, he hoped, and all he had was
a fence.

Unless she had this *Decatur*. The thought caused Usaph to
begin to weep. He left the fence, tottering a bit with grief for
her, for himself. But, of course, he thought, in the midst of
his tears, if that had happened she wouldn't send letters by
him. Anyhow, Usaph Bumpass decided to forget the question.
The posts were bad, letters were meant to be a joy. And you
could chase your tail mistrusting a woman like Ephie.

Its bin a hot summer Usaph here at youre Aunt Sarries.
Youd think you was down in my neck on the woods. Thays
snaiks everwhers, ol Montie lifts a hay bale in the barn
t'other day an they's a copperhead sittin there as if he oned
Aunt Sarries. Still its good to be out of the way of the
Yankees. I sore old Mr. Chales from Mount Jackson the
other day at a funrale hier an he tole me the Yankee cavlry
would of bin over our place at Strasburg twies this summer.
I hates to think of it an so I don.

Everyone says you boys is gone drive that Maclellin all
the way back over to Phildelfier before the first snows.
England gone tell ol Abe to call it quits an leave us be an
youll be back for Crissmas an will be plantin corn in Strasburg agen nex summer. Pray the Lord God it be so. Even
Mr. Deckater Cate a paynter whos bin through thinks it
likly. An he professis to luv Abe. Though no critter could
luve that scowndrell as much as Mr. Cate sais he dos. His
a teese that Mr. Cate, he gose round the farms painting
poortrades of the yonge an Aunt Sarrie payd him to paint

me. When you come home will hang it up in the frunt parler
back in Strasburg.

Done let anythin happen to you darlin husban for yore
wife cudden stan it. I hev made a deal with the Lord so
youll be safe an come back safe. Its paneful to write you
an not be able to touch. Roses is red violets is blue, I swear
to the hevvens I luv you.

Yore adorin spouse
Mrs. Ephephtha Bumpass

Aunt Sarrie sez done worry on the matter of yore pappy's
grave. She sez not even Yankees trubbels graves.

Lovin E. B.

He kissed the letter's open page and dropped tears on its
riotous spelling. She could spell her name, his, the Lord's. But
that was about all she could guarantee.

It came to him that he was shivering. Ephie became a blood
fever, you didn't easily get over a letter from her.

— 6 —

USAPH HAD MET her in the fall of '59. Usaph's daddy, who
was himself ailing, had news of his elder brother, an overseer
on a plantation at Pocataligo in South Carolina. The brother
was said to be dying and Usaph's father felt one of the family
should go and visit him, for there were no other Bumpasses
down that way. He asked Usaph to go, to take letters and
greetings, a bottle of brandy and a little money. Usaph had
never before been east of Manassas Gap. He'd only heard of
the cotton-growing South, of the rice plantations, of the South
of the julep and the great slaveholders, of the unbuttoned,
rundown, rich, steamy, enticing world of the Carolina lowlands. So the journey he took amazed and upset him some.

He travelled by railroads that were to become the framework
of the war he now—three years later—found himself fighting.
The Manassas Gap Railroad, the Orange and Alexandria, the
Virginia Central, the Norfolk and Petersburg, the Seaboard and

Roanoke, the Wilmington and Weldon, and all the rest. On great trestle bridges he travelled through Dismal Swamp. In the inky waters there were alligators; the coastal jungles were thickened by creepers of Spanish moss. He observed Southern gentlemen drinking cocktails and mint juleps with their breakfasts in the saloon car, and outside the foul water and the swamp thickets blurred past. Here, according to the legends white Southerners tormented themselves with at night, runaway and renegade slaves hid and maybe planned a war against their owners, but the dogs of the slave-hunters and malarial miasmas and the alligators usually broke up those plans. Yet one could never be sure. It looked like the place out of which some nigger king, some unconquerable black man with mad eyes and savage thews and a great manhood that threatened all Southern womankind, might come some day.

Everyone had a cigar in his teeth on those coastal lines and talked of politics and the fine nature of Southern institutions. In a mean village smelling of turpentine and the pine woods of North Carolina, a Tarheel Congressman left the train and spoke to the crowd of poor whites and to the gentlefolk who had come out of the woods on fine horses in well-cut clothes. The women were wearing crinolines in this balmy Southern winter; and the slaves carried the bandboxes and portmanteaux and babies.

"We are an agricultural people," proclaimed the Congressman, only a little drunk, "pursuing our own system, working out our own destiny. We bred up men and women to some better purposes than to make them vulgar and fanatical and cheating Yankees. Let me tell you, my friends, about the Republicans, who have risen in the North like a plague. Their women are only hypocrites if they pretend they have real virtue. Their men are only liars if they pretend to be honest. They're nice people to have in your home if you don't mind your littl'uns corrupted, your wife vitiated, your principles compromised. They have no gentry up there as we have, and so they have no order. We have a system that enables us to reap the earth's fruits through a race which we saved from barbarism in restoring them to their real place in the world as laborers, while we are enabled to cultivate the arts, the graces and the accomplishments of life . . ."

The poor whites, sallow from malaria and from their trade of extracting resins and turpentine from the forest, looked at him soberly, and the tall planters too, their eyebrows lowered a little. Even then, two and a half years back, the battle lines were being drawn in the winter air by tipsy Southern Democrats and by crazed Republicans.

The Charleston and Savannah had gotten Usaph to Pocataligo one brisk dawn, and without eating breakfast, he hired a horse at the livery stable and got directions to the Kearsage plantation, where his uncle was said to be dying. The man at the stables talked reverently about the Kearsages. Mr. Kearsage had once been a U.S. attaché in London and was even known to have written a book so deep no one in Pocataligo had ever read it.

Mist sat on the low rice fields and hid all but the stookie tops of the cotton bushes when Usaph rode out of Pocataligo eastwards. Soon he met long lines of slaves moving along the road, shovels on their shoulders, to work on the sluice ditches in the rice fields. They were singing—just like all the books said they did—in a subtle harmony they took for granted.

"Ah mah soul, ah mah soul! Ah's goin' to the churchyard to lay this body down.

"Ah mah soul, ah mah soul! We's goin' to the churchyard to lay this nigger down."

He'd never heard the massed African voice like this. Why, in the Valley no one owned so many slaves. A wealthy Valley man might have as many as three slaves or even five—house-staff and a ploughman and a wagoner, maybe, if he transported his own produce. But Valley niggers lived far apart and in small numbers and never sang in such voice.

After two hours, Usaph reached a plantation settlement, screened by trees and standing up in the rich mud flats of the Combahee River. The big house was two stories high, there were creepers up its walls. It was part-timber, part-brick, and had that unapologizing air of blowsy elegance he had, on his train ride, gotten used to seeing. A house-black in a wig and britches opened the door, but there was a large bustling woman of about forty coming down the central staircase, a glass of liquor already in her hand at this hour. For some reason she came straight to the door. Usaph knew through some instinct that if he'd been a planter, or dressed as a planter, he would have been asked in, for she seemed anxious for company. But he was just the son of a Valley farmer, a wearer of solid plain stuff, neither white trash nor white gentry. If he had to live down here, he'd likely end up as a clerk or an overseer like his uncle. And the tall woman knew it at a glance.

He explained he was looking for his uncle. She bit her lip, put her glass down and called on her black maid to fetch her wrap.

"I hope this ain't any trouble," Usaph had said.

"No, no, come with me."

As she passed him he felt on his ear her hot brandy breath. In the Valley you drank in the morning only if you had to go out at the peak of winter, or had had an overnight fever. Yet in the Carolinas, he could tell, it was booze for breakfast, summer or winter, well or ill.

She led him through a kitchen garden. Beyond a narrow road were the shacks of the slaves, a whole village of shacks, shingle roofs, unglazed windows, fading whitewash. Garbage middens stood by the doors, heaps of oyster shell, old rags, broken boots and crockery and chicken feathers. Some old slave-wives sat by the doors laughing their laugh. Their laugh was melancholy and rich and feminine. They tended almost naked pot-bellied slave children, future workers for the Kearsage plantation.

"I sometimes feel badly about your uncle, boy," Mrs. Kearsage said. "I see him little enough. I hope he understands I have my duties to the slaves. People talk of my having so many slaves. I tell them it's the slaves who have me. Morning, noon and night I'm obliged to look after them, doctor them, and tend to them in this way and that. If Calhoun and Yancey are right, sir, and we ever have to fight for our way of life, I reckon I can manage the commissary as well as the medical side for the whole militia of this glorious state. There's your uncle's place. I won't come in. But you're to give him my warmest and best wishes."

She turned and walked away, an elegant gait. The hut she had pointed to wasn't much different from those he'd seen in the slavequarters, though one of its windows was glazed. Flakes of white on the grey and weathered surface of the timber showed where—about 1845 Usaph would guess—whitewash had once been put on. He knocked. He knew there would be no liveried negro answering at this door.

A white girl answered instead. She was dressed in an old crinoline. She was dark-complexioned and her eyes were dark. There was something wifely in the way she stood on the door-step—that was Usaph's impression, that she was a young wife his uncle had picked up and since she was so beautiful he felt a spurt of jealousy for his uncle. Later, after he'd married this dark-eyed girl, that impression—that she'd opened his uncle's door in so wifely a manner—still tormented him.

"Miss," he said, "I am Patrick Bumpass's nephew, Usaph."

"You come right in then, Mr. Usaph." She stepped back, hanging her head shyly as if she didn't believe in her own beauty.

He passed into the murky, torpid interior. The floor was of packed mud. On the undressed walls were unframed prints of Jefferson and Ole Hickory and various fire-eating Southern Democrats. It looked as if Usaph's Uncle Patrick, having lived by the peculiar institution of slavery, was determined to die by it, with pictures of its patron saints all over his walls. The uncle lay on a bed by the one window. He'd once been a big man, and his wasted jaws jutted aggressively even now, while he was hard up for breath. He watched his nephew. On a stool by his bedside was a copy of the *Charlestown Mercury* and a near-empty bowl of oatmeal. Usaph knew the lovely girl had been feeding it to him.

"Sir," said Usaph reverently, "I'm your nephew, Usaph. I'm your brother Noah's boy from Shenandoah County, Virginia."

The man's breath rasped. "You are welcome, son," he said and tears came into his eyes.

"My father—Noah—is poorly. But he wanted you to have a few comforts..."

Usaph got a bottle of brandy from the valise, and a deerskin purse with ten dollars in it. He put the bottle and the purse on top of the *Charlestown Mercury*. The dark-eyed, dark-haired girl watched, and Usaph smiled at her in a tortured way. If the luxuriant, humid, magnolia-drugged lowlands ever got together to create a lush woman, this woman was close to what might result. She had already infested Usaph's blood, she was already a lowland fever in him and he found it hard to look at her.

"I saw you once," said Uncle Patrick Bumpass. "It was at the depot at Charlottesville and I looks up and sees my brother and his bride toting a littl'un and waiting for the Staunton express. And goddam if that littl'un weren't yourself, Usaph... Usaph it is, ain't it?"

"Yes, Uncle Patrick. Usaph."

The old man began weeping. His tongue darted in and out of his mouth as if to catch tears.

"Thank my little brother," he said in a slow voice you could barely hear. "Tell him that-there's my monument money." The tears increased. "Tell your daddy you found his brother living in a nigra's hut. All his savings lost in a damnfool enterprise called the Combahee Drum-Fishing Company."

"Don't fuss yourself, Mr. Bumpass," the girl said in a low, soothing way.

"This-here's Ephephtha Corry, nephew," the old man told him. "Her daddy's been my truest friend. He sends her in each day to nurse and housekeep."

For some reason the idea repelled Usaph. "Mrs. Kearsage," he said to change the subject, "Mrs. Kearsage said to send her wishes."

The old man laughed at this. "Mrs. Kearsage. There was a time when Mrs. Kearsage liked being around me more than now. But we run head-first here into one of them ironies of the God-ordained system of slavery. An ailing overseer ain't worth the nursing, since he has no value on the market." He laughed again, but it turned into a choking fit.

"If I had market value," he went on, still chuckling and choking, "the way a nigra has, I'd get nursed then by Mrs. Kearsage; I'd be an investment, see, and she'd feel anxious for me. Them slaves, she wipes their fevered brow, but if it weren't for Ephie here my goddam fevered brow could go unwiped till my poor ole brain rotted."

His chest heaved as he tried to get back the breath he'd expended on this speech. "When a man is young and lusty he don't think on these peculiarities of our way of life."

Then, not being strong enough to grip, he laid a hand on top of Usaph's. "You ought to wed this Ephie, nephew, she's by way of being a tender girl."

Behind them, Ephephtha Corry laughed awkwardly. It seemed as if she was shamed somehow by this endorsement from Uncle Patrick. "Mr. Usaph Bumpass don't need no swamp girl, Mr. Patrick. Mr. Usaph is a plain-as-day gentleman."

He could tell she meant it. He was no gentleman to Mrs. Kearsage but to this Ephephtha Corry he appeared a well-mannered and well-off visitor from the mountains. He liked himself in the role; he felt himself get more worldly as he sat there. It's been said that if a woman gives a man a new picture of himself, then that's the start of infatuation. A nervous infatuation had already got itself going in that little shack, and Ephie's view of Usaph as a gentleman certainly helped it along.

"He can do his own arranging," Ephie said in a whisper, both shy and savage, to the uncle.

Now, two and a half years later, in the lines before Richmond, it still worried Usaph that the first idea of a closeness between himself and Ephie came out of the mouth of his dying uncle.

While the old man slept, he and the girl sat together in the sun. Her mother had died—she told Usaph—when she was three; she'd been raised by her father who fished the estuary of the Combahee River and sold his catch to the local villages. He was to have been Uncle Patrick's manager in the ill-omened Combahee Drum-Fishing Company. Uncle Patrick planned to buy a nice cutter, to bring wealthy men to the Combahee and take them out to sea to find drum fish, for drum fish were a great Southern sport.

Miss Corry was serious, shaking her head slowly, when she spoke of this folly. "God didn't mean it to succeed," she said.

"Why not, Miss Corry?"

"I don't know," she said, her head still hanging. "I jest know He didn't much care for that enterprise and that's all."

"Doesn't the Lord like Uncle Patrick?"

"I don't think He likes too many of us Combahee river-rats. And He don't much like some gentlemen neither."

"You mean me."

She grinned slowly, looking up under her black lashes, her smooth forehead. "No, not you. Other gentlemen he don't like."

She had the look of a girl who'd been allowed to raise herself. So she was an odd mix of rough and polish. Her hair was clean, and her dress; but the dress was old, maybe one of Mrs. Kearsage's cast-offs, patched with sacking. You almost expected her to be barefoot, but she wore little black mules on her feet.

Somewhere she'd got some education and knew something of the Bible and enough of her letters to read the editorials in the *Mercury* aloud to the uncle. Fishermen and raftsmen and their women, on coastal rivers or on the fabled Mississippi far away, were said to be shiftless and lacking in morals, and the idea that she might not be a virgin was already starting to torture him even as they sat there.

During the early days of that stay in the region of Pocataligo, he could not look her full in the face, his desire was so cruel.

One noon when they strolled the river flats she pressed up against him almost by accident, but he started away. He thought, if I caress her here, I'll be lost. I'll be out of all control in a strange land. So he tried to pretend for a while that the only thing uniting them was that they both tended and comforted his wry and dying uncle.

Each evening, after Ephephtha had cooked them their meal, she would leave to find her dug-out canoe and skim away downriver towards her daddy's home. Uncle Patrick would grow sullen after she went. He never seemed to sleep much, and Usaph, lying in a bedroll on the packed-earth floor, would wake often to hear the old man raving or coughing or rasping like a saw.

"What's the matter with you, boy?" Uncle Patrick wheezed in the middle of the third night.

"There ain't nothing the matter with me, Uncle Patrick."

"You wouldn't goddam say so? Can't you at least escort the lady to the riverbank? Or maybe go the whole hog and paddle her to her pappy's place. If such a pleasant exercise is beyond your powers, then I pity your generation, boy, that's all I say, I pity you all."

The next day he did what his uncle suggested. It was more than a mile to the river. The dug-out felt unwieldy to him but he made her let him paddle. Sometimes she grinned at him because of the unfamiliar way he plied the instrument. She guided him under trailing magnolia and amongst swamp oaks and forests of dead trees rising white-trunked out of the black water. Soon Usaph was lost in these dark reaches of swamp, but Ephephtha Corry seemed to know where they were. He surely hoped so, for the light was going.

What sort of country is this? he asked himself as he steered the dug-out. The frogs drum even in the fall. A great floppy rain-crow flew past, booming, and this ripe dark girl sat chortling at him from the bows of the canoe.

"Do you have gators up in the Valley?" she asked him.

"We sure don't. Do you have them hereabouts?"

She pointed at a spot about a yard from his left elbow. "What did you take that for?"

Well, as people do in books, he'd taken an alligator for a piece of swamp-rubbish, and he saw now it was a swamp monster there, shunting along on round about the same course as the dug-out.

"Don't you fret. They all know me, them gators and all their tribe."

"They know *you*?" he asked, staring at her, and fearful. A woman who believed that giant armoured swamp beasts knew and wouldn't harm her was in some danger. He looked again at the dim gnarled back and was himself afraid. He didn't tell her that, he didn't want to break any charm she had been travelling under.

"They knew me," she said, "since I been four years old. We's ancient enough friends, Mr. Bumpass, them and me."

The surface of the water broke well off to the right of the dug-out and a big snaky head rose with a mud perch thrashing in its jaws. "Why, that's my friend Jefferson. Ole Jeff is the king of the whole Combahee. Two axe-handles, he is, across the shoulders and that's no lie. Why the niggers're so scared on him, the story goes they feed a baby to him each full moon. Now that . . . I don't know if it's true." She called across the water. "You fancy juicy slave-baby, Ole Jeff?"

But Ole Jefferson had vanished. He might well be under this dug-out right now, Usaph thought.

"There," she said. She pointed to a sandspit. A sort of house was there, propped up on stilts above the water and the mud. It looked to Usaph like the unhealthiest place any man could choose to live. There was no light showing from it, its windows were shuttered.

"Oh Lordie," she said and looked at him with a real worried look on her face. "My daddy's away."

"Where?"

"Why, he's off on some tide," she muttered. "Meeting them drum fish." She closed her eyes and shook her lovely head. "He'll come back soon," she said, but it seemed she didn't really expect it.

"I don't know how to find my way back to Uncle Patrick's," said Usaph.

"That's jest it. You can't. But he'll be back soon to keep you company."

"I'd be happy," he said, starting to go all sweaty with his daring, "with jest yourself for company."

"Yes, well . . ." she said, and as the dug-out kissed the sand just beneath the stilt-house, she frowned again. And Usaph wondered, why did Uncle Patrick send me if he knew there was no way for me to get back?

They climbed a rotting ladder to the planking that served as a porch. Inside she found a lantern and lit it, while Usaph stood there twitching and sniffing the moist smell of mould and mud and fish-guts.

The house was simple as he'd expected. Against the far wall was a fireplace and a chimney made of beaten-out hardtack tins. Smoked fish hung like drying washing above the fireplace. A swamp rat had been feeding on a piece of cornbread and it looked up, and Usaph saw its mean little teeth. Yet the table was clear and showed the marks of being scrubbed daily. His mother used to say you could tell if a woman was a slut by whether her kitchen table was scrubbed good and regular. Ephephtha Corry had passed one of Mrs. Bumpass's tests.

The girl began to show him around, proud as a farmwife. Her father slept at the seawards end of the house—he said there were shifts in the tides and currents that he could hear better lying there. Her bedroom was the far side of a length of canvas sail hung from the roof like a curtain.

She touched him first, taking him by surprise, as they sat at table eating bacon fritters. She touched only his wrist but it came to him like a permission. He began to kiss her in a manner that hadn't ever occurred to him before, keeping his mouth as wide as he could, as if his intention was to devour. His hands raised her old green dress and cupped the fine melons of her buttocks and used them for their own sweet contour and also to drag her to him. He'd never acted like this before, so quick, so unshy, and he was already halfway frightened of him.

At first the girl was more than willing, lifting one leg from the floor, standing ostrich-like the better to fit him to her. But then her body and her mood changed, just like one of her father's tides.

"Please, Usaph," she said. "Please."

Over Usaph Bumpass's shoulder, she saw the walls of the shack the way she'd seen them the night those two drum-fishers misused her when she was but thirteen years. Her father had fetched them from the railroad at Jacksonboro—they were two Charleston gentlemen. They wore watered silk waistcoats under their jackets and they smoked Havana cigars and laughed all the time secretly with each other and took long pulls on sterling silver whisky-flasks they carried on their persons. Anyhow, Daddy Corry took them out fishing in his little yawl of a boat and got them back to the shack just as a hurricane struck. Ephie and her father and the two gentlemen sat up late listening to the wind howl and the downpour, and feeling waves—waves in the swamp!—breaking against the stilts of the house. The two gentlemen drank from their inexhaustible flasks. At midnight the little yawl was being whacked up against its pier, so Daddy Corry went out to moor it in the lee of the house. The two gentlemen weren't capable of helping and he wouldn't hear of Ephie coming with him. She was left to huddle here, here by this table where Usaph was now hugging her to the point of breathlessness, while the two businessmen coughed and whispered.

Then one of them got up and went to the window, peering out at the bobbing light of Daddy Corry's lantern. The other one also rose and walked towards the end of the shack, but as he passed Ephie's chair, he bobbed to the side and grabbed her by the elbow. He lifted her then by both arms and sat her on the table and unbuttoned himself one-handed and brought forth the terrible red slug of his manhood. How she screamed, but Daddy Corry couldn't have heard it, not with the hurricane winds and the crash of water, both from above and in the shape of waves as well.

When the first one was finished, the second came to her from the window and wanted his use of her. By now the first gentleman, who likely had daughters of his own and was a little sobered by what he'd done, said: "Why, Saul, she's so tight and she's bleedin'. I wonder if once ain't enough." But the second man demanded his chance and told her he wouldn't stand for her caterwauling the way the first had.

Ephie got so angry with her father for taking so long to save his yawl! When the second one had finished, he stroked her hair and said: "Now you get to your bed an' sleep sound. Go on, get to your bed." And he made threats about what would happen to her if she told her father anything.

When Daddy Corry came in at last, looking like a drowned man, Ephie was in her bed, weeping secretly, and the two men sat sleepily at table. "Your daughter was feeling poorly," they told him, indicating the girl's curtain and bed.

"I'll jest see if she's warm," said Daddy Corry. Taking his lantern, he drew the curtain back and stood over her bed. He saw the vomit on her pillow and the quivering shoulders and the bruise on her cheek and knew what had happened. He touched her hair like a conspirator. Then he closed the curtain, said, "She's jest fine," to the men, grabbed his shotgun and ordered them out into the storm. They went because they could tell how close he was to shooting them. Then he gave Ephie coffee that must have had whisky in it, for she slept, and all night the men were stuck on that little wharf, wailing for mercy, and *their* screams too being gobbled up by the racket of the hurricane. In the morning, when the wind dropped, he sent them off in a dug-out with them yelling threats of death and legal action at him.

Since that dreadful time she had sometimes let other men lie with her, mostly out of politeness, but without joy. There had been a few times with Usaph's ailing Uncle Patrick Bumpass. But it was not this that made her beg Usaph to stop now. It was that somehow his sharp desire reminded her bodily of the other gentlemen visitors those five years back; and so confused her.

"Please," she said again, and he stopped. Nothing she'd ever learned of men up till then gave her any idea that men could stop. But Usaph stopped so politely, his member still half-crippling him, but him frowning and asking so softly: "Did I hurt you?"

"No," she said. "No. No, you didn't. Tomorrow, Usaph. Honest. Tomorrow maybe."

That seemed to make him so happy. It came to her for the first time in her life that she, in her ole green dress, with the malarial fever in her blood and with all her sorrows, had the power to give happiness.

They talked for a while, then she went to bed and he slept on a rug on the floor. Before midnight she woke him and said there was no need to wait till tomorrow.

When they lay clasped together on her truckle bed, he forgot once and for all to ask himself the question honest farmers are meant to ask about the women they love—the question of whether she was virgin. His knowledge of the body of woman up to that point was imperfect and derived from two whores he had visited in Winchester one market time and from the thirty-year-old wife of ole Travis, the Bumpasses' neighbor near Strasburg.

At the end of their first hour of coupling, it was already three times too late for him to ask Ephephtha Corry any questions about other men and other fornication. He had since wanted to, but never dared. A solemn boy like him could easily lose such a woman, he felt, by asking the wrong questions.

They were both back in their proper places when Daddy

Corry came in before dawn and looked at them with suspicion. He was a little man, leathery from his profession, and he hadn't taken many fish. He wanted a meal and Ephie got it and sometimes smiled secretly at Usaph.

"The Lord hisself couldn't get no miraculous draft out of that there," he said, pointing east, towards the Atlantic ocean. And because the father was so low and tired, it made them all the happier and higher. When they set out for Uncle Patrick's again, they were like Adam and Eve travelling on the face of the waters, and somehow the gators didn't frighten Usaph at all, they were like so many harmless creatures in Eden.

The same evening he returned to the shack with her and told the fisherman he wanted to marry her. Pappy Corry grunted a lot. "There ain't no dowry," he said. "If you can find any dowry in this place you're welcome to it, boy. You can have a half share in my nets if you care for 'em." Late in the evening he said: "Your pappy's the one who won't go for it." Later still, he growled: "I'll have to get me in a woman to cook my victuals for me." And at dawn, when Usaph woke stiff from a chaste night on the uneven floor: "Ephephtha can't think of leaving your poor Uncle Patrick alone till his sufferings're over."

Usaph couldn't wait in the Carolinas that long. He still had to get in the last of his father's corn before the first snows fell in the Valley. He could wait only long enough for Ephie to assure him that they weren't about to have an early child from their coupling. Then he went homewards in deep sorrow, believing he might never see her again, and grieving that she would spend most of her time in the next few months with that uncle of his. But he was caught. How could he deny his father's brother the comforts of a nurse in his last days? It would be unnatural to do so.

Ephie too felt she was seeing the last of him and wanted to flit with him. But she too was bound to the dying and unlovable Uncle Patrick. She was sure from what she'd heard of Uncle Patrick's upright brother Noah, Usaph's father, that the Bumpasses wouldn't let Usaph marry her. She was dowryless trash. The only thing was that she had the gift of happiness in her keeping, and she wished there was some way she could tell ole Noah Bumpass that by letter.

Usaph and his father argued for two months about Ephie. Noah Bumpass could name a tribe of Valley girls of known family that Usaph could wed. People that live in river estuaries have poor morals, said Noah, and carry diseases. Usaph couldn't predict the griefs a swamp-rat wife would bring him, said Noah. "The fact that this Pappy Corry is your Uncle Patrick's best friend ain't any recommendation at all, I'm afraid."

And in that two months and ever since, Usaph went on remembering that it was Uncle Patrick who, by a sort of knowing suggestion, had brought on their first lovemaking. As if his uncle had known more of Ephie's swamp-girl ways than a mountain boy like him, his brain touched by the ice of the high Valley he dwelt in, ever could.

As it happened, Uncle Patrick died in winter and Usaph went straight away to fetch Ephephtha. He took with him as chaperone his mother's sister from Winchester, a joyless widow he disliked. Ephie was clever enough to know she had to behave perfectly, and be skilful and helpful, if she was to win the Bumpasses round. She was all these things. By the time Noah Bumpass died, he went believing she was the best nurse and sweetest girl he'd ever met and was even envious of his son for possessing her beauty.

And now here was this painter, this Decatur Cate, this Union funny man, who talked like a master's student from Charlottesville. Usaph knew, just by the look, by the mocking ways of this goddamn conscript, that Cate and Ephie would have laughed together. And that they might have understood each other as Cate dabbed the pink paint on the canvas and told her to be still and obedient.

— 7 —

SERGEANT ORVILLE PUCKETT of the Rockbridge Artillery, a college boy from Lexington who came towards the sinks from the cannon park that afternoon, saw the tall blond rifleman with rough blue patches on his jacket, leaning against the fence of the slave quarters, groaning, dripping tears. Orville surprised himself by getting a sort of sexual excitement at the sight of the poor boy. But he remembered the principles of Socrates he had learned in Lexington, and thought of good order and, composing himself, passed behind the screen of cedars and dragged his breeches off quickly, as his diarrhea demanded of him.

Orville Puckett commanded a gun in Captain Edward Brynam's battery of the Rockbridge Artillery. In the Rockbridge most of the officers were professors and the gunners mainly undergraduates. So up to the Easter of the college year of 1861 Captain Brynam had been Professor of Ethics and Geometry at Washington College in Rockbridge County, and Orville Puckett had been a student of classics there. There were many such college boy units in the artillery of the Confederacy, for when the war began college people, from their acquaintance with mathematics and trigonometry, considered themselves the natural-born and ordained cannoneers to the army of the infant nation.

Puckett remembered as a lovely, innocent sort of dream the way he'd got mixed up with cannonry during Saturday afternoon classes.

A sweet spring Saturday. When . . . ? Well, as it turned out, just last year. The last Saturday before Virginia left the Union. Old Kenton up on the platform droning away on the subject of Cicero's ovations, using his dullest, most peevish classroom voice as if this were just any Saturday.

And one of the junior-class men came running up the green slopes to the lecture hall and stuck his head in the window and said that the cadets from the Virginia Military Institute were marching downhill towards Lexington to fight the town militia.

That particular Saturday afternoon the people of Lexington were of all shades of opinion. The mayor was still flying the U.S. flag from the City Hall, the townsfolk wanted Virginia to stay snug in the bosom of the Union. The professors and boys of Washington College wanted to fight against that craggy, uncouth lawyer from Illinois who was attempting to coerce Virginia's sisters, to tyrannize over Carolina, Georgia, Alabama, Mississippi and all those other Christian and sovereign states.

But if the college boys were hot against tyranny, the cadets of the Virginia Military Institute, sharing with the college a hill above the town, were hottest of all.

All morning that Saturday there had been arguments on the street corners, and fist fights between cadets and town boys, and—about lunchtime—a rumor reached the Military Institute that a town boy had killed a cadet. At once the cadets took their muskets from the dormitories and marched down on Lexington, marched right past the window of the Institute's president, Colonel Smith, who had pneumonia and couldn't move. The Mayor of Lexington, warned of this invasion of armed cadets, sent a message across town to the Captain of the Lexington Rifles. These were local boys, still, at that stage, in favor of the Union. They were drilling as they usually did on Saturday afternoons on open ground to the west of town. Some civilians joined in with the Rifles now and a battle line was formed on the edge of town facing the cadets' line of march.

Once the junior classman brought this news to Dr. Kenton's lecture-hall window, the ageing don found himself without a class. The exits were rushed; some boys even left by the windows. Soon Orville Puckett and others were down on the banks of the James, watching the cadets cross by the bridge and march in column towards the place by a tavern on the edge of town where the Rockbridge Rifles were drawn up.

Then a few professors from the V.M.I. came scuttling out of their houses in the town, past the town yokels who whistled and catcalled them, and halted the column of cadets. It was the first time Orville had really noticed that gangly professor called Jackson, who now tried to pacify the cadets, talking low and hard to them. According to what Orville found out later, Tom Jackson had been planting celery that afternoon in his back garden with his wife Anna, as if he wanted to believe he'd still be there to pick it at the end of summer.

Orville booed and hissed as hard as anyone when Tom Jackson made the cadets wheel around and march briskly back to the Institute. But if there'd been firing that day, it would have been no replay of a town-versus-Institute ballgame. The townsmen would have been killed. Down in Charleston Harbor, Fort Sumter had been falling bloodlessly all week to the artillery of the State of South Carolina. But this here, on the edge of Lexington, wouldn't be bloodless. The Rifles were armed with old flintlocks and screwball muskets from the days of the Indian Wars of President Andrew Jackson. Such weapons as those were slow to load and inexact beyond fifty yards. The cadets, however, carried Enfield muskets, good over hundreds of yards, made in the armory at Harper's Ferry. Each cadet had, as well, seven rounds issued earlier in the day for the Saturday afternoon target practice. They knew how to fire by order, whereas the Rifles were just a sort of drinking club.

That aside, the incident filled the college with a high martial ardor. The same evening various professors went round the dormitories taking names for a regiment of volunteers to serve the State of Virginia. By the time Virginia seceded from the Union the following Wednesday, the regiment—which existed only as names being carried in professors' pockets—was being called the Rockbridge Artillery.

Major Jackson, his loyalty now being to Virginia, lent the Rockbridge two gun carriages from the Institute on which to mount the town's ancient smooth-bores (War of 1812). He also sent down two bright cadets to give artillery instruction. They were wonderful days, those days before Orville found out what artillery could do to human flesh.

Orville had first found out something of that at that fight at Manassas, where Southern virtue, Southern individuality, Southern forthrightness routed the Union. And where the cannon-hungry South captured 28 U.S. guns. Cannon as such were the manufacture of Northern mills. Sure, rural ways kept the Southern States rustic, pure, American in the old sense of the word. But hard-up for artillery. The cannon taken at Manassas were a gift of the gods.

The gun Orville Puckett commanded these days, a Napoleon twelve-pounder, was one of them. But Orville had changed since the fight at Manassas. Today, the day he saw that infantry man weeping, he didn't know any more if Southern virtue could last a war that went on beyond this coming autumn. And he surely didn't know if he could last it himself. He was getting thin, he had stomach cramps all the time and ceaseless diarrhea.

The war was wasting him. It was wasting the South too. It was turning the South into a sort of war factory, a greedy and wasteful manufacturing. He'd seen what had happened to Richmond, where his father was now a clerk in the War Department. Prices were pumped up, just as they were in the markets of New York; candles, flour, coffee, lumber, copper were hoarded and speculated in. Richmond might just as well be Boston.

He adjusted his trousers and took from his pocket the captured toilet soap his cousin in Jeb Stuart's cavalry had given him. If I can just get home to cornbread every day, and some ripe apples and honey and Thanksgiving turkey and other niceties, I'm going to be all right. He coughed and noticed that there was phlegm on his chest. He felt frightened straight away.

I've got to be careful of that. I wonder can I buy a flannel
undershirt. With a flannel undershirt he might be able to last
out the autumn and early winter. And that should do it.

The weeping soldier had vanished. Orville went to Thomas's
stream and washed his hands, making a face at the human
excreta all up and down the muddy bank. "Too many goddamn
Irish." He began to sluice his hands and his face.

The idea came to him, sharp as a pain, and he began to
cough again. These boys who had fouled the stream would live
on to inherit the new nation, but he doubted he could himself.
He wanted to weep into the water, but he had already seen one
boy weeping today and that was enough tears. Besides, he
couldn't be sure he'd ever stop weeping once he got the way
of it.

Sergeant Orville Puckett was a month less than twenty-one
years, and wound taut to last the summer out.

— 8 —

IT BECAME A night of fireflies and mosquitoes. Gus Ramseur,
the music master, had stopped raving. Usaph was schooled in
the ways of fevers and knew that they were least high at the
onset of dark. So he didn't ease off on his care; he went on
now and then putting a flannel-wrapped hot brick into Gus's
blankets, at the same time tormenting his own heart with the
idea of Ephephtha and that conscript.

And they came at him all evening. Murphy and Judd, and
that evil old man Bolly Quintard. "Nice news from your wife,
Usaph?" "Nice news the conscript brang you, Usaph, from
your own sweet spouse?" "What's your wife's opinion of conscripts, Private Bumpass?" He didn't answer them. At supper-
time there was cornbread, baked crusty in the fire by Joe Murphy, and hanks of ham and good coffee. But when it was ready
Usaph fetched his and took it to Gus Ramseur, and ate it beside
Gus. He could see those others making ironic faces at each
other. He thought, if Gus Ramseur don't come round, what
will I do for gentle company? Even Danny Blalock, though
a gentleman, seems to side with them.

After the meal one of the Irishmen got out his fiddle. He was some fiddler, that Irish boy. He had learned as a baby on the Dingle Peninsula in County Kerry, playing in the public houses while the farmers danced. When he got to Newport News in 1858 and jumped his ship he found in Virginia the music he was used to in Dingle. For the music of Virginia was all Scots and Irish. He could play any air on the fiddle even if it had crazy Virginian words to it now in its new habitat, and a wild American name.

The fiddle he played tonight he'd found in a farmhouse near Gaines' Mill, and if the army moved again he'd no doubt leave it here in Thomas's pastures. But for a moment he hugged it and brought out its sound as if he had owned it from boyhood. He began with a tune they all liked, something like Dixie, with words they felt they had a right to sing.

> "We are the sons of ole Aunt Dinah
> An' we go where we've got a mind ter,
> An' we stay where we're inclined ter,
> An' we don't care a damn cent. . . ."

Next he played the other sure-fire favorite, more sentimental, more restrained, making even brutes like Bolly think of soft women.

> "The years creep slowly by, Lorena,
> The snow is on the ground again,
> The sun's low down the sky, Lorena,
> The frost gleams where the flowers have been,
> But the heart throbs on as warmly now,
> As when the summer days are nigh."

Men holding their shirts over the campfires, singeing the greyback lice, sang and let the tears fall down their cheeks. Just because lice inhabited your armpits and made a city in your crotch didn't go to say you had no soul left at all.

"That song," said Danny Blalock, when the whole six verses were finished, "was given by a Trappist monk in Kentucky." He could always give you that kind of information.

"A monk you say?" Bolly murmured. "A goddam monk?"

"He became a monk in Kentucky when his girl married another man. In no time the other man died and left her a widow. But it was too late then."

Bolly whistled. Then he turned onto his other elbow and called to Usaph, "You might jest encourage that conscript feller to enlist with the monk, Usaph."

The trouble was the humor was too low to answer. Usaph saved up his rancor for the conscript Cate.

When Bumpass didn't answer, the others just forgot him and sat there trading their usual stories of hot widows and wartime adulteries. Ashabel Judd told how he had gone out into the Pendleton County Hills looking for the tracks of a stag. "Christmas, two year back. And like a dang fool I ventured too far and had to find a house to bide the night. Well, the houses in Pendleton are few and I found this quiet place, no paint, mountain trash, you know the manner of people they might be. Well, that door was opened by a wild red-haired widder. There was just herself and her poor simple sister. . . ."

"Oh, you service simple gals, do you, Ash Judd?" Murphy asked him.

But Ash was shaking his head, and there was something true about the way all bravado had vanished from his tale. "No," he said, "Not the simple gal. Not her, poor thing."

"I," said Murphy, "once met a girl in a field near Charlottesville." He lowered his voice as if it were all a secret, but it wasn't so secret Usaph couldn't hear it. "I'd gone off looking for chickens and found herself culling early berries—she had, oh my dear Lord, sweet fingers. After I'd rode her bare-assed in edge of the woods, right there in the goddam sedge-grass, she says to me without blushing, d'you know Sergeant So-and-so my dear husband. He's Captain So-and-so's right hand in the 3rd Virginia, except it wasn't the 3rd Virginia, if you take my meaning, it was a regiment closer to home than the 3rd, but I ain't intending to specify further which one. Right there, off pat, with my fresh spunk in her, she says it." Murphy adopted a feminine voice. "D'you know my dear husband Sergeant So-and-so . . ."

"All right, all right," called Usaph, sweating freely, wanting to *know*, that was all. Wanting to know. Never wanting to know. "The story's taken, for God's sake, the story's understood!"

And that made Ash and Bolly hoot and Murphy look mean.

Looking away, Usaph saw the fiddler studying the huddle of conscripts. The man began signalling with his eyes and eyebrows to someone, and the thin young conscript, maybe eighteen, that he'd shown an interest in earlier, stood up and walked over to the place the fiddler was playing and sat down near him. The fiddler and the boy stared at each other for some ten seconds until all around them disgusted hisses and grunts started to rise. There might have been some arguments about that kind of behavior if it hadn't happened that all over the bivouac other fiddles were starting up, and from the 5th Virginia's camp site a little distance away a battery of tin whistles swelled the sound, for the 5th Virginia was all Irish.

It seemed to the tormented Usaph that everyone but him began singing "Just Before The Battle, Mother." But they used the words that made a mock of the song.

> "Just before the battle, mother,
> I was drinking mountain dew.
> When I saw the Yankees marching,
> To the rear I quickly flew,
> O I long to see you, mother,
> And the loving ones at home,
> That's why I'm skedaddling southwards,
> While there's still flesh on my bones. . . ."

The fiddler could tell that the evening was spoiling on him. Just because the others didn't like him giving favors to a conscript. So he went on to a real spell-binder. "All Quiet Along the Potomac," written in the North but imported South in smuggled copies of *Harper's*. It was—as boys said—"one of them songs against officers."

> "All quiet along the Potomac, they say,
> Except now and then a stray picket
> Is shot as he walks on his beat to and fro,
> By a rifleman hid in the thicket.
> 'Tis nothing, a private or two now and then
> Will not count in the news of the battle;
> Not an officer lost—only one of the men,
> Moaning out, all alone, the death rattle . . ."

Under cover of the general absorption provided by this anthem, Usaph put another brick in Gus's blankets and moved quietly across the meadow to the loveless corner where the conscripts sat, talking low, eating their grits and cornbread. He tried to keep out of the light of their fires, just in case Bolly and the others saw him, and he called as he walked: "Cate!

Cate!" All conscripts who weren't Cate averted their eyes.

Cate was out of the firelight, sitting against Thomas's railing fence. It was a bright enough night for Usaph to recognize the tattered clothes Cate was wearing as Murphy's old rags, minus of course Murphy's Southern Comfort Society shirt. Usaph was pleased to see Cate humbled in the Irishman's lousy tatters.

"You itching, Cate?"

"I've killed all the lice in these rags, Mr. Bumpass," said Cate quietly. "There was—I can tell you—a multitude of them."

"And they'll come back. Their eggs're still probably there in the threads. Just when you get a bit hot on the march and your body gets foul, they'll come back—young 'uns—in their hosts."

But he couldn't understand why he talked lice. Lice could bite Cate's balls down to a stump and it would mean nothing to Usaph if the man had already had Ephephtha Bumpass.

"Get up, Cate. I want a word of you."

Cate looked up at him with a species of wary irony.

"You don't want to sit by me here? None of your friends will see. . . ."

"Oh sweet Jesus, I tell you, friend, get up here now and jest follow in my tracks."

Cate obeyed, though like all such men he had a way of making his obedience seem one way or another an insult. Usaph itched and it was not entirely his own population of lice. It was the itch that comes from knowing you can't win against a particular man, that you might never get replies that satisfy you.

He led Cate over the zigzag fence.

Through a line of oaks they got to the entrance avenue of Thomas's plantation. Fireflies winked nicely amongst the foliage of the oaks.

"Let me tell you something first, Cate, I don't want no funny answers. Do you catch my drift?"

Cate seemed to fluff up in front of his eyes, the way a turkey does. Is the man crazy? Usaph thought Ephie couldn't really tell the difference. Ephie would just as like think crazy was clever.

"I give funny answers only to funny men," the conscript answered, like an actor in a travelling play. "Men like your friends. Don't you think I knew how to slip that letter to you, that you wouldn't want it to come to you in public and by the hand of a conscript? Do you think I'm blind to your code, sir?"

Usaph had the terrible feeling that what Cate said was all mockery, but you couldn't be sure, because the conscript frowned while he talked, like an earnest man. It was just there was nothing to grab on to in his manner. He was about half a hand taller than Usaph and bent over him, looking hollow-cheeked and solemn as a traveling preacher foretelling doom. But you couldn't help noticing a sort of unheard laughter from somewhere in the area of the son-of-a-bitch.

Usaph said low: "You know nothing of my code, sir. Keep your goddam tongue off my code."

"As you say, Bumpass."

They kept silent for a while. The bits of song came to them still. The army sounds so goddam contented, Usaph thought. I happen to have enough goddam heartburn to give a ration to everyone, to make every man goddam heavy at heart.

"How do you know my wife, Mrs. Ephephtha Bumpass?" Usaph asked suddenly, as if Ephie herself had said nothing of it in her letter.

"Why, I painted her. I'm a traveling portraitist, a limner of quality with prices according. Your aunt met the bill though. She likes Ephephtha—Mrs. Bumpass."

"You don't mean my Aunt Sarrie gave you a record of her likes and dislikes?"

Cate thought about this. There were a lot of cogitative flex-ings of his hollow jaws. "Well, she displayed what might be called suspicion at first. But we got to . . . well, *respect* each other."

"How long was it my wife sat while you put the paint on?"

"Well, I would say it must have been eight days all told," said Cate, bunching his eyes up, calculating. "A portrait can't be put together quick, Mr. Bumpass. Oh, I know your average mean rural portraitist might do a likeness in two days. But the genuine article is not to be rushed."

"I hope as sure as yesterday's sun that there was none of that Union talk you come out with this day. I hope, and may I say, Decatur Cate, your goddam life hangs on it, that you never spoke your goddam black Republican thoughts to my bride."

"Do I look like it, Private Bumpass? Do I look the species of man who'd tamper with the political fancies of a good woman?"

In the dark under the oaks, Usaph trembled. But I won't

hit him yet, he thought. I'll let the son-of-a-bitch come to a head.

Cate heard Usaph's grunting and fuming. "I am in a fix, Private Bumpass, sir. Nothing can I say that doesn't hit you like an insult. And through no fault of mine. Am I guilty in carrying a letter from wife to husband? Are the mails of this Confederacy so prompt that I shouldn't be used to carry a letter?"

Usaph waited, still breathing noisily through his nose.

"You are," Cate went on more quietly, "a man I am not and may never be. You are a man beloved of a sublime woman, sir."

It seemed to be time to punish the conscript. Usaph pushed Cate against the trunk of a plantation oak. Because of the man's excessive beanpole height, Usaph had to raise his elbow somewhat to trap the artist's throat against the bark. He listened to the man gagging and it gave him an uncharacteristic pleasure.

"How'd you come to fetch up with this regiment of all regiments, you whoreson, you pig's ass? How come this very company? How come?"

He was surprised Cate *could* answer, had the calmness to answer straight.

"They told us," said Cate, coughing in a manner that sounded stagy to Usaph, "they told us in Staunton that we was natural enough meant as new blood for this Shenandoah regiment." Cate raised his eyes and there was still that sort of mockery in them, Usaph thought, but it still wasn't the kind you could be sure about and all it did was key up your hollow anger. "I couldn't believe my good fortune . . . since I meant to hand the letter in person. Then when the officer wrote me down for C Company, I swapped my place there with a boy . . . one who'd got written down for Guess's Company and didn't care either way."

"Why? Why in hell's name did you do that?"

Cate stared straight at Usaph, in a dead level way for once, and the eyes were sort of bleak. "I knew no one else. Not a soul, Bumpass."

"You know not me, you goddam scum!"

Cate's long head, imprisoned still by Usaph's forearm, gave a little nod.

"I feel I might, Bumpass. That's all. I feel I might know you, from your wife's words."

Usaph released Cate, pulled away as if he weren't fit to

touch, then shaped to hit him but despaired of it doing any good.

"You might be funny, Cate, when you stand there talking with paints in your goddam hand. We'll jest see how good you'll make with the jolly jokes when your Republican friends in the army of the Union are pouring cannister at you."

Not knowing what else to do, Usaph turned and at first felt a little easier. But before he was fully back to his own campfire he understood that the question of Cate and Ephephtha still stood. Seeing two young conscripts talking over a dying fire, he kicked the skillet out of the hand of the one who held it, he kicked the chunks of kindling wood out of the fire. There was a cascade of sparks in the conscript boys' faces and so much fright there that Usaph felt ashamed. Had his father raised him to treat people this way?

He got back to his own fire. The Irish fiddler was sawing away at some sad love song, but no one seemed to be listening any more. The conscript boy still sat beside him and the only good things were that Gus Ramseur, the true musical talent, was cooler, and that mocking Bolly Quintard was working at dropping off to sleep under the tree where he and Joe Murphy had opted to spread their blankets.

— 9 —

ON THE SAME evening that Bumpass and Cate had first tussled with each other, an English journalist, the Honorable Horace Searcy, was riding down the Charles City Road towards the Thomas plantation. Searcy resembled Cate in being a lonesome soul and in having a father who disapproved of his son's trade. He also had, like Cate, been expelled from a university, in his case the University of Oxford, for wounding a fellow student in a fencing match involving épees with no protective tips on them. It was not that Horace Searcy was a vicious man. He had daring, that was all, and misfortune sometimes attended his daring.

Searcy's father, Lord Grantham, was in some ways a reformer—he helped ease the Bills doing away with child slavery in mines and factories through the House of Lords. Just the same, he thought journalism was a vulgar profession, but he had had enough influence at the time to have Horace taken onto the staff of *The Times*, which was the nearest thing to a proper newspaper.

Then, to Lord Grantham's pain, his son became a storm bird, and began to attend wars as if they were boxing matches. His first war was the Crimean, then the war in Italy in '59, and finally the most vulgar of all wars, the conflict between all those former British colonies in North America.

In later days, people would call Searcy a war correspondent, but there wasn't such a term then, for Searcy was just about the first of the species. As his trade demanded, he travelled without much luggage. In his saddlebags he carried whisky, three shirts and a pair of drawers, a sketch book and two novels of Fielding, *Joseph Andrews* and *Tom Jones*. In his heart any affection he carried was for his three-year-old daughter. She was what people called a natural child, a bastard. She lived with her mamma on the edge of London. But she was not the only secret to be found beneath the journalist's ribs.

One of his profounder secrets was that he detested Southern institutions, that he had all the passion of an abolitionist, and that he carried a secret commission from U.S. Secretary of War Stanton to gather intelligence. It was a sign of his world-wide reputation that he sported, in his breast pocket, letters of introduction and safe passage from such Confederate generals as Longstreet and Magruder. He rode his horse comfortably, a dark, solid young man who resembled an Elizabethan pirate; and he looked forward to seeing once again the remarkable Tom Jackson.

The Confederate lieutenant escorting him pointed to the Thomas house. "That's it, Mr. Searcy. That's Jackson's head-quarters."

Searcy thought, not for the first time, what a plebeian war this was. American generals often as not headquartered in broken-down farmhouses with peeling whitewash. It wasn't like that French-Austrian War of a few years back. Nothing but castles suited an Austrian general and even the French never camped in anywhere less than a hunting lodge. Searcy approved more of these democratic knock-about Americans, North and South, than he did of European generals. Only the bad ones here—McClellan and Fremont say—expected castles.

Whereas any decaying tidewater house suited the good ones, suited Burnside and Phil Kearny and Longstreet and Jackson.

"No palace," said Searcy to the young staff man.

"Palaces ain't so common in Henrico County."

"I expect you're right."

In the plantation avenue the air seemed full of methane, the stink of swamp water mixed with the stench of excreta. Searcy had travelled freely North and South and had seen both Union and Confederate camps. In a report to British readers he had said that Confederate soldiers were on average smellier than Union ones—"malodorous" was the word he'd used. It was partly that toilet soap was in short supply in the South, partly that most Northerners had the chance to change their linen more often, partly that they were often more worldly. It was partly the Southerners' suspicion of latrines.

But, whatever their rustic personal habits, Rebels were better behaved than Yankees. They did not regularly steal fence rails or chickens or pigs, whereas, when the Yankees turned up in any farmyard, they would steal a gnat that hadn't been properly hidden away and behave like angels of the sword and the flame—as, however blind, stupid and ill-tutored about the facts they might be, they *were*, in Searcy's eyes at least.

His escort turned back towards Richmond. At the Thomases' front door a soldier took the reins of his horse and a slave in yellow-stained livery with a ratty powdered wig on his head led the two gentlemen into the hall. Searcy pressed his card into the slave's hand. "Tell the General the Honorable Horace Searcy begs an audience."

"Yassah," said the old slave. "Mastah Thomas and the General is at the dinner table, sah."

"So much the better," the journalist said. "I won't be taking up his working time."

Because the Confederacy believed its chances depended on British good will, because that good will had (according to the South) not been evident, Searcy was used to being badmouthed, as a representative of vicious Britain, by Southern gentlemen. Generals who would have seen him willingly and talked to him freely in the spring, were now less free with him. Jackson had never been easy to speak to in any case, and would be even less so now.

While the slave left him standing in the hallway, Searcy found himself stamping his foot and jolting his head. The liveried slave appeared again. "The gentleman can go in," he said, bowing in a way that wasn't quite like the bows of the footmen at St. James's Palace.

In Thomas's living room the air was hot. There weren't any women—Mrs. Thomas, it seemed, had been sent out of the room. Thomas himself sat at the end of the table. He was a Southern type Searcy had described often enough for his English readers; a heavy-drinking, malarial man who looked sixty but was likely only 45. A tobacco-chewer who, when drunk, would likely expectorate the juice on the carpet. His collar sweat-stained, his suit stained under the armpits. No wonder he drank! As the crickets started up on these quiet magnolia-scented plantations and a man with half a brain could feel the stir of the slaves and hear their evening singing and their strange enslaved shouts and yelps, any owner might feel a prisoner and reach for the whisky jug.

Besides Thomas, Jackson sat at the table with members of his staff. In a grudging way Jackson introduced Searcy to the others, to Surgeon Maguire and to Douglas and to Hotchkiss, the mapmaker, and to Quartermaster Harman and to Mr. Thomas, the plantation-owner himself, who half rose, yelled "Honored, sah!" and sank back into a coma.

They all avoid my eyes, Searcy noticed. All except the General, who bored at him with those dark globes of his from beneath those dark brows. Tom Jackson didn't look unlike John Brown. They both had the look of backwoods prophets. But Jackson was a different sort of killer than Brown. He killed his men with marches and too much green corn for dinner and with wild daring battles in a bad cause. Yet he was still the sort of man who, when he looked at you, gave you an urge to confess something. What? That you are—well, not a spy, that's a dramatic American word—but that you sent back information to Secretary Stanton.

"Mr. Searcy," the General said without a smile. "It must be about a year since I last saw you."

It was Searcy who smiled, a faint aristocratic smile. He looked cool, but he was struggling a little underneath. He had to go on remembering that *he* was the one with breeding and with the right perspective on history, whereas Jackson was a backwoodsman from Lewis County in the Appalachians, a wild unlettered stretch of country.

"It was in camp near Centreville," Searcy supplied. "After the battle around Manassas. I remember you had wounded your left hand, sir. May I enquire, were you able to save the finger?"

"Doctor Maguire did the saving. Splints, water treatments." Jackson held up the middle finger of his left hand and flexed it. "I'm grateful for that."

"Our fortunes have not been similar since that day, General," said Searcy in an ornate British way. "You were a brigadier then, now you command an army. Whereas I...I am still merely the correspondent of *The Times* of London."

Jackson yawned. "Your government hasn't changed much either. They're still dragging their feet. I mean, Mr. Searcy, in relation to this conflict...."

"I am not personally responsible, General Jackson, for the behavior of my..."

"Still, it makes you English gentlemen a...well, let's say a less agreeable proposition. A year back you could come to us and say speak up to me and I'll make sure our government in Westminster hears. But we've seen no results of their hearing. I suppose the Prime Minister, Lord Palmerston, reads *The Times* of London."

"Every Englishman of influence does, General."

"I'm pleased to hear it. I suppose you'd like another interview now, but I'm not too sure I would care to give it. Apart from that you're welcome to be a guest in our camp. I trust you've brought quinine with you. This is a malarial locale."

At an interview Searcy had had the week before in a private room of a restaurant on Pennsylvania Avenue in Washington, U.S. Secretary of War Stanton hadn't given him many specific orders. "It would be folly of me, Mr. Searcy, to do so," Stanton had told him. "All kinds of odd information comes to a journalist, and we would be happy to receive any of it. But there is one thing you can likely find out for us."

It appeared that the U.S. Ambassador in England, Charles Adams, had a spy in the British Foreign Office. Through this spy Adams had found out that the British Prime Minister, Lord Palmerston, and the Foreign Secretary, Lord Russell, planned a secret cabinet meeting for early in October. The business of the meeting was to decide once and for all whether Britain should recognize the Confederacy as an independent state. The reason the meeting was secret was because Palmerston and Russell didn't wish to have U.S. and Confederate agents milling on their doorstep, trying to cajole or influence them.

Well, the U.S. knew about it, but a more important question was whether the Confederates did. If they did, they *would* almost certainly try to invade the North before October, so that they could influence that far-off meeting at Palmerston's town house in Green Park.

Searcy had now taken a glass of brandy Surgeon Maguire had poured for him. "I would like to be able to raise this glass and say, here's to the hope of your government and my government coming to terms. But I think my government has decided to let the textile towns of England rot. And I believe they do not even talk about the Confederacy any more."

Harman, a heavy middle-aged man, Jackson's quartermaster, flattened his hand down on the table. "Oh no? Is it that way, Mr. Searcy? Really?" He had drunk more than all Jackson's other staff, but then he was older than all of them and freer in his ways. Even Jackson was a youth beside him. "You haven't heard that your goddam Prime Minister Palmerston and your confounded Foreign Secretary Lord Russell have set a date in October to decide once for all whether to *recognize* us. Recognize us, goddamit! I mean for Christ's sake, we're here, ain't we? *Recognize* us!" Harman subsided. "Anyhow, there's this-here meeting and I would've thought an important gentleman of the press such as yourself would have known about it."

So easy, thought Searcy. So easy. It's as if they don't give a damn.

Searcy turned to Jackson. "I take it this means you will try to march into the North?"

"Why would we march into the North?" Jackson asked, still without a smile.

Thomas belched and grunted in his coma and Jackson went on looking at Searcy, unblinking.

"Why, to influence Lord Palmerston."

"Trying to influence Lord Palmerston hasn't proved a very useful activity," said Jackson. Yet Searcy knew he didn't mean that. He would march to Canada and back to make an impact on that squinty-eyed Prime Minister of Britain.

"May I report your disenchantment to the British people?" Searcy asked the General.

"As long as you don't make a meal of it."

Kyd Douglas, the wise and natty young aide, often had to take the sting out of his General's bluntness. He began to do it now.

"I know the General wouldn't want to offend Lord Palmerston. Lord Palmerston has after all permitted the building of three Confederate frigates in British shipyards."

Searcy said: "Indeed he has."

"As I said," muttered the General, "don't make a meal of it." He looked at his plate. There was a carrot left on it. He had eaten nothing but carrots this evening.

Drunken Thomas began muttering at length, and the General decided the meal was over. Kyd Douglas, in his role as Jackson's pacifier, led Searcy out into the night and offered him a cigar, which Searcy refused, lighting instead one of his own cheroots. Down in the meadows campfires were burning out, but you could still hear laughter and violins—one violin to the west playing "Juanita," another from the fence by the Charles City Road sawing away at the "Grand March Innovation."

"The boys are well rested now," Douglas said.

"And going to remain so, by what the General says."

"You know the General. The summer isn't over yet. The bloom, Mr. Searcy, the bloom's still on it."

"So that anything can happen?"

"Bet your boots on it, sir. It's our slow government that's holding us here. But by the time they get enough letters from Lee and Jackson, they generally arrive at the right idea."

"Which is to invade the North."

"That's dead right, Mr. Searcy. Of course everything I say to you here is as a friend."

"But aren't there men in the Confederate Army, Virginians, North Carolinans, who enlisted to defend the Confederacy but would shy off marching into the North?"

"On every march you lose men. The footsore, the sore in spirit and all the rest."

"You come from Maryland, don't you, Mr. Douglas?"

"That's right."

"You hope to be home by autumn then?"

"That's right. Though I don't wish to have that idea ascribed to me in your journal."

Then something happened that took the edge off all Kyd Douglas's brave talk. Over the snuffling of horses, the chirring of insects, the burr of mosquitoes, the grate of fiddles, the drowsily sung songs, they could hear a man nearby who was weeping beyond all comfort. Instead of looking for whoever it was, they coughed and pretended not to have heard him, and walked off towards the staff tents.

— 10 —

THE FOLLOWING EVENING, Mrs. Dora Whipple was drinking tea in her living quarters, when the black girl came and said there was a soldier in Ward 17 who wanted to see her right away.

"You wait here, Sally," she told the girl, "right here at my table and if a Mr. Searcy comes—an English gentleman—why, you make him some tea."

Then Mrs. Whipple pulled a shawl over her pretty but narrow shoulders. "And, Sally," she said, "offer him some of that broth the boy in the Georgia ward wouldn't eat."

She rushed out of her little house. It was not so much a house as a two-story lean-to stuck on to the end of Wards 1 and 2, and it had been built of green lumber. As the timbers had seasoned and shrunk, spaces appeared between the boards of the wall and the floor. When there was a high wind even now, dust or rain swept in through these spaces. Next winter, she guessed, snow might too.

Now she walked the dusty avenue between long white huts. For this was Chimborazo, the great military hospital. In fact, the surgeon-in-chief and many of Mrs. Whipple's friends in Richmond society said Chimborazo was the biggest military hospital in the world, and she supposed that was true. By moonlight she could see the white wards stretching away to the western stars. Chimborazo wasn't just one hospital, it was five, and each of these five had its dozens of wards. Mrs. D. Whipple was matron of Hospital No. 2 and her charges were Virginians, Marylanders, Georgians, Alabamans. Experience as a matron had taught her to keep them apart in their own wards, for if a Virginian saw a Marylander getting attention he would complain. It was true both of boys on the mend and boys who were dying. In her first two months at Chimborazo, a dying Georgian used some of his small allotment of breath to complain that he saw a wounded Alabaman being tended more than he was.

So No. 17 was a Georgian ward. She didn't feel warmly towards Georgians, because they were fussy eaters. Just today Mrs. Whipple had requisitioned three chickens and made them up into a rich broth, cutting up the raw meat herself, something she would never have thought of doing with her own hands in happier days, when she kept house with her late husband Major Yates Whipple. While she prepared the chicken, she had got an orderly to *steal* parsley from the nearby market garden so that she could season the broth. She'd been so proud of her chicken soup with parsley that she went herself into the Georgian ward with the orderly to see that the ones who needed it most got it. And there were many in Ward 17 who needed it. D. H. Hill's Georgia regiments had suffered many wounds at Gaines' Mill some ten days past.

Yet one grey-faced boy shook his head at the broth and told her: "I was never much of a hand for drinks." Another, a ghost of a boy with a chest wound, pointed to the parsley: "My mammy's soup was not like that much. I might jest have worried down a little of it if it weren't for all them weeds a-floatin' round."

This evening Ward 17 was quiet. Many of the boys were already sleeping. Lamps burnt softly on ledges over the beds. The floor was clean except for a few crumpled-up tract pages. Preachers handed religious tracts out in the day, and their brown absorbent pages—so bad for taking print—made first-rate handkerchiefs. There was a taint of urine and human waste about the place, but not a tenth as bad as when she'd first taken the matron's job. When she first came here, she found that some assistant surgeons would drink the men's whisky supply during the morning, and then lock themselves away in their offices all day singing and smoking and telling vulgar stories, while men died in their cots and the chamber pots overflowed with human filth. Now Mrs. Whipple kept the whisky supply under lock and key in her quarters, and some of the assistant surgeons hated her for it.

She could see who it was that had sent for her. It was a lean up-country Georgian, jaundice-yellow, sitting up awkwardly on his cot. His shoulder and upper arm were imprisoned in heavy bandages and his throat was also bound. Wispy and foul yellow hair hung all over the bandages. Mrs. Whipple had seen him before—he'd been wounded by shell casing at Fair Oaks. He was a lucky young man in that he had the sort of wounds that were left alone by surgeons in the field, and the

first one to lay a knife on him was the surgeon-in-chief at
Chimborazo, who was said to be the best surgeon on the North
American continent. Now, however, the Georgian's blue eyes
were fever bright. Mrs. Whipple believed she knew half the
cause, for at the cot beside his, orderlies were wrapping up a
corpse in its bedclothes.

"You what they call the matron?" the boy asked Mrs. Whipple.

"I am. You know that. You've seen me in this ward before."

"I swear to you on my maw's honor I ain't ever lit eyes on
you."

"You were likely in a fever."

"Maybe so. Can you write a letter for me?"

He reached out his hand. The nails were long; they were
like claws.

"Why don't you let the orderlies cut your nails?"

The boy ignored this. "I thought," he said, "that since Hec
there perished, I'd better get *some* letter or other off to my
folks."

"Don't be so stupid, sir. You'll have lots of time for letters.
And for clipping your nails as well."

The Georgian looked down at those claws. "But I ain't got
no spoon and I been using them instead."

"I'll get you a spoon. And that hair of yours. You can't get
better with all that dirty hair hanging over your wounds."

"Ma'am, I can't get my hair cut, cause as how I promised
my maw I'd let it grow till the war be over. It's unlucky as
the devil hisself to lop it off, ma'am."

The superstitions of poor whites! thought Mrs. Whipple.
"Then I can't write a letter for you," she said.

From the next bed, two orderlies lifted the corpse now and
carried it away. They seemed to do it easily, boys wasted to
nothing after wounds, and half the surgeons didn't seem to
know what to feed the ailing to stop them rotting away. Wide-
eyed, the Georgian watched the orderlies toting their package
down the ward and out of doors. "Farewell, Hector," he called
too loudly, and some of the sleeping stirred and complained.

"I promise you, sir," said Mrs. Whipple, putting on a face
as severe as she could manage, "that you are not going to join
Hector. I shall call an orderly to cut your hair while you dictate
your letter to me."

She did so. The orderly was a pimply-faced boy who didn't

like doing much after dark, but he and all his colleagues feared her, because she had power to complain to the chief surgeon. It was said too that she spent her days off at the house of the Secretary of the Navy in Richmond, where she got to speak with all manner of generals and the Secretary of War himself.

Soon lumps of dirty golden hair were falling on the Georgian's pillow and on the floor. The boy began his dictation, and Mrs. Whipple wrote.

My dear mah,

I hope this finds you well as it leaves me well. And I hope I shall get a furlough at Christmas and come and see you, and I hope you will keep well, and all the folks be well by that time, as I hopes to be well again myself. I myself had a little damage on the shoulder and neck from the Yankees at Fair Oaks but the surgeons treated me passable and I was strong as Peterson's bull again so no cause for any fretting. It was some fight at Fair Oaks but they've all been passable fights according to the boys. A friend I met here called Hec...

He couldn't speak more than that. His eyes grew more fevered still. She slapped his wrist.

"Come now, private, let's leave Hec to his God."

His eyes came back to her face and fixed on it and grew wilder. "You married?" he asked.

"I was. I am a widow."

"You're but passable pretty but you're a nice woman jest the same."

"I thank you, private."

"I would marry a sweet thing like you if'n ever you felt the need."

Behind the Georgian's left ear the orderly began to snicker. Dora Whipple looked coldly at him and he quickly stopped. She finished the letter, folded the coarse army paper it was written on. She found a 5¢ stamp in the small purse she wore at her waist. Half her small income went on 5¢ stamps. "I am honored by your offer, sir, and shall remember it." She looked at the orderly. "Don't forget to sweep the floor," she told him.

Back in her quarters, she found a young man sitting at a table, reading one of her books. He was clearly a gentleman. As he stood up, she decided that he was handsome. There was a square yet delicate face, a big cavalry officer's type of moustache. He was broad in the shoulders, and not of more than average height.

"Mr. Searcy?"

The young man nodded. "Mrs. Whipple," he said.

Searcy saw a little narrow-shouldered woman with a pug face. Yet she had a lively sort of aura that made her seem much bigger. Mrs. Whipple asked him would he like tea and he said no. Therefore she sent the black girl off to bed. They could hear her tramping around upstairs. Searcy didn't want to say anything important in those circumstances, and began to make small talk.

"I must say," he began, "that I expected Chimborazo to be a scene of confusion, what with all the casualties . . ."

"The confusion extends between the battleground and the hospital gates and stops there. If we let it spread into the hospital itself we would never get rid of it. But please speak as you wish, for if you're worrying about my black girl eavesdropping, then you needn't. I've known her for years, and it's against her nature to eavesdrop."

"Pardon me, Mrs. Whipple, but it's not only your slave girl. You understand I can't be overly careful. I don't know how to say this, but how can I be assured of your standing in the . . . in the Union chain?"

"Then how would I have known to send for you? Unless certain important people in the . . . what did you call it? . . . in the *Union chain* told me to do it."

Searcy laughed and rubbed his elbow. "You'll have to forgive me once again . . . but it seems that you could equally be an agent of the Confederacy trying to encourage me to give myself away. You're from North Carolina, I believe. . . ."

"I was born in Boston, sir, and schooled there to the age of fifteen."

"Yes, but you married a North Carolina man. A man who rose to the rank of major in a North Carolina regiment and who was killed at . . . Ball's Bluff, wasn't it?"

"Ball's Bluff, yes," said the widow through narrowed lips.

"Of course I feel deeply for you, madam, in your loss, and I wouldn't like to do anything to revive your sorrow. What I *am* saying is that you seem to have little reason to love the Union."

"The Confederacy killed Major Whipple, sir," she said tranquilly. "By its rebellion—which he loyally followed—the Confederacy killed my husband."

"I am told you are a great friend of the Secretary of the Navy and his wife. . . ."

"My husband and the secretary grew up together."

"Also with General Gilmer and his wife. And that you frequently take tea with Mrs. Jeff Davis herself."

Mrs. Whipple screwed her little face up and grinned at him. "So you think I'm spying on you on Mrs. Varina Davis's orders?"

"What I wonder—and yet again you must forgive me, madam—is this. If you are an agent of the Union, how much do you feel towards all these good friends of yours? And how do you feel towards the soldiers in the wards of this hospital?"

The widow closed her eyes and the lips narrowed again. "That, Mr. Searcy, is none of your business. In general I feel that in anything I do for the Union I am helping my friends and helping the boys in the wards. Because the rebellion cannot succeed, sir."

"Not everyone, even on the Union's side, is so sure about that, ma'am."

She punched the table with her fist. "I am sure, sir. *I* am sure."

They sat in silence awhile and he looked at her wanly over his big moustache. She laughed. "Come now," she said, "I suppose you're one of those people who want to judge me because I own inherited slaves. History and Mr. Lincoln will free the slaves, sir. In the meantime, I find your timidity a little excessive. What if I did rush straight to Jackson with the news that the Honorable Mr. Searcy is a Union spy? Let me tell you, if I did that nothing bad would happen to you. The Confederacy is so busy courting the British parliament that they would not for a moment consider shooting a renowned British journalist whose father is also a peer of the British realm. You would be sent politely away, sir, that's all. Whereas I . . . if my connections were known, . . . well, even if they spared me a noose or a bullet, I doubt I'd last a month in prison."

She thought awhile about that with her head bent. Her already tiny shoulders seemed to shrink closer to each other. For a second he wanted to touch her in pity, for he could sense the great moral torment inside the tiny body.

He smiled remotely and at last took notes from his breast pocket. They were general notes on the strategic situation, but there were items there as well about what divisions were camped where. His recent chat with Jackson and Kyd Douglas was reported there as well.

"On this occasion only, I must insist that I retain these jottings of mine. You will need to make copies."

"Of course, Mr. Searcy," she said. "That is quite reasonable."

She got up from the table and went to fetch a writing portfolio from the far side of the room. Returning with it, she began to copy his notes in her cramped little handwriting, the handwriting of someone who is trying to save paper.

He coughed. "It is all intelligible?"

"Of course."

"Include the estimate I made of the size of Lee's army."

Again a sigh. "I'll put it in. It won't stop our Union generals multiplying it by four."

At last she finished copying his notes and handed them back with a broad smile. My God, he thought, you are an appealing little girl in your funny pug-nosed way. He said: "It seems to me, my dear Mrs. Whipple, there is nothing I could tell you that you couldn't find out from your distinguished friends."

"Not so, Mr. Searcy. A single woman can find out very little from generals and Congressmen. Unless one is a wife or a courtesan one discovers nothing of specific value. And I am too attached to widowhood to find either role very attractive. The men go off and drink or play billiards after dinner. Oh, I've been patted on the shoulder by Judah Benjamin and told not to worry my fey small head about military matters. Such advice hardly amounts to hard intelligence, Mr. Searcy. You are lucky to be a man, to be able to drink with staff officers. And to have a licence to ask them questions. Whereas I am little more than a mere channel. I wish I were more. I wish it very much."

"You must be careful, Mrs. Whipple," he warned her. For he wondered how much information she *did* get from the houses she visited and from the men in the wards as well.

"Yes," she said, "I must." She coughed and her eyes now looked bruised with tiredness. "As matron of this hospital, I feel disposed to prescribe you a measure of medical whisky, which I'd be honored if you drank before you left."

After the ration of raw spirit, he left glowing. Riding back to his hotel in Franklin Street he wondered if she'd been a spy as early as the battle of Ball's Bluff and if she'd ever been haunted by the idea that the news she passed on northwards had helped in any way to bring on her husband's death wound.

Later in the night he found himself waking, her pinched face showing up sharp in his imagination. "My God, you've a weakness for nurses, old boy!" he told himself. For the mother of his three-year-old had been a nurse in the Crimea. He no longer loved that one, if ever he had. But Mrs. Whipple's features returned to him all night like those of a familiar face he had travelled a long way to see, and found—by good luck— in a barbarous place.

BOOK TWO

— 1 —

THE GRAND MOVEMENT northwards began because of the actions of a Union general. It did not begin because Tom Jackson, Kyd Douglas, Ephie Bumpass, Danny Blalock and *De Bow's Review* believed it should; but because General Johnny Pope of the U.S., the one who was mocked because of the rumor that he sent dispatches from "Headquarters in the Saddle," began to move south from the Washington area. His orders were to shield Washington. He moved his divisions well. By the time Richmond knew anything about it, he was concentrated around the town of Culpeper, some sixty miles southwest of the Union capital, and just a little more than that north of Richmond. Culpeper was a main depot on the Orange and Alexandria, and anyone could see what Pope was trying. For if you follow the Orange and Alexandria south, it meets the Virginia Central beyond Gordonsville. The Confederacy needed the Virginia Central both for feeding Richmond and for sending troops and finished products to other areas. Tom Jackson was told to make Gordonsville secure.

"They don't give us rest," said old Harman, the General's commissary officer. "They're always knockin' on either our front door or our goddam back."

Tom Jackson, who had lived such a quiet life for ten years as professor of optics at the V.M.I., now he was a general took idle days as an insult. He was full of a quiet ecstasy as he packed up at Thomas's place.

"Battle is a Heraclitean thing," he told Kyd. 'πάντα ρει, as the Greek philosopher Heraclitus said. Everything changes in war and if you don't believe so, you lose."

Kyd knew he didn't talk at such lengths and quote Greek philosophers unless he was very happy.

One of the less amusing sides of the "Heraclitean thing" was getting eleven thousand men out of the encampment they'd been enjoying for two weeks and on to the road.

It got to be Tuesday noon before Lafcadio Wheat's regiment marched into the crowded depot in Broad Street, Richmond, and climbed on board the third-class carriages of the Virginia Central. Usaph Bumpass and Gus Ramseur had been waiting at the depot overnight. Because of his respect for Gus's talents, Usaph had got the adjutant's permission to bring Ramseur up to Richmond by wagon. It happened that one half of the depot porch had been set aside for the Southern Comfort Society, and from dawn till midnight each day, nice young women of Richmond served cookies and cakes and ham between slices of bread, and as good a coffee as you could find, and lemonade to the boys who were passing through.

Usaph and Gus had spent all yesterday evening and all this morning feasting at the hands of those nice young women. Whereas those boys who arrived at noon were lucky to get one small wedge of pie and half a cup of coffee, Gus and Usaph had spent last evening and all that very morning eating whole pies, had joined the queue at the Comfort Society's bench so many times that the girls had got to know and favor them. By the time the officers crowded them with all the rest of the regiment into those plain timber railroad coaches, Gus and Usaph felt fat and spacious, and Gus said he was sure he had his wind back.

These third-class coaches meant hardwood seats. If they'd had glass in their windows when the war started, then soldiers had soon attended to that. It meant though that at least the insides of the traveling compartments got plenty of air. And that was as well, considering the way transport officers crammed them out.

"Move up there, son!"

"Why, sir, captain, this-here seat's already full."

"Full. You call three boys *full*? Why, that seat is patented to take six fat gran'mas. Move on up there!"

When the seats were full, those officers would sit a hundred, a hundred and fifty boys down in the aisle, so that the only exit you had from the carriage was through the windows. Yet no one seemed resentful. Danny Blalock had picked up a smuggled copy of the *Knickerbocker* at the depot and read through the whole journey. The others laughed and sang and the Irish fiddler who had played in camp took up the fiddle he still had but which he would jettison as soon as the marching got hard. The conscripts were allowed to sit on the floor, and sometimes a veteran would show his power by walking from one end of the carriage to the other across their shoulders and their knees. The conscript boys spoke low because they knew anything they said could be idly mocked. Though their clothes were as bad and maybe worse than the veterans, you could still tell them by the relative softness of their complexions, even the softness of the complexions of those who'd been farmers. For nothing harshened the skin more than long marches and the kind of outdoor sleeping soldiers did. How much the softer was the painter Decatur Cate's face, which Usaph often watched secretly from his seat. Cate, whose harshest tool up to now had been a paint brush!

"Enjoying yourself down there, Cate?" Bolly would sometimes call to the artist.

"Why, I pity you up there, Mr. Quintard, sitting on that hard seat while I'm down here resting in finest grade dust."

Usaph didn't like the change that was coming into the way the others looked at Cate. They saw him as a sort of Mister Interlocutor who said things that riled them in a pleasant way and let them try out their wits. It seemed Cate angered yet fascinated all of them and the idea of having a pet Lincolnite around the place—you could nearly say—*tickled* them.

Cate understood this and sometimes said things to provoke them from his place on the floor of the carriage. "You gentlemen should by rights welcome us boys," he said at one time. "After all, you lost 20,000 in front of Richmond. Do you think you can afford to write off 20,000 of your brethren like that?"

Old Bolly always replied first, and did so now. "Where do y'get that manner of number from, son? Some goddam paper in New Hampshire? Why, we lost mebbe 5000 out of all the army, not a boy over 5000, I tell you."

"Why, let me break it to you softly that according to the back page of the *Richmond Enquirer* you lost 5000 on the afternoon at Malvern Hill alone!"

Now sometimes Cate would go close to the bone, as he had now. And they all sat quiet. *20,000.* A figure that made your breath catch.

Even Danny Blalock, who'd started off with Cate a week ago by going into a fine old state of Virginian outrage, had now gone mild on him. Looking up from his *Knickerbocker,* he murmured: "The conscript's right. 4000 deaths. And given the surgeons we have, some of the wounded will join that number quick enough."

Secretly, Cate felt burdened and sickened by all the afflictions of his soul and, specifically, of his heart. What am I doing, riding by train to take up a position against the Union? Sometimes he looked for a second in Bumpass's direction and, in the one second, hated him and wanted him for a friend.

"You ought to be kinder to these boys," he said loudly one time, to the coach in general. "These bounty boys and substituters and us Lincoln boys too. Don't the figures show clear enough that you need us? Why, I am affronted there is no society for the comfort of conscripts."

Bumpass noticed this was answered by hoots, but not angry ones.

"Where is there a sock-knitting committee to supply us poor mercenaries?" Cate shouted.

"Where is there," Ash Judd said, "a society for proddin' your asses with bayonets?"

Every so often the train would halt for five, ten minutes, and the railroad embankments would be dotted with squatting Confederates easing their afflicted bowels. Sometimes those suffering the worst forms of camp diarrhea could not wait for the luxury of a stop. By the time the train got to Hanover Junction in the late, blazing afternoon, the carriage reeked of sweat and excreta, and there were even tears on the cheeks of some of the new boys, as if this kind of travel weren't a whole sight better than marching.

— 2 —

THEY CAMPED THERE in the fields around the little depot for
some days. It was not till the Saturday after Bumpass and Gus
left the encampment outside Richmond that Wheat's regiment
moved further and lit their fires in the lovely meadows around
Gordonsville, facing north along the Orange and Alexandria
rail-bed that ran all the way to the edge of Washington. The
hills were low and pleasant round Gordonsville, the mosquitoes
weren't there in such swarms, and there was no scum or methane or blood in the flow of crystal waters rushing down from
the Blue Ridge.

Yet there was always the chance of Union cavalry striking
down from Culpeper, and everyone had to do his picket duty.
One evening, when the hills to the west were turning a royal
purple, Company B, Guess's Company, of the Shenandoah
Volunteers, went out to the north-west of Gordonsville, to a
fringe of forest, to stand an all-night picket stint.

Captain Guess led them out. He was the Valley dentist
who'd let Usaph visit Ephie that time months ago. This last
month, in fact since the fights around Richmond, he'd got
sullen and smelt of liquor a lot, whereas before that he had
been a pleasant, quiet man who lent newspapers around.

Guess arranged the picket duty so that some of the veterans
could keep to the rear and boil up coffee on low fires. For the
rest he ordered that each soldier of experience stood beside a
conscript.

"No exclusive goddam clubs," he muttered.

This mixing-up took Usaph away from Gus, and somehow
he ended with a conscript either side of him. One was a thin
boy of at most eighteen years of age, and the other was Decatur
Cate. Usaph suspected Cate had arranged his place in line so
that Guess *would* appoint him to Usaph rather than to any other
veteran.

They stood in the shadows at the northern end of a forest.
"Thing is," muttered Usaph to his two charges, "you spread

85

off aways from me—some seven paces at most for now. After a time, an officer will pass along telling how one of us can sleep. When that occurs, why we spread out a little more to take up the slack." He snorted. "And you can sleep first of all, Cate."

The air in front of their picket post, above the gentle pastures, was a deep smoky blue when Usaph and the others took their post amongst hawthorn and sumac. The moon would rise early tonight. Lucius Taber, the new officer and former Immutable, went along the line shooshing people who knew better than he did how to be quiet. Soon he left, he had to go back and dine with Colonel Wheat, and low, low talk began, since the veterans knew talk didn't carry so far. It was the sound of disturbed underbrush that carried.

Usaph knew you had to talk to stop boredom getting you. He was damn sure he wouldn't talk to Cate.

"What's your name, son?" Usaph asked the boy three yards on the other side of him.

"Joe Nunnally," the boy hissed. He hadn't moved anything like seven paces off. Maybe he was scared.

"You a substitute, Joe Nunnally? You get a few hundred dollars from a rich boy?"

The boy didn't answer. "I ain't asking for the sake of meanness, boy. I'm jest curious."

Close to Usaph's other side, Decatur Cate started murmuring. "If he's a substitute, it means he's taken blood money. If he's a mere conscript, why he's a coward or a Lincoln-lover. You can't expect people, Mr. Bumpass, to answer questions if there's no benefit in any of the answers they can give."

Usaph coughed in an irritable way and spat and didn't reply.

The boy said, "I'm a substitute. What of it? $200? That ain't goddam likely. Sixty I got from a lawyer's son over to Raleigh County."

Usaph whispered: "That ain't what the papers say you ought to get, Joe Nunnally."

"I don't read no papers."

"Sixty ain't much."

"It is to my maw."

"Coming from over to Raleigh, you'd be one of them black Republicans like some other people," Usaph stated. He still would not include Cate in the talk. As for looking, he looked all the time at the hills before him, without even thinking about it, and Nunnally found himself doing the same, since he believed this must be veteran's behaviour and everything veterans did—he supposed—was aimed at avoiding death.

"Maybe I am one of them black Republicans," he said. "But then maybe I jest got hungry kin. The hungry don't give a hoot about no politics."

Usaph laughed soundlessly. Here he stood with a Yankee picket either side of him. That's what conscription had done, put a Northerner on one flank and one of those Union-loving boys from the western counties on the other. If Lincoln or McClellan could know that tonight, how they'd laugh over their goddam brandy.

But these political thoughts of Bumpass's, the amusement they gave his mind, were a mere surface thing. The deep tumor, the question that wouldn't cease its throb, was still whether Ephie had lain with his dead Uncle, that dead boozy man who had engineered Ephie and him together, and now whether Cate had dazzled and possessed her.

Guess walked behind them and said one man in three could rest.

"Cate," Usaph said in the edges of that thicket. *And may your dreams reek, and may snakes rise from them!*

Cate went without a word, but Usaph believed that he was smiling in the dark.

Virginia, as Usaph Bumpass had learnt, was a mass of clearings cooped off one from the other by thickets. The moon rose and lit up the particular thicket beyond the field that Usaph and Joe Nunnally faced. You could hardly hear anything from the other pickets and the only shuffling was the busy shuffling paws of raccoons and possums all around you, and the only real buzz was the buzz of insects.

Usaph and Joe Nunnally didn't say anything for some fifteen minutes. Then Joe Nunnally coughed. "If they come—I only ask—if they come, they'll be on horses?"

Usaph smiled at the moon. "That's how they'll be, Joe."

"I only ask," said Joe.

There was more silence, though Nunnally twitched somewhat. Usaph knew Joe Nunnally would be all the time sighting phantom horsemen amongst the far shadows and then screwing up his eyes and finding them to be illusions.

"Joe," said Usaph after a further time.

"Yessah."

"You know, it's shaping to be over by Christmas. All them knowledgeable people will tell you that."

"That's the best news since the dog whelped."

"So there's something I mean to ask, Joe. See, I got this nice wife to get home to. Now you wouldn't ever run and leave a man like me, would you, Joe? Not between now and Christmas, would you?"

But Joe wouldn't say.

"Well, Joe?"

"Well, I suppose no one runs from them that've got kind words. But how do I know? To be blamed cowards is men's nature, that's what Preacher Hinton's always telling us out to Raleigh County."

"Well, Joe?"

"How can I make any such promise, Mr. Bumpass?" Joe Nunnally groaned, his eyes fixed too hard on the distant end of the moonlit pastures. "Why, I don't even know what it's like . . ."

There, Usaph thought, there's a good honest will there. There might be good enough and honest enough wills in the lot of them conscripts.

Usaph had first gone into what people liked to call a "pitched" or "organized" battle on an afternoon in April near the village of Kernstown. From it alone he knew Joe Nunnally was correct to consider battle a mysterious event that could take you in any direction.

The afternoon of Kernstown all the thoughts that were supposed to steel a soldier's heart were operating on Private Usaph Bumpass. Only the day before, the Confederates had entered Strasburg again, the town from which Mrs. Ephie Bumpass had been driven six weeks before. Kernstown was just up the road from Strasburg. Usaph Bumpass was fighting for his own meadows and for the graves of his father and mother. Compared to any Yankee, to whom this stretch of the Valley was just a stretch of valley, he should have been firm and ferocious and mad with outrage.

What Usaph Bumpass learned that afternoon in fact was that there wasn't always much difference between the standfast and the man who ran. Even though presidents and colonels and preachers tried to tell you otherwise, the standfast and the runner were often the same man on different days or at a different hour. So from two to three o'clock in the afternoon of the battle he had moved up a ridge near Kernstown, found a stone fence to stand at beside his fellows, stood there from three to half past five against whole brigades of Union soldiers and was resolute enough to take cartridges out of the boxes of the fallen, and then spent most of the last hour of light scrambling, if not running, back down towards the wagons near the pike.

Usaph had, before that afternoon, experienced brief skirmishes, and he thought that a battle would be just a skirmish times five or ten. But he had not been ready for the real elements of battle—the cannon shrieks, the feel of the air when it is raddled with musket balls and you feel that if you sniff you'll breathe one in. You could not ready yourself for the wild varieties of damage men suffered or the range of grunts and groans and roars they uttered. You couldn't picture to yourself beforehand the thirst or the sort of terrible daze you stayed in while you held a line of fence, or the speed you'd panic with. You couldn't guess the craziness with which you might roar up towards artillery if ordered to or the equal craziness with which you'd run. And you couldn't most of all imagine how it was to live through your first battle and look back on it.

It was said most boys who shot themselves did it after their first battle. They did it because they felt accursed; like—in the manner of ole Macbeth in the well-known play—they had murdered sleep.

The night of Kernstown—which people now, only a season later, talked of as a "small fite"—Usaph walked back some five miles south to Middletown. He was crazy with tiredness but his eyes were locked open. Unsprung ambulance wagons trampled past him, and blood dropped through the floorboards and made the road muddy, while the boys inside called awesome things. "In sweet Christ's name, a bullet, a bullet!" "Jesus, put me by the road to die." Usaph Bumpass felt that night like the ordinary world of farms and girls and steeples and milkchurns had been carried away for good. He believed no soldier could ever see God's face. He was as terrified of the stars and of Gus Ramseur at his side as he was of any cavalry that might burst on him out of the oak woods. And he believed that if ever he were to be sane again and to have a half a minute's happiness he had to desert and flee a great distance towards the land of bees and babies and old men in cane chairs, towards the land of Ephie.

"I tell you what, Mr. Bumpass, sir," Joe Nunnally said

now. "I'll do what I can by you, that's the best I can say."

"You're one honest boy, Joe," said Usaph. And after that they spoke little.

Later in the night Cate was roused up and Joe went to sleep. Cate took up his scarecrow stance amongst the low trees. Usaph was glad it was not one of the artist's talkative nights. Even so, Cate's presence was itself sort of a loud torment and Usaph's eyes kept coming back to the man's shape and to the side of his face all blue from the moonlight.

That way an hour passed. At one time Usaph hunkered for a period. At another he urinated against a tree. Joe Murphy brought them each a mug of acrid, stewed coffee, and they drank it without talking. The moon was so high now that the meadow ahead seemed bright as a ballroom and someone with a watch passed on the word that the time was past one in the morning, as if he was saying nothing can happen at such an hour and under such a wide flood of moonlight.

About that time, Usaph got drowsy and jolted upright when he found a hand on his elbow. Cate's.

"You get back, Cate."

"I thought you was about to fall, Bumpass."

"Then that would be my own concern, wouldn't you say?"

Cate nodded and swallowed and studied the other man's face, the features so familiar now that they could have been those of a hated brother. But Cate didn't feel any particular hate tonight, or the need to make bright, bitter talk, even though Bumpass, around the mouth anyhow, resembled that old bitch of an aunt of his.

At the moment Cate was just pleased that the night was going on so harmless and bright, that the hour hadn't come when he had to fire on the Union or choose sort of conspicuously not to.

"Let's settle this," Usaph said. "You going back or not?"

"Before I go back," said Cate, "there's this information you should have about me."

"Goddam!" Usaph muttered. But he was thinking, *Information? Is this where I'm told? Is this where he poisons the goddam earth?* And he knew that if it was that kind of information, then he would have to shoot Cate, there could be no help for it, and that that act would sour everything. "What goddam information would I need of you?"

Cate stared at him. Usaph couldn't tell whether there was

mischief or goodwill in what Cate was saying. Cate himself couldn't have told.

"To make the boys laugh," said Cate, "I sometimes masquerade as a black-hearted Lincoln man. Yet I'm what they call in the North a copperhead. In truth, Mr. Bumpass, I believe no Northern army should come South and no Southern army should go North. And that's just about the sum of my beliefs."

Usaph laughed crazily, more high-pitched than a boy should in a picket line. "Hokey, if you ain't a solemn bastard, Cate! Why should I care if you was a copperhead or a horny toad."

But the whole thing still made Usaph's blood creep. For Cate always behaved as if he and Bumpass had confidences between them, and so ought to know something of each other. And Bumpass could not have thought of anyone in the continent he'd less like to keep secrets with or know close.

"For Jesus' sake, Cate! Why don't you jest run off from the army?"

Cate considered this like a serious proposition. The moonlight lay on his right eye, the rest of his face stood in shadow. "I know nowhere to hide," he said like an orphan. "I've got no kin who'd hide me down here. I'm not made for living in the wilderness; I never hunted squirrel in my life. Besides that, I'm told that when you veterans desert you get a second chance, you're maybe bucked and gagged for a while or have half your head shaved, and that's it. But if a conscript deserted and was found again, there'd be no such indulgence."

"They happen to be the meanest reasons I ever did hear."

"I am mean, Mister Bumpass," boasted Cate dismally, like one of those Roman philosophers, "since I am human."

Usaph was about to tell him to get the hell back to his place when, from between them and just by their ears, they heard a hammer cocked and a shot fired. Cate thought the noise would knock him over.

It was Joe Nunnally, who'd been listening and not sleeping, firing towards the north. Before Usaph could complain, other firing like that began up and down the line. After a few seconds, while Joe Nunnally was thoughtfully reloading, Captain Guess came through the underbrush screaming for silence.

"Who fired first?" he yelled when the spatter of shooting stopped. "What blackguard fired first, eh?"

Joe Nunnally said coolly, "There was a thing climbing over the further fence yonder."

"A *thing*? A goddam *thing*?"

Across the pastures a small whisper, almost a whimper, came to them. "You, Bumpass, take this boy and see. And bring it back, whatever it might be."

Me? thought Bumpass. Why should I make a target in a moonlit pasture for the sake of a substitute from Raleigh County. But of course he went. He knew the army worked by ordinary men taking a risk on crazy commands this once and promising themselves that they'd argue and disobey the next time. That was the way of it. And so he stepped from cover and went with the boy.

Out in the moonlight they felt naked.

"You goddam ask me afore you ever shoot again," Usaph said. "You hear?"

"I seen it," said Joe. "You and that perfesser couldn't see it cause you was jawing. I seen it."

They climbed one fence and then another, finding behind it a dead pointer, a fine dog who'd been maybe doing a little rabbiting in his own right and who'd been transfixed through the shoulders by Joe Nunnally's shot.

"Oh Lordy," said Joe and began to cry. "Oh Lordy I'm ashamed before you, Usaph."

Usaph laughed. A dog was better news than a cavalry man.

"No, Joe. That's a shot you fired! Holy Betsy, what a shot!"

Joe gathered the dog up closely in his arms, not caring about stains, and Bumpass carried his musket for him. Captain Guess was waiting for them back on the picket line.

"A dog. *A goddam dog!* Say, there's cavalry over there, boy. They know where we stand now all because you had to shoot a goddam dog!"

Joe Nunnally still had tears on his face. He weighed it a terrible thing to kill a working dog.

"You take that dog back to camp, boy," Captain Guess told him, "carried in your own goddam arms, and stand beside my tent with it until noonday tomorrow, and then you bury it and when next you see a pay wagon, you pay me three dollars to replace it to its owner."

Joe started to limp away straight off. Usaph caught him and slung the rifle over his back. "Don't weep there, Joe," Usaph whispered. "That was one shot, that was!"

— 3 —

As Joe Nunnally carried the dog back to camp, grieving for it in its own right but also because it hung in his arms with the dead weight of an omen, the brandy bottle was being passed at the end of dinner outside Colonel Wheat's tent. Dinner had been cornbread and fried chicken and sweet yams and grits served by Colonel Wheat's orderly. Wheat drank whisky with each mouthful and young Lucius Taber felt bound to do the same. By coffee time Lucius's head reeled and he felt like a happy child on a carousel. But the fireflies off amongst the beech trees seemed to be blurs to him, not point of light, and he should have taken warning from that.

He noticed that Captain Hanks, the middle-aged Valley lawyer, who with Lucius had brought the conscripts to camp, drank pretty carefully. At first, like a true Immutable should, Lucius despised Hanks for this. But after some six or seven ounces of brandy on top of all that whisky, Lucius stopped comparing himself with other officers and began to worry about his own nausea. Soon he began to dream of being sick the way you dream of a sweet release. But he went on trying to listen to each of the colonel's words, for the colonel had called this dinner to inform Hanks and Lucius of certain rules of thumb that apply to military compaigning.

"... the percentage of hits is always very small," said the colonel. He dropped his voice. "As low as a half of one per cent, the ordnance officers say, though I don't know where they get the figures and I don't want it mentioned to the men. They also say the Yankee figures are even lower. Abe is lucky if one in 400 rounds that his boys fire off strikes flesh. Now the Lord's decreed that here in the South we're short of lead and powder and copper, and so the customary reasoning runs like this. Don't give the men breech-loaders, even if we beg and buy and steal them. If you give the men breech-loaders the waste of lead and powder and copper will be more than our means can tolerate. So goes what passes for the ordinary wisdom!"

And Colonel Wheat took another gulletful of brandy. He looked at the regimental surgeon, Abel Oursley, who was also full up with one of those medical stimulants he often used in amputations, namely whisky. Abel nodded over the table, sometimes waking to say a few words about his profession in a thick voice. The adjutant, Major Dignam, sat straight, tall, round-faced, sipping a glass of lime juice. All at once Lucius envied him that tall Methodist glass of lime juice, wishing he himself wasn't an Immutable and wasn't bound to a career of whisky-and-brandy gobbling.

"But look at the question from its other side," said the colonel. "The Southern rifleman is likely a farmer or a farm boy. He's been since babyhood shooting squirrels and coons and, in our part of the Confederacy, goddam bears! He's a natural marksman, that is, unlike the low-grade immigrants and slum-boys that oppose our cause. . . ."

Captain Hanks frowned and put in an objection. "But they shoot squirrels and coons and bears in Michigan too. And in Ohio and Minnesota and Wisconsin. And in upstate New York the country's, why, full of marksmen."

Hanks was clearly a traveler and wanted Wheat to know it. Wheat nodded. It was a brushing-aside nod. "But, capt'n, the gift of marksmanship just ain't the rule in the North. Sure as hell it might be the rule in the backwoods, but most of the Yankee rankers ain't from the backwoods. They're goddam Germans straight off the ship. They're goddam Irish. They're slum-boys and degenerates who can use a knife or a brick from behind but have not in their lives before been called on to be marksmen."

Hanks gave a nod that was halfway a shake of the head and halfway respectful. The colonel sighed and his parroty eyes took in Hanks in a way that said, I hope we won't have any more trouble in mid-argument. "What I was reaching for," he went on, "was the proposition that given the Yankees *as a rule* ain't marksmen an' given that our boys are *as a rule* marksmen, wouldn't it be clear enough to a purblind jackass that if our boys were armed at all costs with Spencer breech-loaders, the casualties we'd cause would increase by the power of the follow-in' factors—first, the greater percentage of hits we already enjoy, second, the increased accuracy-cum-muzzle velocity of the breech-loaders, an' third, the increased rate of fire. Oh, I can see young Lucius there saying to himself, why we'd use up a few years' supply of lead, powder and copper in the one year. Weren't you just thinking that, Lucius?"

Lucius nodded and wished he'd brought a notebook for that *first, second, third* of the colonel's. He sat swaying in misery, sure that he'd missed out on vital news.

"Well, I say one year's supply is all we'd need, Lucius. Northern mothers would end the war. Northern casualty rates, Northern goddam grief. That's the way it seems to this mountain lawyer anyways."

In the silence the surgeon, Doctor Oursley, raised his head.

"When I get boys coming to me on the march, why I've got a ball of blue mass in my left pocket and a ball of opium in my right . . . a ball of blue mass . . ."

"Good for you, Abel," said the colonel, and Abel Oursley went back to sleep.

Wheat went on with his reflections and advice. They should never, he said, fret themselves too much if they saw boys throw their bayonets away. "To be of use in battle the bayonet—on the chance of a charge from either side—must be attached to the musket during loading, as any fool knows. That means men are likely to spike their hands while loading, to cut a finger off maybe at the knuckle, or to wound their neighbors as they lift the long apparatus to fire. Believe me, our regiment ran through all its ammunition at Kernstown and the first thing the boys did then—and it was, mark you, instinctual—was grasp their muskets by the barrel and ready them for use as clubs. And I promise you, gentlemen, that the damage done thereby to the first of the Yankee slum-boys who got into our section was as worthy as anything the bayonet could do."

Hanks felt appalled by this little oration, and his sense of being lost amongst barbarians was made worse as Oursley, the surgeon, raised his turtle-like head again and finished the speech that had defeated him ten minutes before.

". . . blue mass in one pocket and opium in the other," Oursley persisted. "And when they come to me on the march and say, Doc, I'm ailing, I say are your bowels open? If so, I administer a plug of opium; if shut I give a plug of blue mass. On the march you jest have to reduce the practice of medicine to its lowest . . ."

But his forehead hit the table and soon he fell out of his chair and was left snoozing away on the ground. Lucius Taber thought, even in his whisky daze—what if ever I'm wounded and one day am brought to that drunk lying there?

And that moment a boy passed thirty yards off, carrying a

bundle in his arms. The colonel was distracted. "What you got there, feller?"

"It's a dog, sir."

"You meaning to devour that dog are you, boy?"

"Sir, I shot this dog thinking it was the enemy."

"You know you got to pay the owner?"

"I've been told that, Colonel."

"That's the way the Confederacy does things. We ain't no race of plunderers. Now bury that dog."

"Sir, Captain Guess told me to stand before his tent with it in my arms till noonday afore buryin' it."

"Who'm I to contradict the captain. Lucius, give this poor lad a sup of brandy to stand him in his long vigil."

Lucius got up, urging himself to be steady, and poured the boy some brandy in a tin mug. "You teetotal, son?" Major Dignam asked Joe Nunnally just in case, but Joe shook his head, dropped the dog's corpse on the ground and drained the brandy. Then he replaced the mug on the table, bowed to the colonel, lifted the burden again and went off to stand in front of Guess's tent.

Wheat said: "Ole Popeye Ewell once said, the road to glory can't be followed with much baggage." Lucius wasn't sure whether Wheat was speaking of the toting of dogs or excess equipment like cartridge boxes and such. But there wasn't any mistaking what the clicking of the colonel's fingers meant. He wanted the brandy bottle. Taber passed it and, to his horror, got it back after the colonel had used it.

Feeling obliged to pour himself another belt, he did so, looking at it in the mug and saying to it, not with his lips but with his stewed brain, you're the one that's going to kill me.

"Now one last thing," said the colonel again. "It might be a thing of merit to try to explain the constitutional issue for which we fight to simple farm boys, but there's very little use. I believe there is jest no question that low anger is the finest stimulant and every general, even teetotal Tom Jackson, knows that it outranks whisky itself as the primer of the tired and frightened soldier."

At the word *whisky* Taber got up, excused himself and walked fast away into the shadows, towards the far cool Blue Ridge, into the forests. He found he wasn't out in some soothing unpopulated darkness, but standing amongst the shapes of sleeping men of the Stonewall Brigade. The gush from his belly fell on the blankets of two Irishmen of the Twenty Seventh

Virginia. They woke instantly as veterans have a gift to do, and in his helpless spasms, he could hear them complaining and looking round for the source of this discomfort.

"Oh Jaysus, Jimmy, thet's him there, the bastard."

Jimmy got Taber by the collar and Lucius began shaking and was ill again. "What in the goddam name of Hell?" Jimmy asked.

But the adjutant had arrived. "Let go of him, son," he instructed. Jimmy obeyed but not without making a speech.

"But it's hard enough, Yer Honner, sleepin' in shit without havin' that ordure there atop ye."

Taber retched on in front of them. Oh God, I am so shamed. What sort of Immutable am I now? My colonel has done for me with a brandy bottle.

— 4 —

THE ENGLISH CORRESPONDENT Searcy came up to Gordonsville with some officers of Ambrose Hill's division, arriving the morning after Joe Nunnally shot the dog.

Although he'd thought it was his duty both as journalist and agent to go up to Jackson's headquarters, he hadn't liked leaving Mrs. Whipple. He visited Chimborazo two more times after that first meeting. The first of these two occasions he took with him a few diagrams of the way Longstreet's half of the army had placed itself around Richmond. These practically valueless drawings were his excuse for visiting. He sat in her little kitchen and felt his soul expanding under the influence of her liveliness and her good sense and that bunched little smile of hers.

"Is it a good thing for us to be friends?" she asked when he was going.

He'd look her full in the eyes. "Don't even question it, madam."

Just before he left Richmond—his horse was already loaded aboard a freight train—he'd visited her a last time.

But it hadn't been a very happy visit. Orderlies and nurses kept coming to her door with messages and requests; and twice in the three hours he had spent there she had to leave him to himself—or at least to the company of her black maid—for more than half an hour at a time.

"Your mistress is kept very busy," he'd said to the black girl.

"Yassir, them slack surgeons, they get Mrs. Whipple to break the news to boys when they's dyin'."

Searcy didn't like to think too closely about what *that* must do to the brain behind the small pug face.

Perhaps there were Mrs. Whipples all over Virginia who would meet with him and collect whatever he had for them. If there were, he didn't know who they might be or how he would know them. It might end up that he'd have to cross the lines himself with any special knowledge he'd got together. He didn't like that prospect, for pickets on both sides fired with a nervous quickness.

Jackson's headquarters was, predictably, a white frame farmhouse, pleasant, its lawn and rosebeds trampled and grazed out by the horses of visiting officers and couriers.

Searcy was sitting on the stoop of this house one stifling Tuesday morning. He chatted with any officers who came and sat there to mop their faces or fan themselves with their hats. As he sprawled, making what mental note he could of what was said and lazily chewing on a sour cheroot, he saw a sort of mobile haze coming across the meadows towards the house.

It was a cavalry detachment traveling cross-country, and soon it had drawn up at the gate, the troopers swearing and stretching in their saddles and reaching for the corncob pipes in the saddlebags. Their officer got down from his mount and came in through the gate. A typical cavalry colonel of maybe Searcy's age, his uniform part military and part the outfit of an elegant traveling gentleman. Whoever he was, some of the other officers in the garden knew him and called to him.

"I gotta see ole Jackson," he told them.

"Why he's locked in his room."

"Then root him out, my friend."

The officer stomped up the steps and ran into Sandie Pendleton, the General's aide. After an argument, which Searcy could not overhear, Sandie fought his way up a hallway, crowded with officers and riders, and hammered on the General's door. Jackson emerged in shirtsleeves and, after a while, followed Sandie. Such was his presence that every officer there in the hallway breathed in as he passed.

"Colonel," he called, climbing onto the porch. The colonel

was still there in his high dusty boots. "Come with me into the garden."

Before they left the steps the colonel was talking. Searcy could hear stray words and the names of Federal generals— Alpheus Williams, Sigel. The name *Banks* was heard a few times too. Tom Jackson had once said of U.S. General Banks: "He's always ready for a fight and he generally gets whipped." Was Banks moving on Jackson? And in what numbers? And did he understand Jackson's strength?

Tom Jackson and the colonel had walked clear out of the front gate by now and the General, though still and silent, seemed to quiver in the light of the dusty road. The cavalry squadron could tell it, could tell that some decision governing all their futures was shuddering into shape inside Stonewall.

At last the invisible quivering, which was visible as a barn to the horsemen, stopped and Tom Jackson turned and walked fast towards the house. "Sandie, Kyd."

Sandie reappeared quickly on the porch, but Kyd Douglas had to be hollered for, since he was deep in the house and perhaps cat-napping.

"Kyd," Jackson called, "there's that court-martial of Colonel Bright going on over on the Madison Court House Road." Searcy had heard something of the court-martial—something about cowardice at a little battle over in the Valley. "General Ewell is the court president. Tell him the court will disband immediately."

Kyd, diplomatic as ever, suggested: "He might want a reason."

"Tell him the army will march, that's his reason." Sandie was at his side with a message pad ready. "To all brigade and division headquarters at once," Tom Jackson grunted, but audibly enough for Searcy. "Generals to have their men ready for the road by three this evening. They'll receive more details in an hour or so about what country and main roads to travel by and what fords of the Rapidan to aim for. In the meantime each man to draw and cook three days' rations..."

The rest of the orders were lost to Searcy, and Sandie was already reaching for the reins of his horse when Jackson yelled: "Tell them all I'll be at the Jones house north of here in an hour's time. That's all, get everyone rushing."

It was like kicking an anthill, for Searcy saw more brigadiers and colonels than he would have ever guessed were inside, crushing past each other to get out the door of the white house.

Amongst them, Searcy noticed a young Georgian brigadier called Andie Lawton leave by the window. For most people that had ever had anything to do with Jackson knew that the sins he didn't forgive were the sins against speed.

Searcy himself went looking for his horse, as if he too was a devoted member of the General's staff.

— 5 —

WHAT THE YOUNG cavalry colonel had said was: he had ridden right round the Union army at Culpeper, taken prisoners, and could tell General Tom Jackson that there was but two Union divisions in that locale—a force commanded by General Nathaniel Banks, whom Tom Jackson had—as he'd said—whipped regularly in the Valley. Sure Johnny Pope had other men further up the railroad at Catlett's Station, and there was Sigel's German Corps over in Sperryville and King's division coming up from the east tomorrow or sometime or never. If all these elements coalesced, it would mean an army of 40,000 men. "But you know what they're like for moving themselves, them Union generals," the young cavalry colonel said.

Besides knowing the mental habits of Union generals, Tom Jackson knew too the mental habits of the men in Washington: Seward, Stanton, Ole Abe. If Banks were chewed up fast enough, the Washington set would demand that McClellan pull away for ever from the Richmond area. This would free Lee from his steamy garrison work around the capital. And while McClellan went home, it would be like a gift of time to the Confederate army. A gift of time while McClellan embarked his army on the James River, a gift of time while it was at sea, a gift of time while it regrouped itself round Washington, and equipped. And in that vacuum of time, Tom Jackson knew, something could be done to put a new complexion on the war. To consume Banks and Pope, to panic the Washington statesmen. If the movement was to be quick he had to use the Culpeper pike, but he did not care for the practice of walking straight up to the enemy's face like that. For he was a dancing man. He waltzed round a flank. Both of his wives, dear dead

Elinor Junkin, blooming Miss Anna Morrison, could tell you that their stolid spouse, when he decided to dance, could dance something fantastical, was as light as Ariel.

To Tom Jackson the situation didn't feel at all waltzy. But if you wanted 18,000 boys to walk thirty miles in a day and a bit, and mount a battle at the end of the hike, then you were forced to use the best and most obvious roads.

First the boys had to be fed. Soon the meadows around Gordonsville were fragrant with the smell of cush and of baked bread.

Handsome Ash Judd ate his cush-stew as if *that* were his line of business. Joe Murphy, watching him, thought that the way Ash applied himself to his dish, as if there wasn't room in the world for any idea or consideration, was a sign of the boy's slow wits. In fact Ash ate with that amount of care because he knew he would need his stomach for some years after the battle of this summer. He knew, that is, that he was safe. He'd seen the old man again on the Madison Court House road the morning before last. And the witch he'd slept with as a seventeen-year-old in the mountains of Pendleton County had promised him that while ever he met the old man he would be safe.

It had been when Guess's Company were on their road back to camp after standing picket duty, just two mornings back, and there by a fence corner the old man was standing smoking a clay pipe with a wise indifferent look in his eye. Ash, by looking, couldn't have told that the old man was any more interested in him than in any other boy in the ranks of Guess's Company. That was the old man's cleverness, not to recognize Ash, even though he and the old man were known to each other so well and bound together in such a compact that no Yankee marksman nor even the world's widest-bore cannon had power over Ashabel Judd.

Jackson's army got eight miles behind them that afternoon and made their camp around the town of Orange, a town like all the other piedmont towns they knew so well, a town like Gordonsville and Charlottesville, white, a rich verdant even at high summer, and lying there amongst the hills like a promise of the decent life. Tom Jackson himself rode up the main street just an hour or so after his cavalry had ridden through. He dismounted at a little green in front of the courthouse. There was he and Sandie and Kyd and Hunter Maguire, and the body-servant Jim Lewis. While the others looked at maps, Jim went off looking for food and came back with some bread and cold chicken and a pitcher of lemonade he'd got from a private house. "But they tell me, Gen'ral, that all the bedrooms in dis town's been reserved by other officers."

The chicken didn't come to much when Jackson had divided it with his three staff officers. They stood about with a small fragment each in their hands.

"You could go into any house, General," said Hunter Maguire; "you could cancel any junior officer's right to a room."

"This is supposed to be an army of democrats," Tom Jackson said, grinning at his chicken. As the sun went down, he draped himself over a stile on the town green and slept there for a few hours as guns and men crept through to the northern edge of town. He awoke at ten again and dictated orders for the next day's line of march, and was writing away there when a gentleman called Willis, a shopkeeper, came out and invited him into his house. He stayed awake till three in the parlor, discussing the nature of the land ahead with Major Hotchkiss. About then Kyd, who was sleeping on a truckle bed in the upstairs hall, found himself hollered for and came downstairs to write down the General's new orders for Dick Ewell's division.

After that Tom Jackson fell asleep again. He was elated by the risks he was taking, the old familiar risks which were wine to his teetotal body. Tomorrow his soldiers would cover the twenty miles to Culpeper. There couldn't be any doubt about that. The risks demanded fast work and everyone, down to the last wagon-driver, knew about it. The General was in for a disappointment. Of his three generals, one—not sick young Charles Winder, not Popeye Ewell who'd gone blackberrying with Tom Jackson, but the third one, Ambrose Hill—would get the orders mixed. So he'd move his boys too late in the morning out of their encampments, into the pike, which then would seize up with traffic—Popeye's and Winder's and Hill's boys and guns and wagons all clogged together between the embankments of the roadway.

— 6 —

BEFORE REVEILLE THAT morning, at a time when Usaph was in his deepest and sweetest sleep in a field by the turnpike, Ash Judd woke him.

"Saph, Saph!" Ash hissed at him. Usaph came awake so slowly and his mind was mixed, he thought for a time it was Ephie waking him.

Ash was full of pop-eyed excitement. "Danny Blalock and me, today we're going off on our own swing and we was speculating as to whether you'd also care to come."

Usaph wished he hadn't been robbed of sleep for so bad a reason. "Goddamit, Ash, you know how I have to care for Gus."

"Bring Gus along. Ain't he better out in open country, and out of all that dust?"

"And he gets sick out there, say, and we can't catch up? What's Gus and me then? Goddam deserters!"

For there were, as Cate had said, certain rules of thumb in that army. A man could absent himself for a day if his record was good, he could go off looking for chickens or even for women, as long as he was in his place the next morning. Two days' absence began to be the sort of offence you got bucked and gagged for or forced to carry a rail through camp. Three days and you were getting towards a floggable offence, and four or more you might as well stay away altogether, for with bad luck you could be shot dead and you would at least get a month of humiliation, a shaved head, a branding of the face or hand or hip, and bucking and gagging for weeks on end.

"Then," Usaph said, "there's Yankee cavalry out there on any swing you two care to make."

"Come now, Saph. You know how dust kills more than any horseman ever did."

As he was going, Usaph called to him lightly across Gus Ramseur's sleeping shape. "You two get back safe, you understand me!"

Ash and Danny traveled by the hilly and nameless copses between the two roads Stonewall's army was using. Sometimes hawthorn and sumac and poison ivy blocked their way, but mostly there were clear spaces between hemlocks and oaks, and the leaf mold made a sweet road for them. They would come on clearings and pastures and cornfields, they would climb old stone fences and, as the sun rose, would believe that all dust and threat, noise and madness were way off to either side of them. And of course everything seemed, by that light, likely. "What if we find a young widow, Danny?" Ash asked the schoolteacher. "A woman crazed with grief?"

"Do you think," Danny said but with a half smile, "it's the act of a civilized Southern man to take a crazy woman?"

"I mean, not full-born crazy . . . I mean, seeking that well-known solace."

"From two men at the one time?"

"Well, well. You might jest have to abstain, Danny."

And by their laughter they knew it would not happen. They were old enough to know that fantasies don't, yet not old enough to know that sometimes they do and then turn on the dreamer, as wild animals might. Meanwhile, they managed five cross-country miles before the sun came up, and drank water they found in a little run by a cart track, and chewed on a little hardtack for breakfast. At eight o'clock they'd still not seen any habitation and so they rested an hour at the edge of a thicket. It was as they rose from their rest that Danny saw, at the far edge of the clear land they faced, a U.S. cavalryman staring at them. Danny, a crafty man, immediately raised his rifle and yelled at the forest behind him, "Get down there, boys!" And himself crouched, withdrawing a little behind some berry bushes.

They lay for two minutes, Danny and Ash Judd, staring at the opposing forest. They couldn't see the horseman any more. Perhaps he had gone. From what Danny had heard of Yankee horsemen, it would be like them to veer away if they thought there was a whole line of riflemen ready for them.

"If they come out after us," Ash whispered to him, "and there's say a whole squadron . . ."

"Don't count on them being a whole squadron," said Danny, the rational man. "If there was a whole squadron, we'd be able to see one or two of them."

"He was dressed like a French goddam prince, that son of a sow. Did you see it, Danny? Them great thigh boots, for

Chris' sake, and his natty hat and his repeating goddam rifle."

"He's likely a new boy," Danny whispered in his savage schoolmaster's whisper. "Dressing like that. You know how it's a sign of a new boy, Ash."

So Ash Judd didn't speak any more.

"Avast there, Reb!"

It was a voice not unlike their own coming to them across the clearing. When you hadn't met a Yank for some time you got to imagine they spoke an indecent language of their own, but here it was, clean English.

Ash got the laughs but kept them well in. *"Avast?"* he hissed, spluttering. "Goddam *avast?"*

"Yay, Billy Yank!" called Danny. Maybe he hoped to learn something by answering.

"You don't mean to tell me you got a whole skirmish line in them woods, do you, Reb?"

"I got a whole damn company here, Billy. So come and try our fire."

"Goddamit, Reb, I been looking at them woods with my binoculars these past minutes and somehow I can't see none but you and your friend, and these are goddam good Chicago binoculars I got here at my pommel."

"You're a talker, Billy," Danny called. "I suppose you won prizes for oratory up there in Illinois."

"Illinois? Goddamit, I'm an Ohio boy."

Danny laughed privately into the branches of his berry tree.

"Listen to me," the cavalry man called again. "I don't want to call you a stretcher of the truth, Reb, but there's jest me and Henry MacManus here and you and your friend there. There ain't no sense in fighting no equal-odds battle. Even if Henry and I shot you dead with our nice repeaters, what would it mean to anyone but us? So Henry and I are wondering if you two boys're inclined to trade and fraternize a little. Henry here now is busting for a scrap of plug tobacco. You got any plug, Reb?"

"You got any coffee, Billy?"

"Goddam, it's brimming to the lip of our saddlebags here."

Danny shrugged at Ash who made a face back. There was a strange excitement wrapped up in talking with the enemy as if they were neighbors, in checking on their features.

"We got your word then, Reb?"

"Our word's better than yours, Billy. But do we have that?"

"Why, d'you goddam Dixie boys think you *own* honesty?"

The two horsemen rode out in the clearing, but only to the edge, sitting their horses and waiting there. One was a sergeant, the one who'd done the talking. All else you could tell about them at that distance was their youth and how fine their equipment was.

Danny and Ash Judd also emerged but only to the same extent as the Ohio boys had. Everyone was ready to run.

"How's old Jeff Davis now?" the Ohio sergeant called.

"Come to Richmond and see," Danny called back.

All four boys laughed. By these insults each side knew it was safe with the other.

"Ain't you Rebs got a new general? Didn't I read that somewheres? Something about General Starvation?"

"What about you Yanks? You all got nigger wifes yet? Ash Judd called, pleased with himself at getting into the dialogue between the two more eloquent men.

"What's Confederate money worth?" called the young Union private.

"What niggers command your brigades?" asked Ash, sure that nigger jokes were the best offence. "And listen, have them niggers improved the Yankee breed yet?"

The sergeant laughed and stood in his stirrups. "Ain't you got no better clothes'n those I see you in?"

"Do you suppose," said Danny, "we put on our good clothes to go and kill hogs?"

And that sally succeeding, each side decided it was now safe not just to be in the same clearing, but to approach each other. The sergeant even dismounted at a bound and rummaged in his saddlebags, his back to Danny and Ashabel as if trust came easy to him.

"I take it," he said, holding out a fat pouch of coffee, "that you boys are foraging and not wanting to desert to the great armies of the Republic?"

"You take it goddam right, Billy!"

"It happens my name *is* Billy. And this as I said is Henry."

"Danny," said Ash. "And Ash."

"Fine," said the sergeant, taking his hat off, pushing his hand towards Danny. He was a dark-haired, thick-faced boy and Henry was squarefaced and freckled and uncertain.

"No offense, Billy," Danny Blalock said, "but you can get back on your side of the Potomac and then I'll make a train journey up there to shake you by the hand...."

"Why, I suppose you can't manage fairer than that," the

soldier told him, "given the bone blindness of you Southern boys."

They sat together in the grass. Ash gave Henry a plug of chewing tobacco and they eyed each other and ruminated and spat.

"Reb," said Billy sergeant, "I don't want you to take this as mere talk. It comes from me to you as from one American to another. Goddamit, Reb, we got so many men up there, just twenty miles off . . ."

"Keep your secrets to yourself, Yank," Danny warned him.

"God, but I hate to see men die for nothing."

The trouble was the sergeant meant it. His blatant sentiment was ruining this little picnic.

"God, I pity even your rags, boy," he said.

"Now listen," Danny told him. "We won't sit here and be treated like poor relatives. And this isn't talk either—we're on our way, my friend, to get ourselves new suits in Philadelphia."

"In Philadelphia?"

"Or in Baltimore," Ash Judd said. "It's a matter of indifference to us."

"Well," the sergeant told them, his amusement throwing him back in the grass. "God bless your innocence! I can see it's no use laying a meal of truth for you, so we might just as well waste our time on chatter. Is it true your orders are to cut prisoner's throats?"

"What?"

"To save food. Do you cut prisoner's throats? It's a simple question, ain't it?"

Ash stopped chewing, sat with back arched and staring eyes, as if he might fight a duel over the matter.

"Well, we heard you boys were the cut-throats," said Danny. "Out at Fair Oaks *our* wounded had their throats cut. That's what we heard."

"Goddamit, I know it ain't the truth. I had a brother at Fair Oaks in FitzJohn Porter's artillery."

"I guessed it was newspaper talk," Danny Blalock said. He slapped the rigid Ash Judd on the knee, letting him know it wasn't a point of honor.

"Goddamit, you can't trust no way what colonels and newspapers tell you," the sergeant said. "Henry and me, we're in the Fourth Ohio. Colonel O'Grady. General George Bayard is our general of brigade and I tell you he's a fine man. Why, Henry and I have been down on the Culpeper Road looking

at your brothers. Holy Jake, it's a tangle down there. Wagons.
The men all held up, sitting on the sides of the road. There's
lots of cussing going on down there, I can promise you that."

Ash Judd asked him, "Why didn't you capture the whole
goddam wagon train, you and Henry? Make a name for yourself?"

"Oh, there's your cavalry watching it. But I tell you General
Burford's Pennsylvania boys did a raid this morning, about
six. Shot a few wagoners, you know the kind of nonsense.
Now, I would've thought Henry and me, we'd have to rush
like hell to git back to Barnett's Ford by noon. But the sun'll
be low before that tangle gets anywhere near the Rapidan.
Why, there are boys dropping down there with the heat, I tell
you."

"Is that a fact, Billy? You wouldn't ever lie now?"

"I tell you, Reb, it's the word of a friend. If you had to
catch them up, I wouldn't be possessed by any unholy rush."
The sergeant spat. "That's the spitting goddam truth, Danny.
Now, tell me who you boys work for?"

"We work fer Stonewall Jackson," said Ash, as if it were
a small matter. Even quiet Henry MacManus sat up when he
heard it. "We're from the Shenandoah which you boys have
now and then despoiled and now and then got driven from."

The sergeant admitted soberly, "I can imagine to myself
how Henry and myself might feel if you boys were marching
up the Sandusky. But *Stonewall Jackson . . .*!"

"We're," said Ash, "members of the Shenandoah Volunteers which is a regiment in the Stonewall Brigade and the
Stonewall goddam division!"

"Goddamit, Henry!" Billy told his subordinate. "Will you
take that in? These boys are Stonewall Jackson's boys. Goddamit, it must be something to march under a winning general."

"I thought all you boys loved Pope and McClellan," Blalock
remarked. "According to the Northern press, you wouldn't
work in anyone else's hands."

"Ole Mac looked after the boys, but goddamit! Where's all
the success they promised us? Look at us. Good mounts, fine
boots, clean drawers, repeating Spencers. Look at you—no
offense, but you wouldn't tell me you represented the best in
goddam Southern tailoring. Yet you boys are the ones who've
had success up to the moment. Not . . . not that it ain't all going
to change arsey-versey. I think though that Henry and I can
say we are honored to meet you boys."

"And I can say," said Danny Blalock, "speaking I'm sure for Ash as well, that it's more pleasure meeting you two than we would have thought. . . ."

But Danny got on to schoolmaster sort of subjects then. "Ohio is flatter than this, isn't it?"

"That's dead right," the cavalrymen admitted. "Ohio is flatter. But it's fine land as well, you know."

They talked then about the Shenandoah and a little politics. At last Billy said it was time for Henry and himself to go. Standing, he said: "It's a hot day. You boys know your apples ducking away like this. Soon you'll get on higher ground. The mountain you see ahead is Clark's Mountain. The river's just down round the corner of that. You boys want to go straight on, so Henry and me, we'll go diagonal. It wouldn't be a good thing stumbling into each other again and maybe feeling for our weapons."

The cavalrymen were half vanishing into the forest when Danny called out.

"Hey there, Billy!"

Billy pulled his horse's head up and listened.

"You could go into politics, you're such a good goddam orator."

The Culpeper road was a funnel of dust. The lice in Usaph Bumpass's shirt and the crabs in his crotch got lively with the heat, but he tried not to scratch at himself, the way the conscripts did, getting desperate and drying out their mouths with heavy exasperated breathing.

No streams or springs presented themselves in this stretch of road, and Usaph could see Ole Bolly purple-faced beneath his parasol, and hear Gus wheezing. He himself just went on shunting his small ration of saliva around a parched mouth.

He knew by now that he should have woken Gus and gone off with Blalock and Judd. He imagined Ash and Danny doing what they were in fact at that hour doing—finding thickets of blackberries and bursting into their luscious, moist, staining meat; searching for sweet liquid huckleberries which hid with an almost feminine wariness on the underside of the branches of their bushes; plucking and moistening their mouths with sky-blue boysenberries.

It was noon when Ash Judd and Blalock saw the small white farmhouse on the western flank of Clark's Mountain. For a time they observed it, for it looked so neat a little house that you'd expect to find Union cavalry there, since cavalry had a way of finding all the better places. There was, they saw, a barn with a pig pen at the back, but no sign of the hogs themselves. In the front garden, however, some chickens wandered in a melon-and-cabbage patch, and there were two heifers in a meadow.

While they were still watching, a man a little older than themselves came clumping crookedly down the front steps. His method of walking was to thump one foot down and drag the other behind him. His arms were painfully bent as if there was very little play to them, his hands had the fingers spread and bent with the effort of his progress.

"A cripple," Judd whispered.

The young man disappeared into the barn, but Ash and Danny did not move yet. When the man came out of the barn five minutes later leading a saddled horse and carrying a shotgun—that was the moment Blalock chose to show himself.

"Sir," he called. "Sir, I wonder could you advise us...."

The young man lifted the shotgun with his crooked right hand and rested its barrel across his crooked left arm. It pointed wildly 25 degrees north-west of where the two soldiers had revealed themselves.

"Sir," Blalock said again, "I take it you're a Virginian. Well, we're Virginians as well."

The man, dark-haired, dark-eyed, his lips moist, corrected the alignment of the barrel.

"What we were wondering is, could you sell us maybe a chicken or two, or some bread if your wife is baking or maybe some preserves to break the monotony of hardtack?"

"I own no wife," said the boy. The disease had muffled his voice as well as doing some nasty work to his limbs.

"We ain't looters," Ash Judd explained. "Not like them blue-bellies. The law of the army prohibits looting, but even if it didn't..."

"This is our country," Danny Blalock concluded for him.

"Maw!" the young cripple called towards the house. "Maw!"

From the house there appeared a woman of maybe forty. She was a smooth ample woman, her breasts hung like calabashes inside her gray dress. The woman stood there with that wryness about the eyes and mouth that characterizes women who've seen everything, heard every promise utterable to a woman and seen it broken as well.

"You boys deserters?" she called.

"No, ma'am. We're from Stonewall's column and we're going all the way to Philadelphia."

"Is that so? And I suppose on them grounds you come to plunder us."

"Ma'am, if we plundered, we'd get flogged. But if you have anything you could spare, we can pay."

"Come an' let's see you close," she commanded.

They advanced to the steps and the young cripple hobbled behind them. "You sit on the steps there at my feet," the woman commanded them. When they sat they stared up at her. She was a feast of a woman.

"I got lemonade, first of all," she said.

"Oh, ma'am," said Blalock, Ash willing to let him do the fancy talk since he sounded a little like an aristocrat. "Lemonade would be a delight to us. Isn't that so, Ash?"

The woman looked down the steps at mannerly Danny. She could tell he was no ravening deserter. "It's a long time since we last saw you boys," she said. "Keep sat there!"

She vanished and came forth again with a crock of lemonade and two small pannikins. As she poured, Ashabel spoke up clumsily to her son. "How do you go on horseback, sir?"

"I go on the goddam saddle, soldier."

The mother laughed. "Don't you blaspheme there, Arlan. I'd say they're nice boys and intend no harm." She raised her chin and wiped the sweat from her gullet.

"We can't spare no chickens, maw," the son told her.

"We can sell you a little bacon," she announced. "And you can have a loaf of my flourbread jest because you're local boys."

"From the Valley," said Ashabel.

"My, my. Nice people from the Valley. Arlan, you go fetch that milchcow, go on, son. I'm safe enough with these Valley boys."

The son lowered the shotgun and hobbled an uncertain step.

"Our milchcow broke loose last night," the mother explained to Danny Blalock. "Arlan'll have her back here in two shakes or sooner maybe."

Arlan still wasn't sure. Danny thought, he dislikes us like hell for being whole. Maybe even for being the soldiers he can't be. Poor deluded boy.

."They'll keep to the steps?" Arlan asked.

"Oh, Arlan, honey. What if it rains? But you know your maw can manage them."

After one more stare, Arlan hauled himself crookedly up the flanks of his horse. It was painful to watch, but even Ash Judd knew better than to offer help. In the saddle, with the reins in his crooked claw-like hands, Arlan all at once became more masterly. He turned the horse on the patch of dust it occupied and cantered it out of the yard.

"Fell on his head, poor child. Thrown by a horse. When he was no more'n eleven years. Couldn't move much at all at first but he had a purpose to him, always has had. Look at him now. A horseman. And what I'd do without him, with the war on and all the rest, and milchcows bursting out...! For his paw's been gone for four years."

"My condolences, ma'am," said Danny, courtly as he could manage from the stairs.

"Oh," the woman laughed, "he ain't dead. Leastways as far as we know. He lit out to Venezuelie. 'Course, they have the yellow fever in Venezuelie. How does it sound to you, a meal of cheese and fresh baked flourbread?"

"Now? Now, ma'am?"

"When else? Come inside now and make sure your manners are as they have been."

"You have our guarantee, ma'am."

"Here," she said, when they were in the kitchen sitting at the scrubbed table in front of the big hearth whose heat, even today, was welcome somehow. "I think Arlan and I get so few visitors..." She lifted a wet patch of canvas from the corner where it lay crumpled. A jug lay beneath it. "So grab a cup an drink it up," she sang girlishly, "that fine ole mountain dew!"

And so as they ate they drank the burning white liquor, the ferocious distillation of wheat and rye. She got their names from them and they talked of the army and she talked of her battle with the perfidy of men, especially with her husband. An hour and a half passed this way and all three of them were florid and hearty and convinced of the sweetness of the day. And at a certain point Ash Judd did a thing that amazed Danny. As the woman talked he lifted his hand and ran it by the fingertips down the top of the woman's spine, the bit he could get at above the back of the chair. The woman seemed at first not to notice, not even pausing in her speech, but after some

ten minutes of it, she began to give little pleasured flinchings
as Ash's hand worked.

There we are, Danny thought, I'm the one that understands
the exact terms of the Confederacy's struggle, but Ash is more,
much more, at an understanding with women. Even at his
young age, even with his diminished intellect, he *knew* women.
How did he know? Danny wondered. How did he know when
he lifted his hand to stroke the woman's back that she would
not bridle and order him out of the kitchen?

Then Ash was up against her right side, having moved his
chair, and his hand was right round her shoulder, and they
were both beaming across the room like children beneath a
mistletoe. To save himself embarrassment, Danny rose and
said he needed to take the air, a gentlemanly statement of his
desire to use the outhouse. Once out in the brazen afternoon,
he chose not to go to the woman's white-washed sink but to
walk thirty yards further and to urinate in the fringes of the
forest where shade fell on his moonshine-heated face. "Oh that
Ash!" he kept saying, shaking his head. "Oh that Ash Judd!"

When he returned to the kitchen they were gone upstairs.
Danny could hear their footsteps and then other noises, questions and laughter and creaks. He sat at the table, clasping one
hand in another amongst the crumbs. But through the flimsy
ceiling he could hear every whisper and deep sigh. Oh God,
he thought, send Arlan back. Yet don't. No! What would he
himself say to an Arlan who came in at the door this minute?
Oh afternoon, Arlan. My colleague Ashabel Judd's upstairs
explaining the options of the Richmond Government to your
maw!

At last Danny got beyond bearing it and stood up. There
were desires in his belly he'd never known he had up till then
and there was an intent there. He would, if asked about it
earlier this morning, have considered it un-Southern. Goddam
it, he would share the woman with Ash. It was the only way
he could bear her little whimpers. Up and beyond the poky
stairs he found the top floor all one attic, and Ash in no more
than his shirt was heaving bare-assed atop the woman. Her
dress and chemise were up to her armpits and her whimperings
were so loud up here under the roof, they seemed a sort of
homage to manhood. Her little cries both begged off and they
begged release, and they came to Danny as an admission that
there might be a part to woman—to all women, not just to
camp whores—which was an animal part far out beyond the

seas of respectability. This was not such a grand discovery on a world-scale, but it was a fact on which Danny had not been up to now adequately informed.

He expected and feared the mother would drive him away then. Instead, on seeing him, she extended a hand a little way as if making him welcome. As he began unbelting himself, he thought, Ash will give her crabs, Holy Hallelulah! Such a case of crabs! And I shall but add to them. But she didn't seem to be thinking twice about that!

In the column on the Culpeper Road, a large boy from the 5th Virginia dropped dead beneath the sun. They brought him, as they brought the others who had fallen over in the heat, to the embankment beside the road. They took his boots and left him open-mouthed and squinting up at the killing sky. There was no sweat and not even a death clamminess on his dusty face, Usaph noticed in passing him. He was a man with no moisture left in him at all.

Colonel Wheat dismounted, climbed the embankment and inspected the dead boy's face. He turned to his halted regiment. "That goddam Fifth Virginia. They didn't even close their brother's eyes." He didn't himself and beckoned two riflemen out of the column, "Cover him with his blanket, boys. Go on, shroud his poor damn face."

Gus Ramseur, thirsty at Usaph's side, did not even see Colonel Wheat's mercy. He sustained and tormented himself with the music in his head. There was a day in Staunton once when there'd been a parade, and during the parade a man who'd been court-martialed for cowardice was walked in front of the division and two bands played at once. At one end of the parade field a band played "The Rogue's March" and at the other end another band played "Yankee Doodle." The coward was marched in his shirt sleeves into the parade square, barefooted, the left half of his head shaven, a placard on his chest and another on his back saying I AM A COWARD. The discord of the bands was meant to shame the man all the more, but Gus thought instead, as the notes of the brass clashed with one another, that this was more like the music of the age. It was the music you heard in cities like Philadelphia, where Gus had once visited; it was the music you heard in factories from the discord of the machines; it was the music you heard on the battlefield, the conflict of cries, whistles, whirrings and bangings. So they were not really shaming the coward on that parade ground, they were really treating him to the music of his times, the music of the machine of war which, in making those noises and invoking certain brute protests from the men who were crushed and crippled, had made the coward run away in the first place. Sure there were still, somewhere, women and fawns, streams and mountains to write music for, but a man who wanted to write the real music of his age ought to write out of that discord and that dissonance of the bands made on the day the coward was paraded.

Gus therefore had in his blanket, wrapped in a wallet of oilskin, a thick wedge of notes and annotations for his war symphony. It could not be written properly, this symphony, till the war ended and he had learnt more theory and composition and gotten back to a piano. But that would all happen next year if the experts were right. I have just to shift my saliva and save my breath and keep my mind cool during the marches. Then new year I'll be back at my piano, making my notes between visits from students. Mama bringing me in too much coffee and shortbread and telling me not to strain my eyes. He knew his symphony might not be popular, but it would be true, that was most important. He meant to call it *The Fourth of July Symphony*.

Usaph Bumpass had often seen Gus humming and making his annotations on ruled notepaper. That was how Usaph had got to his conclusion that Gus was a man of great talent who had to be saved from the slaughter. Education of any kind awed Usaph. Gus felt that if ever Usaph was in a situation where there was Usaph himself and a graduate of the University of Virginia, and one of them had to give up his life for the other, Usaph might give up his on the simple grounds that the other man had a Bachelor of Arts degree.

Anyhow, as Ramseur kept his brain coolly turned to the music of discord, the cripple Arlan rode into the yard of his mother's farm towing the milchcow he'd recaptured. He could see no sign of the two stragglers around the farm and the silence frightened him. He got down from the horse, left it and the cow tethered, and dragged himself towards the house. There were ways he could walk silently if he took the care and the time, if he did not clump his foot down in impatience.

The kitchen was empty, but the crumbs of the meal were on the table, and the jug was there too. He could hear overly quiet conversation from the attic. He hauled himself to the stairs with great stealth and made barely a noise until he was on the last two steps. At that point he began to hurry, he tottered across the floor, saw his mother half-stripped lying between the two bare-assed stragglers, and in an instant later loosed off the two barrels of his shotgun. Shot went into the wall above the bed and through the roof. If he had had more control in his hands he would have done some grievous work to all three of them with that shot of his.

Before the explosion, Danny had been lying there thinking how natural it was for them to have this big woman between them, praising himself for being unbashful about lying there with her and with Ash. Now he danced up, wearing nothing but his shirt and more pained and ashamed than he'd ever been in his life. He got to Arlan, whose face had gone fish-white beneath his farmer's tan. He flung arms round the man, half caressing him, half stopping him from reloading. "Arlan," he said. He himself was burning red; he could feel his blood burning in his face and at the rims of ears. "Arlan, please!"

"Get dressed and go," the woman commanded, as if it were entirely Danny's fault and Ashabel's. She was already up, shaking her grey dress down over her haunches, becoming again and very fast a distant and forbidden woman. "Arlan," she said, "your maw's very weak." She came up to Arlan and extricated the shotgun from the tangles of Danny's arms and her son's. "You boys dress an' go quick."

"What if he shoots at you again, ma'am?" Ash Judd asked, dragging on britches.

She raised her voice. "Allow us the dignity, boy, of settling all that for ourselves."

Ash and Danny dressed as quickly as the events and their shame demanded, Danny in the corner up out of the range of Arlan's eyes. They were ready in ninety seconds. The woman stood holding the shotgun with one hand and caressing blank Arlan with the other. What would I do, Danny Blalock wondered, if I found my own mother between two boys of the Stonewall Brigade? But the question was too painful for him to deal with.

They were clumping downstairs to fetch their muskets when Ash stopped, mindful of something. He called up the stairwell to the woman. "Ma'am, you mentioned something of bacon you could spare us."

"Get out!" she screamed.

Danny wanted to spring away from that farm but Ash insisted on going slow, with some dignity. In the yard he bent to a chicken, getting it all at once in his hands. He screwed its neck and tied it with a cord from his britches' belt.

"Oh, Ash, that's not decent," Danny said, but Ashabel shrugged. He knew the woman was too busy explaining herself to her offspring to care for the moment what happened to her chickens.

When they were back to the fringe of the forest, Danny said: "What you did, Ash, is worthy of a Yank."

Ash grinned. He took it as a compliment. He had started the day as a lesser man than Danny on account that Danny was a reader and knew so much about generals and politics. But this afternoon had made him the superior for his management of the woman and the remorseless way he'd asked for bacon and destroyed a chicken. If he felt any pain for Arlan—and he did—he was not about to admit it to a clever man like Danny.

— 7 —

ASH AND DANNY got to the ford easy, took their shoes off for the second time that day and splashed across. Some of the cavalry were swimming from the north bank, others were brewing coffee. Vedettes were posted beneath the crest of the first hill. All this meant that the Union horsemen had been driven off, Billy the Orator and Henry MacManus with them.

It was not till after eight in the evening that the Shenandoah Volunteers, less its stragglers and its heat-sick, crossed and found an encampment a mile north of the ford.

That evening Tom Jackson wrote to Robert E. Lee. "Some regiments of Winder's and Ewell's divisions marched as far as eight miles today, and most of Hill's barely two. I'm not making much progress. I regret to tell you that Union cavalry were today allowed to make raids on both Winder's and Hill's wagons. The heat has been oppressive, and General Hill's unfortunate confusion over my movement orders permitted the sun to take a high toll on the health of my men. Tomorrow I do not expect much more except to close up and clear the country around the train of the enemy's cavalry. I fear that the expedition will, in consequence of my tardy movements, be productive of little good. . . ."

Yet next morning, when he got up before dawn, he began to suspect the elements were shaking together properly. Robertson's cavalry was out harrying before four a.m., Ewell's division took the road by five, and Winder's marched behind it, then Hill. All the wagons, 1200 of them, traveled to the rear, making cumbrous time and guarded by two brigades of Georgians. The whole column stretched out for seven miles on the Culpeper Road; but it made good time.

At noon Tom Jackson seemed to be asleep in Old Sorrel's saddle but pointed all at once to a hill off to his right, a steep one for this rolling country. The mapmaker Hotchkiss didn't have to consult a map yet. He knew the place, he said. It was called Slaughter's Mountain.

Old Popeye Ewell, who'd been riding that morning with Tom Jackson, said, "Not a promising name, that one."

Hotchkiss said, "It's just the name of the family who farm it."

It was another of those fierce noons, and the ominous name was still settling redly in their minds when a cavalry officer came down the column, flogging his horse. The poor horse seemed in a frightful lather and spat foam in a way that said little for its chances of lasting the afternoon. Up there, this officer said, beyond the mountain, beyond a stream, the enemy were occupying a ridge in copious numbers.

Tom Jackson and his group reined off to the side of the pike and crowded up against a worm fence which bounded someone's timber lease from the public road. This action allowed the infantry to go on marching, while Hotchkiss rummaged in his saddlebags for the right map. He found it quickly and pointed out its features to the General. The stream was called Cedar Run. It flowed down from the Blue Ridge, running north-west to south-east.

Dick Ewell said that if anyone wanted to anchor a line of battle, Slaughter's Mountain over there with its deep green, wooded slopes, would be a good feature to anchor it on. He seemed pretty pleased when the cavalry officer told him the enemy weren't on it. He kept saying, jabbing at the map: "That's our anchor. Yessir, as anchors go, that anchor's as good as anyone could want."

And while he was still repeating himself, everyone heard

Yankee cannon speaking far up the road. Tom Jackson didn't raise his eyes from the map.

A new disposition came over humble soldiers though, and rumors zipped with electric speed down the seven miles of army and then zipped back so transformed that even by the men who'd started them they could not be recognized.

"It's McClellan up there," went one rumor Usaph heard. "He's got himself back from the James already."

"Goddamit, if it ain't a solid army of niggers up there. Ole Abe's gone and emanicpated the beggars."

"I heard Abe's got himself down from Washington to watch Pope and Banks face up to us. Rumor is he says the Union can't pull back from the Rapidan without them goddam British reckernising our cause."

They were all lies you could laugh at afterwards. But when you stood in that crowd of shoulders, with little knowledge except of whose head was in front of you, blocking your view, then maybe you took some of them as gospel.

Jackson and Popeye and their retinues had taken to the road again, jogging in the dusty space between two of Popeye's brigades. They did not halt till they got to a little rise in the pike from which the stream and the Union ridge behind it could be seen. Again the General turned off the road. There was a more spacious clearing here, the sort of place where travelers on the pike could pull off at noon to chew on a bit of bone or suck from a jar.

Tom Jackson sat there silent for a time and Popeye knew not to ask him questions. They used binoculars on what they could see of the enemy.

"A fine ridge they got themselves there," Popeye muttered, making calculations in his head of the lines of blue uniforms he could see over there amongst the trees.

"How many of them would you say, Dick?"

"I'd say two divisions. And that's minimum, Tom."

Another cavalry man visited them, his horse in better condition than the earlier one. It seems the cavalry'd caught a poor Yankee picket urinating in a wooded stretch of Cedar Run. He'd said he belonged to Alpheus Williams's U.S. division, but that there was also General Chris Auger's division there on the ridge, and Rickett's Pennsylvanians were said to be coming down from Culpeper.

Tom Jackson thought to himself that Ewell could have the

right of the road, including the mountain he'd been so keen about as an anchor. Popeye was used to getting by on the bare letter of Tom Jackson's orders. He didn't get much more than bare letters now.

Jackson leaned down way over Sorrel's mane and squinted. "Dick, you can have this side of the pike. The nature of the ground suggests an attack on their center. Let me know when your boys are deployed."

"You'll be with Winder, Tom?" Popeye asked, wanting an address to send messages.

"Right first off, Dick."

And Jackson just rode away then, as if they'd been discussing some idle deal in real estate. Dick Ewell believed he understood Tom Jackson's purpose just the same. He—Dick Ewell himself—was to pin his line along the base of the mountain and, as Tom Jackson had said, punch at the middle of the other people's line. (Dick Ewell always called the enemy "those other people,' perhaps because he had so many old friends over there.) Meantime Tom Jackson would no doubt send Winder's boys off amongst the blind woods and low hills over to the left, with the idea of taking the other people from the flank. It was exactly what had been tried at Kernstown last spring. Except that today there were more reserves—there was the whole of Hill's division coming up the road, and it could be used as needed.

Popeye saw the guns of a battery he'd sent for come straining up the Culpeper Road. The horses weren't so fast but they looked goddam sturdy. Each cannon with its caisson was driven through a hole in a fence a hundred paces ahead of where Dick Ewell stood. The guns were unlimbered in damn quick time, and the battery officers knew Dick Ewell was watching them and approving. The horse teams were taken back to an edge of forest, and there stood the six guns, loading up with solid shot or shrapnel!

Dick Ewell watched them send off one round, then another. And then another 25 seconds later. Within another 25 seconds there was shot and long-range shell from the other side falling and banging away all round the battery. Dick Ewell saw no one hurt yet, but a maple tree was cut in two near the place where the horses were tethered.

Surrounded by aides, dictating messages and talking to colonels, he still had time to tease his brain with ideas about the ironies of battle. When young—in the days before his stomach gave way—he had fought in the Mexican war. Up the thorny cliffsides of Churubusco and Chapultepec had gone the young Popeye, blinking at the flash of Mexican cannon like a man mildly and reasonably annoyed. After that he spent years in garrisons from Maine to Florida; and inland, escorting the mails on the great ice-bound plains of Kansas. In other words, he had had time to reflect on those mad Mexican battles, and to reflect also on the way the anatomy of a battle is set by accidents.

For example, by the accident of whose division took the road first this morning. There'd be mothers' boys from these regiments passing here in brown bagging coats and torn hats who'd be dead tonight because Jackson trusted one Popeye Ewell more than he trusted Ambrose Hill. But the accidents didn't stop with that. Popeye Ewell had a brigade commander called Jubal Early, a lawyer, foul of mouth, ambitious by temperament. Just the man to push forward up the little slope ahead and down to Cedar Run. So there'd be mothers' boys in Early's brigade who would likewise perish or be maimed because Popeye Ewell liked the style of Jubal Early.

Now, as Early's brigade marched by him, some of them on the road, some of them on a cross-country line across the meadows, five regiments, three Virginian, two Georgian, Popeye watched the boys' faces out of the corners of his eyes to see if their destiny that day was any way marked on them.

Half an hour later his adjutant came up. All his fifteen regiments, the adjutant said, were lined up like a sickle between the road and the far side of Slaughter's Mountain.

He hoped it was the truth. But when you had colonels who were elected by their regiments and learned warfare as they went, you could never be sure they did things properly.

Bumpass and others, marching blind in the column of dust, heard the Union guns about noon. At their first sound, Cate scooped up the dust from his bottom lip with a harsh tongue, looked quickly at Bumpass two ranks ahead and told himself to flee or pretend to be ill, and did nothing, stayed there locked in place, locked in the marriage of Ephephtha and Usaph Bumpass and so locked in the war.

At the sound too, a pretty young conscript staggered from the line and slumped on the embankment of the Culpeper Road and sobbed. The Irish fiddler who had befriended him stood by him, trying to wheedle or reason him back into line.

Joe Murphy, passing, mimicked the two of them. "Ah, don't desert me," he yelled in a falsetto voice, "and don't drop dead of the heat, me darling. Oh, what would I ever do without your plump pink cheeks."

Murphy could talk and josh because he was a veteran, and could tell the cannon were far up the road and that as yet the risk was akin to the risk of being struck by summer lightning.

There was a point Usaph got to in the road, trudging along in a mêlée of other boys, which was the same one where Dick Ewell and Tom Jackson had recently been talking, and where Dick Ewell had had his thoughts about chance and the follies of colonels. From this point, in spite of the dust and the distance, you could see the Federal cannon smoke on a far ridge and, some seconds later, you would hear its bang and whistle. Here Usaph and Gus and the others got one of their rare views of a Confederate general. General Winder sat there in a meadow, resting against an artillery caisson. The top buttons of his jacket were opened to help his breathing and he looked gray-faced, as if he needed the rest. He had only just caught up with his division. His adjutant, a genuine tidewater aristocrat, stood by him and instructed the colonels as they drew level with him. Usaph saw him talking to bird-like Colonel Wheat and Colonel Wheat nodding, nodding.

Railings had been ripped out of a stretch of fence here, so that soldiers could march off leftwards, sideways away from the enemy you could spot way over there on the ridge. The general's adjutant had come right down to the gap in the fence now and was waving Usaph and the others through and telling them to do it at the run.

"We're on a flanking move here, Usaph," Gus panted. It wasn't a hard conclusion for any veteran private to come to.

"Goddam," yelled Ash Judd gaily, knowing he couldn't be killed himself, "ain't it exactly the sort of nonsense that jest about got us all killed at Kernstown."

Now, as the regiment went over a narrow pasture and in amongst cedar stands, it wasn't possible any more to keep even the loose ranks they'd kept in column down the avenues of maples and quaking elm all morning. Usaph began to look around to see if Cate had managed to straggle away and hide, but there he was, over to the left. The Shenandoah regiment had lost boys with lameness and dysentery and some had slipped off into woods and hidden, the Irish fiddler and his boy amongst them. But of all those who could have fallen by the way and straggled off, ole Bolly with his parasol in his belt and Cate, the two scourges of poor Usaph, had kept on as if with a purpose—and it seemed to Usaph of course that their demonish purpose was to go on reminding him of his dead uncle and of the portrait and of the manner the letter from Ephie had come to him by.

"That general back there," Cate said in his resonant college-boy voice.

"His name's Charlie Winder," said Bolly.

"I don't think he looks like he'll last the day." Cate sounded like a truly concerned Confederate.

Usaph remembered seeing some Irishmen who'd been punished by General Winder two weeks back for straggling. Usaph had come across them one day by the side of the road, a stick under their knees and their arms passed under its protruding end and tied with rope in front of their legs. They looked ridiculous. The fiercely tied cords cut into the flesh of their wrists. While men laughed and called jokes at them in passing they cussed back in their Black Irish ways, and one of them called: "Keep an eye on Charlie Winder, you whoresons! Next battle the bastard dies by my goddam bullet."

And that was about all Usaph Bumpass knew about General Winder. But he hoped the man would not die of illness or Irishmen during the afternoon, and that his head would stay as clear as ordinary boys had a right for it to be.

They went loping along in open woods and now came to a cleared and gentle hillside. There were a number of colonels waiting out there on horseback, right in the open, Colonel Wheat amongst them. There was no one but colonels there. Even the man commanding the Stonewall Brigade today was a colonel called Charles Ronald. There was no general available. The thing was A.J. Grigsby, the regular substitute brigade commander since Garnett was dropped, had dysentery today. That was it, you never knew whose orders you might die under. You looked at their faces hard but they were always the faces of strangers.

First the boys dropped their blankets and haversacks and left them in piles and then formed a firing line, under the direction and the curses of Captain Guess, the dentist who had been changed so much by the conflicts around Richmond. The adjutant—Reverend Major Dignam—and Guess and sober Captain Hanks and young Lucius Taber stood amongst the lupins and daisies, viewing the whole process and with their backs to the North, as if they were supposed to be indifferent to anything Union snipers could send their way.

"Don't bunch, goddamit!" Guess snarled in the under-growth. "Two paces apart! Two paces apart!"

If Guess got through the war whole, his old customers would come back to his surgery to get their rotten teeth out. They would remember him as a gentle man. Well, they'd be in for a shaking, shuddering shock once he got his pliers on them next year. "Don't bunch, goddamit!" he'd scream at them.

Other regiments were marching across the front of the Volunteers, right across the clearing, calling stupid things Usaph did not even listen to. He noticed now that he had Gus Ramseur on one side of him and Joe Nunnally, the boy who'd shot the dog, on the other. Then—as if Cate had worked at it—goddam Cate. Beyond Cate, Ash Judd and Joe Murphy and ole Bolly yelled insults at the Irishmen of the 5th Virginia who were marching west across the middle of the clearing.

Everyone in other regiments yelled and hooted when they saw Bolly. Bolly was a favorite with anyone. And he got a sort of animal joy, the old blackguard, out of keeping marching when younger men fell out. He loved to turn up in the battle lines with his dirty yellow parasol hooked into his belt so that men could see him readily and then judge what stuff he was made of. "Hey, Bolly, rumored you was with a plantation lady in Orange!" they called. "Weyhey, Bolly Quintard! There he be, neat as a goddam parson with his 'brella hangin' from his whatsis."

Later, a whole *brigade* of Winder's division went the same way, mashing the daisies with their feet. These boys vanished into the woods way ahead. Everyone started to decide that this meant the Shenandoah regiment was in reserve.

"Is it a good thing, this-here reserve?" Joe Nunnally asked Usaph in a low breathy voice. For all around some were expressing pleasure at the idea and others disappointment.

"I think it may be, Joe," said Usaph. "Let them goddam Irishmen do the plowing and we'll take in the crop. If you take my meaning."

In the next hour Usaph heard fresh Confederate cannon opening up to his front. He had no way of knowing that this was the Rockbridge Artillery, way up along the Culpeper pike, lined out in a meadow and answering the cannon of the enemy.

"Orville, what do you say?" called Patrick Maskill, Puckett's handsome friend. "You're a goddam philosopher, boy.

Do you think they mean to stand or will they probe and run?"

All around them boys were working; *working* wasn't quite the word. No one was bursting his bone cage. There were boys milling round the limber chest, looking in at the shells and charges like they were seeing what mother had packed for the picnic. There were boys swabbing thoroughly, but not too rushed, the black mouths of the cannon. Orville Puckett saw it all as an example of the strange, cool, easy way men often began battles.

Maskill noticed how Puckett stood a little stooped from the cramps in his belly, reaching out and with his fingers indicating to a young artilleryman the length of match the boy ought to cut. "I think, Patrick," he said, "they're in big numbers for people who mean to run."

"That's what I think too, Orville," yawned Patrick Maskill. "You got belly-ache, Orville?"

"Some," admitted Puckett. He felt they—the six guns of Brynam's battery—stood a long way up the road and that feeling didn't help the cramps in his gut. But General Jackson had this habit of pushing his artillery way out to the front, instead of stringing it out in the rear, as generals used to do in far-off 1861.

Orville bent to the elevator screw of his smooth-bore Napoleon and adjusted it a touch. The effort cramped his belly. Turning his head sideways with the pain he saw Pat whistling.

He just about hated Maskill for that.

In a second, Captain Brynam would finish talking with that aide of General Winder's, who'd been sent up here on a visit from the sickly general. Orville knew what the aide was saying. "You're well forward here but we'll send infantry to protect you."

They always said that and it was only sometimes the truth.

Anyhow, when the aide had finished whispering these half-verities, Brynam would give the order: "Fire at will, two rounds per minute." And the boys who were now reading the instructions pasted inside the lid of the limber boxes, all that stuff about how much powder to use with how much shot, and anyone else who was lazing about, maybe leaning against the wheel of a caisson, would come rushing up to serve the guns.

At last Brynam looked up and called the expected order.

These Napoleon smooth-bores could fire five rounds in a minute, but they wouldn't be firing at that rate yet, they were still feeling out that ridge beyond the stream. Puckett's gun was aimed on a diagonal across the road and into the center of those far-off flecks of blue. Back in the edges of the woods the six horses of Orville's gun team snuffled and stayed docile in their harness. There was a boy called Ellis back there, who would talk to them through all the noise.

Puckett himself was sensitive about horses. He had a feeling for them. He believed the worst things of all he had seen in the war happened in the early days when, in obeying the instructions in military manuals, you took the horses a bare twelve yards back from the place where your gun stood. The slaughter of the horses was then frightful. Orville remembered a beast he saw at Manassas, a good broad-shouldered artillery horse struck in the withers by solid shot. He remembered how it struggled up on its front legs out of a swamp of meat and cartilage. Its screams were as high-pitched and piercing as a child's. It was Private Orville Puckett's task, given that his place was with the horses, to cut it out of the traces with his bowie knife, to saw through its leather harness and separate it from the other five mad-eyed, rearing, kicking survivors.

So the Rockbridge had learned you kept the horses back—even 200 paces wasn't too far in Orville's opinion. They could be brought up quick enough if there was need to move the guns. In like manner you kept the limbers back more than the six yards the textbooks had suggested. If a full limber box was hit, it could scythe down its whole gun crew from behind.

A private taking spherical shot up to the cannon shoved it under Orville's nose. Orville was supposed to inspect it and give it the nod. It looked all right to Orville, though his sight blurred at these times. This shot was done up in a long linen tube, the shot and powder all in one linen container. There was a fuse screwed into the surface of the shot, a circular fuse of metal with numbers on it, and you could turn a pointer to the right number. The boy back at the limber box had correctly set this fuse at five seconds. This meant that if the powder was of even quality and if the fuse was well made and was not knocked out of its socket by the explosion inside the gun, or did not fall out in flight, then the shot should blow itself into vengeful fragments over there above the ridge and rain its harsh manna down on poor Yankee boys. But you had to have a lot of some sort of faith for that to happen.

The others seemed to be amused by the uneven quality of Southern powder and the unpredictability of Southern fuses and long-range shells. But when Orville was faced with them he felt a feverish helplessness. He didn't find it amusing that the missile he inspected now might, in twenty seconds' time, blow up anywhere between the mouth of his cannon and the distant enemy.

Orville saw his friend Maskill moisten his lips. "Hot work, Orville!" yelled Maskill in gaps in the noise. To Orville's stunned ears the words sounded hollow, his head floated with an excess of sunlight.

As Orville stood, inspecting shot, calling advice and order in what could be called a well-oiled daze, a round of spherical case shot fired from his own cannon exploded at the muzzle. The crack was amazing and stopped Orville's weak heart. Breathless, he could see fragments of the shell-casing whipping the low vegetation two hundred yards ahead. As the gun whipped back and the smoke cleared he expected one or two of the gun-crew to show wounds. In fact the one injury was far down the line of the battery, a boy working one of the Parrott rifled pieces. He held his hand up tranquilly and three fingers were missing. One of his friends began wrapping the mess in a shirt. The boy just stayed there whey-faced. Orville's gun-crew took little notice; maybe some of them didn't know. It was no use making apologies. The blame was on the gimcrack factories of the South.

Men from Maskill's gun started shouting at Orville's crew. "What was that one, eh? Full of sand, was it?"

"Lordy, one or two more like that, boys, and we can go into the lumber business."

Orville started to smile, a boy brought another round of spherical case from the limber chest and shoved it into his sight; and all at once, because of the great anger he felt, the smile became a grimace.

He shoved his right hand into his jacket on account it was jerking. Oh God, but do I need a woman, a wife, someone to soothe me! One of these nice Lexington girls whose fathers are theologians or physicians and you get invited round to their place to eat cake, drink coffee, sing songs, argue politics or God in a mild sort of way on a Saturday evening. One of those girls who could herself sing and sample, play the piano and make jokes in Latin if that was what you needed.

"Shall . . . shall we try another round, gentlemen," he managed to call.

He saw his friend Sergeant Pat Maskill smiling towards him, carefully sharing the joke, and could tell Pat Maskill knew: that it was a moot point what would happen first with Orville—his mind go or his heart burst.

Under the grin of Sergeant Maskill, Orville Puckett got some of his health back. "Next week," he called to Maskill, "we're going to try Christmas puddings. The components, sir, the components are more reliable."

Maskill laughed in some sort of relief. Orville remembered a time in Lexington when they'd spent too long in a beer parlor and Maskill began weeping in front of everybody about the death of Shelley. He was sure touched by the circumstances of Shelley's death—the poet's corpse being washed ashore on an Italian beach and cremated right there on the sand in the pink dawn by Lord Byron and other great men. When did that happen? Forty years past? Well, the world had lost all its innocence since then, and no Northern boy who was struck by Maskill's fire, or by his own, by Orville Puckett's, made any sort of decent corpse, any touching corpse at all. Any boy that was struck by Maskill's fire or Puckett's, be he the equal of Shelley or not, turned into a foul thing. His own mother wouldn't want to look at him. His own mother would swear that that steaming meat there in the meadow was no flesh of hers.

"No. 3 gun," called Captain Brynam, "should elevate by a degree."

— 8 —

ABOUT TWO O'CLOCK Colonel Lafcadio Wheat began to ride along his line giving advice to his boys. Sometimes he would stop in front of a particular company and deliver himself of a speech. He stopped for example in front of Guess's Company, settling himself in the saddle like a farmer about to have a good talk, and stared about with his hawkish eyes. From these mannerisms alone Usaph knew that he would hear some oratory. It was very still in that clearing. All the noise of batteries seemed to be distant and lazy, and the lack of business to the front meant that everyone must be in his place, and still, and at his ease.

"Boys," said Colonel Wheat now, "there might well be

more noise soon than the night Cousin Carrie lost her virtue. Now you may have guessed we're in reserve again, being that we're the boys best suited to save a day or to point up a goddam triumph, and I'm sure it's the latter we'll be employed upon today. I want you now to keep fixed between your ears these few considerations. No matter what noise descends on this peaceful segment of our Virginia, you're to keep where you been put, right there, fixed in place. Lest any of you conscript boys consider you have more to fear from the enemy than you have from me, let it be said clear that any skulker or backslider can fear from me an inferno that will make the Union muzzles seem like his mammy's lap. Goddamit, I bit the tit off a whore in Charlottesville and I'll bite the head off any one of you, or to save my goddam incisors, I'll shoot it off! So there it is, boys, the grim talk first."

No one spoke. There was still the far-off thudding and the noise of wagons or of masses of boys moving down there on that road. But even veterans were listening to each of Wheat's words. And the conscripts listened like they were about to get *the* essential word from him, the one that would save them.

"Now the sweeter news. It's my suspicion that none of us is going to be hurt this afternoon unless we manage it through our own unregenerate laziness. You know the rules. You don't go shooting too early, you wait till the range is what we call *effective*. Ain't that so? Newcomers wait till the veterans fire, they know when, and if they goddam don't, let 'em remember that goddam titless whore and see in her defaced state the image of what will befall them if they go firing at a crazy long range. Now fire deliberate—no closed eyes—and aim low. This entire goddam brigade is susceptible to overshooting as if there's something wrong with getting a man in the kneecap. Aim for his goddam kneecap and you'll get him, and if you do but wound him, so be it and Hallellulah! For he'll need to be taken off the field by sound men."

Usaph saw Joe Nunnally frowning for fear he might not be able to take in all this good advice.

"Well, the other rules is merest horse-sense. Single out an individual adversary for your fire, some man you never met but you were destined to make inroads in his life. Pick off the enemy's officers, particularly the ones like me who are mounted. Because it might strike you, by observing the poor servant of the Confederacy who sits mounted before you right now, that it's generally field officers who sit on horseback. If you can pick off the artillery, get their goddam horses. If you get their horses, they can't get the cannon away when you advance, as advance you will, sure as the Trinity and twice as slick!"

Some of the boys, Usaph could see, even held Bibles in their hands while they gave ear to Wheat's profane speech. All his blaspheming on the edge of the battlefield took away the breath of the godly and diverted the ungodly from the mortal danger in which they stood.

But there was more noise now from batteries on the other side of the road and lots of Ewell's boys seemed to be firing off their muskets over there. The colonel looked around him, like a parson who knows he might not have time to polish off his sermon before the roof of the chapel falls in.

"Any man who pauses in battle for the purpose of plundering the dead deserves the bullet he shall assuredly get, if not from a Yankee then from me. Do not heed the call of wounded friends. If they can holler it's likely they ain't too bad and that therefore they call out in mere shock. Details have been made to pick up the wounded and your best way to protect your friend is to drive his enemy clear off the field. That's flat. Do your duty, boys, in a way that becomes the heroic example your regiment has gone and set on other battlefields. Remember that the enemy you engage has no feeling of mercy. His ranks are made up of Indians, lovers of nigras, Southern Tories, Kansas Jayhawkers and hired Dutch cut-throats. These bloody ruffians have invaded your country, stolen and destroyed your property, murdered your neighbors, outraged your women, driven your little'uns from their homes and defiled the graves of your kindred. Do you gentlemen need to be told what to do?"

There was a yell from the regiment. "Whe-hee-hee-hew!" It was a wild tribal sound that rasped the blood and cleared out of your ears the echoes of the cannon.

Cate of course abstained from this yelling. All the time he secretly watched Bumpass, wishing him dead yet wishing him also to be safer than any other man on that field. Look at me, goddamit! I can't be avoided, Usaph Bumpass! But Bumpass did not notice him.

Through a minute view down past the distant forest, Usaph saw blue skirmishers way over beyond the road making their way in a firm but wide-spaced line down from their ridge to the banks of Cedar Run.

Gus had seen them too, though probably no one else but the two of them in the whole regiment were so angled as to get this glimpse.

"I jest mention it again," said Gus. "About my notes. You know the man to send them to, Usaph?"

Those music notes that Gus carried in his blankets were his will and his goddam inheritance. Usaph nodded. "Dr. Jerro in Lexington."

"Dr. Guerreaux," said Gus.

"There can't be more than one Dr. Jerro in Lexington."

"I just mention it. I know you ain't so good at Frenchy names," said Gus. He spat some phlegm. "If you sent them to my ma, she jest wouldn't know what to do with them."

"Look, Gus, goddamit it!" said Usaph, remembering that you shouldn't say *goddamit* before a battle. Only colonels could get away with that. "The same deal is on, boy, as ever."

It was just the deal to search for each other after the conflict if a search was needed. You couldn't trust what the colonel had said about the ambulance details. They were never too numerous and most of them weren't outstanding for their devotion. And that was the worst fear of all—to be bundled nameless into the earth with a heap of othe. dead boys whose names were unknown to you. And then no one ever knew where *you* were lying. So that no woman could ever know that mound by *your* name or honor it with blossoms. So that no one for the rest of time knew what your injuries and agonies had been, and whether you went with a look of acceptance on your face, or flinching, or with a sort of frozen scream upon your features.

"The same deal," Gus said, coughing. Not worried. Just wanting the question settled.

The sick young general, Charlie Winder, had arrived at Brynam's battery and was standing behind Puckett's and Maskill's guns, talking to Captain Brynam and looking with him through binoculars at the Federal ridge. Now and then he would make a suggestion about elevation or ask what charge was being used. He had his coat off, it was slung over the front of the saddle of his horse, which stood back near the gun teams.

Through all the racket Orville Puckett could hear snatches of the general's words, even though they came out labored and wheezing. The general was sweating, but he seemed professional in his head.

"Percussion fuse . . . that Number 3 gun's a little . . .

elevation . . . 1.5 would do it, wouldn't you say?"

It seemed the Rockbridge was having some success against that far ridge, and now Yankee batteries began to bear in closer and harder on it. The whistling of some shells seemed to Puckett to be very intimately intended for his own gun and crew.

". . . rifled pieces," Puckett heard the general calling.

"That's right, that's right," Puckett started muttering, though no one could hear him. "Rifled pieces."

He hated that shrieking they made. The rifled shells had lead sabots at their base and the gases of the explosion in the barrel flattened these to the limits of the bore, and the rifling made little flutes and grooves in the lead, which then screamed thus as the shell tore a hole in the hot afternoon air.

So there were engineering reasons for that fierce noise, but it didn't ever sound just like engineering. It sounded as if it had been personally arranged by Satan.

Since the gun was well sighted in, and since the gun-crew were now working blind in the dust to get off three rounds a minute or even four, Puckett, crazy with the noise and gagging from dust and cramp, worked democratically a little way back from the gun, at the limber box. A boy called Moore would take the linen-cased charge out of the one limber chest and Orville would take the fuse out of the other and screw it, deft and quick, into the nose of the shell. Behind him, behind the limbers and caissons and the horse-teams, the shells of the Union were exploding in the maples and oaks and hickories.

Glancing back for an instant in between fitting fuses, Orville saw branches falling. As yet the success of those Yankee artillery sergeants over there were limited to foliage. They would get results though, here by the road, either amongst the horses or amongst the guns, just by a touch of their elevation screws. Or a little variation in the powder charge would take care of it. They were likely twiddling the screws and doing their mental arithmetic right now.

Puckett heard General Charlie Winder yelling more than an ill man should, and looked around. The general was pointing off towards the Yankee slope. Then he pointed to Puckett's gun and Maskill's, but the noise both sides of the road was too steady for him to be heard.

"Give the general my respects," Puckett screamed like a sane man to young Moore, "and ask him would he mind telling you what he said?"

Young Moore went running across towards the place Winder

stood. The general was all crooked about the shoulders with
the effort of yelling and thinking and waiting. His face was
a bilious white which dust and powder smoke hadn't changed.
Moore saw him put his right hand up to his mouth to shout the
order again. Puckett too, inspecting the fuse in the next round,
had half an eye on the general in that instant when a 3-inch
shell, well-tooled in the armories of the North, came down
beneath Charles Winder's raised arm.

Then the general was there on his back on the ground.
Puckett was horrified. A general on the ground! A general on
the ground hadn't got any authority. Winder's side was all
meat, and fibers of his white shirt were mixed in with the blood
and the grey organs which stood all exposed. No one's safe,
thought Puckett. No one is safe here. He wanted to run, and
even took a few quick steps south before something in him
stopped the movement.

The general's body fluttered on the ground just like the
shock had given him a fit. He had raised his left hand and the
second finger and thumb were together, as if Charlie Winder,
who had a reputation as a scholar, was trying to define something to himself. One of Winder's aides and young Moore as
well were fussing about him with a blanket. Sergeant Pat Maskill didn't seem to have noticed what had happened to the
general. He screamed and pointed to the enemy's ridge.
"They're all changing position!" he yelled. He saw that Orville
was standing helpless. He himself detailed Moore and four
other boys from the gun teams to lock arms and carry the
mangled general back to the field surgery along Culpeper Road.
It had to be done, though everyone could see the man was
beyond help from surgeons.

It had happened at the worst of times. The rite of battle had
got going properly now. Jackson was waiting half a mile down
the road from the place Winder had gone down. He was still
in the saddle, and Sandie and Kyd, Hotchkiss and the surgeon
Maguire were with him. They'd all just been watching Early's
boys go down to the banks of the stream where the Union
cannon had started into them, putting them on the ground,
junking them.

Now Winder's aide rode up with *this* news. Tom Jackson
kept a long silence, staring now and then at the aide as if he
were thinking, this man's lying and if I turn on him full force
he could be made to admit it.

"Well," he said in the end, as if he'd been hunting around

in his mind for the best words to say, "I expect God takes the best to stop us getting too ecstatic about war."

All his staff put on somber faces as if everyone was going to sit round in their saddles for at least a minute mourning young Charlie Winder. Instead of that, without saying a word about what his ideas were or his plans, Tom Jackson spurred Ole Sorrel across the main road, fair through the middle of one of Ambrose Hill's regiments. They were North Carolina boys marching into the woods to support dead Winder's regiments. They had to halt all of a sudden and step back on the toes of the men behind them, and there was some profanity about this. Sandie and Kyd and Doctor Maguire came on behind the General. They heard the cuss words of the infantry. But Tom Jackson himself was way ahead.

He couldn't know for certain but he had this feeling from what had happened to Early's boys that, over on Winder's front, beyond the place where the Stonewall Brigade and the Shenandoah Volunteers waited, in a great triangle of woods, things might be going to the devil.

The General was halfway across a meadow on his way towards the Stonewall when there were all at once running boys all around him. Their mouths were open, their jackets were—he noticed—good grey cloth. Green boys.

"Who are they, Sandie?" he asked.

Sandie yelled: "An Alabama brigade. Fresh up from Selma."

"Stop them," said Tom Jackson.

Sandie wheeled his horse to try to obey that preposterous order. It seemed that Banks had just opened the Confederate line like a book, and would now force it back on its binding, break it apart at its spine. "Kyd," Tom Jackson roared. "The Stonewall. Over there in a meadow. Tell them to go forward." His brain kept singing *Kernstown, Kernstown,* because at Kernstown they'd done the same thing to him.

Kyd kicked his horse and went up the funnel of fleeing Alabamans and Virginians, always nearly colliding with some stark-eyed boy who didn't seem to see him. Kyd could feel those strange vibrations in the air that come when the atmosphere is thickly sewn with minie balls, so many you just couldn't worry about them. He thought, it happens at the moment I'm the only creature in the Confederacy who's going in anything like a northerly direction. He saw an officer here and there talking to a clump of men, detaining someone by an elbow, trying to get this or that boy to focus on him. Saying, we can make a line here. But the men always seemed to drift off, or get washed away. And it was beginning to rain.

Back by the road, Tom Jackson got out his sword, something he hadn't done since a dress parade a year back. He yelled to the drifting men all round him. "Here! Here, boys! Get together here. Go forward with Jackson. Come on, go forward with Jackson."

But it was more than the old-fashioned and gallant lines he said. It was the speciality of his aura. Even in that noise and in all the dust not yet settled by this spit of raindrops, men some fifty yards away from him were held up by the wild prophet's eyes that he laid on them as his horse spun round and round like an Italian ringmaster's. "Here, boys, Jackson will lead you. Who'll go with me, eh?"

He'd never once behaved like this before, like a general in an opera. An officer nearby was ordering boys into line. The boys who'd been stopped by the sort of waves Tom Jackson gave off.

Sandie Pendleton rode up to him from one side, big Bill Telfer from the other. They were both yelling good news at once. Their voices made one long sentence of good news. "Thirty-seventh in good order . . . Tenth holding the flank . . . Hill's Second Brigade gone in over the road . . ." And all round the General boys had made a line, all roaring and cussing at the tops of their voices, beasts just wanting to let their rage out, nearly all of them moving their lips, snarling. Jackson knew that men enraged like beasts were a gift to a general. Yet men in a Christian state were never meant to be enraged like beasts. Out of tensions and contradictions like this came the Lord's great day of justification and judgment.

Big General Telfer had his horse just five paces from Old Sorrel. He could see the battle had nearly gone to the other side once already this afternoon because of a general's death. He didn't want another death, not Stonewall's. Why he feared being bereaved again was that if Stonewall was shot, the whole Confederate left, everything this side of the road, would be in his, in Bill Telfer's hands; and that idea terrified him, the idea of being promoted twice in an afternoon.

"You can't stay here," he screamed at Jackson as if he hated him. "This isn't any place for you, for God's sake. You've got to go back, right away. At once."

He waved his arm wildly as if he might start beating Jackson if he was disobeyed. The General's eyes came back to focus, that is they came back to being ordinary eyes. It seemed to Bill Telfer they hadn't been that way up to then, they'd just been there in his head to deliver lightnings with.

The General nodded. "Good, good," he said in a docile way. He turned his horse around and went at a canter back down the road.

— 9 —

WAITING IN THE meadow with the others for the word from Jackson, Cate (naturally) chewed on the circumstances by which he came to be here. For one thing, he was a Northerner through birth and education—his father happened to be a wealthy silversmith, watchmaker and realtor in Lancaster, Pennsylvania. The family had begun as Germans and Cate was an Englished version of Kathner adopted by Cate's grandfather to improve the family's business with the gentry of Pennsylvania.

Cate never got on with his father. He'd been the sort of child who spoke up amongst adults and needed a father who'd give him a pat on the head for his cleverness but a swat on the ass for being gawky. Well, Cate got plenty of swats but a bounty of humiliations as well from his father. By the time Cate senior enrolled his boy in Franklin and Marshall College, the son was determined to fail. Decatur survived his freshman year but was expelled as a sophomore for neglect of his studies, persistent drunkenness and for painting too much.

He's taken up the painting just because he knew it was best suited to irk a good Pennsylvania German like his father. He understood he wasn't so talented at it. But then his father cut off all allowances, and he was left with it as the one thing he could do to earn his bread.

Now Cate was the sort of man who believed that everything that happened to him and would happen in the future was a judgment, and all his talk and bravado—he knew this too—was but a means of concealing that painful fact from himself. He saw his disinheritance therefore as part of that judgment.

He had enough money to buy a small rig and a good horse, and in the summer of '59 he became a travelling portrait-painter. He worked his way through four of the southern counties of Pennsylvania. He understood he wasn't accomplished enough to paint the wives and daughters of the big mill-owners and landholders. Besides, his father had had so much respect for the gentry that young Decatur had a set against them. So, instead of the houses of the gentry, he would call at rich-looking farms. He'd have a copy of one of his works under an arm and a dossier of appreciative letters from former customers.

Those years from '59 to the start of the madness were fine times in the Republic of the United States. Ordinary people could read and write and keep money in bank accounts and have tenfold the riches of any farmer anywhere in the Old World. And the land was full of plump white farmhouses. Because Cate talked like an educated man and had manners to match, the farmer was generally willing to put him up in a guest room while he portrayed the wife or daughter of the house. Cate could usually depend on doing two $8 portraits a week, on eating well and sleeping warm as a guest of the house, and on spending many hours with females of varying shyness and attraction, who would let him dazzle them with talk. Two of them even visited him in the night.

In the Fall of 1860 he crossed into Maryland and—early in 1861—into Virginia. In towns like Culpeper he was able to charge $10 per portrait, but he found the farmers in the central counties of Virginia very political and bloody-minded. And so, in search of more congenial subjects, he crossed the Blue Ridge by Swift Run Gap and began to work his way down the Valley. He had got to Staunton when the war broke out. Even the war seemed to be good for business at first—it made most people feel pushy and one of the pushiest things a man could do in this world was to have his womenfolk painted in real oil on real canvas.

But as he worked down towards the rich town of Lexington, the tensions of the war began to show in the manners of farmers. They began to ask if he was a Lincoln man and whether he meant to volunteer. One day, between a farmer's place near Steele's Tavern and his next calling place, he drew up his rig at the side of the road and practiced a good limp in a clearing. When he presented himself at the next farm door he believed he had a pretty likely hobble. By the time he hit Lexington, a town full of shopkeepers who sold goods to the college and to the Military Institute just up on a neighboring hill, the limp had become a habit.

It was as well. Some of the citizens of Lexington, mostly old men in militia uniforms, some of them veterans of the 1812 war against the English and others of Andrew Jackson's campaigns against Indians over in the mountains, would fall on young men who were slow in joining the army and have long talks with them about it. These gray old soldiers were usually powerful men in town and could prevent ordinary town boys who resisted their suggestions from getting any work or contracts or from selling their produce.

At the other end of the scale of the ages of man were the young cadets from the Virginia Military Institute—hardly any of them more than fifteen years of age. If they saw a healthy male in the street they'd just stand there talking out loud about what a confounded cowardly whimperer he must be.

So months before any conscription law was laid before the Congress in Richmond, Lexington had just about been stripped of young men unless they were lame or ill. Lame Decatur Cate was left to go about his business, but it wasn't the fun it had been. That was why, about the end of April 1862, Cate took the lonely road west, hoping to find some saner county, a county like the counties he'd known before the war began.

Yet even on his way through mountainous Goshen Pass, where the forests were just bursting into summer bud, he met bunches of lean fair-haired boys marching or being marched under ancient militia officers eastwards to the war. One of them told him that just south of Millboro Springs on the Cowpasture River there was a wealthy widow called Mrs. Sarrie Muswell who'd likely go for a picture of herself to hang on the wall. Or if not of herself, then maybe of her niece who was living with her on account of her—the niece's—husband being off with Stonewall. "Though if Stonewall is as sweet a bedmate as that gal is, the soldier said, "I'd be right surprised."

That was how Cate came to meet Mrs. Ephephtha Bumpass, the subject of the last portrait he would do that year.

— 10 —

ABOUT THE TIME Bill Telfer was talking Tom Jackson into being sensible, Captain Guess walked along behind Usaph and Gus and the others, snarling at them: "Load! Load your goddam pieces!" He made it sound as if they delayed doing that out of malice, whereas they'd been waiting, dry-mouthed, for the order, listening to all the screaming from the woods ahead.

Now, in a cooling sprinkle of rain, Usaph hunched to protect his powder and bit at the cartridge paper. I'll remember that taste on my deathbed, he believed. The pungency of cartridge paper and the few grains of powder that came with it. He poured the powder carefully, still in a hunched stance to keep the rain off it. He pushed the ball down with the ramrod.

Then Lafcadio Wheat yelled a few things, they weren't distinct, and the whole line stepped out across the clearing. The rain fell in big slow drops out of a sky that was thundery at its apex. But it was clear in the west and the sun still stood high over the Blue Ridge and lit it sharp as a knife-edge. And from this west, not yet reached by the storm clouds, there was a blinding dazzle of gold. As soon as he stepped out across this farmland, Usaph felt that old molten feeling in his belly. The lust to see the enemy's face. He would confess and confide it to no one. He thought it wasn't natural, that feeling, and in a way he feared it more than wounds, yet was grateful for it.

Crossing the clearing was easy work. But the moment they stepped into the woods, there was the wreckage of the regiments who had catcalled Bolly earlier, and men hobbling and with hanging arms and with blinded eyes being shunted along by friends. These boys passed through the brisk lines of the Shenandoah Volunteers as if the Volunteers weren't there, as if they could have been already dead and ghosts for all the Volunteers meant to them. Just by Ashabel Judd, there was a boy walking along hatless with a leg wrapped in a blanket. You could see the stump sticking out of the end of the blanket and he talked to it as to a baby. By a tree an astounded Cate saw one of the Irish battalion sit with his insides in his lap and ask for water. "Don't stop! Don't stop!" Captain Guess screamed, and no one stopped for the boy. "You ain't about to like it up there, no sir," the boy said levelly, without complaint, as Cate passed him.

Then there were men who, though they limped, you could tell they were unharmed, but beaten in soul. They turned their eyes away as your line passed them, they lowered their shoulders and flitted by you. There was a flicker of blue ahead, between the trunks of trees. It was sharp, live blue. At the sight of it just about everyone, maybe Cate excepted, maybe some of the other conscripts counted out too, but just about everyone, without being able to help it, began to yell their long animal, demonish yell. And just about everyone stood still and fired at that electric flicker of blue, and then reloaded, yelling. "Who-ho-ho-ho-ho-whey-ho-ho-ho!" they yelled, even delaying biting the cardboard end of the cartridge just so that they could finish this yelp.

Cate sighted his musket but chose not to fire. No, not yet. If they mass and rush me, maybe I have no choice. But not yet. Not on the blue of the Union, which to him, as to most Pennsylvanians, had a sacred meaning. Neither did he yell. He was not afraid yet. He was playing with the idea that a bullet would acquit him of his love of Ephephtha Bumpass, and that would be no mean blessing.

Beside him, Joe Nunnally fired and reloaded quick. The Confederacy had bought itself a good rifleman there. Cate had a sense of hundreds of Yankees up there amongst the hickories. But you got the sense that after they fired once, they dropped back further through those trees they had captured so quick an hour past.

So the Shenandoah Volunteers walked forward still. Cate stepped over a fallen Union man, some damage to his jaw. He did not inspect the shape too closely. Then there was another in his path, and a third. My God, he thought, it must be that Joe Nunnally. He looked around at Joe, who was standing still a second, pouring another charge of powder down the barrel of his Enfield. Joe was very studious about it. Cate saw the powder flow easy, for there was very little damp or rain in here amongst the trees. "Go easy, Joe!" he yelled.

He felt a sting across his flanks then. The boy lieutenant Lucius Taber was right behind him and had whacked him on the hip with his sword. "Fire your weapon, you goddam conscript!" the boy yelled.

Decatur Cate saw that there was hardly any color in the boy's eyes, they were all pupil. He could guess Lucius Taber was grateful to have someone close at hand to be angry with. Decatur, anyhow, raised his weapon and fired his first shot northwards, just off into the woods, seeming to aim, not aiming. It seemed there was a scream then and the scream was connected with him. But he could be wrong. There were yells and screams everywhere. But if it was a scream connected with him, he thought, as the tears stung into his eyes, what a comedy! And whose amusement is it supposed to be for?

They were back at the fringes of that arc of wood then, the angle the other brigade had been driven out of an hour before. It came to Colonel Ronald, as it did to Lafcadio Wheat, that they were as fit to be nipped off as that other brigade had been. But Ronald gave no order to halt. They went on out amongst the shocks of corn. The stubble was, as you'd expect, littered with blue-clad figures.

From the east came a long shriek and a shell burst apart in the light rain above the regiment on the Volunteers' right. There were noises of animal protest from those who were struck. A message went up and down the line. Everyone was to run a little way forward and drop on his face.

The clap of shells above Cate's head were themselves like a wound in the brain. Cate was frightened now. Beside Joe Nunnally, he had dropped down a yard or so from some dead boy. For ten minutes while Cate lay there, he recognized the presence of the thing. He felt that if he raised his head to inspect it he would draw himself the whole attention of the United States Artillery. At last he understood that by putting his head sideways, digging his left cheek into the lumpy earth of this farm land, he could inspect the boy.

Well, it happened that the boy was a U.S. second lieutenant with new shoulder straps, silver-leafed. They must have cost him a week's pay. He wore a good frock-coat; even in that dust it still had the gloss on it of something new, and its tails were pushed back either side of him as if he'd been sprinting when he was struck down. He lay on his front, his knees pulled up a little. The wound must be to his front, for Cate could see no damage on him. Where was he from? Cate looked for shoulder markings. He found a little square of linen on the sleeve. 19th Mich., it said.

That amazed Cate. What did it really matter to a boy from Michigan if South Carolina or Virginia wished to manage itself.

What did it matter to him if there were slaves in the South? God Almighty, Decatur Cate had been to Michigan. There were more forests there than whole populations of the earth could fell in a lifetime setting their minds to it. How could it count with this boy if South Carolina went its crazy way? Why didn't he stay home and cut lumber? Cate felt sure this dead boy was, in the springtime he got this coat of his measured and cut, just about like most other Northerners. If they wanted slaves freed, it was for religious and moral reasons, as much because it debased Southern whites as for the fact it enslaved blacks. Or had there been in fact a scalding desire for the equality of blacks in this particular boy's chest? Well, it was lulled now.

As the terrible wedges of noise went on above himself and the corpse and Joe Nunnally and Usaph Bumpass, Cate found himself cursing aloud. In a low voice, beneath all that noise, he cursed the eyes and livers and genitals of those men who'd pushed the issue to the extent that boys from Michigan came down to the farms of Virginia to be killed among the corn.

Some three hundred paces off, a long line of blue appeared behind the furthest end of the farm land, presenting themselves, a Yankee brigade who looked fresh and unstained, who might have waited all afternoon in reserve. They had the look about them of people who meant to stand.

Usaph heard someone near him utter the foulest whoop he'd ever heard, before he understood it had been himself. The whole line of the Stonewall stood and fired at the blue. Cate fired off into the treetops and reloaded, pretending a conscript's clumsiness. Even so he had to fire off four rounds in the two or so dazed minutes the Stonewall stood there. And he began to judge that the rate of fire from the Yankee line was not up to the rate of fire from the Stonewall.

While he rammed his fifth ball home, his musket was hit at the top of the stock and blown in two. He stood dumbly with the dismembered barrel in his hand. Captain Guess came up to his shoulder, snarling at him. "Pick up a new rifle."

"A new rifle?"

For he thought he ought to be exempt now, he ought to be allowed to go back through the woods.

"For God's sake get a new rifle from someone that's down!"

Guess indicated with an irritable sweep of his hand that Cate was to go along the back of the firing line, looking for

a fresh musket. Cate obeyed drunkenly. He turned westwards
without knowing why because an instinct told him there was
a lesser danger that way. He passed ten men in a row, all
standing, all fussing coolly at their muskets, sometimes trilling
their ridiculous cry between rounds, but more now as if they
were singing to themselves.

He came to a conscript whose name he knew. The conscript
was sitting on the ground weeping and holding his arm up by
the wrist. A ball had struck him on the point of the elbow.
There was no way he could hold the arm to soothe the broken
nerves and he wept loudly from the throat. "Hoddy?" Cate
asked the plump boy. "Hoddy?" The boy did not look at him,
being far off and very likely out of his body, as people will
be if an injury be too much. I should give him at least some
water, Cate thought. He was unbelting his canteen when Guess
turned up beside him yet again. "Leave that boy *be* there!"

"I was getting him some water," Cate screamed. "*Water!*"

Guess took a Colt repeater from his belt and put its barrel
right against Cate's forehead. It felt cool and greasy. "You
black Republican son of a bitch, Cate. Get his musket and take
his place."

So he picked up Hoddy's Springfield and stood beside him.
The musket seemed to be loaded, and he put it to his shoulder,
aiming high as it was expected a newcomer would aim. But
he couldn't keep the goddam barrel steady. For it came to him,
if my musket was shot in two, I was damn near shot in two
myself. This goddam fixed idea I've got about Bumpass and
Ephie Bumpass, it has to go! I can't stay here shooting at
goddam foliage. It's a war to be deplored, but it's in progress.
Look at what I've seen today. Oh Jesus, it's in progress! And
I stay here, waiting for Bumpass to die, waiting to rescue
Bumpass, in two minds and the both of them mad. And if so,
then I have to fire on the uniform of the Union. And I can't
fire on the uniform of the Union; therefore I have to desert.

So Cate fired high again, then took a cartridge from his
pouch, bit it, poured the powder down the barrel, dropped in
the musket ball still in its wads of paper and jammed it in tight.
Then he capped the hammer with a copper cap from his cap
box. Next, in this great confusion of mind that was his, he
lifted the musket, fixed aim at the legs of a Union sergeant
and put a bullet right through his chest.

— 11 —

"OH HEAVEN AND HELL," said Usaph Bumpass. "Why ask me, Bolly?"

Bolly admitted it—he was an old man and tired and was making no bones about being stretched beyond his powers this evening. "I'm aged, Usaph, and the business is beginning to tell on me. If I find the boy, how can I carry him?"

"Ask Ash Judd, for God's sake. Ask Blalock!"

"Goddamit, they're already sleeping, Usaph."

Usaph looked about. It was the truth. They were all sleeping. This camp was in a field a mile up the Culpeper Road from the corn and wheat fields where they'd decided their arm of the battle. Few campfires had been lit. Many boys had just thrown themselves down amongst the furrows and the corn stooks without benefit of blankets, such was their brain-tiredness. Gus laid himself down like that on the earth that was moist but not muddy, and a light rain fell on him. The clouds had gone their way west, and above the encampment, if you wanted to call it that, a harvest moon sent down a tranquil blue radiance over the bodies of all these fatigued boys. Usaph wished it was sending down a radiance on his own fallen shape. But goddam Bolly wouldn't let him rest.

"Everyone knows it, Usaph. You're a good ole boy. Everyone knows you're a sweet soul."

"But where the hell is he, Bolly?"

"When we was going forward back there in that goddam cornfield, Usaph. I heared him call out and I stopped by him and there he was. It had come from the side and the jelly of his goddam eye was all over his cheek and his nose bridge, here," Bolly tweeked his own nose, "was gone. I bent to him but goddam Guess said, don't touch that man, like we'd all fit to die if I laid a hand on poor Joe."

You could hear the tears in Bolly's voice and see them on his moonlit left cheek. It just showed you, gross men like Bolly and Joe Murphy could be close. As close as Gus and himself were close. "I don't know if I can make all that distance back there myself," wailed Bolly.

"What if them ambulances have toted him back to the surgeons already?" Usaph suggested.

"When did the goddam ambulances ever find a soul?" said Bolly.

"He might have jest walked back to the goddam field surgery himself," Usaph suggested further. And there I go blaspheming once more, he thought, but I'm too tired tonight to start a blaspheme-free life. "God blast you, Bolly. You like well enough pretending to all the boys in the brigade that you're as good as any young man. Don't goddam come to me pleading to my heart because you're an old man. I tell you, Bolly, it don't go down!"

Frankly as a child, Bolly began to whimper now.

He can't be goddam tireder than me, Usaph thought. Usaph and Bolly and the others had been going forward over cornfields and through woods since their triumph at dusk. But at every cornfield there'd been a few squadrons of Yankee cavalry to pour in a quick and delaying scatter of repeating-rifle fire. Sure, a few volleys of musketry would scatter them and no one you knew would have been hurt. But it was wearying work. Oh how weary was the loading drill when you had that bone tiredness that follows a great combat. A great combat that won't break itself clean at sunset but has to drag on into the dark.

None of it ended until eleven, when there was cannon fire from ahead and solid musketry; and you knew, by the feel and sound, that the Yankees must have had one of their other armies converge with Banks's beaten one. Colonel Wheat then halted you in a wood and at last told you to draw back a mile and sleep. Some of Ambrose Hill's unbloodied boys would do your picket duty for you. Oh how nice! Except that Bolly Quintard had to go looking for his friend Joe Murphy at this time of night and there was no way Usaph could avoid helping him. Well, there was if Usaph would just let himself drop in the cornfield and be instantly asleep as were all the others.

Bolly said: "I *am* a goddam old fool, Usaph, with my posturing and the rest of it. But I swear if you come with me now seeking Joe, that I'll go seeking you and Gus if you ever get caught in that condition."

"In that condition, Bolly? What do you think it is with Joe Murphy? D'you think he's about to have a child?"

Bolly laughed low and moist.

"Goddamit, Bolly," said Usaph, "let's go!"

Stumbling south, Usaph and Bolly passed a few hundred paces from the place Tom Jackson waited by the Culpeper Road with Hotchkiss the mapmaker and with Surgeon Maguire and a few others. A cavalry sergeant, just back from scouting far up the road, found the General there in a light spit of rain. Tom Jackson was sucking a lemon and was all ears. The cavalry sergeant had talked to a dying Yankee boy up along to the right of the road. This boy had assured them that they were in for it now, 'cos Sigel's German Corps had got in from Sperry-ville—sure, a Virginia farmer gave them bum directions but they'd hanged him for taking them the wrong way and now they were deploying for miles in front of Culpeper and the goddam Rebs wouldn't ever get to see Culpeper again. So said the boy whose own chances of ever seeing Culpeper again were so low.

Jackson was happy there by the road that evening. He knew well what hysteria there'd be in the War Department in Washington next morning and in the White House. His own President, Jeff Davis, so nervy with neuralgia, might have begun to behave the same way as Lincoln if he had had the same resources of men. The General understood how it was *lack* of men that made the Confederate War Office more daring than the U.S. War Office, made Confederate Secretary of War Judah Benjamin tougher-minded than jittery Edwin M. Stanton.

Tom Jackson had kept himself awake till now with the tart juices of the lemons he carried in his saddlebag. Now he tossed a lemon rind off into the dark.

"That's all there is to this day," he told Maguire and Hotch-kiss. He climbed onto his horse, they climbed onto theirs. They watched him sway along in his saddle, bouncing in and out of sleep, as they rode south.

Officers who'd known Tom Jackson when he'd been a professor told Maguire that he'd needed ten hours sleep a night in those days and used sometimes to fall asleep at the podium just the same. He always sat straight up, his back not touching the chair, in the cockeyed belief that would keep his innards from bunching up. He used to bore people with talk about his dyspepsia, and at the age of thirty got leave to go to New York to see the best doctor on the problem. So when young Doctor Maguire was sent to Harpers Ferry last year to be the regimental surgeon of Colonel Tom Jackson, men had said to him: "You'll need a staff of three surgeons just to deal with Crazy Tom's complaints alone."

But it hadn't developed like that. Once the marching over the mountains and down the Valley started, the maneuverings and the face-offs, Tom Jackson forgot his dyspepsia and his rheumatism as if they were the complaints of a dead uncle of his.

There were three or four farmhouses they passed, off in the meadows now, all with lights blazing. There were wounded lying all round them, not in rows, more like they'd been dropped by orderlies wherever there was space. You could see the big fires orderlies were burning a little way from the warm buildings. If you looked close, you saw them putting on one fire clothing too bad stained to be of use to anyone. Someone was stoking the other with a human leg or arm, and the terrible cannibal stink of blazing human meat was over the countryside. There were boys who trod amongst the shapes in the meadows, looking for the dead so that their bandages could be used again. There wasn't much noise of protest coming from the ground outside these surgical stations, just sometimes the high voice of some boy protesting to a surgeon and the tough deep voice of the surgeon or the orderlies in reply. It might be some time *after* midnight that the ones who had got beyond the shock of it and had not yet bled away would begin their yelling, and all the woods and fields would be full of strange wild noises.

At each of these farmhouses, Hunter said: "They could clear a corner for you to lie down, sir."

"No," Tom Jackson would say. He wouldn't give any reason. If the moans of boys irked the General's conscience, there was sure no sign of it. Well, they certainly irked Hunter Maguire's conscience. Through the wide-open window of one of the farmhouses, he could see a regimental surgeon called Abel Oursley working by lantern light. Now Oursley was one of the better ones. He'd joined up from a medical practice in Staunton, Virginia, to get away from his goddam wife, as he said. He was, at least, no quack or mountain pig doctor. Though given to the bottle, he kept sober for battles and would have been a brigade or divisional staff surgeon if it weren't for the fact that most of the time in camp, where superiors had leisure to watch him such as they didn't have in battle, poor old Abel was stewed. There was this about him too, he panicked on nights like this, as most of them panicked. Hunter Maguire knew that if he was in there, maybe he'd panic too. Surgeons were faced with so much mess and moaning that they would amputate anything they could rather than attend to a wound in its own right. And what old Abel couldn't amputate he probed with hands that had too much of a tremble to them.

There was no doubt that Hunter Maguire, M.D., University of Pennsylvania, was a sight better surgeon than Abel Oursley though, and it would have been madness to pretend anything else. Therefore Maguire always had the urge to get down off his horse and go into the farmhouse and take the scalpel and saw from Abel's hand. But he knew that even if Tom Jackson let him go into that butcher's shop of Abel Oursley's he would lose what control he had over the circus. It would be an act of too much passion. Not only unworthy of a Virginian gentleman and a high-rating tidewater doctor of fashion. It would also mean more boys would die in the end.

It was strange though that he'd got down off his horse today only for a case beyond hope. Late afternoon he saw a Marylander he knew, a Baltimore lawyer called Snowdon Andrews, lying half-covered by a blanket at the edge of the Culpeper pike. Two soldiers kept him company but Snowdon's face was to the ground and his mouth made little private movements as if he was confiding in the dust.

Well, you had to get down at a time like that, when you saw an old college friend. One of the soldiers waiting at Snowdon's side told Maguire, "It's fearful, doctor," and when Hunter lifted the blanket he saw it was, for a great mess of Snowdon's viscera was tumbled forward into the dust.

Hunter saw Snowdon Andrews looking at him sideways. "I'm grieved to see you like this, Snowdon."

"I'm not too tickled about it myself, Hunter."

"I have to tell you . . . there's nothing I can do for you."

"Yes, that's what you fellows always say."

So Hunter Maguire had sighed and turned the man over and got water from a canteen and rinsed Snowdon's viscera off and returned them by hand to the abdominal cavity while Snowdon watched him, grey in the face but calm-eyed. And then he'd sewn him up and fetched a stretcher and sent him off to die of it all.

A case beyond hope and the only surgery he had done all day!

They were now beside some vacant pasture land on their left. Jackson swung his horse under the shelter of some trees,

for the rain was starting to have a bite to it now. Hotchkiss
said: "D'you want us to fetch something to eat, General?"

The General was already dragging his cloak out of a saddlebag and spreading it on the ground. Then he fell on it face
first. His words came out muffled by the cloth. "I want to rest,
just rest," he said.

— 12 —

BOLLY AND USAPH, bone-tired, found the cornfield at last,
recognizing it from the way that farmer had stacked the sheaths.
They'd already stumbled past a lot of other boys who, hearing
them moving or seeing them by moonlight, called out to them.
But you couldn't answer those boys. Bolly and Usaph moved
past, following their narrow purpose, the way Hunter Maguire
was following his a mile down the road. Those other boys must
have friends and so had to be left to their friends. In Bolly's
brain and Usaph's there was room only for a sort of animal
concern for Joe Murphy.

Bolly's memory of the event got them to that angle of the
field where it had happened. If Usaph had been a little less
weary it would have been nice to watch how Bolly did it. He
had a memory for little differences in this place or that, just
like an Indian's memory. It was easy to find Joe then. They
could hear him sort of sobbing, and he could hear them approach too. "Coming for me, boys? Coming for me?"

He was sitting like a child, his legs spread in front of him.

"I'm blinded, Bolly," he announced. And he already had
that way of lifting his ear that a blind man has. He was dazed
too. When you looked at him close you saw his right eye
hanging by a sort of wormy stalk out of his cheek, where it
was stuck in a sort of paste of blood. The sight brought up
some bile into Usaph's mouth and he had a hard, gaspy time
swallowing it. "Bolly then?" Murphy said again, "Is it Bolly?"

"It's me, Joe."

"Goddamit but I been waiting a long hour for the footfall
of a friend, you son of a bitch, Bolly."

"They wouldn't let me stop, Joe. You know how they harass

a man who tries to stop for a friend."

"Both my eyes gone, Bolly. Jesus, Mary and Joseph, both the bastards! Who is it with you there, Bolly?"

"Usaph," said Usaph.

"Usaph is a good and brotherly boy," said Bolly.

"Well, you're out of it now there, Joe," said Usaph. "You can go home and live now at rest."

Joe Murphy spread his fingers like someone seeking, seeking. "Think you so, Usaph Bumpass?" he asked. "It's rest, is it? I can sit back I imagine and read the goddam newspapers, I suppose."

There wasn't any way *that* could be answered.

"Now listen, Bolly," said Murphy. "I want to talk serious with you. You know damn well there's no place for a man without eyes. There's more place for a man without a dangle than there is for a man without eyes."

Bolly didn't answer. Nor did Usaph.

"I ask you, Bolly, what you'd ask me to do if you was in the one situation I'm in. I'm asking you Bolly to save me from the gangreeny an', even if I lived through that, from the shame of goddam darkness. Of needing goddam hands to guide me all me days when I ought to be out walking like a seeing man."

He began weeping a gale. Out of them smashed eyes? Usaph wondered.

"Now?" Bolly asked in a small voice. "You mean right now, Joe? You want to be . . . relieved from misery, son?"

"While I'm at peace, Bolly. While I'm at peace. I tell you that there Frenchie goddam Jesuit in the Louisiana Brigade told the boys that God ain't about to turn away any boy who's after dying in battle for such a good democratic goddam cause. Now them Jesuits knows a powerful lot more than your average priest. The Lord won't turn away Joe Murphy even if he's been a profane and shameful braggard." There was silence. "I'm at peace now, Bolly," Murphy repeated after a time.

"Well . . . *where*, Joe?" Bolly asked in a pained voice, awake now with all the sharp weight of the task Murphy had laid on him.

"You know, Bolly. The back of this misused and degredated head. You're after doing it for enemies so they don't even feel pain. Do it for a friend, Bolly!"

Bolly thought awhile. Then he got out a cartridge. It seemed that in that hot battle he'd only used some twenty rounds, if that, and still had plenty to do the job for Joseph Murphy. He

bit the cardboard cartridge secretly, half turning away, just like
a man trying to slip a plug of tobacco in his mouth in polite
company and against his wife's orders. He sprinkled the powder down the dirty barrel of his musket.

Usaph was dead against it, he couldn't say why, for he
wouldn't want to live blind himself. He wouldn't want to be
shunted round by Ephie and never see her special beauty. And
never notice the other men looking at her and deciding she
must be ripe for a suggestion, seeing as how she was stuck
with a blind spouse.

"Jest tell me when you're all ready," Joe asked.

Usaph said "Whoa up, Bolly!" He didn't know why he did
it, seeing he approved of Bolly's act of mercy in principle.
Anyhow he got his neckerchief off and poured the dregs of
water on it from his canteen. Usaph was a man of more than
normal thirst and carried a canteen of U.S. make, like two
dishes soldered together. To the dregs of water he added his
spit. "Is there pain there, Joe?" he asked, pointing to the face.

Though he could see nothing, Murphy understood. "No.
God is merciful. There's no pain to speak of, Usaph. Well,
when I say no pain, I mean no screaming pain, anyhows."

Usaph felt an urge to lever the hanging eye off the right
cheek and pack it back in its socket. God knows it might work
again. But no, he kept away from that side of the face and
began to wash Murphy's left cheek, gently, expecting protest.
By the chin he moved Joe's head to catch the light of the moon,
that was still shining down between thunder clouds. There was
such a paste of powder and blood and soil on Joe's cheek.
"Bolly, you got water?" Usaph asked, but Bolly said no. So
Usaph unbuttoned his britches and urinated on the cloth.

"Fod God's sake, Usaph," Bolly protested, wanting to get
his task behind him.

The urine-soaked cloth stung Joe's forehead above the left
eye. He yelped. "You hit a cut right there, Bumpass. It won't
be troubling me much longer."

"A cut there, that's fine, Joe. But does *this one* hurt you?"
He laid the cloth fair on that eye and Joe said nothing. He
began to ply the cloth, cleaning up the socket with a will, and
still Joe did not complain. And after a few seconds, Usaph
could see that the eye was there, sure enough, in its place, and
it seemed unmarked. And as he made this find of the eye buried
under all the battle muck, Joe reached out his left arm slowly
and gripped Usaph's rag arm by the wrist. "Goddam it!" he

called. "Oh Jesus, Usaph. I can see yourself there, you son
of a bitch!"

He hopped up, still with his right eye on his cheek. He
bayed under the moon with pleasure.

"Goddamit," he cried. "I'm going to be one of them grandfathers with a glass eye, and you take it out of your socket and
roll it in your hand to frighten the littl'uns. Goddamit, I'm
going to be one hell of a scary grandfather, oh Mother of God!"

Usaph and Bolly clapped and chortled and yippeed and
danced with him. He made a strange dancer. But when they
stopped celebrating with him, the cornfields seemed full all at
once with fevered wails, the midnight screams that Maguire
had expected. The joy of Bolly and Usaph for Murphy had
brought all those damaged boys in that place out of their merciful daze and now they were raving under the moon like men
who couldn't wait another second for peace or water or bandages.

In the morning a natty Yankee officer came across Cedar Run
under flag of truce to ask that the day be set aside for finding
the last of the wounded and for putting the dead in crowded
but Christian graves.

Usaph was not put on burial details, but he could see the
parties working in the meadows round about, wearing masks
of linen over their faces. The dead were starting to bloat, Usaph
could see, and to burst the seams of the vests and trousers
they'd died in. They were all barefooted under the sky—they
always lost their shoes to needy Confederates.

The sight put Usaph in a black mood, which deepened when
Guess sent him in a detail back to the wagons for cases of
Springfield cartridges. But he went and fetched a case and so
came back, the sun biting into one of his shoulders, the cartridge box into the other.

Along the embankment in the sun, calling on passers-by for
water, were whole lines of stragglers bucked and bound. Usaph
heard one of them calling to him by name *"Usaph! Mr. Bumpass!"*

Usaph paused and looked up at the embankment. There was
the Irish fiddler and his fancy-boy, knees locked up over a
stick by their bound hands. The soft-faced boy had lost his hat
and his face was beginning to blister.

"You know me, Mr. Bumpass sir. I'm Sean and I think I

can say I've brought ye pleasure with me bow one time or another."

Usaph wasn't gracious. "What of it, Irish?"

"Bumpass, I've the diarrhea."

"And I suppose that makes you different from the rest of us?"

"If I could have a little water, Mr. Bumpass. And if you could take me hat off me head and put it on poor Walter's..."

Well, there were flies all over the fiddler. He had the diarrhea right enough.

"We'd all like water," said Bumpass.

"Come, Bumpass. Ain't we practic'ly brothers?"

"If we're brothers, why did you straggle off yesterday, brother?"

The fiddler said nothing. He let his head fall, for he'd come to the conclusion that Bumpass lacked mercy.

"Goddam you, Irish!" yelled Usaph, and put the ammunition by the roadside. He climbed the side of the road, dragged the fiddler's hat off his head and pushed it on to the soft boy's. "You're the victim of an unholy goddam passion, fiddler," he said, and for some reason thought of himself and Cate. He was just starting to feed them water, and other bucked backsliders were also beginning to yell at him for his bounty of water when a young officer, riding down the pike, screamed at him. "No water for them people, son," he screamed. Son? thought Usaph.

"We're all goddam sufferers," he snarled at the roped boys as he stepped over them, but they groaned and whimpered back, and he was pleased to take up again that box and totter up the road. "An honorable goddam burden," he muttered to himself once.

Back in the encampment, in a field of trampled corn, a thick-shouldered boy with dark hair and a big dark moustache was baking bread and chatting with Bolly.

"Hey, Usaph there," called Bolly. "This-here's my friend Hans Strahl. Why he's my partner now that Joe's gone and done that to his eyes."

Usaph looked at Bolly there, sitting cross-legged on a blanket and, it seemed, fiercely pleased to have a new friend, any friend. "What's the name, boy?" Usaph asked, peevish.

"Hans," said the dark young man, wanting to be neighborly. "Hans Strahl it is." There was something a little German about his way of speech. But he wasn't any conscript, for his face was familiar from before the time of conscripts.

"Another goddam Dutchy," Usaph grunted and looked up to see Gus Ramseur staring at him. Too late Usaph began to laugh as if it had been a joke all along; and then he turned away red in the face.

"You must watch out for that Bolly," he called in a sort of strangled joviality to this Hans Strahl. Then he found his blanket, climbed a stone fence and slept deep all afternoon. Falling asleep he kept muttering: "You goddam hayseed, Bumpass! You goddam club-fisted hick!"

— 13 —

MRS. WHIPPLE HAD a distressing morning. It had begun in fact about 3:30 a.m. when Mrs. Coleman went into childbirth in the laundry.

Mrs. Coleman had come up from North Carolina two months back to visit her husband, a typhus-sufferer, in Ward 8. She'd picked up her sister along the way and brought her along too, and the both of the women had stayed ever since. They were lean unlovely country women—"'bout as pretty as a pair of shingles," one of the boys in Ward 8 said of them.

But although she may not have been a beauty, Mrs. Coleman was the only one who had ever won a battle of wills with Dora Whipple. What had happened was that Mrs. Coleman had just refused to go home. On the very first night of her stay she'd come knocking on Mrs. Whipple's door.

"There must be a place for my sister and me to sup and lie down."

"This is a hospital, ma'am, not a hotel," Mrs. Whipple said, icy as she could manage.

"Well, they seem t'have found a place for *you*. And you ain't married to no one."

When it was clear to Mrs. Coleman that there was no place for her to stay, she and her sister just camped out all night on the steps of Ward 8 and got pretty wet, for the spring had come in rainy.

When Mrs. Coleman and her sister threatened to stick to

the steps the following night as well, Mrs. Whipple had unwisely let her use the laundry. Mrs. Whipple knew it was
foolish, but Mrs. Coleman had shamed her into it.

After that there were always reasons for Mrs. Coleman to
stay on at Chimborazo. Her husband got a new fever, and Mrs.
Coleman didn't want to go home till that had worked itself out.
And when it had and Private Coleman was sent back to Daniel
Hill's division, Mrs. Coleman said she'd dreamed her husband
would be back within a week with a wound, and could she just
stay till the big battles round Richmond had "fit" themselves
out? Well, it made good enough sense, for the woman had
already been in the laundry three weeks and another week made
little difference. Within the week, Private Coleman was back
as his slant-browed spouse had dreamed, and there was a wound
in his neck he'd got at Malvern Hill.

Of course now the wife had to stay on till she knew whether
he'd live or develop the "gangreeny." By the time it was clear
that the wound was healing, she was so close to what she called
"whelpin'" that she couldn't be moved. Just at dawn that morning, Mrs. Whipple, helped by a sulky and hung-over assistant
surgeon from Ward 8, delivered a hearty boy-child to Mrs.
Coleman. Mrs. Coleman said she meant to call it Malvern
Chimborazo Coleman. And of course she did and little Malvern
Chimborazo would have to stay on a few more weeks yet, she
didn't want the wee thing fetching a fever on one of them slow
trains down to North Carolina.

After the baby's birth, Dora Whipple left the laundry which
had been set up snug with beds and didn't look like a laundry
any more, thinking, *I'll never get rid of that woman,* and
feeling already tired and desperate, even though the day hadn't
got going yet.

Mrs. Whipple hadn't reached the doors of her quarters before she saw one of the medical orderlies running towards her.

"It's Mr. Greenhow," he was calling. "In Maryland."

Maryland was Wards 30 and 31. She'd put all the Marylanders together in there because soldiers from other states
seemed to resent them. Mrs. Whipple liked Wards 30 and 31.
None of the boys in there were like Private Coleman. Most of
them were cultivated gentlemen from Baltimore. And Captain
Greenhow, a lawyer from Baltimore, was one of the gentlemen
in Maryland that Dora Whipple liked best. She hurried down
the alleyways between the wards with the orderly hobbling
behind and rushed up the steps of 30. Inside, most of the boys

were still asleep. Alec Greenhow was in his bed, his eyes clear and wide-open, and the sheet over his lower body sodden with blood. Dora Whipple tore the sheet away and lifted Greenhow's blood-wet nightgown and saw that all the mess was pulsing out of a little hole high up on the boy's thigh.

"Wake the surgeon," she yelled at the orderly, and he went to do so. In his absence, Dora Whipple looked at Alec Greenhow, and Alec looked at her. He was twenty or so years old and he knew what had happened, and so did she. He'd had a hip wound and had been waiting here four months for the shattered bone to knit. She had designed a sort of cast of cardboard and wood that let him hobble a little way on his shattered hip. But now a splintered edge of bone had cut a deep artery.

"I'll just put my thumb on that little nick," she said briskly, but only because brisk was her nature. She located amongst all that gore the exact spot from which the mess was rising—it was only a small opening in the flesh. She forced her thumb down on it as she had promised. That was enough to stop the surge.

After a minute the surgeon came in, a young one, a good one, a Marylander himself.

"Sprung a leak, have you, Greenhow?" he asked brightly. "Just take your thumb away, Mrs. Whipple, let us have a look."

She did it and he stared awhile, and felt the hip with the tips of his fingers. Then he got Mrs. Whipple to come aside, leaving the orderly to thumb the puncture in the thigh. He said in a low voice, "It's one of the deep arteries, Mrs. Whipple."

"Well, what can you do, doctor?"

"Nothing. It can't be reached. If it were lower down the leg, I could try to amputate..." He shrugged and bit his lip. "He...I can't tell him, Mrs. Whipple."

He bowed jerkily and walked, almost fled away down the aisle. Alec Greenhow's eyes followed him and seemed to know exactly what it meant. Oh God, Dora Whipple thought, what is it about *me* that people always think *I* can do these things. My shoulders are only nineteen inches across.

She moved back to the bed. "I'll take your place," she told the orderly. "Please get Captain Greenhow new sheets."

"New sheets?" asked the orderly, frowning. He knew they'd only be fouled with further blood, and that he might have to boil them up himself.

"I said *new* sheets!"

The orderly shrugged and nodded and went off to obey. Captain Greenhow looked her full in the eyes again. "How long?" he asked.

"We can arrange for a series of orderlies to hold the place . . ."

He smiled. "To keep their thumb in the dyke?"

"I'm sorry, Captain Greenhow. But there may be . . . letters and so on for you to write."

He shook his head. His lips were dry and hard to form words with. "I couldn't write letters. Perhaps you can send a message to my folk. The address is in my things."

All at once Mrs. Whipple found she was crying. "It isn't fair," she said. "Four months healing. And now this."

He had this terrible calm. "It's the way of things," he said. He didn't mention God or destiny, and she wondered was he perhaps an atheist. "You can let go," he said, and it was more like a sentence on her than a permission.

"No!" she said. She pressed her thumb harder. "No. I'll stay here all day."

"Please let go," he said, and he took by the wrist the hand that was holding the artery. She said, thinking desperately: "The orderly isn't back with the clean sheets yet."

Alec Greenhow grinned as if she'd said something very feminine. He looked so young. "All right," he said. "But *then*."

The orderly was back awfully quickly, and Mrs. Whipple wondered why he had to be so damn efficient this one time. He pulled the saturated sheet away and lay the new ones carefully as if Alec Greenhow was going to be occupying that bed a week or more yet. He showed some delicacy of feeling at last, that orderly, the way he did it. The main sound Dora Whipple could hear now was her own blood drumming in her ears. "You can go now," she told the orderly, and he went.

"So?" said young Captain Greenhow then. "No!" she said. Her thumb was biting into his flesh.

But he reached out with both his hands and, an inch at a time, forced her hand away, yet staring all the time at her eyes as if those were the only terms on which he could die properly. She heard the terrible dull splash as the interrupted flow began again, and at that second her hands and feet tingled in a way that terrified her. There was a surging in her ears, and her lips, this summer's morning, turned frost cold. She knew she was falling and losing her hold on the world as sure as Alec Greenhow was. She felt her right hip and shoulder crash against the floorboards.

Later she knew the young Marylander would have been glad she fainted, for she would have made a spectacle of his death if she had had her way. They carried her back to her quarters on a litter, and on the way past the laundry she was still too numb to hear the yelling of Malvern Chimborazo Coleman.

When they carried her in, the widow lay still and numb on her bed. But after half an hour she was beginning to stir. Her black girl brought her a cup of sassafras tea and roused her and handed it to her.

"Ma'am," said the black girl, "the surgeon . . . he's azwaiting to see you?"

"What surgeon, Sally?"

"Why, the boss surgeon, ma'am."

"The surgeon-in-chief? Oh my heaven!"

She stood up instantly. Her strong soul had somehow absorbed Alec Greenhow's death and now he was just part of the history she would carry around with her. She shook out her dress and punished her hair into shape.

"Ask him in and make some tea for him."

She sat herself down at the table and flexed her mouth to get the wrinkles of recent grief out of it.

"My dear Mrs. Whipple," said the surgeon-in-chief, entering. He was a tall man of about fifty years, totally clean-shaven—he was one of those progressive surgeons who thought a doctor ought not to get his whiskers in his work.

"Sir," she said, standing and smiling so calmly he couldn't have guessed that just forty minutes past she had fallen in an hysterical faint.

"I'll be brief, Mrs. Whipple," he said. "Do you feel you can leave here?"

"I don't understand you, sir." Have they found out? she wondered. Are they testing me?

"You might have read that three or four days ago there was a fight north of Orange. It sent Pope scuttling off beyond Culpeper. Just about our whole army has moved up that way, and it's struck the Surgeon-General's Committee that a hospital should be got together at Orange. Nice little town, Orange. You could take in wounded and sick from whatever campaigns are fought, either campaigns in the valley or ones up along the railroad. And the Committee was wondering if . . . well, if you would care to be the matron of the Orange Hospital." He rubbed his clean jaw. "Not that I shan't be distracted to lose you . . ."

Dora Whipple studied him for a while. Is it an innocent proposal? she wondered again. Have they caught someone else from the intelligence chain?"

"All my friends are in Richmond," she said. And so is the thin little man who wears a beaver hat and a frock-coat and meets me at ten o'clock every Thursday evening on open ground west of the hospital, and makes a note of what I can tell him. Perhaps I want to be separated from him now. Perhaps the Alec Greenhow business has changed my mind on spying.

She tested this idea and found her mind had not altered. The spying business was no flirtation which she could take up and put down whenever she wanted.

"I must refuse," she said. "I . . . I must confess I need the recreation which Richmond offers."

He smiled frankly and stood up. "I understand perfectly," he said. "I'll tell the Surgeon-General to find someone else. Might I say, Mrs. Whipple, I am pleased to keep you."

She smiled and left her kitchen, along with the surgeon-in-chief. He went off towards the administration block, and she was on her way to the cookhouse to oversee the breakfast preparations. Passing Ward 30, she noticed that an orderly was toting a bundle of blood-fouled laundry down the steps. "Oh what times these are," she muttered.

Now it was sometimes a bad thing to be too close to powerful people. She had sometimes met the Surgeon-General Jonathan Moore at Richmond dinner parties, and spoken up frankly to him about Chimborazo and its many problems—the skimpy food, the lack of drugs, the reused bandages, the shortage of fuel. Now she found out that Moore was speaking up to her— in a letter that arrived in the hands of a good-looking sergeant early that afternoon.

My dear Mrs. Whipple,

The campaigns which shall end this war will be fought rather to the north of Richmond and therefore it has been decided to set up a major hospital at the town of Orange. A girl's seminary and two warehouses have been requisitioned for the purpose, and further wards will be built at the edge of town in due course. I am therefore asking you, my dear Mrs. Whipple, as a personal favor, to forgo the company of all the admiring friends you so justly enjoy in the Richmond area, and to act as the matron of this new hospital. It will be hard work indeed, and at first your quarters will be little short of primitive. I can but repeat: would you do this for me as a personal favor, Mrs. Whipple, and as a service to our young nation? Could you please let me have your answer as soon as possible?

> Yours with warm regards,
> J. H. Moore,
> Surgeon-General C.S.A.

She sat with her eyes closed for a while when the letter was read, and then she smiled wistfully. She couldn't do anything now except send a letter saying yes. The little man in the beaver hat would wait for her in vain on the open heath next Thursday night unless—as he probably would—he saw a mention of her new position in the *Richmond Enquirer*.

It was only after she'd sent off her reply with the handsome sergeant, that she realized that Orange would put her closer to that English journalist who was up there with Jackson's army. The idea of this excited her. She wondered should she write and tell him, and if she did, what would he think? In the end, because she was an adventurous woman, she wrote anyhow.

— 14 —

AUNT SARRIE MUSWELL *née* Bumpass wasn't, and hadn't ever been, a beauty. But that hadn't soured her against Ephie at all. Sarrie just wasn't a jealous woman. She'd had old Muswell who'd loved her in spite of or even for her average plainness. Dying, he'd left her wide enough logging lands to keep her well all the rest of her days, and in addition to that there was a half share in the profits of a tavern in Goshen and in yet another in Raphine. Aunt Sarrie Muswell had no reason to blush either for the beauty of the rose or of young riverwomen from South Carolina.

When Ephie arrived at Aunt Sarrie's place in the wild and lovely Cowpasture valley she brought that ailing old black woman with her. She was looking yellow and fevered herself. . . . Aunt Sarrie had been on the Ohio to Cairo, Illinois and down the Mississippi to New Orleans. She knew that most river people were jaundice-yellow a good part of their lives. So the yellow skin was in character.

"If you didn't have that stain of color, gal," she told Ephie, "you'd be jest too ravishing for contemplation and Usaph could by no means have safely let you travel."

But Ephie was sickening for malaria, which river people also carried with them even in places where the air was sharp and clean, even up in Bath Country. The fever struck on a night soon after Ephie's arrival and she had to be nursed for a week by Aunt Sarrie and by Aunt Sarrie's slave Bridie. As well as that, in that first week the slave Lisa got some sort of fit or stroke and lost power over her own bladder.

Aunt Sarrie didn't seem to mind the extra bother at all. Ephie, in the clear patches of her malarial fever, worried about it, about what Aunt Sarrie might think of her. She wanted to a piteous extent to be patted on the head by Usaph's relatives, and malaria was such a low-grade white-trash sort of disease. She worried too what she might say during fever, for all the wild men of her girlhood haunted her delirium, and she raved at them, she knew she did. And one of these men was Aunt Sarrie's own brother, Patrick Bumpass, plantation overseer.

Whomever Ephie ranted or pleaded with in her fever, Aunt Sarrie didn't seem to take much notice. Ephie, when she got better, was respectful to Aunt Sarrie and that didn't hurt either, for the older woman had a weakness for being treated with respect.

Ephie was helpful, didn't question Aunt Sarrie's generalship over the farmhouse, and didn't boss Aunt Sarrie's two slaves. She helped the slave Bridie attend to the messes poor old incontinent Lisa made, and spoke of her soldiering husband Usaph regularly and with clear affection. For all these things Aunt Sarrie liked the girl.

On the day Decatur Cate arrived at her gate, Aunt Sarrie Muswell's household was operating in a way that would have delighted those who wanted to argue that slavery was a humane and Christian institution. In a wicker chair on the porch sat Usaph's old slave Lisa, crooning to herself. Her crippled hands were all tortured and indented by rheumatism, but the summer sunlight sat on her lap. If he had been able to see through to the kitchen, Cate would have observed Ephie Bumpass working the butter churn. The gurgling and whumping of the churn was a background rhythm in Lisa's quiet song.

Upstairs he might have seen Aunt Sarrie herself making the beds with her slave Bridie; and Bridie's husband, Montie, a strong man of about fifty, down in one of the river meadows planting corn. It was a democratic household, everyone working in together, and the fiction that Ephie *owned* Lisa and Aunt Sarrie *owned* Bridie and Montie seemed to bring none of the parties any particular hubris or grief.

If Aunt Sarrie had been thinking about her ownership of slaves this morning, her opinion of it would have been like that of many another well-off but not rich farm wife from that side of Virginia. She'd been thinking some ten years that slavery only worked for the rich. But the fathers and grandfathers of women like her, coming from England or Scotland and settling in these westward counties, caught on quick that slaves were a sign of success in lowland Virginia and so had gone to a lot of trouble and expense to buy a few of their own. The trap was that many people could only manage to have that true Virginian high-handedness with slaves if they owned a few hundred of them. If you owned a few, those few tended to become members of the family. You couldn't rightly sell them even in bad times, because when you tried they wailed and begged you not to and it was like selling a brother. You fretted through their layings-in and their births, through their illnesses and their long dotage. And some of them sure had a long, long dotage!

Neither Decatur Cate approaching the house, nor Aunt Sarrie nor Ephie inside it, were thinking of the ironies of the peculiar institution that leafy spring morning when Decatur Cate left his surrey at the gate and limped up to the house carrying a big portfolio under his arm. Bridie, Aunt Sarrie's slave, answered his knocking and went and fetched the mistress.

Aunt Sarrie was taken by the quiet well-mannered tones of this limping man, and asked him into the parlor. "I work in a manner reminiscent of Copley and Rubens," he told Aunt Sarrie, showing her a canvas he'd done in Pennsylvania of the sister of one of his drinking friends. "This is one of my early portraits, ma'am, but my work has improved since I painted it." The girl had died also since then. Consumption devoured her. He didn't mention that to his clients.

Aunt Sarrie wanted so much for this strange gangly young

man to paint Ephephtha. For Ephie was so lovely that sometimes Aunt Sarrie herself wanted to reach out her forefinger
and, just like an artist, trace the lines of the girl's face. Aunt
Sarrie told Bridie to fetch Mrs. Bumpass, and while they waited
for Ephie to put in an appearance, the widow looked at the
bony boy and thought, he ain't up to much. Not even a young
wife would desire a man like him.

She did not understand how much Ephie had known and
hated men who were loud, big-boned and heavy-fisted. She
did not understand how much Ephie might decide to lean towards any man who wasn't that way.

When Ephie came in she saw Aunt Sarrie sitting there just
about twitching with the excitement of the gift she was about
to give this fair young woman.

As for Cate, as soon as he saw Ephie come into the parlor
and stand under the tintype of dead Mr. Muswell, he fell in
love with her in that way that suited his obsessed nature, fell
in love that is, the way other men catch a disease. The world
became as unclear to him all at once as are the outer limits of
an old painting. Only this dazzling girl stood out sharp and
clear at the center. He could hear Aunt Sarrie chattering away
and it meant nothing.

"You realize," Aunt Sarrie was saying, "that it would be
no way proper for me to have you as our house guest, sir. But
my man Montie . . . he'll set up a camp cot for your convenience
in the barn and the nights're getting so passable warm that I
do believe the arrangement will meet your comfort . . . meals
you can eat with us. . . ."

Aunt Sarrie saw him straighten himself. He seemed to become in front of her eyes a little less lame.

Cate knew that he'd soon be turned out on the road if Aunt
Sarrie sniffed out the passion he felt for that·young Mrs. Bumpass. He did not want to be turned out. He wanted to do a
slow sketch first and then a slow portrait, and he wanted to
take at least a week about it, and towards the end of that time
to manage to tell her how she was breath and bread and water
to him. He could sense in Ephie that she could be led, and he
meant to lead her in a particular direction, namely California,
a place undivided by war and unstained by brotherly hate. You
could still—so he had heard—get to California from New Orleans. Even though the U.S. Navy sat off the delta of the
Mississippi, there were English ships that slipped in and out.

Ephie, like Bumpass himself, had a terrible respect for

learning. In Bumpass, it led to him seeking friendship with
men like Gus Ramseur. In Ephie it made her listen with respect
to Decatur Cate. At table Cate mentioned painters and books
neither of the women had heard of, raised ideas they weren't
familiar with, explained artistic matters to them and told them
stories. Aunt Sarrie had always gone for practical men, and
all Cate's blather just helped her to write him off. But Ephie
was enchanted.

"Your limp seems to be getting better, Mr. Cate," said Aunt
Sarrie on the second morning at breakfast.

"Why yes, ma'am, it was but a kick from a horse."

Aunt Sarrie let him use the parlor for the sittings. The first
part of the process was a charcoal sketch, then a water-color
sketch. As he had planned, he worked at a slow pace. He
explained all the mysteries and magics of beginning a painting
while she sat before him. Aunt Sarrie tried to be in the parlor
with them as much as possible—just for decency's sake. But
she was busy. First she had to have conferences with Montie,
for there was ploughing of two meadows, tending of beehives,
milking of cows, feeding of hogs, curing of bacon to be attended to. Montie had a funny place in that household. He and
Aunt Sarrie knew each other backwards, and he lived in the
house with his wife. He didn't exactly eat with the women,
even his wife Bridie treated him as a nigger and gave him his
meals separate. But at least half a dozen times a day Montie
and Aunt Sarrie would have to meet in the vegetable garden
or in the kitchen and discuss farm business like two old friends,
which in fact they were. It was like Montie had just about
forgotten he was owned.

As well as that, Aunt Sarrie and Bridie had to talk to each
other about cooking and preserves and butter and so on. And
logging men would come to the door, and now and then a
country lawyer. So Aunt Sarrie couldn't do much more than
visit the sittings in the parlor, and Cate saved all his best stories
for when she was gone and there was just himself and stock-
still Ephie in the parlor.

"I remember a man I painted over in Fauquier County," he
told Ephie, "and that itself is strange, for as a rule men want
their womenfolk painted. But this man, though he had a wife,
looked straight at me and said yessir, I've always desired a
picture of myself. So I painted him—it was hard work because
he kept on rushing to talk to his manager and his slaves. And
it was hard for other reasons as well. He didn't have the sort

of strong features that're meat and cheese, Mrs. Bumpass, meat and cheese, ma'am, to an artist. Well, during my work his wife kept to her kitchen and I barely saw her at all. But at last the painting was done..."

"And how long did that take you, Mr. Cate sir?" Ephie asked, stone-still and through barely moving lips.

"Oh, oh, I'd say ten days or more I was at it," Cate lied. His fingers around the brush were sweating with desire for her. "Yes, as I was just telling you, I scarcely saw his wife until the work was done, and then this gentleman went to the back of the house and fetched her—he was so well pleased with the work himself, I can tell you that, maybe a whole lot better pleased than I was. And he led his wife into his parlor by the elbow to view the thing.

"Well, as I say, up to that time she'd been a shy woman who'd kept her place, but now she began to speak up. She said, oh no, I don't like that there picture, Silas. But she looked at *me* as she said it and I noticed that she never looked at him. On the times before that I'd seen her, if she spoke to him she looked at the wall or the roof as she did it. I can't abide them eyes the artist gen'lman has painted, she cries out. The eyes? he says. I think the eyes is fine."

Ephie laughed in a nervous way for Cate was imitating the local accent as broad as he could. She wondered might he go on to another farmhouse and there imitate her mode of speech.

"It's because it's me, the farmer speaks up, that she don't like it. If it happened to be her confounded son she'd like it, even if it had eyes like a confounded caterpillar! And the wife says to me, looking at me straight, take your painting off with you, sir, I don't want it in my parlor. A pity for you, says the farmer, for it's going to sit wide and proud above our mantelpiece and that's flat. And the wife then began to weep and then she says, I saw eyes like that on the axe killer they hanged three summers back at Warrenton..."

In Ephie's face the dark eyes, dark as jungles and as deep, had just about reached a roundness, the sort of roundness that goes with amazement. If I saw eyes like that in any other creature, Cate thought, I'd say *What a hick! What a bumpkin!* And he sat there pinching the tubes of water color in his fingers and expecting to evaporate from wanting her.

"That is the foolishest thing, said the farmer, that I heard this past ten year. You talk like nothing better'n an ignorant town girl and I can't tolerate it. And he came up to her and

I thought that if I hadn't been there he would have hit her but instead he just bustled her out of the room by her elbow. . . . Could you, Mrs. Bumpass, lift your head a little. . . ."

For the tension of the story was making Ephie's chin fall a little.

"That was Easter," Cate went on. "Easter twelve months. Last fall while I was down Orange way, I saw in the newspaper that my subject, the man I'd painted, I mean—that he had gone to his stepson's and shot the poor young man dead there, right on his doorstep, and then shot the stepson's wife who was, as they say, Mrs. Bumpass, *enciente* . . . with child. . . ."

"Oh Lord have mercy, Mr. Cate!" said divine Ephie Bumpass, almost comically through those unmoving lips, lest she break her pose.

". . . but then he had gone home to his own place and likewise murdered his quiet wife and then shot himself in the head."

"Oh no?" Ephie Bumpass groaned out.

"And I often reflected after the event, Mrs. Bumpass ma'am, how strange it was that he went to such expense to have his portrait done in oil and had just the same decided to destroy his living portrait, so to speak, his portrait in the flesh, and in particular his face. . . ."

And Ephie went on groaning for the horror of it through her fixed teeth.

It was about the time Cate got his slow water-color sketch of Ephie finished that Aunt Sarrie got to see how Cate excited Ephie with his stories. Well, it wasn't a romantic excitement, she decided, it was just a sort of excitement that came with a man who could paint and tell stories, two activities which Aunt Sarrie placed very low on the scale of male talents. But she remembered she had once fallen for an ugly but silver-tongued Methodist preacher, and she began to reflect from her own experience of life how quickly one brand of excitement could become another and more dangerous one.

So she started to smile less at him at the dinner table, and to question him about the war.

"I've little doubt," Cate said, "that a State has the right to pull out of the Union. But since my State doesn't want to do that anyhow, I feel little interest in the struggle. Pardon me," he said, grinning broadly at her, "for my frankness, ma'am. I would not fight to suppress the rebellion of free men, but neither have I any reason to fight for the rebellion."

It was the sort of speech moderates were making all over America that summer. Moderates and cowards as well, of course. It sounded pretty grand in Aunt Sarrie's kitchen. But Aunt Sarrie didn't react for him; she stared at him and he smiled back. He thought, *if anyone thwarts me, it's going to be that old bitch.*

"What then is your home state, sir?" Aunt Sarrie asked.

"Pennsylvania, ma'am."

"But you paint enough Virginians, ain't it so?"

"Virginians, ma'am, are a handsome race."

"You'd say so, would you? But this-here war has a way of claiming people. Of taking their lives over, you get my meaning? What do you mean to do when it goes and takes your life over, Mr. Cate?"

"God forgive me, ma'am, I am not one for killing my brother Christians. I intend to go to California soon enough."

"Oh, California."

Yes, and I intend to take Mrs. Bumpass with me.

About this time Ephie Bumpass began to write a letter to her campaigning husband. It took her so long. She sat there at the table, wincing in her struggles with spelling, seeming so consumed that Cate felt a rage of jealousy and wished he *was* a soldier of Pennsylvania, since that might give him a chance of shooting this unknown Private Bumpass.

— 15 —

JOE NUNNALLY HAD spent the two days after the battle round Cedar Run in that state of hellish anguish that comes after your first fight. He wouldn't eat the hardtack and the green corn and fritters Cate made up over the fire. It wasn't that it was poor food. It had some savour for a boy of his years. Yet he, never one for undue washing, had got this strange feeling that the world had lost its cleanness and honesty now, and he had lost his too.

Now he knew he was supposed to take his pain of soul to the adjutant, Major Dignam, who'd been a Methodist preacher in the Valley. But *this* pain was something a Methodist preacher couldn't touch or talk away; *this* was a pain which couldn't be explained.

Cate had been ill in the stomach himself these past days and had little enough taste for food. "I know what you're undergoing there, Joe," he would say, but he didn't talk further. He couldn't explain this feeling in the normal Cate manner, in the way he'd explained to Joe everything that had happened since they'd been conscripted in Staunton. The reason was he was going through it himself, Joe could tell, and *he* had no power over it either. So there was no way Cate could tell Joe Nunnally to be calm, that it was all just the big forces of history working away, and if you let them big wheels grind, and sat small and easy on their rim, you might escape being mashed down to pap by them. Since the battle Cate'd been pale as a sick aunt and looked like he couldn't crawl out of the way of one of them great wheels if they was to come rolling across the encampment fields right now.

"Sure, I know what you're undergoing there, Joe. But everyone's got a right to feed himself," Cate would say, chewing drily and without joy, and then staggering up and away into the undergrowth. Cate knew that part of the problem was that Joe had a talent prized much in that country—he could see what he was hitting, he hit what he aimed for. Well, it was a talent that was devouring its host right at the moment.

Joe's family were timber-cutters and kept a few cows in the deep green hills of Raleigh County. They cut all the hardwood that grew in those hills, the richest hardwood hills in the world according to what mayors and Democratic politicians always told the people of Beckley. Joe Nunnally's father and later Joe Nunnally himself felled tulip and locust, gum, hickory, magnolia and ash and maple. They felled oak and walnut and cherry and beech and buckeye, sycamore, birch, willow—and they could have had a hundred more types of trees to choose from and still stayed poor working for the Beckley Mills.

Joe's father had always needed to hire some local man to help him with the crosscut, but when Joe got to be twelve years or so he was more useful already than the sort of poor drunken hill-farmer who was all his daddy could afford to pay.

What happened in Joe's family is a common story in timber-cutting families. The boy is working with his daddy, the old horse, shaggy-coated, bought by the father in better and more hopesome days, and older than the boy himself, is hauling on a chain-pulley to lift a log from the ground. The father and son are by to guide the log on to its cradle on the wagon. The horse dies in its traces, like that, in mid-grunt you could say. The log falls, slowed in that it has to pull the dead horse with it but fast enough to put the father on the ground and crush his chest there in front of the boy.

It is spring and there are lots of deer in the Appalachians, deer and elk and foxes, so the family does not starve, given that the boy has a magical aiming eye. So, while there's game in the woods, the family have meat. But there's things the poorest family has to get in by winter. The boy needs to sell the timber and so he needs a new horse. He can't sell timber till he has a new horse and he can't have a new horse till he sells timber. It's a human enough fix, and the boy knows it.

Then, at the start of May, he goes to Beckley to ask the mill-owner to advance the horse money against future deliveries of logs and there's a man there, sitting outside the Renny House in a wicker chair, who comes up, talks to him, and buys him a drink in the parlor. And given that the drink is strong and the boy is young, there's a lot of talk about mutual problems.

"You need a horse," said the man. "Well I've got a son who's been poorly all his days, otherwise he *might* be in the army of the Confederacy. Mind you now, I don't think we mountain people have so much to thank the Commonwealth of Virginia for. Goddamit, ain't it the truth, Mr. Nunnally, that it's easier for us mountain folks to get to New Orleans than to Richmond. The abysmal goddam roads, Mr. Nunnally, the abysmal goddam roads! I mean, you just catch an Ohio ferry say in Parkersburg and you can be in Cairo, Illinois, in three days, and in New Orleans in eight. Or so it was in happier days, Mr. Nunnally. So it was.

"That aside, Mr. Nunnally, my boy wouldn't last more than two weeks in a goddamn camp with them boys of no refinement all round him. Now I'd be willing to pay for a good substitute for him. I'd be willing to go up to $50 or more to find him a stand-in. Could you get a horse for round about that, think you, suitable for your line of work? Mind you, boy, you wouldn't be round to work the horse for a while. But then even the Wheeling papers says this difference between the States ain't going to last too much beyond the first fall of snow. Britain . . . Britain, Mr. Nunnally, . . . has her interests. How old are you, Mr. Nunnally?"

"I'm fifteen years, sir."

"I think," the man said, "that for $60 you could say you

were eighteen years. What do you say?"

"I'd say eighteen years," said Joe.

So Joe Nunnally got $60 and bought a horse with 30 of it, for his mother could make some money hiring it out. The rest of the cash was hid under a rock by a spring the family drew their water from. For there'd been tales of boys accepting substitute money like that, because they had sickly parents or one parent gone, and the bounty would feed a family for a year. And when the boys were gone and sworn in, the men who'd paid the money would come round to the family house and bully the cash back out of the folks.

Now, as the man had said to Joe Nunnally, the mountain people didn't have a lot to be grateful to Richmond for. The roads were bad, you had to go to big towns for the schools. Because the tidewater people counted their slaves in the population when it came to sending men to the State House, the mountains where there were few slaves didn't have representatives in the numbers they should. Mountain Democrats thumping tubs in Beckley would say such things as: "Goddamit, they don't count their slaves as human unless it comes to doing us out of a seat in the Capitol at Richmond. To keep us from our proper power, they'd count a goddam opossum on the rolls!"

You found that the people in the Shenandoah Valley were for Virginia, but as you got into the mountains beyond the Valley, and across into the wild valley of the Kanawha, you met more and more people hostile to the Confederacy. The Nunnallys were, by temperament, hostile to it, but in a way typical of the mountain poor. They did not believe it worth fighting for either Union or Confederacy. They knew they'd be as poor under either. It was in their memory, their grandfathers had told them, that mountain men had been as poor under George III as under George Washington. It wasn't expected ever to change.

Yet these mountain politics had little part in Joe's decision to run. Joe was running out of horror, Joe was running for his soul. Sure, he'd hide in central Virginia till the army passed on. He'd take his Springfield. God Almighty, with this Springfield musket he had he could frighten off any recruiting man or sheriff who came up into the Nunnallys' hills. There were all manner of relatives up there who'd be helpful in frightening government agents. And the man Joe had met in the Renny House had had his goddam value from his $60 already. It didn't matter to the man in the Renny House whether a substitute deserted. Even if it did, he could buy another one.

Anyhow there wasn't any choice. The God who had placed man in the earth, in the rich hardwood hills, would deny him air if he stayed here in the evil column.

Deserting was simple. Green corn and green apples had kept the bowels of Jackson's army in their accustomed state of flux. It was easy to break ranks with or without asking an officer. The affliction was sudden and could not often bide the asking of permission. Even harsh men like Captain Guess, even Lucius Taber knew that.

There'd even been a story going round about young Lucius, as a matter of fact. He had a plague of diarrhea the morning they marched up to Cedar Run and, lest anyone think that the unseemly stains on his britches were marks of fright, he'd lined (so the rumor had it) his seat with three back numbers of *De Bow's Review*.

Anyhow, when Joe Nunnally peeled off out of line at two on the morning of August 14 just to the south of Barnett's Ford on the Rapidan, where forest stretched away to the east, he was taking advantage of the universal disease. Getting behind a tree, he slipped sideways toward another and then was gone from sight. He was moving east first of all, since he knew home was west and thought that if they hunted for him at all, they would hunt that way. He would hide east for a few weeks till all of the two devilish machines of North and South had gone their way up or down the road, or sideways or outflanking each other to hell and back. He knew he had to watch for cavalry, but his hearing was refined, he was sure he could sidestep anything he might meet.

At dawn he began to feel cleaner and happier. He went to sleep right in a thicket of poison ivy at the bottom of Clark's Mountain. He was sure he was safe there, and he'd always had this virtue against poison ivy, he could roll in it without it harming him. He would often roll in it to amuse his brothers and sisters, even though his mother said you could lose your virtue against poison ivy like *that*! There was nothing like the sting people then got from it, people who up to then hadn't felt any harm from the plant. Well, that might be true, but virtue over poison ivy was a nice talent to have on a morning when two armies were over the land, and when it was a nice point which of them meant you the more harm.

He stayed all that night and half the next day in the woods, eating his rations cold. By the next breakfast his hardtack would be gone, and his corn wasn't fit for the hogs anyhow. He moved so slow that it was noon on his second day when he saw the farmhouse Ash Judd and Danny Blalock had visited some five days back. From the trees, he saw crippled Arlan come down the steps and stumble away to the barn. He saw Arlan's mother at a window upstairs, lifting her throat in the still air as if she expected a breeze. Arlan returned to the house after some quarter of an hour. What had he been doing in the barn? Maybe he had a jug of whisky out there.

Later in the day, the big woman came down into the garden, talking nonsense to the chickens that skittered away from her. It made Joe grievously homesick to hear the sweet nonsense she spoke. She got a stool and milked the cow expertly, sighing sometimes and talking to the animal like it was a fellow sufferer, and then she took the pail back into the house. In the late afternoon both she and the cripple sat at their ease on the porch, saying very little to each other. It was as the woman rose to go indoors and make supper, that Joe chose to come out of the forest. The boy picked up a shotgun that must have been at his feet, and the woman looked at Joe sidewise as he came to their gate.

"Not to trouble you, ma'am, sir. I wonder . . . well, I wonder if you could spare me any of your victuals. I've a mite of cash."

Arlan's shotgun wavered in arms that lacked the strength to hold it firm. But his voice, though slurred, was sharp. "What say *you*, maw? What say *you* to soldiers who come up to the gate asking to be fed? What say *you* to soldiers' mites, maw?"

The mother did not move her head. Looking more at Arlan than at Joe, she sighed. "You a deserter, boy?"

"No, ma'am. I'm a one-year man and my one year is now past. I'm free now, ma'am, to find my way home. But I confess I want to keep to quiet places while the armies're round about. I don't want to be re-enlisted no more, on account my pappy died and I have to go home to fell timber to keep maw and the brats."

"What's your name, boy?" Arlan asked him in a poisonous voice.

"You had a bad time with soldiers, have you, sir?"

"Never mind *bad times*. What's your goddam name?"

Joe only then decided to lie, and only on account of the

vicious way Arlan was talking. "My name is Usaph Bumpass, sir."

"And you say you ain't a deserter, Bumpass?"

"I'm a one-year man, sir. Set your eyes on my uniform. There's a year's wear in this." It was true, because he had had his new clothes taken and been given year-old stuff. "And I can help you folks if you but give me a few meals. I can't but notice, mister, your sore affliction. . . ."

"You take your goddam tongue off my affliction, you son of a bitch."

What man spoke in front of his maw that way? Joe Nunnally asked himself. "I reckon," he said, talking fast and grinning as nicely as he could manage, "that in a few days I could set you up with all the wood you'll need till midsummer next. I reckon I could husk corn for you and repair the barn and set myself to a year's worth of odd ends of work."

There was a long silence while the cripple considered this. The mother said, like someone asking permission: "For God's sake, Arlan, he's but a boy."

"You'll sleep in the goddamn barn," the cripple told him.

"That's still heaven by me, sir."

"What did you call yourself, boy?"

"Joe," Joe called gaily.

"I thought you called yourself Asa or some goddam thing," Arlan barked out.

"So I do," said Joe, face burning. "But you see, my friends all call me Joe."

"Come on in then, Joe," Arlan said, and he watched the boy come forward wary as a young animal. That boy's such a poor liar, Arlan thought. For Arlan knew that there were no more one-year boys, that the Confederate Congress had done away with one-year boys, transmuting them all into three-year boys. You just had to go to market in Stevensburg, as Arlan did, and ask this or that merchant when his boy was coming home to be told that much.

So Arlan let him stay a day and a half, till he'd chopped up a useful cordage of wood. And on the third day, he rode off early, leaving the boy whitewashing the back of the house, and he went down through the forest to the Gordonsville–Culpeper road. As he expected to, he met up with a Confederate cavalry vedette down there by the side of the road, watching out for Pope to cross the Rapidan. And part

of their duty as well was to give stragglers a kick along and
to bring in deserters. He said there was a deserter over to his
place. Name of Bumpass.

— 16 —

ALL MONDAY MORNING Major Dignam, Methodist preacher
and adjutant of the Shenandoah Volunteers, watched from beneath an oak in front of General Tom Jackson's tent near
Clark's Mountain. He didn't feel comfortable here, he tensed
inside his grey jacket whenever some passing staff officer
glanced at him. He'd been feeling awkward since seeing Jackson and Lee and Longstreet come riding down from the top
of the mountain two hours back, all looking thunderous as if
they'd been handed the Tables of the Law up there and were
under strict orders from God to force their scriptures on a stiff-
necked people. Dignam had seen them all dismount, three tall
and somber men, and go into Jackson's tent to have some
refreshment or other. The Reverend Dignam had never seen
Lee before and had only read of Longstreet. He'd watched
Jackson pass a couple of times. It was a shock to find that
these great icons of the cause really lived and drew breath from
the very air in that very tent there, the air he was presuming
to breathe himself as soon as he could get in there.

At last Longstreet and Lee had come out and ridden off
south, and Dignam had started buttoning his collar. He wore
a long frock-coat his congregation had given him fifteen months
ago. It was better than butternut—you could at least say that.
Now he watched Sandie Pendleton and Kyd Douglas and the
mapmaker Hotchkiss and Major Harman the profane quartermaster dash in and out of the tent, and hoped and feared he
would soon be called in himself.

Well, that hope and fear got quashed. A general, one star,
but a general none the less, rode up on a good bay and handed
the reins to a guard. Then he barged into Jackson's tent. From
his place under the oak the Reverend Dignam couldn't hear
the details of the interview that was proceeding in there. He
could hear enough, however, to know it wasn't a happy one.

It wouldn't go any distance towards improving the General's temper.

At last the brigadier broke out of the tent, mounted his horse savagely, as if it were partly to blame, and gave it a swat with his reins. He left Jackson's headquarters at a gallop.

In the clearing, Kyd approached Dignam under his oak. The General had some time to talk to him now, Kyd said. He led Dignam to the tent and held back the flap for him.

When Major Dignam passed through into the tent the first thing he saw was the General's back. Jackson was sitting on a camp-table, not putting all his weight on it, for it wouldn't have taken it. The table was piled with sheets of paper. Dignam looked at them with a little reverence. They were likely letters from Jefferson Davis, and Judah Benjamin's office, and such-like.

The General stood, sort of turned and discovered him there. He nodded curtly to Dignam and sat at the desk, but his eyes weren't on his visitor. Lord God, now give your humble servant guidance! prayed the major. The silence went on for a good half-minute before Dignam got the idea that he was the one supposed to talk.

"Sir," he stated, "I'm adjutant of the Shenandoah Volunteers of your old brigade. In my private life I am a Methodist preacher from Augusta County."

There was no flicker from the General's eyes. Dignam thought, God help me, the man isn't even blinking, his eyelids are locked open.

"On that account, sir, I am concerned for the soul of a particular man . . ."

"We are all concerned for souls, Major . . ."

"Dignam, sir."

"Major Dignam, we are all concerned for souls."

"This man is one of the three condemned to death for desertion."

"Oh." The General found and picked up the appropriate piece of paper. "Which of the three. I suppose it's this Joe . . ."

"Nunnally, sir. Yes."

"Nunnally is a conscript."

"Yessir. Very young. Very simple-minded. You know these mountain people."

Dignam went red, remembering that the General himself liked to be thought of as a mountain man. "I mean, sir, the folks from way up and deep in the mountains."

"Nunnally is also a substitute, it says here. The prosecution laid it down straight to the court-martial that Nunnally intended to go somewhere fresh and sell himself all over again as a substitute."

"Sir, he got $60 for acting as substitute for some rich man's son. $60, General Jackson, isn't the sort of amount a cunning boy would be likely to take. If Joe Nunnally was worldly enough he would have known he could have got $200 at least in any big town."

"You make the whole trade sound honorable, Major. How much did you take when you substituted for someone?"

"Nothing, General. I'm a volunteer, you know that."

"That's my exact point, Major Dignam. This whole money-for-substitution business is deep immoral."

"But that's not Joe Nunnally's fault, sir. It's the fault of . . ."

"Yes, of the Confederate Congress, you might just as well say so, Major. But this Nunnally . . . you say he's not cunning . . . . When the cavalry fetched him in he was using another man's name. The name of a volunteer called . . ." Stonewall consulted the page ". . . Bumpass. A veteran of Romney and Kernstown and Port Republic, of the Seven Days in front of Richmond and of this last battle at Cedar Run. Now if he's cunning enough to foul a good man's name, you can be rock-sure, Major Dignam, he's cunning enough to sell himself again, and this time for whatever price those rich skulkers see fit to pay."

"Sir," said Dignam in a small voice, "he told me something in making his peace this morning. He said he deserted on account he felt that if he killed any more of his fellow men he would be cursed by God."

The General's voice came out small too but Dignam felt it was sort of dangerous to be near it. "These people rile me. Could I ask you, is General Lee the accursed of God? Is Jefferson Davis? Is Bishop Leonidas Polk, who holds a general's commission in the Confederate army? Is the Reverend Moses D. Hoge the accursed of God? In the view of all these righteous men this war is pleasing in the nostrils of a just God. And then is a simple boy to come down off his mountain and tell us it isn't?"

The Reverend Dignam, with his Methodist background, was used to the claims of a man's individual conscience. The General's idea that a man had no right to one, that only Jefferson Davis, Bishop Leonidas Polk and the Reverend Hoge had a right to one, seemed almost papist; and if General Jackson hadn't been General Jackson, then Major Dignam might just have found the authority or the courage to tell him that.

"In that case," said Dignam, and he didn't know *where* he got the courage for saying this, "consider your responsibility, General, before the Lord. You are sending this boy's soul to hell."

As he'd feared it might, a terrible silence settled in on the tent then, one of those electric silences you get in woods in midsummer that beg to be broken by lightning. The General reached out and took him by the shoulders, and there was all at once great sideways pressure on the top of Dignam's body, and Dignam, a tall strong man himself, was amazed at the force Tom Jackson had in his wrists.

"That is my business, sir. In a second you will go and do yours, for the sure-fire reason that you're about to be pushed out of this tent. My courts are too lenient. For once they've done the right thing and you ask me to sidewhack their decision. It's been suggested that only one man be shot, chosen by lot, but that suggestion seems to me to be nothing but a foul extension of this army's general weakness for gambling. Let me tell you this. You say you serve in a division that used to be mine. Well, in that division, during the recent engagement on Cedar Run, there were 1200 absentees through straggling, through feigned illness, through absence without leave. In Ewell's division there were 1600 absentees. These are losses inflicted on us by ourselves, Major. So please do not pursue the matter of the sentence that has fallen on this boy. It has fallen with cause. It has also been upheld by General Lee and by the Secretary of War. Do you understand."

Dignam was speechless. He was angry in the way that he wanted to hit the General, but he was awestruck too. At last he felt the pressure on his upper arms loosen off and the General looked at him with something close to friendship. "Now git!" he said. And Dignam, not knowing what else he could do, obeyed. Outside, he staggered up the road some few hundred yards, hid behind a tree and wept, biting his hands to stop the sound of his grief being too clear to anyone who happened to be on the road.

In his tent, Tom Jackson reflected that he'd been more talkative to Toombs and to his Methodist minister than he'd been to anyone, stranger or friend, on any day in the past six months. And he knew the reason. It was because he knew the

army would go out after Pope now and chew him up in detail.
His own three divisions, though thinner in numbers than he'd
have liked, were in good heart as far as anyone could tell. The
invasion of the North was inherent in what God had done to
Pope at Cedar Run, and even in Pope's withdrawal from the
river, the withdrawal from which Toombs would be punished.
The invasion of the North lay coiled like an epiphany in his
bowels and in Lee's, waiting to unravel. Under the canvas of
his tent, General Tom Jackson raised a hand and touched the
fabric of the ceiling. It was like he was welcoming the God
of Battles.

— 17 —

MRS. WHIPPLE ARRIVED at the Orange depot late on a Tuesday
night. She managed to hire one of the few carriages that had
been waiting there for the much-delayed train, and so rode the
short distance to the square brick seminary building across
town.

It was a hot night and the front door of the building stood
open. In the stonework above the door was chiseled "The
Orange Lutheran Seminary for Young Ladies." But all the girls
had gone off to relatives in North Carolina or Richmond, and
a drowsy buzz of male voices seemed to waft down from the
upper floors. Mrs. Whipple left the carriage and walked inside.
Just beyond the front door stood a little glassed office, and in
it sat a young surgeon, reading.

She knocked on the glass.

"Ma'am?" he said.

"I am the matron. Mrs. Whipple is my name."

"Much pleased, ma'am. Curtis, ma'am, head surgeon on
this side of the street. We have rooms ready for you, ma'am."

Curtis showed her through the place, through the well-
ordered and well-scrubbed dormitories and, at the end of each
floor, a surgeon actually on duty! At night! "How many do
you have here?"

"I have 250 of our boys on this side of the road, and on the
top floor some sixty Yankees."

"There's a warehouse too," she said.

"Across the road, ma'am. If...well, ma'am, it doesn't have the human advantages of this fine building."

But she could tell that what he was trying to say was, it is not nearly as good a hospital.

"I'd like to see it."

"Now?"

"Yes." She smiled. "I can see you know that sick men can suffer crises at night. I would be interested to see if the warehouse surgeon has the same ideas as you."

Young Curtis coughed. "I think I'll go with you, if you don't mind, ma'am. The surgeon...Jimmy Canty...he's a harmless enough fellow but a little suspicious."

So, in spite of the late hour, they left the seminary and crossed the street. From the far pavement, Mrs. Whipple could smell the warehouse, that unwashed stink, that reek of urine and slack sanitary arrangements. Curtis knocked on the door for some three minutes before an orderly answered.

"I'm the new matron," Mrs. Whipple said. "I would like to inspect these wards."

"You better come back in the morning, ma'am."

"What's your name, orderly? I should like to report to the Surgeon-General that you denied me entry to my own hospital..."

"Oh goddam! Hoity-toit," said the orderly, and swung the door wide.

"Tell Surgeon Canty we're here," Surgeon Curtis said, as he and Mrs. Whipple came in. They began walking then through the wards, amongst all the sounds of pain and fevered sleep. "You see, ma'am," Curtis said, being loyal to Canty. "There aren't the windows we have. Ventilation counts for a lot, ma'am." In every ward they found boys with diarrhea, some of them excreting in corners because ward-buckets had overflowed. At the approach of Mrs. Whipple, these boys would stand up shamefaced and clutch their britches round their waist. Mrs. Whipple blinked with the stench.

She and Curtis were on the steps to the second floor when a tall man of about forty came prancing down them. He looked sort of florid, and as soon as he started to talk, you could tell he'd been taking liquor.

"Can I help you, ma'am?" he asked pointedly.

She introduced herself.

"I would have preferred, Curtis ole boy," Canty said with

a forced, angry grin, "if you'd waited for me to be fetched."

"The night cans are overflowing, Surgeon Canty," said Mrs. Whipple. "You may not know of it. Would you like me to have the orderlies empty them?"

Canty closed his eyes and shook his head in an amused way that said *fussy female*. "I'll have it attended to, ma'am, if it would make you the happier."

"I think there are some boys in the wards who'd be made happy too."

She saw the way he lifted his head and looked sideways at her. Oh well, dislike, thought Mrs. Whipple. We all have to live with dislike.

On the way back to the seminary Mrs. Whipple said to Surgeon Curtis: "I should live over there."

"But ma'am, it isn't a very pleasant building."

"No. All the more reason I shouldn't use up any of your space. Given that your space is pleasant, Surgeon Curtis, and your hospital looks like a hospital." He grinned and may even have blushed. "Why thank you, ma'am. Canty . . . he's quite a skilled surgeon . . ."

"And a characteristic drunk, Surgeon Curtis. There's one more thing. The distribution of all whisky in this hospital comes under my control from tomorrow morning."

"Of course, I've no objection to that, ma'am."

But Canty will have, she thought.

— 18 —

HOW HAD THEY chosen them? Usaph Bumpass wondered.

The Shenandoah Volunteers came out of a deep forest and into the glare of a big clearing. And there were fifteen men, in a squad, standing close up to a great hole in the ground. And deep in the hole stood three men, still shovelling dirt.

It came to Usaph late, as if he was a slow boy, that the hole must be a grave. Did they make them dig their own graves? That seemed damned wrong to Usaph. It seemed an abomination to make boys dig their own grave.

And then back to the other question. How did they choose

them. Those fifteen boys standing so close up to the hole. Which brigade were they from? Were they chosen by lot or had some officer gone about calling for those who'd like to do the task? If so, Usaph hadn't heard him and was glad not to have heard him.

The afternoon was hot, full of a blur of flies and the screaming of katydids. The vast meadow where they stood was like a sort of history of America itself. It sat amongst ancient forests. It had been cleared maybe about 1760 by some Scot, some Irishman, some sharp Yorkshireman. It had borne more crops than a sow has litters for a century and more, but now its owner did not much esteem it, or was happy to let it rest, for blackberries grew in clumps there, the grass was high, and the forests that had preceded the farmers was growing back at the edges. America was not however easily cancelled.

They lined the Shenandoah Volunteers out, with the rest of its brigade, facing the grave and no more than fifty yards from it. As that happened bands came into the field playing the "Dead March," and then the 2nd and 3rd Brigades were marched in and lined out on either flank in such a way that the graves ended up in a sort of hollow square of spectators. But in spite of all the music and the shouting, the men in the hole in the earth went on shovelling. Usaph wondered what made them keep working like that. He said it aloud without understanding that he had. "What makes 'em keep on working like that?" The bands sounded tinny under that great sky, in that great field.

"What?" Danny Blalock asked nearby.

"Why do they go on digging? Surely there ain't nothing more they can threaten 'em with to make 'em dig like that."

Off to his left and in the rank behind him, Decatur Cate spoke up. "They don't think they'll die, that's why. They think maybe if they work hard, they'll be let off for good spade work."

Danny Blalock said: "This isn't the right time, Cate, for your disgusting opinions." But he didn't press it. He'd changed since the fight near Culpeper Road; he wasn't as sure of his ideas. Usaph stared round at Cate and saw tears in the man's eyes. Let the son of a bitch weep, thought Usaph.

The truth was that Joe Nunnally dug in some hope. Major Dignam had told him to entertain hope and he was entertaining it strongly. As well as that, Frank Weller had also told him to keep hope bright. Frank Weller was a Tarheel who'd deserted twice already. First time he'd got all the way home to his farm in Waynesville, North Carolina. That was last April and Frank had wanted to get a spring crop sown. Not that he would have come back even then but they fetched him back. The State militia came for him one morning and brought him back, and he was sentenced to flogging two days in a row and being paraded with a placard every day for a month. It was hard for a man to keep his enthusiasm for the military life after that. Then his mess-mate, a simple boy called Jackie Swelter, was torn in two by a shell near the Culpeper Road the other day. Frank decided then it was time to go for good. He was sure he could hang out along the Blue Ridge all winter, there might even be willing mountain women up there to warm his solitude, and then maybe in the middle of the next summer he could sneak down to Waynesville by the many back roads of the Appalachians.

It hadn't worked. The cavalry found him after just two days. Like Joe, he was making himself accommodating to a farm wife and to her children, this one being resident on the road towards Powell's Gap. Frank and Joe Nunnally and the other prisoner had spent last night chained together in this clearing. Frank was a brave man and looked like a brave man. He stood above six feet, his face was square and his hair and beard curly. His eyes beamed wild and ironical. It was just he didn't feel a life given for this struggle was a life well spent. He came from the mountain end of Carolina, where people were as poor as the Nunnallys were in Virginia. The specter of nigger equality and Northern tyranny didn't seem such a big scare to such people as it did to the people in the lowlands. He had volunteered while drunk and everything he'd seen on his military travels, and everything he'd seen in that Babylon of a capital called Richmond, convinced him that this *was* a rich man's war and a poor man's fight. Just over the border from Frank Weller's place, just over in the mountains of eastern Tennessee, the Confederacy had had to send troops into towns like Newport, Madisonville, Morganton, Sevierville to hang and shoot the Union men and to burn their farms and put their widows and kin on the roads. Now it seemed to Frank that they were going to shoot *him*, not for being so hot and strong for the Union but for not believing enough in this other cause.

Yet he'd gone on muttering hope all night to the boy Joe. "Why, Joe, they ain't never shot anyone from the Stonewall Division yet. Make an example of 'em, sure. But shoot a man, no. You see, this is meant to be an army of goddam democrats and free men. If it weren't so, why there'd be niggers in the ranks, ain't that so? Now it sits odd with some of the boys in the ranks to have free democrats shooting down free democrats, and so as like they'll march the whole goddam circus up to see us and then an officer will come riding forth with a pardon. Jail and hard labor, sure. I deserve it for my original drunken will to have a hair of this war . . . but not even a goddam colonel would tell you that those boys who'll be looking us in the eye come tomorrow are any way partial to the business of firing on their own."

The guards had backed this up by being kind as brothers to them, feeding them bacon for supper, looking at them strange and almost tenderly.

The third condemned man was also a Tarheel from the mountain border with Tennessee. He was somehow separate because his opinions or some other large accident had led him to desert northwards where, on his capture, he'd straightway offered to put on the uniform of the U.S. The Confederacy had captured him back a few evenings past. Last night he'd kept silent and sat, as far as the chains allowed him, separate from Joe and Frank. He was the thorn in all Frank Weller's arguments of hope, since it was no way likely there'd be any forgiveness for him. He was a thin man, much shorter than Frank, yet the guards seemed to have a special respect for him, as if he'd chosen the toughest, the most principled way, of getting himself before a firing squad.

But despite this man, and because of the help of Frank Weller and Major Dignam, Joe Nunnally dug his grave in as good a frame of mind as could be managed. "Don't think that it's a goddam grave," Frank had whispered. "Think it's jest a bacon pit or some such."

And in this way they worked, sweating like honest farmers, and soon they were waist-deep in a hole that measured maybe seven feet by seven feet and would soon be four feet deep. And now and then, fear would blind Joe, and he couldn't help thinking that if Frank's comforting weren't true, and if Major Dignam was wrong, then he *would* sleep forever, for all time, with these other two, and their bodies and bones would be twined close as lovers' and so they would rot together.

Well, if that happened, at least the Reverend Dignam had given a promise to mark the place with a stone or a cross.

Soon an officer came, inspected the pit and told them to

climb out. The man who'd been found in Union uniform sat down in the bottom and was sick between his legs, which were still encased in their blue trousers. The officer screamed, "Cover that muck! Go on, cover it!" And Frank Weller and Joe Nunnally sprinkled it with loam. But then it was hard for Joe to get out of the pit. His legs felt slack. He came up over the mounds of displaced farm dirt, and not fifteen paces away were the squad who were meant to kill him. "I know none of them," said Frank Weller evenly, inspecting their averted eyes.

There were three orderlies with blindfolds to tie round the eyes of the condemned, and Joe's blindfold was on before he understood that, if Frank was wrong, that was all the world he was ever going to see, and familiar things like grass, stones, trees and katydids were now rarer with him than were nuggets of gold. "Hope, friends, hope!" he heard Frank Weller mutter in his sing-song way.

Joe was taken by the elbow and made to kneel. Oh dear God, what now? This is when the officer with the pardon is meant to come spurring up. But there was instead another sort of surprise altogether. A tough and piercing voice rose in the old farm land. It was a chaplain with a message for those who were not condemned.

"I speak out," the voice said, "not for the benefit of the condemned but for the sake of the honorable. Of all deserters and traitors, Judas Iscariot is without doubt the most infamous of all those whose names have found a place in history, either sacred or profane. . . ."

Joe could feel the clods of earth beneath his knees and the air he breathed seemed gritty with the hatefulness of that parson's voice.

". . . no name has ever been more justly execrated by mankind, and all this has been justly done. Turning to the history of your own country, I find written high on the scroll of infamy the name of Benedict Arnold, who at one time stood in the confidence of the great and good Washington. What was Arnold's crime? Desertion and treason! He too hoped to better his manner of life by selling his principles for money to the enemies of his country, betraying his Washington into the hands of his foes and committing the heaven-cursed crime of perjury before God and men. . . ."

Joe could hear a stutter of hushed laughter beside him and Frank muttered: "Oh Lord, ain't it a grand thing . . . ?" The laughter took Frank over again for a while, ". . . a grand thing to be as famous bad as Benedict Arnold."

And Frank's juddering laughter went on for some time as the preacher raged on.

"I now lay down the proposition that every man who has taken up arms in defense of his country, and basely deserts or abandons that service, belongs in principle and practice to the family of Judas and Arnold. These three wretches! Like you did they come to fight for the independence of their own country. Like you they received the benefits of pay and, in one case, bounty money. Like you they took upon themselves the most solemn obligations of this oath: *I, A. B., do solemnly swear that I will bear true allegiance to the Confederate States of America and that I will serve them honestly and faithfully against all their enemies or opposers whatsoever....*

"These three, they are your fellow beings! They marched under the same beautiful flag that waves over our heads. But in an evil hour, they yielded to mischievous influence and from motives and feelings base and sordid, unmanly and vile, abandoned the principles of patriotism...."

The condemnation rolled on. Joe imagined a smooth fat rabid clergyman whose soul had not been tested ever. He began to tremble, kneeling there, but it was not with shame.

"They took to the woods," the florid voice said, "traversing weary roads by night, hoping at last to reach the places in which they claimed their homes or their strange allegiances...."

The preacher then compared the three miscreants to the Tories of 1776, whose shame had followed them no matter where they ran. "Yea, though they all fled to Canada, it would still pursue them!"

While the preacher exhorted everyone in the Stonewall Division to detest him, Joe went on feeling the sharp bite of the sun across his shoulders and on the back of his head, and wondered if Cate and Bumpass were watching. He felt a trembly peace as he put himself in God's hands, even though the preacher said he had no right to. Joe was sure that preacher must be Baptist or some such heathenish sect. For now, not happy with cursing any generations he and Frank Weller and the other man might beget, he moved on to bad-mouthing the folks at home.

"I am fully satisfied that the great amount of desertions from our army is produced by and is the fruit of a bad, mischievous, restless and dissatisfied, not to say *disloyal*, influence that is at work in this country at home. Some people profess to be greatly afflicted in mind about the state of public affairs. In their doleful wailings you hear such melancholy lamentations as *the country is getting impoverished! We can't make our independence stick. The price is too high. This is a rich man's war and a poor man's fight.* Some newspapers have caught the mania and lent their influence to the evil work, while the pulpit—to the scandal of its character for faith and holiness—has belched forth in some places doctrines and counsels sufficient to cause Christians to blush."

Now, after his short season of peace, panic came to Joe, for he wanted water and it came to him that it was stupid for him to want it. And peace and panic went sweeping in and out of him, changing places all the time. And then, he could tell, the preacher had moved into his summing up. "No!" said Joe aloud, but not too loud. He wanted to raise his voice in argument with the chaplain, but couldn't find the words.

"Take courage then, companions in arms," the preacher ranted. "All things around us today bid us be of good courage. History fails to tell us of any instance of ten millions of free men being enslaved once they determined to be free. When I have seen our brave men in winter's cold and summer's heat, marching from battlefield to battlefield, barefooted as they were born, and without a murmur, I could never doubt our final success. Such men as these were never born to be slaves. Then let your trust today be strong in the God of Nations," etc., etc. There was silence at last except for the noise of insects, and the shuffling of the awestruck Stonewall Division sounded like the shuffling of cattle.

"Joe."

It was Major Dignam's apologetic voice off to Joe's left. "I'll say the Lord's Prayer out loud. You may say it too."

"You told me to hope!" Joe screamed. "You went and told me!"

"Don't curse me for that," said Major Dignam. The man in the blue pants could be heard sobbing. Joe could somehow tell it was the man in blue pants, and not Frank Weller. Frank Weller had shown already that if pushed to the edge he got the stark-staring giggles.

"Our Father, which art . . ." said Dignam.

"Do it good, boys!" Frank Weller yelled. "If it's done, do it good. Three in the heart."

He knew that was how things were arranged. Each victim had all of five men to fire at him, but only three of the muskets would have live rounds and the other two would be blanks. And of the five men who would fell him, each would be able to comfort himself to his death's day that it was likely *his* musket that held the blank. Goddam their comfort...!

"...and forgive us our trespasses," said the Reverend Dignam from an increasing distance. Now the orders must have been silent ones, because a great tearing and a great shock entered Nunnally's rib-cage and he was pushed back on his bare feet and tipped sideways, and after the ringing left his ears he was content to lie there, holding back his breath since he knew breathing would split him down the middle with pain. But he could *hear* breathing and shoes and the call of insects, and the worst pain he had, just about the only one other than breathlessness, was homesickness. "Maw, maw, maw, maw!" he called over and over.

"Goddamit," he heard someone scream, an officer you could bet. "Call yourselves marksmen? Fifteen goddam paces and you don't do it clean!"

"Maw, maw, maw..." The officer came to kneel by the boy and put a bullet in his head, and Joe *did* feel the barrel of the Colt fit against a fleshy indentation behind his ear, but before the officer fired, Joe—with a quiet act of his own will—chose to die; and so beat the bullet and entered a decent oblivion.

— 19 —

IF YOU ASKED Usaph Bumpass he might have said the next move North began under bad omens. First they paraded the regiment past Joe Nunnally's pit to view the bodies there, and somehow it was the worst thing that Usaph had ever seen. For Joe and the other two were tumbled naked together. Someone had taken their trousers. What sort of country couldn't spare a deserter's trousers? The fact their trousers had been taken contradicted all the preacher's blather.

"Why in the name of heaven and earth, Gus?" he asked Gus Ramseur, "why are they so bent on taking the britches off them boys."

But Gus, stronger now and of a stronger mind, wouldn't get mixed up with the question. He wanted to keep the powers of his soul together for facing any future fevers and conflicts and for putting his strange music down on paper. "I don't know, Usaph, why for the britches. But they have reasons, I suspect. Most likely mad ones." And he began humming some clumsy tune before they were a hundred paces past that pit.

Cate was marching along a few ranks behind Usaph and started to utter this bright, bitter speech.

Everyone listened, because it had a sort of authority about it, a sort of outrage, and it vented some of the poisonous feeling that was in all of them. "That's what it's like with these so-named democracies," Cate started ranting. "They tell you all that the state's there by your free and enlightened choice. But if your free and enlightened choice don't fit in with theirs they say then, *Sorry, ole feller, but you have to have your heart peppered up by marksmen at fifteen paces. Why, we're preparing the way for the great freedom and sorry, ole feller, you ain't going to be round to see it. But just take our word it's coming, sure as the Charlottesville Express.* But I ask you, gentlemen, what manner of democracy is it if *they* say when it begins. Aren't you the *demos*? Aren't you the people? Had again, gentlemen! Had again!"

It came to Usaph during the speech, that urge to club Cate, and when Cate drew breath, Usaph marched on some paces, feeling he could leave it to Judd or Hans Strahl or Danny Blalock or Bolly to make reply to Cate. They didn't. They were getting used to him. His crazy speeches were as habitual to them as the buzz of flies.

With a roar that seemed to Usaph to come from someone else, he broke through the rank behind him and swung the butt of his Springfield wildly against Cate's body. It came down against the hipbone; Usaph felt the body thud—through the wood and metal of the weapon—in his own hands. Cate started to stagger sideways and dropped his own musket. Bolly and Hans Strahl straightened him up and picked up his rifle and pushed it back in his hands, for Captain Guess could be heard yelling some way back. "What's that? Is that brawling? Cease that goddam brawling!" Judd and Strahl and Gus Ramseur were guiding Usaph back into his own place in the formation. But a lot of damage had been done. For, in the second Cate looked at him, in that white-faced, sick second, an open boast had come out of the conscript's eyes. The boast said—and Usaph

had no doubt about it—*I had your wife, you son of a bitch!*
The instant after it appeared Cate was trying to change that
look, trying to hide it away, trying to look just clouded, like
a man with a fresh-bruised hip has a right to look.

Usaph was the one that was near falling over now. He felt
like that man in the yoke who was kicked in the belly by a
horse. As the company shuffled ahead, he managed to bully
himself back out of the state of certainty about Cate and Ephie
and into a state of coy doubt again. The one thing he didn't
doubt was that on a day soon he would take the life of Decatur
Cate.

Then, as a mercy, things got so damn hard and hectic that
all thoughts of presages and all doubts about Ephie got ground
out of his mind. They marched, Usaph locked in the ranks of
the Shenandoah Volunteers, twenty miles that day. Usaph
welcomed this hard, numbing march. They got through Culpeper, where Ambrose Hill spotted his home places, but they
didn't stop until the Rappahannock River. Then for two days
they moved west and every strategist in the ranks knew what
they were doing, they were feeling for the flank again. Usaph
and the others saw little. They traveled on country roads
through little hamlets, out of sight of the river most times, and
slaves would come to the fences to watch them with mute eyes
as they went by. West and west they walked and it began to
seem they could march to Canada before they'd get round the
end of Pope's Yankees.

At night Gus and Usaph slept on one waterproof with the
other on top of them, and their blankets and food cached between them to stop casual theft. They had not lived under cover
for a year and to their backs and loins luxury was two waterproofs and flat earth to lie on that was not total liquid mud.
And though it was a regimen that would have killed a town-
dweller, they slept well.

The word kept coming back that you couldn't get round the
Yankee flank. There was a rumor Lincoln had put a solid line
of Germans and slum-boys, two paces apart, from Fredericksburg all the way to San Francisco.

It was the evening of that third day's marching upstream
that Cate came up to Usaph in the midst of a thunderstorm,
when Usaph was trying to get his evening fire going. Cate
stood, watching as if to find out how to strike flame to wet
kindling. "Bumpass," he said softly after a time. Bumpass
seemed not to hear and Cate stood awhile in his weather-proof

cape with the rain in his eyes, and wanting Ephie Bumpass so
much he could have brained Usaph Bumpass with a rock right
there to have her.

Bumpass knew Cate was there. He felt helpless. What will
the son of a bitch tell me? Cate hung over the fire site like a
strange skinny bird. How Bumpass wished he'd go away in
the most complete sense, would die or get a killing fever.

"You have to forgive me, Bumpass, for being so provoking
the other day."

"I weren't affected," Usaph boasted but didn't look up.
"Were you worried I was affected, Cate?" But Usaph didn't
give him time to say why. "Why don't you jest go and desert?
I mean you don't believe in nothing. So what's keepin' you?
I want to know that for once. I ain't asking for the fun of it,
I want to be told, goddamit! What I mean is, a boy like Joe
knows nothing of the world and of railway systems and the
rest, but you could make a fist of deserting. How I wish you
goddam would and rest my poor soul, Cate!"

Cate said: "There's always the chance we could be friends,
you know, Bumpass. Like two ordinary gentlemen."

"Maybe the lion will lie down with the lamb." There was
a merry little flame now under Usaph's hands. He picked up
a twig and flourished it at Cate. "Listen, we had this goddam
confabulation before. A man like you should get . . . Why? Why
don't you jest get?"

Cate thought for a while. Lord, don't let him make any
clean breast, Usaph prayed. "What if I said I gave your wife
certain undertakings . . . ?" Cate asked.

"If you said that, Cate, I'd cut out your goddam tongue."
Usaph stood up the better to threaten Cate. "Ephie has no need
of any of your undertakings. I have Gus to look for my body
if my body goes down, which by hokey it ain't going to." He
began to push Cate hard by the shoulder. "So get! Go on! It's
a positive act of that-there moral turpitude for you to hang
round in the camp of the children of goddam blindness." And
he pushed the shoulder again and again. "Get!"

Cate looked like he would cry, coming over all dismal, and
he turned and sloped off in the rain.

Usaph ran after him and got him by the arm and whirled
him around. There was that ploughboy strength to Bumpass.

"Tell me, Cate. I saw the way you looked, you son of a
goddam sow. Did it happen? Did it?"

Cate started weeping. "Bumpass," he said. "No. No."

"You want to see me die, so you can carry the news to Ephie. Widow's goddam comforter! First in the bed, Cate. Is that the way you want it?"

"No," said Cate. It wasn't fear that worked in him. It was a sort of perverse love of this innocent yokel.

There were tears amongst those raindrops on Usaph's face too. Cate pulled away and for some reason Usaph let him go free.

"And I hope they find you in any event," he yelled after Cate, "and I'll be on that execution detail and I'll make sure I get a musket with one of them genuine bullets for your goddam black heart, Cate! Yeah, you can wager on that, Cate!"

When he turned back to his fire, water had put it out.

— 20 —

CATE REMEMBERED WITH a special sharpness how the widow had got gradually less and less polite to him. He got the idea she only ate supper with him those days to stop him saying things to Ephie. As a matter of fact, one evening, she took to sending his supper to the barn on a tray. By these signs Cate had known he'd have to act soon.

His chance came on a morning when Aunt Sarrie seemed to be readying herself for a trip to town. She appeared to be in a bad mood about it; he could hear her stamping round asking Bridie for pins and where she'd put her—Aunt Sarrie's—best lace kerchief.

Of course, even as he thought away in that meadow near Cedar Run, Cate still thought of Ephie as a beautiful and simple being over whom two intelligences—his own and Mrs. Muswell's—were fighting. In fact Ephie too had been aware of the undertones of what was happening that morning. It looked to Ephie as if Aunt Sarrie was all the time trying to make up her mind to say something, to give some advice, and then shaking her head as if that would be unwise. Ephie saw her however talking deep and earnest with Montie before climbing into her gig and taking off. She had not told Ephie where she was going, just kissed her solemnly. Ephie presumed she was off to see some mill-owner or lawyer in one of the towns about, but guessed that the journey might have something to do with Cate.

When she went into the parlor an hour later, for what should have been one of her last sittings, she discovered all at once that Aunt Sarrie's absence had changed the whole feeling between her and Cate. She listened to him chattering away, but there was some sort of tension between them; her hands were sweating. It seemed to her as if this meeting could only end in a howling argument or . . . or something.

Afterwards she could barely remember what they'd spoken about in that first hour of the sitting. One thing she knew was that she had asked, just like someone pleading: "Ain't I jest about through with this sitting business, Mr. Cate?"

And when she said that, Cate gave an argument why she wasn't through with the business, but she did not even hear what it was. She nodded and nodded, and wanted both to flee and to stay. At one stage too he explained to her how to grind and mix your own oils, but she heard nothing of it, even though she kept saying: "Is that so?" and "Oh, like that?"

Cate himself was in a sweat. When will you do it, ole boy? he was asking himself. And how?

Well, about eleven in the morning, he grasped a brush by its handle and held it up vertically, the bristles towards the ceiling. With the umber paint that sat all over its hairs, it looked a little like a weapon which has just been used. Then, for one of those mysterious artist's purposes Ephie understood nothing of, he advanced on her, one eye closed, bisecting his view of her face with the brush held in front of him. She watched him out of alarmed, dark eyes.

They were hugging each other before Ephie even knew it, Ephie still sitting, Cate lowering crookedly above her. When he dragged her upright, his hands moved wildly around and over her, looking for that point of flesh somewhere—on her back perhaps or her shoulders—which if held would give him the greatest sense of possession. And Ephie . . . she was shuddering worse than someone with malaria but her mouth, a little open, was moving madly over his face.

"You'll come with me to California, ma'am," he said as a statement.

"No," she said, but like someone who can't help herself.

"You'll come with me to California," he reiterated, starting to chuckle. "Because of our great desire, ma'am, our great . . ."

"For Lord's sake, Mr. Cate," Ephie begged him, whispering, panicked, "Bridie'll hear you...."

But Cate was talking quiet enough. Only to Ephie did it seem he was talking at the high top of his voice.

Just like a grandee in a play, Ephie thought in her panic. He said: "This great desire wasn't put there for no purpose, Mrs. Ephie Bumpass. We'd be happy, so happy in California. I would teach you all those things.... I can see in you this wish to be taught, darling Mrs. Bumpass. You can't deny that."

Mrs. Bumpass couldn't, so she just twitched there, caught in his arms, in the parlor. Oh, she wished Aunt Sarrie hadn't gone away to Goshen or Millboro or Warms Springs or whatever town it was. And oh, at the same time, she was so pleased Aunt Sarrie *was* away.

"Our lives would be so different there," Cate whispered. "War would mean nothing there. My queen, my queen...."

"I...," said Ephie, shaking her head, "I can't speak of it."

"Let me tell you this," he said. She was beginning to squirm and pull away towards that chair again, the one in which she was meant to be posing. Cate noticed but thought it didn't matter that some of his paints had come away on the fabric of her dress. "You have never been loved by a man like me," he said in a solemn way.

For some reason this statement worked powerfully on her, but she tried not to let him see it. "Love is a big word," she muttered. She felt she might just choke there, in the parlor, and so she found the chair again and sat sideways in it. And while she sat, there was also in her the urge to run out the door and up amongst the hills that were covered with Aunt Sarrie's timber leases. And, of course, at the same time, the urge to put out her hand to Cate's face.

Cate could see it struck a potent chord. "You haven't ever been loved by someone like me," he repeated. He shook the brush. "You *want* to go with me, Ephie. You can't even hide it. You *want* to."

Ephie whimpered and shook her head and, almost by accident, put her hand along the line of his jaw, part to caress him, part to push him off. When he tried to clasp her again, it was the quickness of her mouth that surprised him, the way it found his lips and worked at them in that strange fated manner that belongs to people who can't much help themselves any more.

Then, using the chair for leverage, she forced herself away and sat for a while with her hand on her forehead, and made those breathy sobbing noises he understood too well, for they begged him both to leave her and to take her.

It was impossible of course to have her in the parlor by day, with the slave outside or upstairs or in the cookhouse or somewhere close.

"You must come to the barn tonight, Ephie," he said. "You know you can't avoid it. When does Mrs. Muswell get home?"

"All she said to me," Ephie told him, still crouched in the seat and caressing her forehead, "is she meant to be home soon as she could."

"Yes?" Cate asked, for she had more to tell.

"But I heard her say to Montie..."

"Yes?"

"That she feared it mightn't be till tomorrow noon."

He'll be watching, that black man, Cate thought. He'll have orders to watch and he'll know what to watch for.

"Is Montie partial to drink?" he asked.

"As much as any man," Ephie said. Oh Lordy, I am making plans with the man. But it excited her. In the pit of her belly it excited her.

Cate said: "I could give him liquor."

"You give him liquor, Mr. Cate," Ephie whispered, "and he'll guess your purpose. For he is no fool."

Cate smiled at her with great certainty, but her eyes were still down and she did not see. "You'll come to me," he said. "You'll come to the barn. After Montie and Bridie have tucked themselves up tonight. You'll do that, won't you? You'll come?"

She raised her face, her eyes bunched close, sweat showing either side of her mouth. She shook her head wildly, like someone trying to come to terms with pain.

"You'll visit me," he said. "I'll wait all night, Ephie. And I'll die if you don't come."

She went over to the mantelpiece and stood there, still nursing her forehead. "Oh mercy, Mr. Cate, how can I ..." But she meant more how could she sit calm for any more painting. Cate came up to try to touch her again.

"Forgive me for bringing you this distress," he said.

But she sidestepped him and shook her head again, whatever that meant.

"I'll die," he said, as if for the first time. "If you don't come ..."

He'd stayed there in the parlor and painted devotedly the

rest of the day, telling himself all the time it was certain she would get to the barn that night, and yes, they would go to California, leaving no trace behind them, except this one portrait to remind Aunt Sarrie and all the other folk of Bath County of the beauty they'd lost.

Alone in the rain, Cate remembered the flavor of the certainty of that morning the way an old man remembers the flavor of a distant June and a vanished girl.

— 21 —

TOM JACKSON HAD got energy to chastise colonels at three a.m. on a steaming summer night from somewhere, and it was from the papers that lay on his desk. Twenty-four hours past Jeb Stuart had taken three cavalry regiments all the way round to Catlett's Station, way up the Orange and Alexandria Railroad. One regiment tore up railway track, another tried to set fire to the bridge to the north, but the drenched timbers wouldn't take flame. A third swept up the main street of the town from two directions at once and made prisoners of a good half of Pope's staff—adjutants, engineers, artillery officers and a clutch of field officers of various rank. In a downstairs hallway of a house just off Main Street a coat was found that had a tag inside its collar with Johnny Pope's name on it, though there wasn't any sight of the general himself. But most important of all, the cavalry found secret papers there, right in that house. Copies had been given to Longstreet and Jackson only last evening, and they lay on Jackson's desk now.

These captured memoranda and despatches showed that at least two of McClellan's corps were back in the Washington area from the James River and, not needing too much re-equipping and reorganizing, would be able to march to join Pope within six days at the most and come under Pope's management within a week. Other forces from Pennsylvania and some traitorous West Virginians (7000 in all) and some further corps of McClellan's would unite with the remaining three corps of McClellan's army. So that, even allowing for the traditional Yankee slowness of movement, it could happen that within ten days at most, Pope would have at his call some 130,000 troops where now he had just near on 50,000.

Now this kind of news should have depressed some men. In Jackson it made for a great and nearly sinful excitement. It gave him back the sort of conditions that suited his soul and his health best, the sort of conditions he'd missed for years as a professor and as a loving husband. It made the taking of wild risks a needed and a proper thing. It made gambling legal.

When the colonels came in to get their ears pinned back, Tom Jackson—anticipating the gamble—had been working at movement orders for his three divisions. He worked through till eight a.m., not even noticing the chimes of the clock or the coming of light beyond the windows. He studied commissary and quartermaster returns, he read the latest reports from his surgeon, young Hunter Maguire, and from his Chief of Artillery, and studied Hotchkiss's reports and maps for a likely line of country to use during the next few days.

At eight a.m. he ate a solid breakfast with Sandie and Kyd, then worked on till eleven, when he mounted up and rode with most of his staff a little way south. After two miles he reached a flat open field where a table had been placed in the sunny middle, far out from the copses that surrounded it. All kinds of staff officers crowded into the shadows of the trees, but only Lee himself was out there in the middle, wearing a wide-awake hat for shade, his leonine head bent down over a large map.

Jackson stepped out to join him in the harsh light, bowed, took a seat at the table and—everyone at the edges of the field could tell—straight away began talking map-talk.

A minute before the due time for the conference to start, General James Longstreet arrived. He could tell as he stepped through the fringe of respectful officers and out into the middle of the field amongst lupins and bees and clicking insects that it might have been a mistake not coming early. Because Lee and Jackson were nodding at each other like men who'd already come to an agreement.

Longstreet was from South Carolina. He was a little over forty years old, a tall man with an orderly mind, and he didn't exactly trust those two, there was a mad streak in both of them. Lee took horrible risks—like when for the sake of hitting McClellan's flank along the Chickahominy, he left Richmond wide open some seven weeks back with only 1500 boys·in the defenses. It happened that the ploy had been a success only on account of George McClellan's weakness of soul. One day the

Union might get a soldier of firm intent and then all these temperamental risks Lee took would wreak quite a whirlwind, yessiree!

As for Jackson, well, James Longstreet didn't respect him much more than Ambrose Hill did. He thought he was given to impulse.

General Lee looked up now and called, "G'morning there, James." And dammit there was already some quiet excitement about him. Longstreet bowed, solemn and proper towards both men, and took a chair at Jackson's side.

"Well," said Lee in a low voice, "you know of our situation, James, and I know already that Tom here knows. At the moment we've got about 50,000 boys of ours outfacing about 50,000 boys of Pope's to no one's particular benefit. We've got here what they call a static front and we want to make it fluid as fast as we can on account of there being some 80,000 Union soldiers on the road to join Pope. Now we've about a week to devour Pope in detail, and we may not even have a week when it comes down to it. Yes, I understand you know all this. I just recapitulate, that's all.

"Now Tom and I've been talking about a ploy, James, and I wonder if you see any value in it. It's this. Tom takes his three divisions and a cavalry screen and clears *way* off to the west and round Pope's flank. He moves at great speed, as seems to be the tradition of his divisions . . ."

James Longstreet thought, it might be the tradition but I haven't seen much evidence of it. He said nothing though.

"Tom has a route already planned," said Lee.

Jackson looked up with those blank, staring eyes. He pointed to one of the maps, showing the country off towards the Blue Ridge and behind the Bull Run Mountains. "My engineer Captain Boswell grew up in the country we'd be traveling," Jackson explained. "He recommends taking a line through Amissville, Orleans, Salem, Thoroughfare Gap and Gainesville to put us square across Pope's rear and communcations at Manassas."

Manassas again. Well, Manassas couldn't be avoided, Longstreet knew. There was a grand junction there where the Manassas Gap Railroad and the Orange and Alexandria met. The O & A was essential to Lincoln for shipping troops south from the capital, and the Gap line for despatching them across to the Valley. The first massed battle of the war had been fought for Manassas and it was sure to be fought for again. It was not the name of Manassas that fretted James Longstreet.

It was the way of getting round to it that James Longstreet felt doubtful about.

"It's a long flank march," he said, a little breathless, because it really scared him. "It's a long, long march"

Lee looked away, a faint benevolent smile on his face, towards the shade trees his staff lolled beneath. "Well, I suggest, James, it's better than the front-on style of attack that cost us so many boys at Malvern Hill and other places."

Longstreet shook his long patrician head. "We've got just about equality in numbers with Pope now?" he said, and Jackson's eyes came over drowsy.

"In fact there are new boys up from Louisiana, from Mississippi and Alabama," said Generalissimo Lee. "We're likely doing just a little better than Johnny Pope at this moment."

"Yes, well that's excellent. But in terms of what's coming Pope's way, General Lee, we're way down. So what you want to do—and correct me if I misunderstand—what you want to do is split up a numerically lesser army—ours—right in two—in the presence of the enemy, in very contact with him . . . !"

"That's a mite pessimistic way of stating it, James," said General Lee.

". . . and on top of that, you want to send nearly half of it on a fifty-mile loop right round the back of the enemy. And I ask for what purpose? I simply want to know. I want to measure the purpose, sir, against the risk."

"Well, I'd say, James, that the purpose was to exploit the situation."

"But this violates the major military principle of concentration."

"God help us all, James, what else can we do? Look, with States like Alabama and Louisiana scraping their barrels we can get together 23,000 infantry and some 4000 cavalry to send off with Tom. And you'll be here with 32,000 in your corps. That's the South at floodtide, James. They are the numbers we've got together by the best efforts we can put forward, by using all the laws in all the States as well as the laws of the Confederate Congress. In a week, as I say, and as you well know, there'd be 130,000 Yankees facing us along the Rappahannock. And if by some gift of God we could fight them ragged, all Abe Lincoln and his War Secretary have to do is call for another quarter of a million boys and put in new requisitions for cannons and muskets. We can't win it, James, by keeping to the principle of concentration that we learnt at West Point. And the reason is, if *we* sit still, they can out-concentrate *us* every day of the week."

James Longstreet bit his thumb and stared off into the middle distance. "I know all that," he told General Lee. "But the danger. My wing could be crushed right here, on this ground, after General Jackson marches off."

"As a matter of fact, James, I don't intend for your wing to linger long here. I want you just to hold the line while Tom gets away, and of course to cause so much trouble along Johnny Pope's front with raids and artillery fire that he won't for a moment think that half of us are gone. And then, allowing two days for Tom here to get poised, you and I will be off too, James, at night. Leaving our fires burning."

Long-faced James Longstreet turned to long-faced Tom Jackson. "You could be attacked on the march and chewed up."

"At the worst," Jackson told him, not using Christian names since Longstreet wouldn't, "I could retreat to the Blue Ridge."

"You could really get yourself swamped in the Manassas area. Why there must be at least some 50,000 of the others on the road up that way right now."

"It will depend a lot," said Tom Jackson, closing his eyes like a cat, "on the work of my cavalry."

Teach your grandmother to suck eggs, James Longstreet wanted to say. But he was a sane man. He could see the reasons for the move if it could be well managed. He doubted Jackson could really manage it well.

"I've already drawn up," said Lee, almost in apology, "the movement orders, James." He handed a paper to Longstreet.

Longstreet read over the details on the page Lee handed him. He took a minute and a half over it, contorting his long lips here and there and giving little grunts. At last he said: "It might work if General Jackson's corps completes the march in two days. That's 25 miles a day. But how can you do that with a wagon train?"

"There won't be a wagon train," Tom Jackson said. "There'll be a few ambulances. And they'll move along! Oh yes, they'll move along at a good clip! We'll feed and supply ourselves from the Federal trains we find in Manassas."

Putting both sets of his fingers against his forehead, James Longstreet laughed a silent and bitter laugh at this crazy op-

timism. These two men, more staid than him, not given at all
to cussing, were like men rendered mad by their initial suc-
cesses at a gambling table.

"We can depend on you, James," said Lee quietly. "I know
that much."

"Oh yes," said James Longstreet, "you can depend on *me*."

Lee smiled. "I suggest you get Dan Hill's division to move
into the camp sites Tom's men vacate tonight. But I leave the
fine detail to you two."

"Very well," said James Longstreet and sighed. "Very well.
I'll talk to Dan Hill."

"James, Tom," said the generalissimo with that chaste smile
of his. "I think this is just about the biggest thing we ever
tried."

"And all I hope," said James Longstreet, "is that the Union
command stays as lax as it has been up to this."

"Amen to that," General Lee whispered.

But Tom Jackson said nothing. He was staring at the maps,
just like a goddam traveller who knows where he'll be at night-
fall.

— 22 —

WHEN SEARCY RODE into that street in Orange a week after
Mrs. Whipple's arrival, masons and carpenters were working
on scaffolds outside the warehouse. Mrs. Dora Whipple, Searcy
thought, has ordered holes knocked in the brute walls, is letting
in the light and the air. Doing for the hospital what she's done
for me perhaps, for the Honorable Horace Searcy.

It was while he was dismounting that the thought came to
him. Why don't you marry this woman. Like that. Marry an
American! He'd never met anyone who'd done that—apart
from other Americans of course. Certainly she came from the
aristocracy of Boston and had married into the gentry of the
Carolinas, but in English society that counted for little more
than being the daughter of a Red Indian chief. Searcy smiled.
If I marry an American, it will confirm all the governor's worst
opinions of me, he thought.

In the lobby of the warehouse he found an orderly in a long

dirty coat. Once it had been white, now it was yellow and dappled with the brown of old blood which will not wash out. Oh, Searcy thought, guessing correctly, the surgeon in this place isn't up to Mrs. Whipple's standards.

"Could you direct me to the matron's quarters, please?"

"Out the back."

"*Out the back* isn't a very exact description."

The orderly looked at him and Searcy could just about see him thinking, *a friend of hers!* Searcy was unrepentant at being thought of that way.

"Come on, ole chap. I asked vou where the matron was."

The orderly got more specific then. Mrs. Whipple's quarters were a newly built lean-to of green pinewood in the courtyard behind the warehouse. Stone walls on three sides of this yard. It would be a bitter place in winter. Maybe, however, she wouldn't have to occupy it in winter. She might be in the North. She might be in England. She might be my bride. Searcy started grinning there, in the courtyard, in his enthusiasm for that idea. And as he stood there, the project grew and sent him to her door feeling a grand elation.

He knocked and heard her businesslike voice telling him to come in. Opening the door he found her at the table, kneading gingerbread and cutting it with a knife. The fragrance of gingerbread cookies came from a small portable army oven in one corner.

As he entered, he noticed a certain expectant flinching of her eyes. He guessed she was worried what he thought of her for writing, for sending on her new address. "Oh, how can I say welcome?" she said. "When I'm all over flour?"

"No need for welcome," said Searcy gallantly, bowing broadly. "I shall take the welcome as read."

She made a mouth. "You see, I promised gingerbread to some of the boys for supper. It's always so important to tempt their appetites . . ."

You tempt mine well enough, sweet lady, Searcy thought.

She coughed. "I thought I'd better write you about my new location," she whispered, "in view of our . . . our professional connection. . . ."

In fact Searcy had been so enchanted since he'd come in that he'd nearly forgotten they had any such connection. "Of course you should have. Can we speak freely? Your black girl . . . ?"

"She's out at market, sir." She smiled and pointed to a chair just by the table. "Sit here. True, a fine layer of flour-dust will cover your clothes, Mr. Searcy. I shall try to compensate for that by giving you the first slice of gingerbread to come from my oven."

"A bargain, madam," said Searcy. He sat and they smiled at each other in silence for a while. When Searcy spoke again, it was in a voice which could hardly be heard, even by Dora Whipple. "You know the connections you had in Richmond? I don't mean the social connections. I mean the . . . *other* connections?"

A seriousness came over her small bunched face. "I know the kind of connections you mean, Mr. Searcy."

"Do they operate here? In Orange?"

"No one has made any contacts with me."

Searcy thought a moment. "I don't ask this in any offensive way, my dear lady. But I wondered if perhaps you'd had a change of heart?"

"My heart is steady, Mr. Searcy; even more so my mind. It's the way I'll stay. No one has bothered to contact me. If you told me anything now I would not know to whom to relay it in my turn." She punched a particularly massive lump of dough. "I imagine someone will come to me in time."

Searcy smiled. "I have nothing in particular to tell, Mrs. Whipple. Except the old, old story. That Lee has some 60,000 troops and that's the best he'll ever do. I've said so in one of my despatches to *The Times*. I wonder if they bother to read *The Times* in Washington?"

"I don't think they can, really," said Mrs. Whipple. "Or if they do, I don't think they believe what they read."

He could see that she'd become very serious. That they had become spy and spy again. He wanted to get back to being man and woman, friend and friend. He shook his head. "In any case I visited, madam . . . because I wanted to visit!"

She looked straight at him. That acute frankness was in her eye. And he wondered what it meant, wondered whether he ought to go to her, be-floured as she was, and solve matters by wrapping her in his arms. But someone new had arrived at the door of her quarters and was hammering.

Dora Whipple wiped her hands on a towel and crossed the room and opened. Searcy saw at the door a tall man with the white, slightly purplish complexion of a boozer. He wore an untidy surgeon's uniform.

"Doctor Canty," said Mrs. Whipple.

The surgeon did not answer. He handed Mrs. Whipple a note, which she unfolded and read.

"I'm too busy with gingerbread to answer this nonsense," she told the surgeon when she'd finished reading. "There are hundreds of men needing a whisky issue many times a day. If you give me a clerk, I can make sure these records you ask for are kept . . . how much whisky is given, when and to whom . . ."

"It is not satisfactory, ma'am," the surgeon told her. "It is too easy for you to play favorites with the whisky keg, as happens with some of them Marylander officers you spend your time with in Ward 4."

"Do I read you right, Surgeon Canty . . . ?"

"You read me any way you like, ma'am."

Searcy got to his feet now, delighted to be able to do something definite for her. "Go before I take you with my fists, sir," he told the surgeon in what Mrs. Whipple thought of as his best Britannic manner.

Surgeon Canty went a dangerous purple. "This is my hospital. I have authority over every square foot of it."

Searcy was so anxious to get at him that he spun Mrs. Whipple aside and took the lapels of the man's uniform. "Apologize to the matron," he said. Mrs. Whipple was close to Searcy's elbow, saying softly: "Let him go."

The surgeon's eyes were bulging but he would not formulate any answer.

"Please," Mrs. Whipple whispered. "*I* have to stay on here with him. *I* have to work with him."

Searcy pushed the man away and was surprised how he toppled. Canty had that strange weakness of the inebriate, the man who drinks more than he eats.

"I shall send a goddam corporal's guard," he was calling, "to evict your guest, Mrs. Whipple!"

"And I, sir, on my return to the army," Searcy announced, "shall mention your charming manners to General Jackson."

Canty turned away and vanished into the hospital. Searcy closed the door, and he and Mrs. Whipple returned to the table, panting fiercely.

"Oh, Mr. Searcy, you've taken my hand," Mrs. Whipple said all at once in a high breathy voice. For he had her hand, pallid with dough, clamped in his, and seemed to be studying it deeply. She laughed. "If you waited half an hour you could have it in its normal state."

But he could hear her excited breathing. He put his lips to her wrist and they came away comically marked with the gingerbread mix. That made both of them laugh. "Look at yourself in the mirror," Mrs. Whipple advised Searcy.

"Marry me, Mrs. Whipple," Searcy said simply.

"No," she said, equally simply. The laughter had vanished. "It can't be done." She nodded over her shoulder. "Boys perish in that place, you know, my dear Searcy. Any need of ours isn't as sharp, sir, as theirs."

"There are other matrons to take over the management, Mrs. Whipple."

"Few as accomplished as I," she told him. "I have to say it. *Few* as accomplished as I."

"Listen to me," Searcy said, starting to argue hard. "Lee and Jackson have to come to grief in the North. There must be a retreat in the autumn . . ."

"And oceans of wounded boys, my dear Searcy. *Oceans!*"

He waved that aside, "Perhaps about Christmas matters will have settled. We can get out to the North with one of the blockade runners. We could go back to England. My father has a fine house in the West Country. Imagine us living there, Mrs. Whipple, in such peace. In such happiness. I have a book to write there about North and South. You also ought to write a book."

"Which book?" she asked, and her laugh was very nearly bitter. "The one about the matron or the one about the spy."

"Come, Mrs. Whipple! I stagger round the earth from one battlefield to another. Like the ghost of Hannibal or someone like that. I tell you, my dear Mrs. Whipple, if I had you, I could happily come to rest. We could live together in a well-ordered household."

She laughed again. "It sounds as if all you need is a good housekeeper."

"I tell the story badly, Mrs. Whipple," he said with a confessional grin. "Let me say this. I desire you. Oh yes, more than anything. I desire you."

And it was now somehow that he decided he had a sort of right to take hold of her. She proved so small-boned, he got the illusion he could force her in between the fibers of his own body, take her over that way. The directness of her mouth on his was like the directness of her eyes. They stood clasped together for at least a minute. Then, like a sensible woman who didn't want to go short of breath, Mrs. Whipple pushed

him away. "Please, let us sit down, Searcy," she murmured.
"Just till our heads are clear."

He did not take her invitation to sit, but he watched her.
Her hands were folded in front of her, not in the way women
pray but in the way of people who are suddenly exhausted.
"Now just hush up, Mr. Searcy," she pleaded. *"Please."*

"As you wish," he said, turning his face away.

"Now come, Searcy. Don't let your features droop like that.
You don't need me to tell you I am honored. You know that
in other circumstances . . ."

"We can make the circumstances."

"No, we can't do that, Searcy. Don't tell yourself we can
make the circumstances as we wish. The war owns us both and
we both know it. We met under its conditions and, unlike most
people, we know it won't end by Christmas."

"We could leave it tomorrow," Searcy insisted.

She put her head down on her hands. "Do you think so?
Look at the life I lead, Searcy. You yourself thought it was
curious when you first met me. I tend the heroes of a cause I
detest. My way of saying it is that I nurse the victims of that
cause. Say I walked off now. How cavalier it would be of me.
How light-headed. I nurse the Confederacy and send information to the Union. I do not have the right now to become
a private woman all at once and to say *enough* to both causes."
She sat up straight. "Of course I would like to fancy you'd ask
me again when this war has let go of us both. I don't presume
anything, though . . ."

Searcy sat there half an hour arguing and pleading with her,
until it was time for her to go to the cookhouse and see to the
evening diets. Then he sat a gloomy hour on his own, chewing
on a cheroot. At last she came back. Walking in, she let her
hand trail down his arm. Then she sat down again herself.
Searcy could tell by looking at her that she had been thinking
of him all that time in the cookhouse, not in any sentimental
sense, but arguing with herself about what was possible and
what was not. And while she spooned broth, she would have
still been arguing and thinking. She was in a ferment all right.

"I believe," she said, giving a small laugh, just like a woman
who knows she is taking a risk, "that marriage is not the only
context for lovers, Mr. Searcy."

He smiled and looked wistful. He did not think she could
have said what she just had. "I've heard that too. But marriage
is the best context for us, dear Mrs. Whipple."

"The best *ideal* one, yes, sir. Men get so solemn about marriage. Yet they are so promiscuous at heart." She coughed again as if she had trouble with her throat, which as far as Searcy could tell, she did not have.

"You mean we may be lovers?" he asked, amazed.

She would not answer straight away. Then she said: "Nothing can happen between us here, my dear Searcy. The one thing Canty, our friend of a second ago, does with any efficiency is to watch *me*." Yet again she coughed. "I believe the situation is that when ladies visit gentlemen in their hotels, they wear a veil and enter by the back entrance. Believe me, Searcy, I would rather not wear a veil, but we labor under the circumstances this war . . . *this* war . . . imposes on us, my dear, dear, Searcy."

Searcy stood up and went to her. He was half joyous and half disappointed. "Yes," he said, kissing her. "Wear a veil."

"Is it true," she asked before he went, "men never marry women who visit hotels secretly?"

"Be assured, my dear Mrs. Dora Whipple, that this one does."

The result was that that evening, in a room on the second floor of the Lewis House in Orange, Mrs. Whipple gave herself to the Honorable Searcy with all the thoroughness he could have wished for. Just the same, in too short a time, she had to leave. She told him that she must be back at the hospital by eleven p.m., for she was bound to make the rounds of the wards every night before retiring, to see who was dying or in distress.

And as Searcy lay alone at midnight, playing with the sadness of her going, it struck him she was exactly right. The war *did* own the both of them as surely as slaves were owned in the Carolinas. The thought kept him awake and fretful till dawn.

— 23 —

AT THREE O'CLOCK that morning there was a sort of party going on in a pleasant field some half a mile down the road from the little yellow farmhouse of Mr. Tilley. Three wagons were drawn up in that field and their tailboards were down. Long queues of men led up to the tailboards of the wagons. The Stonewall Brigade were drawing three days' rations again, and everyone was talking and everyone seemed fresh.

Only Bolly was morose. He snarled at his messmate Hans Strahl and made remarks all the time about Dutchies and what low-grade beings they were. "Old Bolly's gone and decided," said Hans to Usaph, "that he don't want to be seen mixing with no Germans."

Yet contradictorily he hung round Gus and Usaph, as if he did want quieter company now than he'd had with Joe Murphy and Ash Judd. He listened, with puckered lips and a frown, even to Gus's music talk and to anything fanciful Usaph wanted to say.

The business of drawing three days' rations in the middle of the night excited Usaph—he felt there must be special purpose for it, that such lumps of food must mean someone—Jackson, God, someone—thought the whole business of conflict was drawing towards an end.

He thought he'd pass on to Bolly a hopeful rumor he'd got from Danny Blalock, who himself claimed to have read it in an issue of *Harper's*.

"It's said," he told Bolly, "that the Yankees already, while we sit here, have got together plans for this big parade. The same to take place once we have Philadelphia and force a peace on them others. It'll be fire brigades and Yankees and your humble goddam servants, just to show that America is fair at peace again. Why, could you imagine what it must be like to march in a big city like that?"

"They'd shy at you with goddam offal," Bolly moaned. "Them New York Dutchies got no end of rubbish to throw at Christians."

Gus started to talk about a composition professor he wanted to meet, a German who had been in New York since the German riots of '48.

Ole Bolly wasn't likely, in that mood, to let the Germans off the charge that they lived like trash, just because they happened to have a fancy perfesser.

"But, Gus," he protested, under a night sky that was half stars, half low cloud. "You don't need no Dutchy teaching you these things. You're damn fine at the fiddle when you take it in your head to treat us to some tunes. Goddamit, you're so much better than that fancy Irishman." Bolly, so it seemed, had a down on the races of the earth—Dutchies, Irish, the lot.

And so the idle talk went on. "There's a rumor anyhow," Hans Strahl dared say, "we're jest going back over to the Valley itself."

"You heared my friend say Philadelphia," Bolly growled. "Can't you hear proper? My friend said Philadelphia. Why, there ain't anything happening over the Valley."

"Except the Yankees hold it," Hans said, looking away. "Maybe the people in the Valley don't call that nothing."

Over the tailboard of the wagon, each man was handed three pounds of cornflour. There was no standard way though that any one of the boys took it. Judd had nothing better to take it in than his wide-brimmed hat. Strahl had stripped a length of birch-bark from a tree and got his flour poured on that, and then the bark made a good kneading board for making it up into dough. Blalock had a pint pot, and Gus had got a jug from somewhere. Some other boy from the company tied up the arms of his lousy shirt and had the orderly from the wagon pour the ration of flour into the sleeves. And each of these methods were fairly standard ways men had for collecting their vitt'ls.

Some of those whose hats weren't in use for carrying flour used them for the molasses ration—you could eat the gooey stuff up straight away, dipping hardtack in it, and then you could wash the stickiness out of your hat before any vengeful sun came up.

It was a real hive, that field, and everyone was buzzing, talking in the clearing, talking in line, talking while stuffing their faces with biscuit and goo and goober peas. It was no Roman orgy, but it was a Confederate orgy and it had a flavor to it, in that these lean boys now gorging themselves knew it meant big events.

It all went a little sour just before four o'clock when the meat wagon came in, bringing with it the strange hearty smell of fresh meat. Officers like Captain Guess and Captain Hanks and Lieutenant Lucius Taber and the Reverend Dignam hurried the men up to it, saying there was only just time to collect the ration. So with only just time to collect it and no time to cook it, they needed to salt it so it wouldn't taint by noon.

In every wagon the orderlies were calling: "I don't have no goddam salt." "Well, ask the goddam commissary." "Well, salt's going short in the whole goddam South." "Well, if there's plenty in Mobile jest you get down there and fetch us all a peck." And other stuff of that nature.

Usaph had no choice now but to roll up his fine bit of beef in his blanket, but it was Bolly who couldn't bring himself to do that. He stood looking down on his share and shedding tears on it while Guess and Taber roared round the glade punishing delayers with a sword blade on the ass. That boy Taber took to command as easy as you'd expect from a foolish boy.

"Bolly," said Usaph.

"There ain't salt, Usaph," Bolly told him, sounding amazed.

"I know that, Bolly."

"Well goddamit, this could be the last fresh meat I ever see, Usaph."

"Well," said Usaph. It was true for everyone here, that sentiment about the meat. But it didn't do any good to say so.

"Put it in your haversack then, Bolly."

"And I tell you I ain't never going to see a woman again, that I *know*, goddamit!" And he started to wail through an open mouth so that anyone at all could have heard him. "How did the whoresons forget the salt, Usaph?"

Usaph could see Bolly wasn't going to be easy comforted and the fuss he was making would bring those raging officers to him. He began arguing and, turning sideways to make a point, found Cate beside him. Well, that was always happening. Cate said in a reflective way, "For if the salt lose its savor," which though from The Book wasn't much help. But then he pulled a little bag from nowhere. "You can have my salt, Bolly. You can salt your meat while we march."

"*Your* salt?" said Bolly, feeling the bag and smiling like a child right in the middle of his tear-wet face.

"That's it, Bolly, my salt."

Cate began to lead Bolly off into the lane where the lines now formed fast. Usaph now had time to consider that this three pounds of beef he held in his hands could mean *his* life. It took little cleverness to work out that if it rotted, that would just about be the same as going half-lame on the road and under the sun. It was a simple matter now; would he like to die a proud man or could he beg Cate for the ordinary things of life, for salt for his meat?

"Cate!" he called, catching Cate and Bolly up. Cate looked at him very quiet, without smiling. "Do you have enough of that to salt my meat, Cate? I mean, I ask no goddam favors, I have money . . ."

"I would have offered," said Cate straight out, not putting on side. "Except I thought of course my offers was some sort of insult."

By the time the sun got up Bolly Quintard, Cate and Bumpass had all had their beef safe salted, and it was as well. For it became a clear hot day and there was a stink of rotting beef all over the marching brigade. All through the day men were cussing about their spoiling meat and how they'd never get to eat it. But Bolly marched jolly under his parasol, and it was strange, Usaph thought, how a handful of salt could make for this old man the difference between contentment and despair.

Ash Judd, moving in the column, saw his ole man sitting on a porch in the hamlet of Amissville. It was the sort of village where no one who lived there had ever seen much of note, and so the sight of an army coming down among its straggle of white frame houses, its store or two, its two little white boxes of churches, must have shocked the townsfolk this early morn, and now there wasn't a chicken in sight or a dog or a child, every soul was deep in its house except for the ole man, who belonged to no one village, no one habitation. A little before the Stonewall Brigade, Ambrose Hill's division had tramped through, and maybe the good but not too clever folk of Amissville thought that that was the end of it. Now here was another division. Just the same the ole man had sat there calmly, alone, a cold corncob in his hand. Other boys must have seen him but no one ever seemed to wonder what he was there for. Some of the boys called to him now. "You come join us, youngster!" they'd call. "Don't you go skulking there." But the ole man didn't answer them. He seemed to be dozing, and only Ash knew his true nature.

The morning was hot as the Stonewall Brigade came through Amissville, past the ole man. But after last week's rain there wasn't much dust and everyone could see, clearer than they'd ever seen it since they left the Valley, the sharp line of the Blue Ridge, sweet as a letter from home and fair ahead.

When Ash looked back towards the porch where the ole man had been, he saw he had left it and was strolling round the back of the house, for all the world just like an oldster making for the privy. He was a sharp one, that ole man.

Ash had first seen him two winters back. The ole man'd been sleeping under pine boughs and snow then, and his flesh had been blue as you'd expect; but now, in the war's high summer, it had a good color.

That winter two years back, Ash went out hunting two days after Christmas, carrying his old flintlock. His daddy might normally have gone along with him but was ill that day—likely as not from the mountain liquors he'd drunk on the afternoon of Christmas. So Ash stepped out alone into the woods that sparkling morn, into the snowy forests of the hill country on the borders of Pendleton and Rockingham Counties.

Some two miles out in the woods he saw a track in the snow he'd been seeing since the winter of '56, when he himself was a boy of fourteen. It was the track of the great stag who came through there every winter, and it was a standing ambition of the Judds, both father and son, to stalk it and bring it home, not least because it was a hard life for the family at that time of year, and fresh meat was a rarity with them in the months between Yule and springtime. One year they'd tracked this stag twelve miles and had to sleep out, being damned lucky the weather grew mild.

That day then, two days after the Christmas of 1859, he knew it wouldn't do to stalk the animal late into the afternoon. He didn't want to be finding his way home in a freezing night all alone. But there was something about following the trail of a great stag—there wasn't really any one point you could break off and turn back unless nature or man made you, and by three in the afternoon Ash was well over into the Pendleton hills above the raging Moorfield River which ran with chunks of ice but was too fast moving to freeze over. Now there wasn't a town this side of darkness he could reach and very likely there wasn't even a habitation. He knew, though, that he was likely closer to the town of Fort Seybert than he was to home, so he headed up in that line, following the river.

That's how he came to the witch's place. It was a long shack, no whitewash to its boards, but there was smoke from its chimney. There were outhouses but no barns. Likely, Ash thought, these people made their living by odd ends of trade, from moonshine, from cutting lumber, burning charcoal, stealing a cow or a horse here or there. Ash looked at this house for a good while before showing himself. He looked at it with all the snobbery and mistrust of those who live in farms that are whitewashed even if poor.

Soon there wasn't much light and he had to go and knock. He knocked a long time, yelling out homely things to show he wasn't a man to fear. When the door opened, it opened at speed, like a falling trapdoor, and there was a mad red-haired woman in the doorway, her hair sort of blazing and frizzled and her eyes bulging from her head. She nearly scared him away from the place straight off. But in the growing cold he needed to get into that hot kitchen.

"I'm Ashabel Judd, ma'am, from over to Singer Creek," he said.

"Then, Mr. Ashabel, I'm Mrs. Lesage," said the red-haired woman. "I'd wager a pig to a gallon of mud you've heard tell of me."

And he had, by damn. He'd heard women talk about her in whispers. Talk of the strange disease of women which country doctors couldn't do much for but Mrs. Lesage of Pendleton County could mend. Ashabel had heard Mrs. Lesage's name uttered since he was a wee boy, and it had seemed to him that not only were the diseases fixed up not to be spoken of aloud by women, most of all the cures weren't to be spoken of.

When Ash didn't move, just shivering on the doorstep, Mrs. Lesage laughed at him. It was a high, loud, mad laugh. "I've tended kin of yours. Ash, I remember the names of half your aunts, boy. Besides that, it's nice to get visitors this time of year, when a body's got the last of the ham on the skillet."

And sure, the kitchen was full of the savor of ham and batter and potatoes. Mrs. Lesage stood back to let him past the door. Ash did it slowly. He could see another woman in there. "This is my sister, Miss Gassaway," said the witch of women's diseases. "She speaks only in tongues."

A fat girl of maybe twenty-five sat at the end of the table. There was nothing in her face, in her eyes, and she didn't notice Ash when he said, "How do, Miss Gassaway?" and bowed.

"People say to me," said Mrs. Lesage, "how come you can cure them strangers yet you can't cure your own sister? Well, how do I know the answer to that? But Miss Gassaway here can talk in Greek and in the languages people spoke before the Lord Christ was on this earth. Only sometimes, of course, when the spirit moves her. You watch."

And taking up a knife by its blade she rapped her stupid sister a sharp hit on the wrist with the knife handle, and the sister began to speak in what might have been Christ's Aramaic or might just have been a loony language, but at least it had expression. But Mrs. Lesage didn't care to listen to it all, and as the sister raved, the red-haired witch raised her voice over the babble and went on talking with Ashabel. After the ham fritters and the potatoes were eaten, she put her sister to bed in a room on the back end of the kitchen, pushing her along tenderly enough and talking to her in God's English even though the poor fool couldn't understand it. Then the witch got out some whiskey and she and Ash talked and laughed and drank together as snow came down outside. And in the end Ash wasn't sure which bits of the evening were a whiskey dream and which bits really happened.

Anyhow, it went this way. Mrs. Lesage got to looking prettier and prettier, smoothing down her fierce red hair, and they both got to being amorous—her hand in his hair at the back of his head and his on her dress at the thigh, and all at once they were all over each other. As they were coupling on Mrs. Lesage's bed, behind a curtain on that side of the kitchen that was furthest from the fireplace, yet naked and warm and merry, the witch stopped proceedings dead, stopped plunging and rearing, and looked at Ash with the start of a tear in each of her eyes.

"I have such dreams, Ashabel," she said. "Dreams of a time close to now. Dreams of the time when all the young bulls go forth to the slaughter, all the young boys. I have these dreams, Ash, full of the corpses of young bulls, of the young men, Ash."

"War?" Ashabel suggested, for there was the expectation of war even in Pendleton County that winter.

"War? A shambles, Ash. A slaughter-house, boy."

Well, it wasn't a very new thing to have people predict war, but the way she looked at Ash, as if she'd dreamed of exactly *his* sad corpse, scared him a little. There was as well in her eyes a sort of offer of help. Ash didn't know what crazy help it would be.

Anyhow, they settled back to what they were at, and then Ashabel began to doze and opened his eyes to find her standing above him with a knife she'd got from somewhere. He yelled and tried to roll from the bed, but his ankles were tangled in the covers. Mrs. Lesage made a deft wound in the meat of his leg and then threw the knife away. Before his scream was out, her mouth came down over the injury and she drank there as if with a real thirst. "Whoa," he yelled, "what's this?"

Within a little while it began to be pleasant, that movement of her mouth on the cut, and he caught on that it had something to do with her witchery.

When she had drunk till her face was blue, she reeled off to the side of the bed, fetched a cup and spat the quantity of blood into it. Then, while he watched sort of enchanted, she began all manner of mad daubings and paintings of his body with the mixture of her spit and his blood. The whole business wasn't unpleasant and Mrs. Lesage sang songs in tongues as weird as her sister's. Then sometime, in that deep snowing night, she was done and they lay together, panting and sticky with warm blood and warm juice, and they slept deep, worn to a wire by the struggle to make him safe in any battles to come.

But that was nothing beside what happened next morn. Ashabel woke in the witch's bed with the quilt to his ears and his head pulsing and his mouth seeming full of gravel, and the first thing he heard was the witch chattering to her sister outside while they ate their breakfast. After a time he rose, pulled the curtains aside in the corner, and signalled, *what ought I to do?* to the widow-witch.

Mrs. Lesage laughed: "Why, Ash, you could walk through here dressed the way you come from your maw and Missie Gassaway wouldn't know any difference. But quick, take this here bowl of coffee and drink it up while you wash from that bucket in the corner. Quick now. Then dress yourself snug. I've got a thing to show you."

Some fifteen minutes later, when he was washed and dressed warm, she led him out into the grey morning. The snow was just petering out amongst the spruces and maples and aspens on this hillside and the day would come up sharp and freezing soon. He blew on his hands. "Get the shovel from that-there outhouse," the witch told him.

He obeyed and they walked a small stretch to a snow mound. "Scrape the snow back from that," said the widow. "Break any ice."

Again Ashabel obeyed, digging heartily into the mound. "No, no, careful, Ash!" the widow advised him. "You don't want to bark any flesh there."

Beneath the layer of snow Ash found boughs of spruce in a heap. Mrs. Lesage gestured to him to pull them aside. When he'd done that, he saw first the naked blue thighs of a woman beneath the branches, an old woman whose flesh hung slack on the bone, whose paps were dry and frozen to her ribs. Then he saw the naked old man, lying on his back, his eyes closed, no breath fluttering in him. The pair of them made an ancient ice-blue husband and wife, sleeping deep under mounded snow and cut boughs.

"Dead?" he asked the witch. He was taken by the half smile on the old man's face.

"Not dead, Ashabel. These are grand folk, these're the mammy and pappy of my dead love, Mr. Lesage. You know how it is, Ash, in the wintertime. With four people in the house the food gets scarce by now for folks like us. These last three winters Mr. and Mrs. Lesage sleeps out here. At the first decent fall they rill themselves up with applejack and I lays them down out here and cover 'em down decently. In the spring I drop 'em in a warm tub and they jest shakes themselves like an old dog and sit up joking."

How can I believe such a story? Ashabel asked himself. I must git away from here. She's killed those ole folk, nothing surer.

"Quick now," said the witch, "cover 'em up again before the air gets to them."

Ash did it, thinking, I gotta run and never tell anyone I was ever here.

"When that-there slaughter I spoke of, Ash, the one in my dreams, when it comes along I'll send ole Lesage there—" she nodded to the mound "—out to care for you in all them summer slaughters. He's got powers, ole Lesage, by heaven and earth he's got powers. Look for him in the spring and you'll keep seeing him till late autumn, and then you'll know, Ashabel, you'll be preserved. Now you won't forget his ole face, will you?"

He wouldn't ever forget *that*. Ashabel thanked her as polite as he could and then hurried off into the icy forests as fast as he could make his excuses, heading back towards Rockingham County. He'd heard tales of hill people storing their extra mouths and all other parts of the body thereto attached in snowy mounds all winter. But no one really believed it possible.

Ash joined the Shenandoah Volunteers in May of 1861. He began to see the ole man on country roads soon thereafter. Goddam it, he thought then, the proof of the pudding . . . !

— 24 —

IN AMISSVILLE GENERAL TOM JACKSON remembered he hadn't written to his lovely Anna before taking to the road. He stopped at the parson's place to get a real quick letter off to her. He couldn't say her name without his belly becoming molten, his heart a sweet hive. But he had to be quick about writing to her this morning.

He wrote the letter as if he was still in Mr. Tilley's farmhouse. "The enemy," he wrote, "has taken a position, or rather several positions, on the Fauquier Hot Springs side of the Rappahannock. I've only time to tell you how much I love my little pet dove."

Although he wouldn't tell his intentions even to his love in North Carolina, his army wasn't moving unseen. For there was a Federal signal station in the hills north-east of Waterloo Bridge on the Rappahannock, and in the dustless air a dozen men there could see Hill's division and the regimental flags, scarlet and blue against the deep green of a rainy high summer. As early as 7:15 a.m. these signallers spotted the regiments, only some four hours after the movement began. At first the Union signalmen thought it was some small detachment returning to the Valley, but when at 8:30 a.m. the infantry and artillery brigades were still rolling along the narrow roads there off to the west, the lieutenant in charge of the station drafted off a message. A whole division, he said, going north, probably to cross the river at Henson's Mill. Some wagons, not so many.

By 10:30 the Stonewall Brigade had appeared at the head of *its* division and a further message was flashed off by heliograph eastwards—two divisions moving well closed up and goddam fast. By noonday, when elements of Ewell's division had also been noticed, the young lieutenant—who'd been keeping a count of regimental flags—signalled Pope's headquarters that there were 20,000 men on the road to Henson's Mill. Within an hour of that, General H. W. Halleck, Union Chief of Staff in Washington, knew about it all. McDowell's corps, way over to the west, was alerted. For once the Union had been given an accurate estimate of a movement by Confederates.

But those bad mental habits of Union generals again, as James Longstreet had prayed they would, protected the Southern army. Johnny Pope had a habit of overstating, by a factor of at least three, the numbers of Confederates that opposed him. He didn't believe that the movement of 20,000 Confederates was a movement of more than a quarter of the enemy and therefore saw no danger to his rear. He believed it could only be a sideshow. It was beyond Johnny Pope's mind too to imagine that Lee might split half his army away from the main force and send it fifty miles into the rear of an enemy who had some 80,000 men, and more coming up to join him.

So all the good mathematics of the signals lieutenant in the hills above Waterloo Bridge went to waste. Pope told his generals that this splinter force was heading towards Front Royal or Luray townships in the Valley.

On the second morning of that march, before the heat was too bad, the word got back to Bolly and Usaph and Gus, having passed from man to man down a line ten miles long or more, that the column was turning east at Salem. Not west towards the Valley, but in behind Johnny Pope. So it was a northwards movement, a movement to threaten all those fabled cities Usaph had never seen—Washington, Harrisburg, Philadelphia! The regiments sprang along nicely that morning, but by noon everything began to break up as the road rose towards the blue-green range called the Bull Run Mountains.

This road up to the pass rose between tall forests which threw a good shade over the marching boys. It was on the last shadowy and tall-timbered miles to the top of Thoroughfare Gap that Bolly petered out altogether. He gave a little yelp and hobbled away to the edge of the road, to the cliff-edge that is, where dozens of lame or ill or cunning boys already sat panting, vomiting, binding up their feet with linen torn from old shirts, and all this above a nice little forested gulch. Somewhere down there a mountain stream ran deep in its socket, or was it just wind in the beeches and the oaks? Bolly hunched his body down, ashamed of himself, knowing that everyone knew of him, the most ancient veteran of the Stonewall, and everyone would see him there, unmanned by the rise of the road. He looked away. He studied the great fall of greenery below him.

Usaph ducked out of the line to talk to him.

"I'm done proper, Usaph. I'm lame's any old horse and my wind's broke."

"That ain't nothing to feel so ashamed about, Bolly."

Bolly shrugged. Usaph could tell he was thinking on his old lines. Which were, if I can't get up the pass, maybe the boys are right and my wife of 22 summers rides a better bull than me.

Gus too bent over Bolly, and Hans Strahl, tentative, not sure anything he did would be welcome. Then Major Dignam came along. They were all glad it was a sentimental man like Dignam who'd know neither Bolly nor themselves were average stragglers. Dignam just said: "Too much, Bolly?"

"We could take him pick-a-back," Gus said, "to the top. He'd be fine on the downhill."

"Goddamit, Gus," Usaph hissed at him. "When was your own wind as good as that?"

Hans Strahl said: "I can tote him some."

Bolly looked at the three of them, shook his head and covered his eyes.

But Dignam liked the suggestion all right. "It means you've got three boys out of line to carry one. But then I've seen boys earlier today running from the lines to pick green corn in the fields." They'd seen that too. What else could a man do whose meat was eaten or maybe rotted? "I think if men can leave ranks for the sake of unripe corn, they can leave ranks to carry Bolly," said Dignam, like goddam Solomon in judgment.

So they had their orders and Dignam passed on. Usaph took Bolly's musket and Gus's, and along with his own they made a fierce burden in their own right. Then Gus, frowning over Bolly as if he were a piece of cunning musical notation, took the old man's shoes off and slung them too over Hans Strahl's shoulder. Bolly's feet were hard and older than the bole of an oak and more calloused.

"Up, Bolly!" said Gus.

Bolly did not move. "I don't care," he said, "to go over the Gap like a goddam clown or a child."

"And we don't care for this added goddam burden," Usaph

told him. "So you'd best jest sit there till the first snows, Bolly."

"Oh Lord," said Bolly, speaking directly to the Deity, "how you humble the mighty. You gave your servant Bolly an eye more pointed than a hawk's, ears like a hound's, oh Lord, and a manhood like a stag at rutting, but kept in store this-here humiliation. Hauled up a mountain by boys and Dutchies! So be it."

He dragged himself upright and fell so hard against thin Gus that Gus was very near toppled. At last Gus managed to hitch the old man up on his back. "Don't be a goddam dead weight like that, Bolly," Hans Strahl told him.

Gus staggered away and was soon tottering. The path was hard enough even for the unburdened, and few boys had the breath to whistle them or call mocking questions. Gus would struggle along some few hundred paces, then Usaph would take the load, then Hans, and so they made their slow way. And regiment after regiment passed them by and considered them stragglers, which at this late and heady stage of the war hurt their feelings not a little.

Usaph noticed, on account of keeping his eyes low and away from the strangers who were passing, that there was a high number of boys walking barefoot. Some had their shoes tied round their necks and were saving them from this pass road, rather risking cut heels and stone bruises than wear out leather that mightn't be readily replaced. Others lacked any shoes at all and the feet were usually cut about, but their owners didn't seem to notice it.

Usaph Bumpass was therefore reminded of the state of his own shoes. The uppers of his right one were tearing away from the lowers on the outside, the stitching was exposed and soon would break, though it wasn't a matter for grief yet. There wasn't much cure for it either. You could hammer the upper on to a wooden sole that would last you a long time, except with a wooden sole you couldn't bend your feet, as a man walking some 25 miles in a day needed to. You could stuff wads of the *Richmond Enquirer* into the innards but that too crowded the shoe and hampered the foot.

These shoes of Usaph's were the ones he'd got off a North Carolina corpse at Gaines' Mill. They'd looked decent then, but they were wearing fast on these back roads.

He could just about feel the strain on the stitching of those dead man's shoes as he labored up Thoroughfare Gap with Bolly on his back. His brown throat was tense as cedar wood with that despairing burden he carried. It was getting dark, though a corner of the road here or there would catch a golden acre of light and make men think of tomorrow and its danger, yes, but most of all its promise. "Carryin' your own daddy?" they'd maybe call to Usaph or Hans or Gus, now that the crest was near, and whoever was carrying ole Bolly would feel the old soldier's clammy, shamed breath on his neck.

In the long twilight a battery of the Rockbridge Artillery came up behind them on the road. Six scrawny horses hauling each 12-pounder, and leather harness and wooden traces squeaking with the stress of it; and behind each wheel of the caisson and the limber and the gun itself, two men pushing. And a rider on each of the three left-hand horses, striking the flanks with crops and yelling like wagoneers.

On one of the chests on the caisson of Maskill's guns sat Orville Puckett wrappped in a blanket, cruel pain in his jaws from the fever he had, and all his bones aching with the jolting they were getting. He too suffered from a deathly pride and it was such that he wouldn't let his gun-crew see him riding uphill on the caisson of his own gun. So his friend Patrick Maskill had lifted him aboard the caisson of the battery's No. 2 Napoleon, Maskill's own.

Orville Puckett was too tired to protest about that. Pat Maskill thought Orville was likely dying.

Maskill now saw Usaph carrying Bolly, saw Usaph's legs jolt and stumble at the edge of the mountain road and, watching Bolly's shape, saw it was that of an old man.

"Gran'daddy," he called to Bolly. "*Gran'daddy!* What in the name of hokey is a boy your age doing here?"

Bolly muttered, in the loose undignified hunch which Usaph held him. "I marched, boy, from Romney to Harrison's Landing. But nowadays all the virtue's gone out of ole Bolly. . . ."

"My gun," said Patrick Maskill, "weighs half a ton as foundered, and then there's the weight of the caisson and the limber and I don't know if you add in the weight of the wheels or not. That's a question of physics and my bent ain't in that direction, being rather to the law. But what I think is that if we added the weight of one gran'daddy to the weight of this-here—I don't think it would make that much difference to the overall burden."

He ordered two of his gunners to lift Bolly up on the caisson by Orville Puckett's side. Orville saw the old man there but took no interest in him. Unlike Ash Judd, Orville hadn't had any promises concerning old men, and was wrapped up in the question of whether he himself was dying.

Ole Bolly, sitting up like a general, felt belittled. "I'll always be added weight now, Usaph," he told Bumpass.

"You'll be like a spring lamb on the downgrade, Bolly," Usaph promised.

But he didn't blame Bolly for his feelings; in fact he felt some sort of anger against Maskill himself. Sure the man had taken from him a bruising burden. But it was all right for these gentlemen of the artillery with their degrees in law and Latin and Greek to come up to you and say "ain't" and "this-here" like regular boys. Speaking like that to you only because they thought you were an unlettered country boy. Why didn't Gus speak up and show them something of the mental capacities of ordinary riflemen? But Gus never gave officers or college boys the benefit of his mind, standing by instead like an oaf.

So if Bolly hadn't weighed so much Usaph would have had a mind to carry him all the way to the top. You could see Bolly would've liked it better that way. While ever he was carried by friends, he felt he might get his strength back. To be carried by strangers meant he'd become some kind of official burden.

So Usaph and Hans Strahl and Gus all understood but didn't let on to Bolly they did. The muscles of their back and shoulders were paining too much.

— 25 —

ABOUT DUSK THAT day some hundred or so Confederate cavalrymen edged down to the forest on the rim of the village of Bristoe Station. They could see the railway depot just a hundred yards away across a meadow. There was no one there. No pickets, no railroad workers. Beyond the depot the little white town sat on a bit of a rise. The Railroad Hotel stood behind a picket fence just fifty paces or so from the railroad yard itself.

The captain commanding the cavalry put his left squadron to the task of sealing off the north end of Main Street and his right to sealing off the southern. He knew that some of General Henry Forno's Frenchies from Louisiana were coming down the Bristoe road to join him, but it went against the cavalry officer's temperament to wait for them—the noise of their goddam feet would likely give them away in any case.

Over beyond the railroad, in the front parlor of the Railroad Hotel, Captain Pinder of the 8th Connecticut sat drinking whiskey with two of his young officers. They were boys from western Connecticut, from the gentle towns round the foothills of the Berkshires. They were waiting for the innkeeper to come and tell them dinner was ready. Just before seven these three gentlemen heard a shot in Main Street and then a fury of rifle fire. Pinder and the two boys had never been in action before and it took them a struggle of the mind to believe that a test of fire had dropped in on them this summer evening, so far up the Orange and Alexandria Railroad, with dinner cooking.

Captain Pinder went into the hallway. He saw the host of the hotel trembling in the doorway of the dining room and then there were dozens of his own men pounding up the hotel front steps, crowding into the narrow passage.

"Stuart's boys!" they were yelling. "It's a goddam Stuart raid!" and like stuff.

He could tell they thought it was against the rules for cavalry to come down on them at supper-time, and goddam it, Captain Pinder agreed with them. "Front rooms!" he ordered them, and they crowded into the front parlor. Above the firing came the Rebel scream, getting close along the road, and it stung the skin behind their ears and at the backs of their necks.

They crushed up to the open window of the room where Pinder and the two boys had been drinking. The whiskey bottle sat on the table there still. They began firing through the window, a dozen boys firing at a time, a dozen loading up and milling behind them. Pinder thought that it was so crowded in here they'd start killing each other just by accident or through panic. "You others," he yelled into the hallway, "upstairs!"

But there was already a lean man on a lean horse clattering up the hotel's wooden steps onto the porch. There an eighteen-year-old Connecticut boy looked up at him as if he were a horseman from God, rake-lean and impermeable against the setting sun. And he sure looked like something you couldn't argue with. Pinder, some five paces behind the boy, saw the

horseman shoot the boy through the forehead and ride on up
to the front door, leaning in and shooting. Pinder blinked but
no bullet struck him. The din was hellish and Pinder began to
bite his hand. For he could see through the parlor door that
young men were being shot in the throat and the infernal Rebel
cavalry was shoulder to shoulder in front of the hotel, leaning
over their horses' manes and firing calmly and without animus
like boys at turkey shoots. In the hall there was a young man
either side of Pinder, keeping close because they trusted him;
he had once been a popular mayor of New Milford. Both of
them dropped and were groaning on the floor. These boys,
thought Pinder, have families in Litchfield County, Connecticut, and their folk are always going to inquire of me, what
did you do with our sons? With our boys from New Milford
and Danbury and Kent, from Sherman and Canaan and all
those towns with high-steepled churches and village greens?
Their families will never forgive me, Captain Pinder thought.

He found he had his white handkerchief in his hand and he
stepped over the dead and the damaged, waving it at the horseman. "Surrender," he was screaming, not as a demand but as
an offer. "Surrender!"

He sent one of his drinking friends upstairs to tell them
there that it was over, and now there was sudden still. He went
out onto the porch, and a young Confederate officer was waiting for him. "I suppose you're Stuart's boys?" Pinder said,
tears all over his face.

"We're Stuart's boys. But the whole goddam Stonewall
army is just up the Bristoe Road."

Pinder thought about this. It didn't sound to him like the
work of humans. "What kind of man is your Stonewall
Jackson?" he asked in the end. "Are his soldiers made of gutta-
percha or do they run on goddam wheels?"

The conversation didn't develop, for a train whistle sounded
to the south, and soon on a far bend a freight train could be
seen. The Federal garrison were locked up in the schoolhouse,
and already the Louisiana infantry had arrived at the railroad
depot, and had gone a little way south and started piling ties
on the rails to halt the engine, while others were trying to tear
the rails loose. But the train came barging down on them. They
could see *Train No. 6* painted above its cow-catcher. The
driver, a Union soldier likely, or else a Virginian with a Union
soldier standing over him, opened the throttle as the little depot

house of Bristoe Station showed itself. The ties on the track were scattered by the wheels of the engine and *Train No. 6* took in a high freight of bullets. Yet none of them made it pause, and soon its caboose was a small dot, carrying news North.

Now, anyhow, the Louisianans had time to lever out a stretch of track on an embankment just some 300 paces south of the depot. In the twilight a freight train and twenty empty wagons, having run a cargo shuttle to Pope's forces on the Rappahannock, came to the embankment at speed, not intending to stop at the station, and went plunging down the bank, and there were suddenly hundreds of butternut spectators about, waving their hats and yelling like the worst savages, as the engine and the cars lay on their side and the engine hissed. The engineers and their guards crawled out, holding bloody foreheads or cracked knees or elbows.

Then, at first dark, a second engine and further empties clattered up, returning to Alexandria for loading. This one flew off the embankment into the wreckage of the first. The Louisiana boys were chortling and cheering and looking at the wreckage as if it were a work of art.

A little later the last train of the evening came steaming along but paused on the bend before the embankment. By then there were bonfires and the sound of whiskey yells all round the wreckage of the two big trains, and this last engineer didn't have to be very canny to know that there was something uncustomary going on in Bristoe Station. He backed off at some thirty miles an hour.

So the word of the capture of Bristoe went north towards Manassas and south towards Warrenton, but General Forno didn't much worry about that. He thought it would be misread, and events would prove him right. When the reports got to Pope about the firing on *Engine No. 6* and the withdrawal of the last engine of the night, he wrote it off to another nuisance raid by Stuart, and Secretary of War Stanton in Washington took the same view.

What they neither knew nor would have believed was that Tom Jackson was just six miles up the Bristoe Road, sleeping in a farmhouse, in a cane-bottomed chair, waiting for boys like Bumpass and Ramseur to catch him up on the downhill grade from Thoroughfare Gap. That the authority of Tom Jackson was there, two days after leaving the Rappahannock, at the end of 54 miles of marching, and thirteen miles behind Pope's headquarters, and straddling his railroad link!

Dark had barely fallen, yet at that headquarters of Jackson's everyone but the sentries was studiously sleeping. Sandie Pendleton's long shape was stretched on a blanket in the hall of the farmhouse and a young cavalry officer called Blackford lay parallel to him. Kyd dozed in a swinging seat on the porch. His bones were tired but his brain was racing with the possibilities of what they had done these past few days. So his snooze was full of images—he was for example addressing Lincoln's cabinet. His speech was very reasonable and they said such things as, "Well, when you put it like that, Captain Douglas, your stance seems entirely reasonable. . . ."

At 9:30 a cavalry officer woke him from dreams of reconciliation and Washington. After he had listened to the man, Kyd wandered into the hall, tripped over Sandie's ankles and woke him as well. "Sandie," Kyd Douglas whispered, "that General Holmes didn't put a picket at Manassas crossroads. The two following brigades took the wrong turn. They're headed off north."

"Then send a rider after them," Sandie told him, pretty peevishly.

"A rider's been sent but . . ." He nodded to the shape in the cane chair up the hall. ". . . he said to tell him about any units lost or misdirected."

Sandie grunted and went up the hall and touched Stonewall's shoulder. The General woke with the gentle suddenness of a lizard.

"Sir, General Holmes in Hill's division failed to post a picket at Manassas crossroads as ordered. Two following brigades took the wrong turn and are headed off north."

Stonewall said, like a judge passing sentence, "Send the cavalry after them."

"It's been done, sir."

"And put Holmes under arrest and prefer charges."

"As you say, sir."

Then, seemingly hugging his authority to himself, Tom Jackson went back to sleep.

The authority of Tom Jackson, in innocence of which Pope slept the night in a hotel in Warrenton! Johnny Pope, military engineer by trade, lying on his side, his face pointed to the perfidious South. Before sleeping though he ordered General

Heintzelman to send a regiment up to Bristoe Station and look
at the problem. He thought it was only a regiment-sized problem.

— 26 —

WAY BACK ON the Rappahannock that evening, the Honorable
Horace Searcy sat on the porch of a house just a mile or so
up the road from farmer Tilley's place. He was watching what
went on beyond the gate—which was that lean battalions were
going past on the dirt road in their wide-awake hats. It was
Daniel Hill's division of Longstreet's wing of the army and
it was already drawing away from the river, quietly, without
singing or bands or any yelling. It had left its fires burning.

You could be sure that their drift off to the west was unknown to the army of the Northern Republic, who had spent
a drowsy afternoon over there, stretched out round Sulphur
Springs and eastwards towards the railway.

Watching this quiet movement of whole brigades with
Searcy was his host, a small, plump farmer of about fifty years,
not at all like the angular men who were streaming past his
gate. He leaned against a porch upright. "By hokey, they're
heading away, clear out of it. I guess I'll have goddam Yankee
cavalry at my front door by this time tomorrow evening."

"I don't know about that, sir," Searcy told him reflectively.
"I think you might perhaps go unmolested for a while."

"Unmolested? I would goddam hope so."

Searcy could guess what was happening though he hadn't
been told. He had learned much general military science in the
Crimea and elsewhere and could tell a flank march made in
some secrecy when he saw one. He argued with himself
whether tonight he would ride down towards one of the fords
in the Waterloo direction. If he could get across the river he
should meet up with the U.S. cavalry vedettes at the western
end of Pope's army and give the warning that Lee was making
fools of them.

Even if he could flit across the river tonight, he had small chance of flitting back again, so that he could never expect accreditation to work in the South again. And in that case would not see Mrs. Whipple until the war ended. Unlike Usaph Bumpass, Kyd Douglas, Tom Jackson and others, Horace Searcy did not expect the war to end by the autumn of 1862. He was not sure that it would be finished by Christmas of 1864. He did not want to wait two or more years for his next sight of plain but superb Dora Whipple.

He had little doubt that to inform Pope, a mediocre general, of the great flank march that was under way against him was worth sacrificing any journalistic privilege for. The question was whether he was willing to give up Mrs. Whipple for the same chancy reason.

It wouldn't be an easy crossing if he tried it. You could be sure there was a strong Confederate picket line down on the river to shield this march which was going on. He would have to creep through that if he could. If he were a better swimmer he would travel on foot, but then he needed a horse in case he had to cross quickly, in a deep place with currents, and in case he was chased by cavalry.

He reflected how if any of these officers passing the gate knew his true opinion and the work he did for Secretary Stanton, they would certainly come up there on the porch, make a grand Southern speech, and shoot him in the head.

They would tell him before putting the bullet in him that he typified Britain in its hypocrisy, that Britain could never have abolished slavery if slavery had been internal to Britain. But slavery had always been *external* to it—had existed in the British colonies, in Africa, in Jamaica. It was easy to destroy and abolish something that was distant from you. What did it matter to Westminster if the economy of Jamaica was destroyed? Well, sah (they would say before shooting him), the economy of the South is not about to be destroyed to suit the hypocritic feelings of London or Washington. The Southern form of slavery, sah, is the best condition to which an African nigger could hope to aspire, sah! Bang, sah!

Searcy supposed that in Southern terms he deserved a bullet, for he had never felt as strong against anything since child labor as he did against the civilization of the South.

When he first went South in the spring of '61, before the first shot had been fired by South Carolina against the Federal fortress called Sumter, he'd had a vague feeling against slavery but was willing to look on it as he felt an outsider should, as

more the business of the Americans than any business for him.
He started to get passionate about it with his first sighting of
negro field slaves in the coastal lowlands of North Carolina.
Their ragged shoeless condition made the house slaves in their
mock-Georgian wigs and pantaloons seem even more like some
sort of ridiculous human poodles.

Then, on the train from Savannah to Macon, Georgia, he'd
had that conversation with the Reverend Mr. Elliott, the Bishop
of Georgia. Elliott was a big handsome cleric who sat down
in the saloon bar with Horace Searcy and set out to prove to
him that the Bible and the Constitution of the United States
both sanctioned slavery. As the man talked, and Searcy looked
at his large open face, it began to appear to the English aristocrat that this urbane and eloquent bishop ought to be fought,
that his place in history was beside the witch-hunters of the
last century, and with the priests who worked for the Inquisition
three hundred years ago, and who could prove from the Bible
that God *wanted* people racked and tortured.

The bishop and others argued with him all the way down
the line. At every railroad depot where they stretched their
legs, on every boat landing that spring, were advertisements
offering rewards for the recapture of this or that runaway negro,
with a description of the man, the whip and brand marks, the
scars that came from Massa's blows, the cuts that came from
Massa's malicious riding crop. But still it was all God's will,
according to Bishop Elliott.

In every big town you could see the great slave yards with
the massive hoardings outside them.

W. C. Mentor—Money advanced on slaves.
Constant supplies of
Virginia negroes
On sale or hire

And behind the sign, a high-walled depot in the middle of
the nice white houses of Raleigh or Wilmington, Macon or
Savannah, and behind the walls the slave pens where black
humans were kept for inspection.

Then Montgomery, Alabama. When Searcy went there that
spring it was the Confederacy's first capital. On the eve of his
meeting with Judah Benjamin and Jeff Davis and Mr. Treasurer
Memminger in the Confederate capitol, a mock-Greek pile on
one of Montgomery's few low hills, Searcy sat on the hotel

porch amongst gentlemen spurting tobacco juice from their mouths with immense accuracy (but missing the spittoons anyhow very often), and from there watched the sale of a young black man.

The salesman stood on the steps by a fountain in a square outside the hotel. In the midst of the plumes of water stood an Athenian statue of a lady, for these Southerners were big on Greek architecture; maybe they thought it went some way towards proving they were cultured gentlemen. On a crate set in front of this stone woman, from whose feet the jets of water burst, stood a wiry young negro in good muscle. Surprising that the sale of a fit young man could be, more than the image of sad-eyed black women and pot-bellied, "bare-assed" children, the thing that made Searcy feel he must *do something*. It may well have been the way the negro boy carried his little cloth bundle in his hands. What mementos were therein no one could guess, but he looked exactly as if there was no place on earth he could call home.

In the square itself that afternoon, given the heat, the only spectators were a few Irish laborers in a wagon, some volunteers in gray homespun, and about half a dozen gentlemen in black coats, satin waistcoats and black hats, who were genuine buyers. The gentlemen on the verandah, chewing and spitting and sipping cocktails, might become interested if the bidding proved low.

"A prime field-hand," the auctioneer yelled. He was an Irishman and as whimsical as his race. "Why, can't you tell jest by looking at him what a good-natured boy he is. There now..." He took hold of the slave's jaw and turned the black head profile-on to the audience. "...there's docility in that eye of his'n. No scars on him to speak of—you can verify that—except the few littl'uns that come from the normal conversations atween mastah and slave."

There was a lazy guffaw from the verandah.

"This here fella ain't got any problems—nary a taste for licker and no conjugal ties, by which I mean he has no wife, no place to distract his mind from the fitting attachment to a new mastah. Enine hunthred and fiferty! Ah, gentlemen, is your attachment to the divinely-ordained institution of slavery of such a pale nature that you can't do better in the presence of a prime boy such as this than enine hunthred and fiferty. Are we to write to Abe Lincoln and say Mr. Lincoln, you're right about us, take our heartland, for our attachment to our birthright tends to peter out at enine hunthred and fiferty dollars."

There were the sort of amused catcalls you'd expect from the crowd, both on the verandah and in the square.

"That's good, thank you, sir. We have enine hunthred and eseventy-fife and we can, as God pertects us, expect more. We have enine hunthred and... and we have ah-one athousand. We have ah-one thousand. Oh, gentlemen, oh, gentlemen! No more? I have instructions concerning the reserve price on this fine specimen whose owner is selling him merely to employ the sale price in setting up a company of Emerald Guards to fight against the Northern tyranny. Any advance... Reserve is ah-one thousand. Ah-one ethousand is accepted, sir. Would you kindly join the nigger and meself, sir, at the notary's, where the exchange will be formalized. I thank you gentlemen one and all for your attention."

"That nigger went cheap," said a slow-chewing Alabaman voice on the hotel porch.

"Yessir. Niggers is going cheap these days. Why, a man could well speculate in 'em at a time like this, but I for one don't think I will."

What Searcy witnessed a week later on the steamer *Southern Republic*, traveling down the steep-banked River Alabama from Montgomery to the Mississippi, made the passionate exception he took to slavery even stronger. The captain of the steamer was another Irishman called Meagher, the ship a topheavy floating wooden fortress of saloons and smoking rooms and cabins. At godforsaken landings along the way, the steam whistle screamed and the calliope atop the steamer played "Dixie." The framework of the *Southern Republic* was of such raw and resinous pine that turpentine oozed out from the joints; and a visit to the engine room, where blacks naked to the clout thrust pine beams into the mouths of the boilers, convinced you the whole light, over-driven structure would explode any second. In contrast, life on the upper decks was pretty gracious by Southern standards. The whole ship, from engine room to calliope, seemed to Searcy like a great floating symbol of the South itself.

At the captain's table in the dining room, while the calliopes screamed and the *Southern Republic* moved through crowds of mosquitoes and populations of alligators, Southern gentlemen started to speak of the captain's success running slaves to Mobile a few years back. Captain Meagher had taken a ship to the west coast of Africa, loaded up with Ashantis and returned to Mobile. The collector of duty on slaves imported into Mobile heard about the ship, but somehow the sheriff couldn't be found anywhere in the town and the U.S. Marshall was missing, both of them of course well paid by the captain's partners to vanish for a few days. Meagher trans-shipped all the negroes to a river steamer called *The Czar* that night, and by the time the collector got out to inspect the slave cargo there was no cargo at all.

But it wasn't only the collector he duped, it was his partners too. When they asked for their cut of the slaves he smiled sweetly and said he didn't understand them. To show his good faith though he gave them a couple of old niggers each. They were beaten, those partners—there was no one they could complain to, for running niggers illegally was subject to capital punishment. And so suddenly Meagher had had slaves and land and wealth, and he built a fleet of steamers of which *Southern Republic* was the newest and proudest.

Searcy watched the way Meagher listened to the others tell this story about him, watched the broad leer on the man's face. "Well now," he said, winking and nudging, "so you think these niggers I got aboard here come from Africa? I'll show you."

He called to a fine jet-skinned boy of maybe sixteen years. "Jest come here, Bully."

The boy came over. He was near-naked, his cheeks were marked with a tribal pattern of scars and his chest also had tattoos.

"What's your name, boy?"

"Mah name Bully, sah!"

"Where you born?"

"Me born Sout' Karliner, sah!" "There, you see he weren't taken out of Africa. Bully, I got a power of the South Car'lina niggers aboard, ain't that so?"

"Yessah!"

"You happy, Bully?"

"Yessah."

"Show these gen'lmen here how you're happy."

The boy grinned maniacally and started to rub his belly. "Yummy, yummy, plenty bellyful, sah!"

"That's what I calls a really philosophical chap. Now, Mr. Searcy, I wager you got a lot of people in your own country cain't pat their bellies an' say what Bully here jest said."

Everyone laughed except Searcy. It wasn't that he couldn't

disapprove of his own country. It was the boy, Bully, who
interested him. "Did he get those tribal marks in South Carolina?" Searcy asked the captain.

"Why yes, he did," said the captain, winking. "It's the way
them nigger women have of marking their offspring to recognize 'em. Ain't that so, Bully?"

There was laughter, laughter and the spitting of tobacco
juice.

"Mind you," the captain went on, all mock serious. "We're
obliged now and then to let some niggers in to keep up the
balance 'gainst the niggers you run into Canada."

Well, they could laugh. Tonight, the night Dan Hill's division edged west, they might be about to pay for their laughter.
Not their laughter against the Honorable Horace Searcy, who
was willing to believe he might seem a little ridiculous to
Americans. But for their laughter against the black race and
all the blows that were innate in that laughter.

After supper, feeling wistful about Mrs. Whipple, Searcy
loaded his two Derringers and put one in his breast pocket and
one in the side pocket of his jacket. In the dark they made no
difference to the contours of his clothing. He had the farmer's
boy saddle his horse. Dan Hill's division had passed on up the
road towards Amissville. Soon General David Rumple Jones's
boys would take to it, slipping away from Pope's front in the
dark. There was no sign of it yet though.

Traveling across country, Searcy kept off small roads and
lanes and rode over low hills towards the river, veering west
all the time, keeping to tiny foot tracks amongst the undergrowth. He could see fireflies burning in the lower branches
of trees like festive lights, and the air was cool. Virginia was
a fair land, he thought, and he was about to lose it and the
treasure it held—Mrs. Whipple. But no one stopped him.

The paths he took led him down to the flat by the river.
Here it was still quaggy from the recent rain and all the sound
was of chirping insects and the muddy noise of his horse's
hooves in the mushy earth. He thought he must be beyond the
picket screen now. You've got round it, Searcy, he told himself. There is now only the acceptable risk of being drowned
in crossing the river or shot by Union pickets on the far side.
But as he was thinking about this, three horsemen stepped their
horses from the woods to his left. One of them called, "Stand,
friend!"

For a second he wondered if he could outride them, but it was too high a risk. Confederate countrymen were self-taught, yet no trained equestrian such as he was could be sure of outracing them in this manner of country. Maybe if he could stand on his dignity with them they could let him go on or at least send him home. Then perhaps he could attempt it again later in the night.

"What do you want?" he asked, as if they were interrupting what was for him just a pleasant night's ride.

They drew nearer to him. Ragged Rebel cavalry. Most of what they had was taken from the U.S.—their cavalry boots, their harness, their britches, their shirts, and the Spencer repeating rifles two of them had levelled at him. One of them had a bandana tied jauntily round his neck and a lieutenant's bars on his shoulders.

"You British?" the lieutenant asked. His own accent sounded Texan and very likely was.

"I am the Honorable Horace Searcy, correspondent of *The Times* of London. I have accreditation from General Longstreet." He took out of his breast pocket the letter which had been nestling by the Derringer. It said who he was and that the Confederate officer should extend every courtesy and co-operation to him within reasonable bounds.

The lieutenant held this up to the moon and read it with one eye shut. "Fetch the cap'n," he told one of the others. Then, to Searcy, "And where are you going, sir?"

"I was merely riding for my health," said Searcy. "Of course there is always the chance I'd meet up with Confederate pickets and engage them in conversation. You must understand, lieutenant, that the Confederate cavalryman is a picturesque and romantic figure to the average city-bound Englishman."

"Well, I'll be switched," said the Texan drily. "And here I was thinking I was jest average myself."

The third horseman rode back now with an officer in a big hat. "Mr. Searcy," said this officer in a voice which was a little Norfolk and a little East London, a sort of English yeoman voice.

Searcy decided to sound warm and see how far the claims of a common race would get him with this captain.

"That's right, sir. Do I have the honor of speaking to another Englishman?"

The officer laughed at this. "Well, when these boys are

around me I'm bound to call meself a Texican. But I am English, yes, by birthright." He took his hat off. "Sir, I often saw you in the Crimea."

"Oh?" said Searcy, all warmth. "What regiment?"

"I was a sergeant in the 11th Hussars."

Searcy blinked. The 11th Hussars were the Light Brigade that crazy Lord Cardigan had ordered up the avenue of death at Balaclava. They had been told to attack the Russian artillery that was withdrawing from Voronzdof Heights, but the order got mixed and Cardigan sent them fair down the valley at the center of the Russian line. Searcy had watched it all from a ridge just above the hill where the Light Brigade formed up. Despite Lord Alfred Tennyson's silly poem about the event, it was the worst thing Searcy had ever seen in any war other than this one.

"You lived?" was all Searcy, genuinely reverent, could say for the moment.

"Roundshot killed my horse, and I was just trying to get away on foot when some Russian infantry ran out from their redoubt and took me prisoner. I was eleven months a prisoner of the Russians, but it wasn't bad at all there in Odessa, though I got the black fever once . . ."

"And you emigrated to America?"

The three horsemen seemed bored—they'd probably heard their captain's story often enough before.

"The old world seemed a mite dangerous to me, Mr. Searcy. As it is, I own an emporium in Houston now; my wife runs it for me. She's a Texican, sir. They're a different breed of women."

Searcy laughed indulgently. He couldn't think of anything much worse than marrying a Texas woman, but then the man's opportunities in England had probably been a little narrow. Searcy said, "I wonder if I could have a word with you in private, sergeant . . . I mean, captain?"

"D'you mind, boys?" the captain said to his horsemen. *D'you mind boys?* They never spoke like that in the 11th Hussars. Searcy however was halfway willing to admit that that might well have been the 11th Hussars' tragedy.

Anyhow the others rode back into the woods and hid themselves again.

"I wanted to know, captain," Searcy muttered, "if you intend to restrict my movements tonight. I have all manner of private interviews to make this side of the river and I would appreciate being allowed to proceed with them."

"I could give you a section of cavalry, Mr. Searcy sir, to go with you."

"Well, a section of cavalry would tend to detract from the privacy of the arrangement, don't you think?"

"Mr. Searcy, I know I can't permit you, sir, to go about this area without supervision."

"Are you implying something, sir?"

"Of course not." The captain thought awhile. When he spoke he was tentative, because the old English class difference was working on him when he spoke to his troopers.

"Mr. Searcy, I know what I have been ordered to do. In the first place, this is a dangerous area for a man of your reputation, sir. Picket fire is likely to break out at any time . . ."

"Allow me to take care of my own safety, captain. Look here now. You've seen me in the Crimea, as you say. You know I am an English gentleman."

"Indeed, Mr. Searcy."

"If I gave you my word as an English gentleman that my purposes are quite licit this evening, and involve no danger to my Confederate hosts—would that suffice?"

The captain got more thoughtful. "It would suffice no better than the word of any other man," he said in the end.

Searcy turned his face away. "I consider your suggestion an insult."

The cavalry captain thought about this. "I think you'd better go home to bed, sir. I saw an English shipping agent hanged in New Orleans last year as a Union spy. You and I, sir, know these things can happen almost by accident . . ."

"If I don't, sergeant," said Searcy, making no bones about how himself being younger son to a baronet and the captain what Searcy's mother called "an upjumped commoner," "what would you do?"

The captain had taken a pistol out and had it pointed. "Well, there is always arrest, and if I arrested you then your movements would be cramped worse than if you just went back now."

Searcy didn't know whether to be grateful to him or not. If I can't get through the lines, he thought, then I have no reason not to go down to Gordonsville and lay siege to Mrs. Whipple. The only thing was: laying siege, even to a woman like Mrs. Whipple, wouldn't change the history of modern times. Getting over the river might.

"This is ridiculous," Searcy snarled, but turned his horse's head back towards the farmhouse where he was lodging. He could hear the captain breathe out. He didn't have to tax his brain any more on what to do with a renowned London scribe.

The scribe seemed pretty piqued anyhow and had now reined his horse in again, this time (the captain felt sure) to get a parting insult off his chest.

"Tell me this," said Searcy. "What are you doing with this rabble? After what you've been used to in the Hussars?"

"Well, sir," said the captain, letting a little Texas into his voice. "The boys are a mite rough, I admit that, and they're no use at all for parade ground stuff. But for rough and in-dependent work they're adequate."

"But the cause, captain, the cause. What do you think of it?"

"Texas gave me a home. It made me a rich man beyond my dreams. It gave me the rank of an officer. I figure you owe something to a place like that."

Searcy rode round in the dark a little longer, hoping on the long chance that some Union cavalry might raid across the Rappahannock and take him prisoner. By one a.m. it hadn't happened, so the Hon. Horace Searcy took a long draw from his flask of whiskey and went home to bed.

— 27 —

EARLY ON THE morning of August 27, Colonel Wheat led the Shenandoah Volunteers into a field within sight of the depot yards at Manassas. They were now, what with straggling and illnesses, some 247 men in strength. Bolly was still part of this strength, however, and so were Hans Strahl and Usaph Bum-pass and Gus Ramseur. And so was Decatur Cate, conscript, two-minded but strong still in the legs.

As they all eased their muskets and blankets off their shoul-ders and found a place that had shade or was in a fence corner, Colonel Wheat rode in amongst them and made the sort of speech they were used to from him.

"They tell me, boys," he yelled, "that in the depot yards here are two-mile-long trains of goddam provender. Perhaps those of you with sharper eyes can jest about see them from this-here spot."

In fact, just down the road, the depot yard and the long lines of freight cars could be seen even by the short-sighted. Wheat could certainly see them too. And beyond the freight cars there were large storehouses, and between them there were sutler's booths.

The colonel said, "Then, by popular report, there's goddam warehouses stocked through the provision of a foul Washington government and a glorious providence. I think it would appear even to the diminished intellect of a goddam colonel that if everyone was let go into the depot to choose goods at will there would be riot and impropriety. I think likewise that it might appear even to the same stamp of intellect that to forbid *everyone* to visit the depot yard would in the same manner stir up riot. In that case if I were in a colonel's situation who had his regiment within a goddam spit of a plush depot, I would suggest that each company send off some ten men, no more than that, foraging amongst the plenty that's fallen to our lot, while others rested and got their fires going in the event of a famous feast taking place. Of course, I ain't by any means in this imaginary colonel's situation. I mean to say there may be a depot round here for all I can tell, but I regret to say I got grits in my eyes coming down the pass yesterday and my vision is impaired. . . ."

Well, the selection was pretty informal and Bolly seemed to want to go, to see the horn of plenty there at the railroad yard. So for sentimental reasons he was sent, as were Gus and Usaph to mind him, along with Hans Strahl, Danny Blalock, Ashabel Judd and some others.

Two infantry regiments and the cavalry had captured the place the night before, taking eight pieces of artillery and 300 prisoners. As Usaph and the others got down the road towards the depot, they could see some of these prisoners across the yards, in the front of a warehouse, rolling and kneading dough, stoking field stoves, splitting fuel. Telfer was using them to make flourbread for the army that would come here today. And an army it would be, for Ambrose Hill's boys were coming on behind the Stonewall, and Ewells's were on their way up from Bristoe. But when Gus and Usaph and the others stepped into that great quadrangle of store buildings, with the railroad

from Alexandria coming into it from its northern end, and the
shanties and tents of Yankee sutlers, who were either prisoners
or fled, leaving all their delicacies fit for confiscation, they felt
like children who'd got to a carnival before the crowd.

In spite of any sentries, boys from other brigades of the
Stonewall Division were already breaking locks on box cars
(if there were locks) and sliding doors back, and sentries
seemed to be easily distracted in an opposite direction, or
detained on the far side of a line of wagons. The first open
wagon Usaph saw, there were boys in it handing down barrels
to others on the tracks, and when the barrels were open, you
saw cakes and pies in there done up in layers of greaseproof
paper—Usaph had never seen anything like that, barrels of
greaseproof pies as if they came from factories the way cannon
did. It just showed you what matter of society they had up
there in the North.

Someone from Guess's Company put his hands up, took
one of those barrels on his shoulder and disappeared towards
the encampment with it. From a car some fifty paces further
on, bags were being slung down which when you opened them
were full of hams in cheesecloths. Boys began tipping hams
all over the yard just to see more ham than would be got
together in a month of Christmases.

Bolly Quintard laughed and hooted and yelled like his old
self. "We ought open a wagon of our own, boys, that's what
we ought!" he called.

That was done quick by pulling a bar on the car door. Ash
Judd got inside and pushed a hogshead out and Danny Blalock
cut into the lid with his knife.

"Tell us," said Bolly, "tell us what it is?"

Danny cupped his fingers into a brown gritty stuff that lay
inside and tasted what they picked up. "By dang, Bolly, if it
isn't coffee and sugar all mixed ready for brewing."

"Holy spook!" yodelled Bolly. "Them goddam people of
Mammon in the North, they'd put women in a barrel ready
mixed with goddam Spanish fly to make 'em saucy. Well!
Holy Delilah!"

They had an argument who'd take this barrel of sweet mix
back to the encampment, but at last Hans Strahl said he would,
but he'd be back within a minute and a second, so not to find
anything too delicious in his absence.

They found bags of beans and potatoes and desiccated veg-
etables and syrup, and everyone made a trip back with some-

thing, except Bolly. When Usaph got back to the depot after taking potatoes to camp, his colleagues were standing about watching some Irishmen from the 5th Virginia talking to sentries in front of a sutler's shop.

"That's where the genuine articles are," said Danny Blalock. "That's where they have the marmalade and the wine and the lobster paste."

All over the yard and in the same minute, now that men seemed to be fixed for basics, they were crowding up sentries in front of the sutler's stores. Ash Judd put his arm around a young sentry outside a store marked *C. Semmler Army Sutler No Credit.*

"Where are you from?" he asked the sentry.

"I'm from North Carolina."

"And you're a fine boy, your maw must be proud of you."

"No use sweet talking me, you Stonewall boys. What's in this-here store jest ain't our property."

"And who's this C. Semmler then? Friend of yours?"

"You know he ain't no friend of mine."

"Oh I thought you were so partic'lar about poor ole C. Semmler's goods that he must have been kin of yours from the shores of the Carolinas. I thought he must have been a Tarheel after your own stamp."

"Goddamit, you know he ain't kin of mine, you know he's some Yankee Dutchy who skedaddled last night too fast to fetch his goods along with him. Listen, you boys, you keep away from that latch. Goddamit, leave that shutter alone now!"

Usaph flung his arms around the sentry from behind. "You can tell your officer you was overpowered, son."

Now the shutters were down, and everyone could see the cans and the jars on C. Semmler's shelves, jugged and canned and jarred sweet and good things, the tongue, the lobster, the nuts and candy, the pickles and catsup, the mustards, sardines and cigars, and the barrels of oranges and the soap, and those toothbrushes that only tidewater richies used. Usaph and the others climbed over the counter. They knew they'd earned all this, that no Tarheel sentry or even no officer was about to shoot them for taking this. Usaph put candy and sardines in his pocket, then three oranges. Even the act of looting made his mouth drip like a hound's—he wasn't proud to be so hungry for good things but there he was, with dribble down his chin.

Under the counter he found a bottle of white wine with Dutchy writing on it and a picture of a castle. He escaped with

it. Already, in the depot yard, there was a crowd three times
as thick as when he'd first come in. Over by one of those
switches railroaders threw to shunt trains about, a few of the
foragers of Guess's Company—Ashabel, Blalock, ole Bolly,
Hans—were sitting down to picnic on what they'd found.
Usaph joined them, then Gus with a modest jar of marmalade
and a packet of crackers, his good manners still in operation,
even when he was looting.

Hans Strahl had two of those Dutchy bottles of something
called Rhine Riesling and was passing them about and rec-
ommending them. "Call it licker?" roared Bolly after a mouthful. "Why this is nothing better than bottled baby's piss."

Though *he* didn't like it much, Usaph did, and found that
by the time the bottle had gone round some four or five sips
a piece, there was a summery glow in his chest. And he looked
at the crowds climbing into wagons and running about with
both barrels on their backs and breaking into the stock of those
iniquitous Yankee sutlers. "Why this," he said, "must be the
biggest goddam harvest party the world has ever seen. And I
would like to raise my glass to my friend Hans there, whose
kinfolk is responsible for putting this slow white nectar in
these-here bottles."

Strahl nodded.

"It's some feast for them cavalry, anyhow," said Ash Judd,
pointing to troopers loading up their horses with hams and bags
of coffee. And cannoneers were using *their* horses to roll caissons into the yard and were burdening up their caisson chests
with anything that would fit therein or atop.

Danny Blalock joined in Usaph's song of praise after taking
a long draught of wine. "Yes, this is the biggest bazaar in all
the east of the continent. And here it is in the hands and up
to the mouths of the dirtiest, roughest, most hell-fired and all-
eating boys that were ever born in a valley or dropped on a
mountainside."

"Amen!" yelled Ash Judd.

"But I jest hope," said Gus, "someone is minding we don't
get the wrong guests."

"Damn you, Gus!" Ash said. "You miserable goddam
Dutchy." For they knew there wasn't so much cruelty in the
world that starving boys could be set on in the midst of a
picnic. Sure, somewhere on the other side of town there were
explosions now, but of a kind a sane man couldn't work up
a lather about.

• • •

They wondered where Bolly was but then they heard him calling. "Quick, all you goddam slackroots! Quick now!"

At first they couldn't see where he was but then Usaph spotted his hoary ole face staring at them from behind a barred window of a nearby boxcar.

They didn't want to leave their party. "Later on, Bolly." Usaph called.

"No now! Before them other ruffians gets on to it."

"You got something precious there, Bolly?"

"You jest come and see."

They got up, carrying wine in one hand and food in the other, and Bolly, in the middle of all that great riot going on in the railyard, opened the slide door in a secret way and let them in. They stood in a strange interior. There was a great plush upholstered table right in the midst of the carriage. A good part of the roof was all glass and let the light of day straight down on this table. There were cabinets and hampers and chests and swing-out gas lights on all the walls.

Ash Judd said, "Why, is this a cat house for goddam generals!"

"No," said Gus. "This is a field surgery that runs on rails."

Usaph, just pleasantly tipsy, whistled a long blast. "Why you can't beat these goddam Yankees. They're so goddam cunning they'd put the gospel on wheels if you let 'em."

Bolly found his way through into a sort of back room of the boxcar. There was a cabinet in there that he'd broken open and from it he'd taken with one hand a bottle of whiskey and with the other a bottle of Napoleon brandy.

"And there's more," he was chanting. "And there's more."

That was Bolly, never one to keep a good thing to himself. Ashabel Judd had the story that Bolly sometimes lent wives to travelers who took his liking. Maybe it was true.

Bolly was already drinking anyhow, first a gulp from the Baltimore whiskey, then a gulp from the French brandy, and the others stormed into this little annex and found two dozen whiskey there and at least eighteen brandy, for whiskey and brandy were the great specifics of surgeons. Why, they would give it to you for fever or if they meant to cut off your leg, and they used it even if they wanted to clean your wounds. And some of them drank it in quantity too.

That's when the party got wild. Somehow the glass of the cabinets was broken and there were foul songs foully sung and everyone felt wonderful. Gus got sick in a corner and lay there, and as for Bolly, flattened out by the distillations of Maryland and France, he lay back like a corpse on the plush table, gave a querulous grunt in a high-pitched and nearly complaining voice, and wasn't heard from any more. Usaph himself felt fine enough but very hot; he thought he might float round the roof like a balloon. He was still puzzling out this feeling when two surgeons broke in. He recognized one of them straight off as Abel Oursley, the regimental surgeon. Usaph went up and slung an arm round the surgeon. "Is bad luck," he said, like a friend. "We got on to all the goddam hootch afore you could."

Oursley pushed the boy's arm away. God, he thought, they all know I'm a goddam tippler. Well, damn 'em. He knew what he was here for, he was looking for morphine and chloroform. Because a Yankee brigadier called Taylor had been brought to him with but half a chest left, and everyone seemed to think special efforts should be made for this poor bastard Taylor. Jackson seemed to have taken a shine to the poor son of a bitch at a range of half a mile.

Oursley's colleague was already in the annex. "There's good and plenty here, Abel," he was calling.

Oursley looked around at all these drunken boys. "All get out!" he yelled.

Gus went first; he was happy to go, to be under an open sky and have the breeze on his brow.

"All go, do you hear, you goddam drunken whoresons!"

Surgeon Oursley looked like he might hit them with something if they didn't move. So they began to depart, in their slow, swimmy way. Maybe there was an intuition in their muddied brains that they might need his goodwill one day soon.

Only Bolly hadn't moved. The surgeon went and stood over him. Goddamit, there'd be trouble if he touched Bolly!

He was staring at Bolly and *touching* him. "Goddamit!" What age is this man?" Oursley asked.

Danny Blalock answered. "They think he might be all of seventy."

Oursley put his hand on one of Bolly's eyelids. He wasn't angry now, there was a tenderness in the way he did it. "The poor son of a bitch is dead," he said.

BOOK THREE

WHEN THE TIME CAME, Usaph walked away from the Junction with a headache but full of a strange happiness and with confidence in the events and generals that now carried him along. It was a cool evening march, back in a westerly direction. As you went uphill and looked over your shoulder or even upwards at the top of the evening sky, you could see that Stonewall's engineers had set fire to the whole goddam depot. The glow of burning Manassas came from the south-east with a glare that killed off the early stars. Down there everything was burning. The cars burning down to their wheels and axles, the warehouses going up, the sutlers' stores. And Bolly burning up like one of them Viking chiefs, burning up on that Made-in-Boston table under a nice sheet. And the engineers ripping up the rails, you could be sure, and heating them on fires and then bending them round posts. And the goddam radiance of it all hanging in the firmament like the afterglow of that great banquet they had all had down there.

"I think," said Gus, still sentimental from his wild encounter with liquor and in his faintly foreign accent, so that the *think* was *zink*, "that Bolly might jest have died the way he would've chose."

And all around, the other boys began to say pious things about ole Bolly. "He died feasting at will behind this enemy's back. And that ain't so bad." "Death," said Danny Blalock, "came up to him in the guise of a whisky sleep."

"And on a soft surface," said Ash Judd, "and he ain't had much acquaintance with soft surfaces this year past."

None of them were sure why they were moving back westwards again, but no one seemed to resent the movement. They felt it was just part of dancin' Tom Jackson's mysterious plan, and since that plan had netted them the Manassas feast they did not much complain. There was a rumor they were moving back to Thoroughfare Gap to meet Longstreet's boys.

"If it's so, Gus," Usaph muttered, "at least we won't have to carry poor ole Bolly up the pass."

Far down the railroad line, General Johnny Pope had woken up to the idea that it was the whole of Jackson's corps at Manassas. He had been helped in his perceptions by the fact that, when his army woke that morning along the banks of the Rappahannock and squinted through their binoculars, they found no one except a few taunting Rebel cavalry regiments looking at them from the other bank. Longstreet had flitted. Not even Johnny Pope could ignore that piece of intelligence.

The first order he gave was to three of his corps, the German one of Franz Sigel's, McDowell's three willing divisions, and Reynolds's Pennsylvania boys, to get to the town of Gainesville. If they managed that march in two days, they would then be standing fair between Jackson in the area of Manassas, and Lee and Longstreet coming in from the west.

Johnny Pope sent four generals, Reno and Phil Kearny and Porter and Hooker, creeping and converging on Manassas. For he had that disposition of soul called wishful thinking and wished to believe that since Jackson had had the hide to spend all day on the 27th in Manassas, he ought in fairness to wait there on the 28th and 29th for the convenience of Reno, Kearny, Porter and Hooker, who would want very much to surround and swallow him.

In fact, this evening of August 27, Tom Jackson was riding out along a quiet road towards a little hamlet called Groveton and to a long low ridge beyond. Hotchkiss had pointed out the ridge on a map earlier that afternoon.

"Wooded, Jed?"

"Along the slopes, yessir."

"Good for hiding, then?"

Jed grinned. "What sort of hiding d'you intend, General?"

Under their screen of Stuart's cavalry, Tom Jackson's army moved as anonymous as farmers' sons on that thoroughfare, under that sky bright as two harvest moons.

Tom Jackson was sleeping in his saddle as was usual. It had pommels slightly higher than the regulation cavalry saddle and that helped keep him somewhat upright. But even while he drowsed he knew what country they were passing through.

The hill called the Henry Hill rose on the right of the road. This is where his brigade had stood last summer in July when the Yankees came flanking round over Bull Run. Tom Jackson had lost 560 men on that hill there and he'd spent the whole afternoon with a crazy little wound of his own, a needling pain that ran from his left hand up to his brain, on account of his middle finger being broken by a bullet. Now even in his sleep, he remembered how, about three o'clock that day, a Yankee regiment dressed all in red came running along the crown of Henry Hill, and it seemed to him then that they were the red-hot embodiment of the shattered bone in his middle finger of the left hand. In fact they were just the poor New York Fire Zouaves, and the graves of many of them were hereabout, on these slopes.

Whenever he stirred in the saddle he could see the weeds and briars growing round the little shacks in the meadows hereabout where the Confederates had spent that first innocent winter of the war, building these structures about Christmas time, leaving them about the end of March and not knowing how hard the summer could be that was waiting for them.

Usaph opened his eyes to a strong morning light and amongst a babble of talk. In a while he knew where he was. This was the wooded hilltop they'd come to after midnight. It was a strange hive-like noise that was going on all around him; there was something untoward about it. Then he understood there were no harmonicas or fiddles and there was no singing. Well, to a hiding army, all this was forbidden. And there was no smell of woodsmoke, since fires were forbidden. But there was sure a buzz of talk. For talk was free.

Of course, one of the talkers was Cate, but Usaph could listen even to Cate this morning without too much of a stomach knot. Cate was sitting some ten paces away from where Usaph lay and his audience was Gus Ramseur and young Ashabel.

"I don't believe a word of that," Ash was saying. "You trying to tell us that the might of this great army rests upon goddam nightwater?"

"You could say that," Cate admitted with a sort of lawyerish grandeur.

"Well, where was this, Cate?" Gus Ramseur asked soberly.

"Why, this was Loudoun County in this State of Virginia. I spent part of the winter up there, painting an English lady and her little maid."

Goddam you, Cate, for saying *little maid* that way.

"A godforsaken little place called Upperville. And there was this contractor from the Niter Mining Bureau. A fat man like you'd expect a contractor to be. And what was he doing but sending the slaves under their own houses—you know how those slave houses stand on little stilts—to dig up the earth there? They'd dig up about the top three inches, and then they'd percolate water through it into casks, and then the water would dry off. And there it was, saltpeter for gunpowder."

"I don't know if this is at all the truth," Ash warned Gus Ramseur.

"He told me," Cate went on, "that he could get about fifteen pounds from any slave's house that had been up ten years. That is, a pound and a half for every year of occupancy."

"Every year of emptying their bladders," Ash corrected him with that hectic, crazy laugh.

"This same contractor," said Cate, "claimed he got saltpeter from caves as well—I believe it's a matter of bat's droppings."

"Holy Jimmy!" Gus said wonderingly. "I have these forty rounds in my cartridge box and twenty in my pockets, and you tell me it's all the droppings of bats and colored people."

"And not only bats, Gus, and not only black people. This gentleman tells me that before the war is much older wagons will visit every white household and make a collection of the lye. Only natural modesty prevents it from happening now."

"So," said Ash, "them big bladdered women you see in the country . . . they'll be goddam heroes. I see this-here struggle to be one between the bladders of the Confederacy and the goddam factories of the North. . . ."

As if to give a little music to this idea of Ash's, firing started up away to the south, and it didn't seem to be much; it seemed to be some U.S. cavalry stumbling on the flank of the Stonewall, down there a mile or so through the woods.

Jackson heard it too. He was down on the flat land below the ridge where Usaph and the others were hidden. There was a little farmhouse there, and the farmer and his womenfolk, a wife and two daughters, looked out at Tom Jackson and his staff from behind their curtains. They were poor people and had little in store, or so they said, and it wasn't Stonewall's policy to make people give up their milk or eggs or butter, or even to claim shelter under a roof like theirs. So he settled down on a blanket spread under one of those nice oaks you find in Virginia. In a corner of the same meadow tall General Telfer lounged against a fence chewing a cheroot. Bird-like Popeye Ewell paced and talked to anyone who had the energy to pace with him.

In this field, just six miles from Thoroughfare Gap, Tom Jackson had spent the morning snoozing on a groundsheet. He was woken however each time his cavalry came in with a captured order, and there wasn't any doubt his cavalry was working hard that morning, snapping up Yankee couriers as they scuttled between one wing and another of Johnny Pope's army.

About noon one such order was brought into that little farm-yard. A rider came up at a mad pace, just managing not to run into the fence posts, and without dismounting, handed the thing over the fence to Charlie Blackford, the young cavalryman who seemed to have stuck himself onto Tom Jackson's staff. Charlie went and woke Jackson. Jackson read the page that was given him and stirred as if he knew it was the end of his sleep for that day. The captured order he had in his hand was one written out by Johnny Pope's adjutant and it swung four whole corps of the Union army round towards Manassas.

Tom Jackson hitched himself up and sat on the railing fence, thinking away, not saying a word to anyone about his thoughts. After a while he got down from the fence, got on his horse, rode up towards the woods where the Stonewall Division was hiding, then back again. You could tell he was getting madder and madder about something and Blackford was amused by the way Kyd Douglas and Sandie and Hunter Maguire all sat off to one side, letting him rage round, as if they'd got used to living with his moods.

What he was thinking through was a sort of painful military theorem: What if Pope's army all goes off to Manassas and then beyond Bull Run? Within a few days McClellan's troops will join him and there'll be no chance of beating him on his own. Therefore I have to attract him to me now, I have to show myself, this morning's secrecy has got to end. There the theorem ended, but there was a problem attached to it. How can I judge the hour to show myself until I know when the others will join me, when Lee and Longstreet are likely to be here?

Tom Jackson got an image of Jimmie Longstreet's features in his mind and they seemed to him to be essentially cautious features. Tom Jackson hoped Bob Lee was harrying Jimmie Longstreet along at an incontinent speed.

Those watching—Blackford, Kyd, Sandie, the others—could tell he was in a mental fix and that it was acting on him like some form of pain. The General stayed off on his own and in that state for close on two hours. It was one of those endless summer afternoons that seemed to expand before your eyes to about the size of a week.

Anyhow, young Charlie Blackford went strolling round the farm. He was up with two cavalry men, both wearing new blue britches filched from the storehouses at Manassas, both leaning against a worm fence drinking from a crock.

"Where'd you get your sup, boys?" he asked with a grin that showed he thought it was whisky.

"Why, it's buttermilk, cap'n. They got it by the gallon down there." One of the horsemen pointed south. If you went towards the Bristoe Road, he said, and turned west by a little Methodist church, you came to a farm on the left where they'd been churning butter and had buttermilk for sale.

Charlie Blackford could think of nothing more sustaining this long afternoon than a canteen of buttermilk, so he went round gathering canteens from people who wanted some and set off with Sandie and a few troopers to visit the farm. They found the farmhouse just down by the silent main road to the west. They introduced themselves as members of Jackson's staff, and the farmer and his wife wouldn't take a cent for the buttermilk, and the farm wife said if they came back later she'd be done baking, and there'd be corncakes and butter. When Charlie and the others got back to the meadow that was head-quarters, Jackson had got down again from his horse but was still pacing and glowering as if there was a good chance that today's first real explosion would be Stonewall Jackson going up. Charlie Blackford decided to risk going near him with a canteen. "Buttermilk, General?" he asked, and Tom Jackson took the canteen without getting out of stride with his thoughts and took in a long swig of the stuff and then handed the canteen back nigh empty and without saying one word.

Pop-eyed General Ewell came striding up from the place

he'd been keeping near the far fence. "What in God's name you all putting away there?"

"Buttermilk, sir."

"Why goddamit, offer me some!" For buttermilk would be kindly with his jangled guts. Either because he needed to or thought he needed to, little hawk-nosed General Ewell ate nothing but cereal and the occasional luxury of fruit. It didn't seem to impair his energies any. But he believed buttermilk would make a big difference to him today. Charlie Blackford offered to go and get some. He took Ewell's orderly, a tall boy, along with him and the two troopers that had gone before, and a few more as well that had been slumped round about. When they neared the farm this time, they spotted five horses hitched right outside the door. Blackford sent two of the troopers across the fields and round to the back door and then charged from the direction of the road with his three other men. Five Yankees came spilling down the steps of the farmhouse and Charlie Blackford and the others spurred up, and four of the five surrendered straight off. The fifth ran, being fired at; and while his small force kept the prisoners tidy, Charlie ran indoors and began filling canteens with buttermilk and dragging hot cakes off the table into a flour bag he'd brought with him for the purpose. The farmer and his wife weren't to be seen so he just nodded with a sort of crazy politeness towards the interior of the house and ran. He was just mounting his horse when firing started from the woods a hundred paces west of the farmhouse. He and the others rode off crouched, trying not to be sacrifices to Dick Ewell's taste for buttermilk. They drove the four Yankees before them. But after a few hundred paces, when the firing heated up, Charlie yelled: "Let the prisoners go in the rear with me."

So it was done and Blackford got back to Ewell with buttermilk.

Now there were these boys from Indiana to question—they were the flank guard of the whole Union army. They fought in a war where it was thought of as all right if a prisoner told what he knew, and after they had done so, they were escorted over the ridge, through the resting army, down to the quiet valley beyond, where Jackson's wagon train was drawn up.

It was deep in that summer's afternoon, when the sun hung unremittingly in the western quarter of the sky, that a courier came in from Lee. Lee and Longstreet, said the courier, were at Thoroughfare Gap and although there was some opposition, mainly from cavalry, they meant to cross in the morning.

Tom Jackson got up now in a smiling state and began to talk to Telfer and Ewell, grinning at them more than he'd grinned at anyone since Easter.

Half an hour later, by climbing the corner of a fence in the farmyard, the three generals were able to see a Union division strung out and swinging along the main pike just a little way down the hill. They moved smartly and willingly, like boys who had never been marched a terrible distance in all their military career.

Up in the fringe of woods above Stonewall, Usaph and the others could also see this division moving along nicely in the dusk. Although officers came along telling boys to hush, Usaph didn't think that force down there signified much. For the sun was already low.

The Yankee boys saw a few lean Confederate horsemen atop a ridge a half a mile in from the road. They'd been seeing distant Rebel horsemen all day. These two looked, with the last sunlight of the day behind them, as lean and starved as the rest. Yet it gave you a strange feeling in the gut to see Rebels riding up and down like that, like the scarecrow proprietors of the farm of death. But the sun was low and soon everyone would camp and boil up his coffee.

On the ridge, Tom Jackson patted his horse. He said to Sandie: "How do they look to you, Sandie? D'they look like messengers, would you say?"

Sandie barely knew what Tom Jackson was talking about, but grinned as if he did. He followed the General when that mysterious gentleman turned Ole Sorrel's head fiercely and galloped back down to the farmyard.

Telfer and Ewell were still rubber-necking like boys at a ballgame from their corner of the field at the passing Yankees. Tom Jackson reined in by Telfer.

"Move your division out of the woods, down towards the pike."

"And do I attack, Tom?"

"You do. The lead brigade."

"And me, Tom?" Popeye Ewell asked, fortified by buttermilk.

"You support his attack on the left."

It was a characteristic Jackson battle conference, all over in the space of a few grunts.

The leading Union brigade on the pike belonged to a brigade

called Gibbon's Black Hat Brigade of Rufus King's division. They were certainly proud but had never fought before today. This evening it seemed that God had been saving this hour specially for them. For if they looked at the sunset one minute, there was nothing but a proper golden radiance above a black line of forest. And the next there were batteries galloping out into the open to get an uninterrupted line of fire on them, and there were long lines of men, who didn't seem any better dressed or any more rushed than laborers, moving out of the woods up there on the ridge.

— 2 —

THEY SENT USAPH and the others down the slope from the woods, and you could see the Yankees were already flinging themselves down on the road and then being urged into an upright position by their officers. The Rockbridge began its firing and Yankee artillery in plain sight answered from meadows beyond the road.

Then it was all lost from sight to Usaph and the others. A low ridge, the ridge where Tom Jackson had ridden a few minutes ago, put itself between the road and Usaph. In fact, Usaph guessed it ran for more than a thousand yards, and as if guessing that those neat Wisconsin boys might charge it, General Telfer got the Stonewall Brigade to halt there, right in front of it. Any Yankees coming over it would be lit by the evening sun.

Just the same the idea didn't suit the boys, you could feel their desire to be let loose. They still suffered from the crazy belief that from now on it would all be like the feast at Manassas.

Usaph stood by Gus and Gus had his ear lifted to the whine of the shells above his head. Talk started up, but Gus said nothing. Looking down the line, Usaph saw Cate staring at him. God, you might damn well lose those eyes in ten minutes! Usaph thought with a savage lift of his soul. For all the martial demons were on Usaph at times like this, and one thing it did

for him was he could see each blade of grass as a separate
wonder, even in a little sump like this where the light wasn't
good, and he could see and number each wisp of evening cloud
and remember its lines all his days.

Hans Strahl, who wasn't so talkative at the best of times,
had chosen now to be telling a story to Ash Judd, who listened
with a sort of grinning composure for which only he himself
knew the reason.

"You know how these-here Springfield muskets are so goddam well made," said Hans, studiously sounding like a native-
born Valley boy, "that an Irishman in the 5th Virginia was able
to carry whisky in the barrel of one all the way from Manassas
last evening to this very place. . . ."

Young Lucius Taber and the fierce dentist, Captain Guess,
were going about hissing "Silence!" But no one obeyed, they
just chatted a little lower.

"And when he sat down by the road early this morning,"
Hans pursued, "to have a draught of it, he had to put the barrel
in his mouth. And ain't it jest what you'd expect that the
chap ain of the 5th came along then, and he'd have to be one
of them priests of the Irish type, the 5th being all Irish. And
he sees this here boy with his gun in his mouth and one hand
on the barrel and the other down near the trigger and he yells:
'Don't do it, Paddy. Jaysus'll see you through!'"

Usaph noticed that there were boys, as there always were,
leafing through the scriptures, but it was too late for him to
do that; he'd left his in his blanket roll up the hill. Also he
guessed that if he touched a scripture at a time like this he'd
lose his call on those war-hungry devils that got into him at
times like these. And without those devils, he couldn't face
fire.

Before there was time for him to raise any sort of envy for
those boys who, while cool and scared and reading the Book,
still stood waiting to face the enemy, a line of neat boys appeared atop the rise fair ahead. They looked like well-shaped
farm boys—and from their corpses it would be found that their
origins were in Wisconsin and Indiana, and that they came
from no Irish or German sink in Manhattan or Boston.

They were no more than a hundred steps off. Without waiting for any advice from an officer, Usaph shot the one his
eyes fixed on full in the body. He had turned into something
like an animal now, though there was a Christian left somewhere inside him to lament that fact at a later time. Why, a

friend—even Gus—could be shot between the eyes and it'd be midnight before Usaph was human again and mourned him and the waste of his talents. God, he felt so expert, firing uphill didn't worry him even a little. He was some marksman and so were all the rest! And the Yankee boys went on presenting themselves over that ridge. Who was their commander and what did he mean by serving them up like this?

Bumpass, the war animal, fired four rounds before the Union colonels got over their craziness and stopped despatching boys over that small rise. There was a stillness then, apart from the artillery firing which, though loud, somehow wasn't Usaph's business. Usaph looked at Gus; Gus smiled. From the rise came thin cries, a true babble you could barely make out the bits of. There was a boy up there, though, calling, "By Jesus, Andy, I'm hurt," in a straightforward voice like a man commenting on the weather.

One of those delays set in and what ended it was the order to go forward at a trot, over the ridge. The Yankee boys up there on their backs and bellies, putting their hands out for kindness, meant nothing to frothing and trembling Usaph Bumpass. They had no rights. They'd been swept off the table of contents of this battle.

Beyond the rise was a long rail fence and the Yankees had pulled the uprights from it. The last Yankee runners who had lived through that advance were being pulled back into the ranks down there by the road, into the warm comfort of the jostling shoulders of their kin. The Stonewall went on walking through another desecrated fence, and stopped just a hundred paces from the road. Later, Usaph could not remember any order to halt given at that stage, but maybe there was. It seemed to him as if a halt came because the brigade had come to some unspoken animal agreement about how close was the right thing.

In fact, General Telfer thought they'd already gone too far, and the instincts of such colonels as Lafcadio Wheat told them any closer was ridiculous.

Where Usaph and Gus and the others stood, it was an open field, unploughed, and there was bluegrass up to the calves of tall boys like Usaph himself, and the knees of shorter ones like Danny Blalock.

Tom Jackson watched from his farmyard at the edge of the forest. He could foresee lots of maimings and deaths in the way the two lines of boys were facing each other off, but he didn't expect the lines to hold like that too long. He'd send Kyd off to the south to tell a Confederate brigade camped down there by a quiet stream near the Manassas Gap railroad line to hurry round from that direction, cross the road, and roll up the Yankee flank in the normal way.

Tom Jackson, believing he had God's firm approval, didn't think how little this sort of move had worked lately.

Kyd, riding with the order, found the country very broken down that way. He had to ride through ravines where the suckers and undergrowth were up to his shoulders, and his horse would panic and vines would get him by the throat. Four ticks got down Kyd's collar during that ride. There were deep woods too that muffled the noise of the crazy actions down by the road, and night had just about arrived.

The brigade Kyd was trying to find was under the command of General Bill Telfer's cousin, Alex. It was close on eight p.m. before Kyd, no longer a neat and cool aide, but a sweating, tick-infested, irascible boy, collided with some of cousin Alex's pickets and got the message delivered. It was willingly obeyed.

But the same country that had made a fool of Kyd caused this brigade to tangle itself in the ravines and thickets. This company or that kept following the noise of the conflict to the north and stumbled into the meadows behind the Union line, where they could do nothing but snipe.

So the event as Stonewall could see it at its start wasn't changed all evening. Two long lines of boys stood up to each other so close that the artillery of either side couldn't join in any more for fear of striking their brethren.

The Reverend Dignam coolly perceived what a filthy thing it was for two lines to be placed so close like this. He walked down just behind the long string of riflemen. No one looked back at him. It was crazy. Half these boys might run in circumstances not half so dangerous as these. But even the conscripts were standing here, laboring away like mill hands in the great factory of battle.

Sometimes the Reverend Dignam, keeping his cool Christian head in the midst of his promenade, would be bumped by a boy reeling back from the line open-mouthed and grabbing with both hands a pulped eye or a punctured skull, or holding a shattered arm out from the body and looking at it with that gaping, protesting mouth the wounded put on. And sometimes boys would kneel down, as he approached, like tired children falling on to their haunches, and then their heads would go right down in an Eastern salaam, and their hindquarters would point to the sky.

Lafcadio Wheat was standing back some fifteen paces behind Company D. His headquarters was a patch of lupins; the flowers were a nice radiant blue this time of day. He had an orderly with him and Company D's young captain was sitting by his feet. The boy was staring down at his own hand, which lay in his lap. The boy's thumb had been shot away and all the pad of the hand too.

"This is madness, Laffie," Dignam screamed at Colonel Wheat. The colonel grimaced and lifted his ear, meaning he hadn't heard . . . "Madness!" the Reverend Dignam screamed again. "We must get them away from here. Back to that rise. Lay them down. Just over the crest. We should . . ."

"Goddamit, Diggie! If *should* was *could* we'd both be . . ."

He was about to say we'd both be generals, or some such grand thing. Before he got it out, he saw a private soldier turn away from the firing line ahead. "Oh Jesus," said Wheat. "Oh Jesus, Diggie!"

The private had taken a ball in the jaw. He would have been better to lie still instead of encouraging by movement the gush of his life's blood. But with his mouth open and his hands out, he stumbled straight for Colonel Wheat, as if he trusted the colonel to set things right. Wheat's arms went forward and received the boy.

"Now, now. Jest rest there, feller. Jest you rest."

He helped the private down to the ground to sit by the young captain. He looked terrible himself with his coat all fouled and muddy red, and children resting against his knees.

Colonel Wheat yelled, "There must be something coming from the flank." It was the only explanation of why he'd been ordered up here along with all the other regiments for such a close look at the enemy. It could only mean that any moment now there would come a wild Confederate attack on the Union flank. For the meantime he supposed his task was to hold the Union line in place by the shoulders, in a firm wrestle-hold so it would get the full shock of that flank blow.

The Reverend Dignam got a thought too painful to yell out in noise like this. What if there *was* no flank attack—Tom Jackson wouldn't tell them one way or another—and what if the Yankees went on standing?

Dignam knelt down and slid the weight of the boy with the jaw wound off Wheat's shin-bone. The boy fell on his back amongst the stained lupins. His eyes were open but it was mainly the whites that were showing. So Dignam bent over to do some merciful work on them and to close them up.

He was just flexing the muscles at the back of his left ankle so that he could rise again when there came a bad jolting impact on the top of his bowed head, right beneath the crown of his hat. Somehow he knew straight away that his hearing would never be any good any more. But he could hear, just the same, above the ringing silence the remote voice of his good, earthy friend Lafcadio Wheat screaming, "Diggie, for Jesus's sake. Diggie!"

It came to Dignam gently, coming up from his belly, that he had taken a mortal wound. Receive your unworthy servant, he said interiorly.

It was not the dying that frightened him; he was not at all afraid of something that seemed simple and reasonable the closer you got to it. Besides, he believed in the Resurrection of the Dead as truly as most people believe they'll be paid on Friday. But the big knot in his brain as he died was this: In Bedford County, where he'd had a good living and a fine church, he'd wanted and had twice got Mrs. Alison Kane, wife of the presiding elder of the county, Mr. Emery Kane, a dry-goods merchant of Bedford. Alison was a tall woman with a long and subtle mouth and deep eyes. The memory of her face sat in his mind now like a single live and well creature in a doomed house. And he was free to cling onto it all the way down that funnel that opened beneath him and drank him down. Yet even as he fell he accused himself. For soldiering had been vanity and the war had been a gift to him, getting him away from Mrs. Dignam, a fine girl he had failed to love through no fault of hers, and away from the sharp thought of Mrs. Alison Kane.

Colonel Wheat began dragging his friend up not two seconds after the bullet went into the crown of Dignam's head, but from the feel of the preacher's limbs, he could tell already that one of the best and most sensible of men had perished in an instant of time.

— 3 —

"OH HELL, BOYS, will y'look at that," Dick Ewell said, and sat over slowly on his right hip.

It was a little after seven that savage night. Popeye Ewell stood by his horse at that fence the Northern boys had taken the rails down from earlier in the evening. With him he had a few young officers. They all felt they were well to the rear of the battle. They were in fact but a short walk from it. Now Tom Jackson was considerably further back, over the ridge and by the railroad cut, and that was sensible of him. Because everyone would be lost if he was hurt, given that he carried the plan round in his head.

But Popeye Ewell, by his horse, by the fence, didn't feel he was taking any particular risk being where he was. He knew soldiers tended to overshoot in battle, but he wondered if anyone would overshoot to the extent of shooting him up there on that little rise.

One of these young officers standing with Popeye was in fact a young general. A general from Georgia called Andie Lawton. Once, an age or a month ago, Lawton had, rather than be judged slow by Tom Jackson, jumped from a window in Gordonsville. Now his brigade was holding the line just across a field or two, just by the road there.

Before he'd called out, Popeye'd been a little agitated. He kept pulling at the corner of his rich moustache which came down a long way past each corner of his mouth. He kept raising his chin in little jerks, like a man who's not satisfied he's tall enough to get a good view of the proceedings. And he felt a little confused.

That goddam Jackson hadn't so much as told him any flank attack would come in, though Dick Ewell, just like the deceased Reverend Dignam, believed there must be one coming. In the meantime there were too many boys getting felled. But he knew what a withdrawal meant. If you ordered a retreat you had to tell Bill Telfer who was in charge of all those Stonewall

boys. And even if you could make it a good withdrawal, it
was an axiom you lost one in ten men as prisoners or maimed
or corpses through running. For that was the awkward bit. The
boys down by the road were wound up so tight to stand there
swapping fire that if you called them back a hundred paces,
they'd read it as a threat and start galloping. Dick Ewell knew
a lot about how calm standing can give way to flight and rout.

So, before he cried out, Popeye Ewell couldn't see much
alternative for the moment to what he was doing already. And
then the high-pitched minie ball entered his knee. He knew
what it was at once. Some goddam Indiana boy must have been
aiming at an early goddam star. At the goddam Blue Ridge.

Handsome Andie Lawton looked down on his general,
who'd been standing the last time Andie looked. He looked
at Popeye's baggy grey trousers with the blue stripe down
them. They were long on him; Popeye wasn't much of a
dresser. They flopped down well over his dusty boots, even
when he was sitting down like that on his hip. The knee of the
left side had been punctured and was already running with
blood. The wound had done nothing for Popeye's temper, and
he looked up at Andie and grunted. "Look to your own goddam
command, Andie. It ain't no goddam circus for a boy like you
to go gawping at."

Andie didn't go away. He knelt down beside Ewell. "Where
is it?" he asked, though he knew exactly where the ball had
gone. One of Popeye's staff officers called Byron knelt down
with a flask of brandy. That really angered Popeye. He roared.
"You expect me to drink that stuff, boy? That crunchgut? With
the stomach I have?"

The shouting turned his skin grey and his eyes rolled and
he fell right over on his side, whimpering.

Andie Lawton was just thirty and ambitious. But he thought:
"Oh Lord of Hosts, the whole left of this line is now in my
command." So it showed you Popeye's advice about not gawping was not pure peevishness. Andie Lawton thought he had
better go and have a look at his line.

He turned to Byron and the other boy officer there.

"Back there there's that railroad cut and you should find
Surgeon Maguire somewhere along it. Get Popeye—General
Ewell—up there."

Byron indicated with a wave of his hand that gushing kneecap. "How?" he asked.

"For God's sake, there's only one quick way, you know that. Put him on his horse."

In fact he took time off his command and helped them lift the general. Popeye tottered in his saddle and muttered and complained through the half faint he was in. He lay forward against the mane of his horse, and his mouth was crushed sideways by the firm horseflesh. Bryon had fetched a spare shirt out of his own saddlebag and tied it tight around the knee, but the linen got scarlet in seconds and began dripping on the horse's belly.

Andie thought, he won't keep that leg. There'd be a hacksaw job and he'd be away from the army for months or years if not for a lifetime. It came to Andie with a fearful glow that he would command that division for a long time. On a long-term basis the idea excited him, but to become a division commander during this particular crazy fight was something he didn't want.

"You, Byron," he said. "Take him fast. And you, you come with me. We're going to visit my colonels." *My* goddam colonels!

This second officer, maybe twenty-one years old, started to argue. "No, General Lawton, you stay here. I'll find a runner."

"Why in the name of hell . . .?"

"Well, they can't afford another shot commander."

He could see the boy meant it, and was scared of what it might do to the risky balance of that firing line if too many generals got shot.

"Staying here didn't do Dick Ewell much good," Andie Lawton said. "So you better come when I tell you."

Tom Jackson saw the two horses cross the railroad cut at a poor pace. He thought some officer had sent him a few lazy despatch riders. Hunter Maguire, watching too, saw him set his face, readying himself to yell and roar at them.

But at the same second both Stonewall and Hunter Maguire came to the knowledge that it was Dick Ewell there, flopping about loosely on that horse. Surgeon Maguire ran a little way down the slope to this patient who had dropped in on him. He did not drag Dick Ewell off the horse—he could see the horse's withers were slick with too much of the discharge of Popeye's blood.

"Dick Ewell?" Stonewall called. Maguire inspected the knee without touching it.

"The patella, General. The kneecap."

"Bad, would you say, Hunter?"

"No doubt," said Maguire.

A few grooms were round about, hanging on to the staff's horses. So was the surgeon's orderly. Maguire told these boys to lay blankets out on the ground. They delayed about it for they knew the blankets wouldn't be much use after a general or anyone else had bled away on them. "Put down goddam blankets!" Maguire roared.

Jackson drew near to Popeye's horse. "Hullo, Dick," he said. Standing, he was taller than the neck of Ewell's little mount. Dick Ewell didn't answer. "He's a bad color, Doctor Maguire," said Stonewall, as if the information would be of professional help to Hunter.

Hunter had the grooms and his own orderly lift Ewell down. The orderly was a good man and he held the leg in its slight bend as the others dragged Popeye down, and he said the things that needed to be said: "Don't haul him like potatoes! No jolts there, goddamit!"

On a pile of blankets and waterproofs, they laid Popeye down. Hunter's orderly, dropping further blankets atop Dick Ewell's upper body, looked in the mouth to see what was making all the grunting and gagging noise that was going on. He found the general's false teeth askew in the mouth and jammed hard up against the palate. He took them out. He didn't have any bedside stand to put them on, and Maguire was yelling at him to fetch his medical bag. So he put the teeth in his own jacket pocket.

The shiny instruments were laid out. Instruments shinier than most of the wounded got treated with, laid out there on the ground on strips of sealskin. Hunter Maguire cut into the cloth of General Ewell's trousers, cutting close to the left crutch with a sawtooth penknife.

"Can you see all right there, Hunter," Tom Jackson called over his shoulders. His eyes were still on the fight some half-mile off, down past the railroad cut near the road. Maguire was somehow pleased that Tom Jackson wouldn't be staring down at the surgical work. He went on sawing and ripping but gently as he could. If you gave this knee a good jolt one of the deep arteries might spout.

All round the blankets where Popeye Ewell lay, Maguire's orderly was putting down star candles that had been found on the march, and lighting them so there'd be enough illumination.

By their flame, Maguire got Popeye's leg bare. It was a white, wizened little leg with the veins blue high up on the thigh. It was blue too and awfully swollen all round the kneecap which had been hit, as Maguire had guessed, square on. The bone had been fragmented by the minie ball and turned all inside out. The cartilages had been twisted too and it would have looked to a layman like there were strands of rope mixed up in the mess. You could bet, without probing, that the head of the femur was all shattered. There was nothing that could be done to pack those bones back into their correct relationship one to the other. There was no fancy surgery you could try on that mess. The knowing orderly was already tying a tourniquet high on the leg. In the background—because to Hunter anything else than this task was background—Tom Jackson sent Byron off with orders for Lawton. "There's a barn there, well up the road," Stonewall was saying. "I want him to anchor his flank right there." "I think, sir," said this Byron, "that's already been done by General Ewell's orders."

"Then make sure they stay there," Stonewall said.

"I believe the leg must go sir," Hunter called. He uttered the sentence firmly. A lot of generals thought that amputation was the method of quacks and butchers and poor country doctors. A lot of them thought that, if they were shot in the leg or arm, the good doctors they had on the staff could always save that limb, no matter what.

"Go?" asked Stonewall, a subscriber to the general theory.

"The bones are a shambles. I can't get at those deep arteries to stop the bleeding. It has to come off."

Hunter was very sure not to make apologies. His Professor of Ethical Medicine and Surgery at the University of Pennsylvania had always said that apologies were the last recourse of the second-rate surgeon. Once you start apologising, he'd said, you'll never finish. You'll be apologising to yourself in the end, for you're bound to be finished off by the same diseases that afflict your patients and for which you're always saying that you're sorry. If you had to treat President Buchanan for piles, he used to say, and they still pained him after a year's treatment, you might frown a little, but you never said, sorry, Mr. President.

"Well of course you ought to do it," said Tom Jackson. "Here?"

"I wouldn't wish to move him as he is. Not even on a litter."

Stonewall looked down the hill at the conflict roaring along there by the road. "Afterwards? Can he be moved afterwards?" He was thinking all at once of the widow Popeye had courted in Richmond. It wasn't a very passionate business; Popeye firmly called her Mrs. Brown whether he was speaking to her or of her. She seemed a sensible woman and, potentially, a good nurse.

"He can be moved by midnight, General." Hunter said.

There was a straggle of litter-bearers coming through the railroad cut and Stonewall called to two of them. They staggered near. The boy they were carrying was arguing away in a loud voice. His face was lopsidedly swollen; he'd been shot in the right cheek. He was chiding someone, and it turned out it was his maw. "The only thing being, maw," he kept saying. He was arguing with his maw about putting in a share-crop on the river pasture. His maw must have been some arguer. His brow was knitted in an awful fixed frown.

The litter-bearers, one of them with but one good eye and the other pretty thick-browed, stared at Stonewall. He told them to get that boy down to the surgeons fast and to tell them to treat him straight up and then to come right back here and wait. Did they understand?

They both nodded madly. Their mouths were agape. Maguire hoped it was from the labors of litter-bearing but feared it was dimness of intellect.

Dick Ewell woke and saw Hunter kneeling above him. "Jesus have mercy," he said. "It's the Pennsylvania society doctor."

"You'll be well, general."

"It's a hell of a pain, Hunter. It's a goddam county fair of a pain!"

The orderly was already mixing a quarter grain of morphine in a tin cup of water. "Drink this," said Hunter when the solution was ready. Ewell's popping eyes were nearly on his cheeks with the force of the agony. "Holding 'em, Tom?" he called to Jackson.

"Holding 'em nicely, Dick," Tom Jackson said over his shoulder though no one could have guessed whether he meant it. So Ewell drank the narcotic cup and his arms went loose and he sighed a long sigh. Even so, Maguire had the orderly kneel at the general's head holding a pad soaked in ether close up to the beaky nose.

This is the first kneeling-down amputation I've ever done, Maguire told himself.

Hunter plied the long shining scalpel and the file and the bright saw and the fresh bone wax to seal off the marrow when the leg came off. The packages of silk and cord and catgut were open only because he'd used them to sew up that Maryland lawyer, Snowdon Andrews, who'd been disembowelled at the Cedar Run. Apart from Andrews and Ewell and a number of the staff now and then who might have got a hot little slug of shrapnel in his cheek, Maguire had hardly practised any surgery in a long day.

Kyd Douglas, back with a report from Bill Telfer, saw Hunter, in an apron that looked fresh but had a smear of gore across its middle, cutting into the leg. Kyd kept his eyes ahead while the rasp of the bone saw went on, and the filing. When it stopped he turned and saw the surgeon working away with those silken threads in the bloody stump and then, with broad movements of the arm, sealing a flap of flesh back over the wound. It was as well Maguire was fast. The star candles were burning out, the last light of day was just about gone.

Later, turning around again, Kyd saw one of the grooms setting off with a crooked lump wrapped in a blanket. He'd been ordered to take Popeye Ewell's leg back to the field surgeries to be burnt with all the other fragments of this evening's conflict. Though Kyd had seen a lot of boys on their backs this evening, that was the only time he felt bile in his mouth. He thought, if I were that boy I'd throw the thing into the first ravine rather than carry it all the way back through the woods. Then I'd sit down and chew tobacco like hell just to get certain tastes out of my mouth and certain stenches from my nostrils.

Which was just about what the groom did anyway.

About an hour later, the Yankees dragged away across the meadows. They gave up the field that is, but Tom Jackson, yawning, said later that evening that they'd done it in a well-ordered manner. And *that* was a sort of praise.

— 4 —

WHEN CANTY APPROACHED her on the second floor of the hospital that morning, Dora Whipple was feeding gruel to an Alabamaman private who had just come through typhus. Canty stood by the soldier's bed, but looked at Dora Whipple instead of at his patient. That was characteristic of him, she thought.

Raising her eyes, she saw past Cantry to the end of the ward. There was a colonel down there in the doorway, a grey-haired man. Two soldiers almost as ancient as him also waited there with muskets in their hands. Mrs. Whipple had seen that colonel around Orange. If Orange could have been described as having a garrison, then he would have had to be considered the garrison commander. He controlled a few companies of senior soldiers, nearly all of them over 45, the others limpy or lacking a limb. They worked around the railroad depot and kept order amongst the convalescing patients of Mrs. Whipple's hospital.

Canty said, as if it was the best news he'd had in a month: "The colonel would like to speak to you."

"He's welcome," said Mrs. Whipple. "Tell him to come in."

· "He'd rather speak to you on your own."

Mrs. Whipple sighed and put down the gruel beside the boy. "Now you make sure you finish that up," she told the survivor of typhus.

"Only cos you say so, ma'am," the boy told her. "But I can't tell why anyone would eat that mush of their own free will."

They always said things like that, the farm boys. They weren't big on broth or gruel.

Mrs. Whipple walked to the door of the ward. The old grey-haired colonel watched her coming. He must have been at least seventy years and very likely 75. Canty, she noticed, was right behind her, had followed her on her passage up the hospital aisle. "Thank you, Doctor Canty," the old colonel said, as if dismissing him. But Canty would not go.

The colonel sighed. "Ma'am," he said, "what I do is not of my own choosing. I've orders to arrest and detain you, pending a military trial. In fact, it's shaping up to be a special court-martial."

Mrs. Whipple could not think of anything to say which might talk the old man round. But she frowned and opened her mouth. "Don't say anything at all, ma'am. Let me tell you, I cleaned out the lockup down by the depot yard and it's all set up for your comfort. I will accompany you to your quarters here in the hospital right away, in case there's anything you have a mind to bring with you, though mind you, you can't bring more than my boys can carry. There ain't so much room in a cell. I'm sorry, ma'am."

She had part-way recovered now. "This is a fantasy, colonel."

"No, ma'am."

"Don't I even get told what it all means?"

"The charge is such, ma'am," he said, glancing at Canty, "that if I said what it was in a halfway public place, it might not be in the interests of your well-being, ma'am. For these are passionate times."

She laughed. "I'm not coming with you, colonel."

"Please, ma'am. I wouldn't know what the hell to do if you refused—excusing the expression. My boys here wouldn't know what the hell to do. We got our orders. Why don't you for the moment make it smooth for us? In the end you got to come with us in any case—there ain't no way that *that* can be avoided. Let me tell you, I got manacles, ma'am, I don't want to put on you. We can walk through the streets, you and I, down to the lockup like friends or you can go in chains. . . ."

Mrs. Whipple took thought for a while. "I'll come with you, colonel," she said, like someone granting a favor.

He was so kind to her. He made his "boys" walk many paces behind, so that any citizens of Orange who saw them on their way to the lockup that day might have thought they were strolling together. When they reached the lockup, he showed her inside. There were three cells, one of them hung with old green drapes to give her privacy.

"My men," he told her, "are all family men of mature age, ma'am. You'll find you'll get treated with some delicacy. . . ."

"But the reason for the arrest, sir. In this whole ridiculous matter, what is the charge?"

"There's some army lawyer coming to see you, ma'am, in just a moment. He can tell you more. But the grounds for the arrest, ma'am, is that you are a spy." He looked away. "I ain't saying for a second I believe it."

He showed her into the cell. Beside the bed, there was a table with a basin on it full of fresh water, and with a little square of yellow soap beside it. There was a covered enamel bucket in one corner. Somehow it was the niceness of these arrangements that gave her her first onrush of terror. She would have liked it better if they'd thrown her in with other prisoners, into a cell with straw on the floor and a foul open bucket in the corner. They were treating her in a way that made it seem as if they pitied her because there wasn't any escape open to her.

She managed to laugh. "The whole idea is so stupid. My husband, sir, died for your beloved Confederacy."

The old colonel waved his hands at this argument, like a man troubled by insects. "I know all that, ma'am."

He left her, and someone locked the door. When she heard the lock shift, her head became light, her ears cold. She had to resist rushing to that enamel bucket and being ill in it.

She sat there half an hour and made use of the Bible they'd left on the pillow of the bed. She read Psalm 147 over and over, and was just finished it for the tenth time when another officer appeared at her cell door.

This one was much younger than the colonel. He looked as if he had just stepped off the train from Richmond via Charlottesville. He had not done much campaigning, she decided, for his uniform was fresh and well tailored.

"Major Pember," he said, "from the Judge Advocate's Department, ma'am. I believe you've been worried as to the cause for your arrest, so the first thing I'll do is read this to you."

He'd taken from a valise he carried a document which he began to read aloud to her. It was the formal charge of treason. His voice was gentle and ordinary as he read, and took the sting out of the words he was conveying to her. He quoted the Act of Congress under which the charges against her made her liable to the judgement of a military court. When he finished he lowered the paper. "May I come in, ma'am? I've been detailed to act as your counsel."

She smiled and shook her head, amazed. "This cell is no property of mine, sir. You know well you can come in here if you wish."

The lawyer nodded his head to the turnkey, who unlocked her cell door. Then he came through, his eyes looking about in a well-mannered way for a place to sit. There was only the one chair.

"Please," Mrs. Whipple said, "you can sit on the edge of my . . . rather of *this* cot."

When they had both seated and settled themselves he studied her awhile. "It seems to me, ma'am, that we will have little trouble defeating this charge."

"And if I do defeat it and walk free again, what are my chances of surviving the mob feeling, the crowds in the streets, Major Pember?"

"We are not making any grand show out of your trial, ma'am. You will be protected."

"But why was I arrested? And on what evidence?"

"It seems, ma'am, a Union spy called Mr. Rupert Pleasance was arrested in Richmond two days ago. Did you perhaps know a Pleasance?"

"I did not know anyone by such a name."

"A man of maybe 45 years," said Major Pember. "Slight in the shoulders. Reddish hair. When arrested, he was wearing a light seersucker suit and a beaver hat. . . ."

"There are many men of 45 who wear beaver hats," Dora Whipple said. But she knew, of course, that the man described was the one she used to meet on the waste ground west of Chimborazo on Thursday evenings. "Why would anyone arrest me for a connection with a man of middle age in a beaver hat?" she asked ironically.

"The gentleman in question had a notebook with your name in it—other names as well. I believe that all persons named in a certain way in that notebook have been arrested . . . as you have been yourself . . . and charged with treason. Now, ma'am, I do not fully know the prosecutor's case, but it seems to me to be circumstantial. Therefore, do not be too distressed at this stage, my dear lady."

"The man in the beaver hat?" she asked. "Does he have grounds to be distressed?"

"Yes, ma'am. He has already come to a painful end. It might be better if you did not inquire . . ."

"I am no infant, sir."

"Then I have to tell you he was hanged in Richmond this morning."

Her knees jumped at the idea of the rope, and the nausea

she'd felt when first arrested came over her again. The next time Horace Searcy arrives at that door and asks me to go to England, I will not hesitate, she promised herself.

"It is best if you admit nothing," said the counsel. "But I must know. Had you met the gentleman?"

"I think I may have. But as I told you, I did not know him by name."

"Did he perhaps use you—all innocent as you no doubt are—as a kind of source, ma'am, for insignificant news on Confederate military matters?"

It came to Dora Whipple as he uttered this cunning lawyer's type of question that she had no chance of lying to the Confederacy. That she despised it too much to lie to it—to lie to its judges and even to this pleasant lawyer from the Judge Advocate's Department would be to come down to the level of that Confederate cause. The idea that she was above lying did not fill her with serenity but with panic. There are things I cannot do, she thought, and if I am not careful those things will kill me. There are lies I cannot tell, and that is my grand handicap. She thought a little more. Well, she considered, two months ago I wouldn't have believed I could visit a man in his hotel room and perform intimate acts with him. So try, Dora Whipple, try to learn to tell the correct lies, at least to answer blankly. "I wasn't an innocent source of information, sir," she said in a voice that sounded outraged. "I am devoted to the Union. I willingly passed on information of *some* value to this Mr. . . . Mr. Pleasance."

The lawyer stared at her. At the corners of his mouth he began to look a little less lenient. "Very well. You tell me that, ma'am. I do not glory in punishing women, however. I still say this to you: that all we need to do to defeat the charge is not to make straight-out admissions until we have to. And if we have to, to then plead such things as the natural simplicity of the feminine mind, the unsettling grief of your late husband's death—for I believe you've lost a husband in this conflict?"

The mention of Major Yates Whipple made Dora really angry. It was such a pleasing change from feeling ill. "I will not plead any simple-mindedness, sir. My mind is at least as complicated as yours."

"Of course," the lawyer muttered. "I didn't mean it that way." He began to look even more searchingly at her. "It is important for me to know however whether you were under the romantic influence of this gentleman Pleasance, and was that your motive in . . ."

"Do not ask offensive questions, sir! I did not even know the man's name. Let me say it again. It is the Union I clear-headedly cherish."

Once again he asked her not to misjudge his motives. And then he got on to other matters. He gave her advice about answering questions in court which, in her still core, she hoped she'd be able to follow.

"So the worst we have to contemplate," he told her at the end, "is perhaps a jail sentence, and I'm sure your friend, Mrs. Randolph, will ensure the jail sentence is not *too* painful. Mrs. Randolph by the way told me to say she will come to Orange to see you."

"Too kind," said Dora Whipple, once more feeling the embarrassment of being treated too pleasantly.

The lawyer packed his documents away in his valise, and stood up, still studying her. "By the way, ma'am, I do not hate you. God knows whose cause is right. I think it important for you to know I do not hate you."

— 5 —

THE DAY MRS. WHIPPLE was arrested, Colonel Wheat woke in the forest as he had the morning before. It was so exactly like yesterday's waking, the buzz of the boys talking and the sharp summer sky beyond the leaves, that he almost decided that it was yesterday and that the fight by the road was one of those fierce dreams.

It was as his mind cleared that that griping panic of lonesomeness rose up from his belly. I must have someone to sit by me. Now. I don't care even if he takes me in his arms, and shows me by the pressure of his arms that I'm really here.

"Diggie!" he found himself calling. He raised himself on his elbow. "Diggie!" he called again, but only in a tentative way. No one answered. And there were fires burning this morning; a thin waft of coffee fragrance came to him. For boys still had pockets full of coffee and sugar they'd brought with them from Manassas. Some of them had fought last night with coffee bulging in their jacket pockets. "Diggie," said Colonel Wheat softly.

He had himself overseen the burying of the Reverend Dignam down near the road last night. A not-too-deep grave, dug with bayonets by a lot of tired boys. Some of them wanted to drop and sleep, some to stagger on if they could towards the field surgeries over the hill looking for friends. It was no sense moving the body, since Diggie would lose too much of his cerebral matter if he was carried far, even if there had been litters to spare. Somehow it had been of importance to bury Diggie whole.

All Wheat had been able to do was get him into a decent though shallow grave—two feet at the best, though at the ends it was lucky to be a foot and a half. To stop animals troubling his good and saintly friend, Lafcadio Wheat sent soldiers looking for stones; stones could be had round the foundations of an outhouse near by and from a portion of stone fence. With these filched weights Diggie was weighed down till Judgement Day. Then Wheat took a bearing on the corner of the orchard and paced out the distance, and he swore that after the war, next spring say, he'd bring Diggie's widow down here and they could see to a monument of some kind.

So in the morning Lafcadio Wheat sat there under the trees, letting his head clear and his terror settle, and wondering when his orderly was going to bring him a pot of coffee. He remembered then that his orderly sergeant had been shot through the chest, and his messenger killed too. So there was no one to bring him coffee this morning except the boy who normally held his horse, and that boy was back with the medical wagons in a bad way with pneumonia.

Wheat still felt so bereft that he would have welcomed any company and had to stop himself from getting up and going and begging boys to sit by him. Just the same, he was a little disappointed when he saw it was Lucius Taber walking towards him over the leaf mound, up amongst the breakfast fires.

Lucius's face looked smoky, and though he'd smoothed out his uniform and his hair, there was some forest bug on his neck, and a maple leaf stuck to his collar from where he'd been sleeping.

"Nice to see you walking upright there, Lucius," said Wheat, and tears he couldn't understand pricked his eyes. He found his shoes and slipped them on his feet and held out his hand to the boy like a 66-year-old instead of a man of 32 years. "Give me a haul up, would you?"

He stood upright and there was a giddiness like he'd been drinking half the night.

"Cap'n Guess is dead, sir," said Lucius. "He died straight off without pain, that I know of."

"Oh damn. But I think someone already told me that, Lucius." Poor goddam Guess. The practice of dentistry is closed to you now, ole boy. "You were with him?"

"I was, colonel."

Before Major Dignam died last night he'd shamed Lucius by putting him back by a farm behind the firing line to stop people escaping the conflict by the usual device of two whole men assigning themselves to help along one lightly wounded one. Lucius had carried his sabre in one hand and his revolver in the other, but no one obliged him by running.

In the hour he spent on that beat he permitted wounded men to lie or be placed around the foundations of the barn, but not inside it, for it could catch fire and incinerate them all. And it was around the barn that he caught his only skulker of the evening. He'd seen Sean, the Irish fiddler, peeping round the corner of the barn and could tell from the liveliness of his features that he wasn't hurt. It was easy to guess why he was there, sitting amongst the wounded; and sure enough, Lucius found Sean's pretty boy Walter sitting at Sean's side with a bowed but—you could bet—unbloodied head.

So Lucius had all at once something to do. He'd led the fiddler and his boy at gunpoint back to Captain Guess, who was standing fair behind Decatur Cate and presented them to him. Guess lectured them fiercely, though Guess himself could not have heard what he was saying and only snatches got through. "Two goddam sodomites . . . bucked and gagged . . . on parade carrying a goddam placard . . . shoot the pair of you . . . musket off the dead . . . see you fighting."

The fiddler had bent and picked up a Springfield and gone into the line without looking once at his fatal passion, the boy. The boy sank onto his knees. Guess opened his mouth again, but was shot in the heart and knelt down himself at the boy's side like he meant to make an effort to comfort the boy (it seemed to Lucius), but then fell over on his side.

Once that had happened, Lucius saw gangly Cate had turned around and was watching Guess. He wondered how the ball had found Guess without first travelling through that black

Lincolnite conscript. There wasn't any justice to it.

"Keep at your work, Cate," Lucius had yelled.

"Where'd you bury him?" the colonel was asking now.

"In the woods hereabouts." Lucius paused. "I guess that makes me commander of Guess's Company now."

Lafcadio Wheat began laughing, and his laughter was as always a bit of a mystery to Lucius. One thing Wheat was laughing at was the mathematics of the fight last night. He'd taken 210 men down to the road, which was the best he could get together, having lost some to drunkenness, straggling and illness since the feast at Manassas. And of those some 210, he had lost some 92 or 93 killed and wounded during last night's madness. This broke the rule of thumb by which it was said that one in five was hurt in a fight. And the rule of thumb might go by the board again today. So was there any such thing as Guess's Company left? If there was, here was a boy who wanted to be its sovereign goddam voice.

"I guess you are the commander of poor goddam Guess's Company, which he got together in the spring of '61, boy, in that season of hope. I guess you *are* the new man for Guess's Company."

Well, there it was. But somehow Lucius didn't feel as happy about it as he felt he ought to.

"In fact," the colonel went on, "if you hang round you could end up inheriting the whole goddam brigade. Come with me now and we'll look at a few of your boys."

The Shenandoah Volunteers were chirping round their campfires. This was one of those good and endless summer days you get in Virginia, and boys who'd woken horrified from their deep, blood-sticky sleep were feeling better now as the sun got higher. There was animal pride taking over, pride in living through the last evening. And each of them was telling himself secretly, whispering it to his own ear, that there was no bullet now that could stop him. That was the type of kindly lie by which, in telling it to himself, a soldier got ready for a new day. And what a goddam day it might turn out to be. For Pope would try to get these woods today. Meanwhile there were robins everywhere, pouncing down among the resting men, and woodpeckers doing their daily work near by. And in a light breeze the redbud and the pine, the hickory and the maple and walnut kept up the ancient murmur of their leaves.

"What I need," said the colonel as they walked, "are two good men, one to act as my orderly, another as my runner.

Given the way this-here brigade is shrinking, he won't have
to do so much damn running. But still a colonel needs a
runner."

Gus Ramseur and Usaph were at that time sitting by a little
fire of sticks. They were making up a small mess of corn and
bacon in the pint pot and looking quietly at the flames and
thinking.

"Them two," said Wheat to Lucius. He pointed towards
Gus and Usaph, and it seemed to him that their faces were
ones he'd known since childhood, the very sort of face a man
wanted around him in hours of despair. He wanted to stick
those two close to him. They could be trusted like brothers;
he could talk to men like those two! He could divert them with
tales of his scandalous gran'daddy. "That's Ramseur, ain't that
so? And old Bumpass? By hokey, them two are old hands
now."

Ignorant Lucius wasn't much impressed by them. Wheat
could tell. That was highly in their favor. "Fetch 'em," he told
Lucius. "Boys," he said when they were standing, a little
amazed, in front of him. "Would you care to work close to
me?"

"Why," said Usaph, as if there was any choice, "I would.
Gus?"

"To be sure, colonel."

They stood in the forest's mottled light. Two flattered boys.
Wheat loved them for that. "You, Gus," he said, "you can put
on a sergeant's stripe now—paint it on your goddam hat with
an ink ball. And you, Usaph, you can write and tell your spouse
over in the Valley you've been made a corporal. Not that it's
such a fine thing to be hanging round me. Hanging round
colonels ain't a profitable business. You may know, boys, that
my friend Colonel Johnnie Neff and my colleague Colonel
Lawson Botts suffered death wounds last evening. And . . . and
some others as well."

Lafcadio Wheat was silent for a moment. He remembered
the day last spring when it had come time to elect new colonels.
Colonel Cummings had been in charge of the 33rd then but
didn't want to stand for re-election, so Johnnie Neff stood
against the major and the lieutenant-colonel of the Regiment,
even though he was only a captain. And they'd elected him.
Well, he'd died for the honor last evening.

"Now you got certain duties straight off, boys. For one
damn thing I want coffee. You'd find some in my saddlebags.

And I want some flourbread baked up crisp from the same source. Now with your rank, you ought to be able to bully some conscript into doing most of the chores."

He turned and went away. When he'd gone ten paces he heard Usaph hoot. "Goddam!" Usaph squealed to his friend the music teacher. "We'll be well off as goddam house niggers!"

Well now, the colonel asked silently. Will you be?

He was aware what he'd done to Usaph; he knew Usaph would stick like glue to anyone that uttered any sort of faith and trust in him. That German musician was calmer, more worldly. But Usaph would find it hard to pursue a fate separate from his colonel's. So if I'm dead, Wheat thought, so is that boy. Until then, I'll have his closeness.

At dawn Tom Jackson had 18,000 men in the woods. Guided in by the cavalry overnight, they stretched along that woody ridge for two miles.

By now Johnny Pope, over in Manassas where the air still stank of fire and loot, had heard all about last night's fight. He'd chosen to see it in the rosiest terms—General King's recruits had stumbled on Stonewall while Stonewall was in retreat. What had to be done now was pound the man while he fled.

He sent Sigel's German Corps in first.

Searcy, from his headquarters—a little circle of rocks in the woods up the northern end of the ridge—saw them coming. He didn't know quite why he was there—he'd never put himself this far forward in the Crimea, nor in northern Italy.

So what was the reason? Well, he could answer that in part. You have given yourself up to this conflict, Searcy old chap, by running intelligence to Mr. Stanton. It is only proper you should stay here a few hours and feel the furnace heat! Not so long that Mrs. Whipple will lose a lover. But for a time.

Apart from staff officers who huddled and smoked cheroots in nearby clusters of rocks, he could see, over the shoulders of Ambrose Hill's soldiers here in the woods, the Confederate front line down the slope a little. The Confederates were making use this morning of a railroad cut that ran all the way along the base of the ridge. This railroad cut was the front line. Ambrose Hill's youths lay in it and behind its fills, and waited for the Northern battalions.

There's no argument, Searcy old chap (so he told himself).
You're damned well placed.

So placed, Searcy saw swarms of Union troops emerge from
distant woods and run at the cut. Those who reached it were
clubbed or shot and, falling into it, made a squirming, whimpering surface for their brethren coming on behind. The young
boys of the Army of Righteousness and the young and likewise
precious boys of the Army of Blindness fought each other in
the cut for a while with stones and rifle butts, and tried to
choke each other. Then the boys of the Army of Righteousness
would drag away and leave the cut to these others.

This sickening rite repeated itself till ten o'clock.

Searcy worked through. He wrote copy that showed a genuine sense of outrage and which would appear in *The Times*
25 days later. He even made sketches in his notebook, diagrams
of the country, quick impressions of what he could see of the
cut.

A little after ten the boys of the Army of Righteousness
flowed over and through the cut—from this distance they came
on just like a mulberry tide, on which Ambrose Hill's reserves,
just fifty paces ahead of Searcy, drew a bead.

He saw it all with the blurred and slewing vision of a drunk.
He would have got up and run but he couldn't be sure of his
legs.

Then there were blue individuals there, just ahead, and
animal conflict with bayonets and stones, and rifles swung as
clubs.

Still he felt the mysterious duty to stand on, near blind with
smoke, blinking, stupefied by the noise.

When it was over and the Northerners escaped in pitiable
groups of two and three, Searcy the correspondent went strolling along the back of Hill's lines. He scarce heard the strange
cut-off yelps of joy or pain. Turning left and stepping out from
amongst the trees Searcy saw a Georgian unhinging the cartridge belt of a young German who had been shot through both
legs. "Don't take my pitchers, mister," the wounded man was
calling. "Don't take my pitchers, plis, mister."

The Georgian handled him almost gently. "I ain't intending
to take yore goddam pitchers," he snorted. "What'd I want
with your goddam pitchers? I got pitchers of my own, you
know. You goddam Dutchies ain't the sole owners of goddam
pitchers."

All over the slope Confederates looted the dead and wound-

ed for cartridges. The sight for some reason set Searcy weeping.
He wanted, he itched to get at Tom Jackson. And say, sir, in
European armies I have known, a general would see the fact
that his troops were scavenging the dead at 10:30 in the morning
for the wherewithal to continue the battle as a sign that he'd
soon have to surrender or withdraw. But Tom Jackson seemed
to see this sort of thing as no more than a proof that his boys
meant business.

So why didn't I cry and start trembling like this in the
Crimea? Well, I'm older now. And this is . . . yes, it *is*, Searcy
old boy . . . this *is* a holier war.

Searcy wandered on across the slope. He was still working
as a journalist. He knew the various badges Union soldiers
wore on their sleeves. Some of the dead down near the cut
displayed the oval insignia of Sigel's German Corps—they had
been killed early this morning. The men who had fallen in the
past few minutes and were just getting accustomed to their
wounds and wondering if the pain and terror could be managed,
they wore the diamond badge of General Jesse L. Reno's IX
Corps. Hill's division had by some means held out two corps.
It was axiomatic that that sort of thing couldn't keep on happening. Someone ought to go and state the axiom to Tom
Jackson.

Searcy did not do so straight away. He spent some time on
the slope, letting his rage against Tom Jackson build. From
his tin canteen coated with the fur of arctic seal—an explorer's
special from the Army and Navy Stores—he fed water to those
who cried for it, even to boys with belly wounds and a bloody
froth already on their lips. He pushed the water fatally and
unwisely down their throats, as if it were the only gift he was
capable of, and he'd be damned if he didn't give it.

About a mile south of where he'd spent that early part of the
morning, Searcy found Tom Jackson in a clearing in the forest.
Searcy had intended to come rushing up and start straight off
raging at the madman, but it could not happen that way.

Tom Jackson was at the time sitting on a caisson behind
some of Andie Lawton's Georgia batteries. He had a pad on
his knee and was writing a despatch. Sandie Pendleton and
Kyd, and some others Searcy didn't know, stood around the
caisson like a protective wall.

"General!" Searcy called, dismounting in a flurry. Sandie

put a hand up to halt the journalist. "Shh!" Kyd said, hardly turning towards Searcy.

A shell hit the forest floor on the far side of Tom Jackson's party. It was maybe the length of a small church-aisle away and Tom Jackson's shoulders and the page he was writing were showered with grit and pieces of leaf. It didn't surprise Searcy that the General just shook the page off.

"Searcy," said a large cavalry officer, stepping from the group around the General. The way the man said his name, it came out Zeerzy.

Searcy flinched and inspected the officer. It was von Borcke all right. "Ve git drunk, der last time ve zee each der odder. Dat vas in Milano in '59, ain't it so?"

"Yes," said Searcy. Why did I ever drink with you? "I'd heard you'd come to this war."

"I am wit Jeb Stuart. I turn up in Richmond wit der letter der introduction from Cheneral von Montauffel und here I am, ridink wit Stuart."

Von Borcke wore a big grey hat with a plume in it and a grey jacket of ornate and non-Confederate design from one of the many armies he'd belonged to. Searcy wanted to say: "When I got drunk with you, you Prussian bastard, I didn't know what a foul thing a mercenary is."

And then he thought, aren't you a sort of mercenary, Searcy old chap? Oh yes, you don't do it for pay, you do it for the moral thrill of being in a great war of liberation.

The air von Borcke likes is air laced with the stink of powder, the presence of dead young boys and open wounds. What sort of air do you like, Searcy old chap?

At heart von Borcke was a European though and would understand better than Americans that Jackson was breaking the rules.

"He has to give it up, Heros," said Searcy in a voice that was louder than he wanted it to be. "He has to give it up, for pity's sake."

Some of Jackson's staff turned and began looking at him. Good! thought Searcy.

"There've been two corps beating up against your left flank." Searcy found he was yelling directly at Jackson. "They have Kearny's and Heintzelman's in reserve and God knows what else.... Ambrose Hill's men, Heros, are depending on the dead for ammunition. I saw, sir ... with my own eyes ... I

saw a major gathering pebbles of a calibre suitable for muskets.
It's not even noon. For God's sake, this line can't . . . simply
can't be held."

There was a sort of hush, even though artillery was banging
away all around. Tom Jackson himself got up from the caisson
and, still holding the despatch pad in his left hand, came up
to Searcy. He reached out his free hand and put it on Searcy's
wrist. My God, Searcy saw with surprise, my damned hands
are trembling. There was a frightful kindliness in Jackson's
eyes.

"I'm touched by your distress, Mr. Searcy, but you mustn't
fret." And then a slow country smile rose from beneath the
dark whiskers. "Longstreet's arrived," the General whispered.
"General Hood's Texans have just turned up down on the
Gainesville crossroads. We have the means, dear sir, to hold.
The means . . ."

Patting Searcy's wrist once, Jackson turned back to his seat
on the caisson. Searcy heard him say: "Give him some brandy."

— 6 —

ORVILLE PUCKETT LAY on a waterproof blanket that morning,
on the shaded side of McFail's ordnance wagon. Even while
he drowsed, his head was full of pain and he kept his eyes shut
against the mild sunlight in this clearing. His knees were held
up towards his chest to ease his stomach cramps. Already his
stomach had rejected the little bowl of corn gruel McFail had
fed him for breakfast.

McFail was a Scot. He'd grown up in the Highlands somewhere and had this thick way of talking you could just understand. He was grey and tough and well in his forties. In the
poor white section of Wilmington, North Carolina, he'd owned
a grocery store, but his wife had sold it some ten months past
and gone further south, taking with her McFail's ten-year-old
son and the sale price and a Cherokee lover. McFail was hungry
for money to start his life afresh. He'd taken $10 from Patrick
Maskill to mind Orville in these last few days and to carry him

in his wagon. As well as that, Maskill had said that if Orville was still alive in a week, McFail would get $20.

"Orville is the sort of boy we need to have alive," said Maskill.

McFail had whisky from Manassas in his wagon. He'd been saving it for the time that was bound to come when boys would pay $2 a half cup for it. Why, he'd heard that in the army of the Tennessee they were already parting with $2.50 for a sip of the stuff in a tin can. While waiting for the price to rise, he fed Orville a slug of it three times a day. Not just because he had a fatal kindness, but also because the war might come to its close before the big prices came in, and then boys would be able to buy as much of the stuff as they wanted for $2 a bottle. A prize of $10 in a week's time just for keeping a gunner alive was worth thinking on.

McFail stood amongst the wagons speaking of fast money this morning as every morning. Every time Orville woke, which was about once every two minutes, there was McFail talking about the way this man or that had been visited by divine wealth.

"I'm told there was a driver of sixteen years, a mere bairn. He was serving in the army of the Confederacy in Kentucky this past spring, and what does he do but go to a Union general by night and he offers to deliver forty Confederate wagons for money. Well, one night these forty wagons is eking along south of Perryville and this traitorous bairn is driving the lead wagon. And some Union cavalry comes out of the woods and makes captives of the cavalry escort at the front of the column and then leads the whole wagon train in a circle to the North. That boy became the happy possessor of $1200 in U.S. treasury notes jest frae that wee enterprise."

"If you mean," one of the other drivers said, nodding towards the noise of cannon from the ridge, "to go and make deals with General Johnny Pope, the time is now. For there seems to be so much conversation going on atween them and us right now."

"Why, there's more ways of making fortunes than that," said McFail. "I was reading in a copy of *Harper's* that a sergeant of 24 frae Chicago dreamed up a wee false hand a mon could use to do up his buttons and hold his member with while pissing. Why, this war augurs to make so many one-armed people that the baby sergeant will be the richest mon in all the continent."

"Goddamit, McFail," someone called. "Them Yankee horsemen might come around this morning and deliver you from all your dreams of wealth."

For there was a sort of anxiety in this clearing amongst the wagon-masters. There were litter-bearers around there too, trying to delay in the shade on the edges of the forest, skulking from their surgeons and their officers. Amongst all of them there was this funny feeling about the battle up there on the ridge that was beyond their influence. And they often spat tobacco juice, the wagon-masters, and said with what sounded almost like real hate that they hoped the goddam infantry was doing its job up there. "I hope they can hold that goddam line," they'd say occasionally, as if the boys up there would just give it all up if you let them have half a chance of so doing.

Well, Orville understood these feelings in a way. For the soldier, the wondering and the frowning ended once the firing started. Back here you could wonder and frown all day, and nothing happened to ease that tautness of the brain.

A little after nine o'clock by that jangled watch Orville Puckett carried in his trouser pocket, and which he sometimes squinted at when the cramps or the sharp voice of McFail woke him, a whole force of Union cavalry—just about three regiments of it, came riding into that clearing. They were horsemen who'd spent the morning creeping away from Longstreet, and so they'd come over Catharpen Run and by a series of country lanes to the edges of these woods. What they saw before them was a goodly part of the supply and ordnance wagons and the medical side of Jackson's army. It was said later that they were Germans, for they didn't hold surgeons sacred. They leaned in the saddle as they galloped into the clearing and shot a Georgia doctor in the face while the man had a bonesaw deep in the marrow of some poor boy's leg. Loitering litter-bearers were shot by their empty litters. McFail and his friends ran to their wagons. They were not meant to be armed, but they were, better than any infantry man, with breech-loaders they'd acquired by what was called alienation of supplies; that is, by bribing officers or cavalry men with whisky. McFail stood by the axle trees of his wagon and fired off one round. Then the rifle seized, and he was working its lever when he was shot through the chest.

The clearing was now full of blue cavalry men. Orville thought, I can clear the mechanism of one of those. He rose from the blanket and the cramps kept him bent. But he took the rifle from McFail's side and, working the lever, got rid of a stuck round and then shot a young horseman clean out of his saddle.

Now no one except cavalry officers kept sabres, and even then few officers carried them in battle. But all at once there was an officer coming at Orville and gesturing with a sabre. He was about the same age as the boy Orville had just killed and he was coming to punish Orville for that death. Even without his cramps, Orville couldn't run, being backed up against the axle tree like that. Orville thought how he didn't want to kill this young subaltern, but he could see the horseman's mouth set like an old wound. And the idea came that if only he and the cavalry officer could go aside from all that heat and fire and speak with each other they might find they were both Americans and mutually forgiveable. The other consideration was that the Spencer had seized up once more. No wonder someone had sold it to goddam McFail—it choked on every second round. I am defenceless, O God, thought Orville, backed up against enough ammunition to keep a brigade in the line for a week or so.

The boy officer came on very savage. Orville was frightened by the hate that was there. He worked the lever but then it got properly stuck. The boy struck Orville at the side of the neck at the moment Orville was thinking of saying something to conciliate and soothe him. Orville felt the deep bite of the metal. Deep enough! he wanted to say. And his breath went out of him along with his first blood. The blade was halted at the front by his collar-bone and, amazed, he felt it grate against the bone atop his spine at the back. Dear Christ, I'm halfway beheaded. By this old-fashioned device.

He couldn't remember the blade coming out, but Orville noticed the boy had gone away; and you could see the bloody steel raised high.

He sat down and drowsed off again before he knew he had done it. His well-stored blood spilled out by the split in the collar of his artillery jacket. But the deepest blood, the blood that shouldn't be poured away, went on its easy way in Orville's jugular, which the blade had run beside but not sundered.

A railroad cut has its own specialities. Sometimes it is higher than the surrounding fields and in these parts it is called a fill. Then it slices fair through little hillocks, and there it is called a cut. Ordinary people tend to call the whole thing a cut. This

railroad cut—of which Wheat was thinking that it would be
very likely the scene of the worst railroad accident in America,
with no locomotive even involved—had no tracks laid in it and
was all cuts and fills, one after another. Some boys opted to
lie atop the high embankments, others behind the tall fills.
Fifteen feet high. At their base officers could stand on level
ground if they wished, and call up for news.

In the hot noonday along their stretch of railroad cut the
Volunteers were left alone and relished it. It was a mysterious
mercy and they made use of it, some sleeping, some playing
poker down in the bottom of the cut, some talking, some
reading bartered and yellowed newspapers.

Usaph and Gus lay with Lafcadio Wheat atop an embankment, on their bellies, their ribs tickled by the spiky grass.
Wheat could see blue regiments in the woods off to the north
and he lent Usaph and Gus his glasses so they could see them
too. Usaph began to think, but it was a fine thing to work with
a colonel and discuss probabilities with him and be privy to
the mental side of battle.

"They're pushing away up there, them Lincoln boys,"
Wheat said, pointing north. "You can be sure as a tune on a
fiddle they mean to make a push at us down here."

Yet all day Colonel Wheat's boys were left untroubled. A
Union general called Porter was meant to have fallen on their
end of the line with his whole fine and numerous corps. But
although Usaph, Gus, Wheat and even Jackson did not know
it, Porter had had an argument with Pope that morning and had
reached the conclusion Johnny Pope didn't know for certain
where any of his corps were or what they should be doing.

So he did not move. Later he would be court-martialled for
his kindnesses to the Confederate lean right flank.

About mid-afternoon, when butterflies hung from the lupins
with folded wings and the heat lay on Usaph's shoulders like
a fierce but tolerable garment, Wheat began to talk about his
gran'daddy. It amazed Gus and Usaph. They felt exalted and
a little uneasy, being let look through Colonel Wheat's field-
glasses. It didn't seem right to them that now they were being
invited into the secrets of the Wheat family. But soon they
could sense that in some ways the colonel needed to tell them
of the scandalous ways of that first American Wheat, as if the
best fate he could envisage for himself was to grow up to
become just such an old man.

"Now my gran'daddy," said the colonel, "was a wild-haired attorney from Clarksburg, and his name it was Hugo Wheat, and he was such a big man and could nigh-on dig post holes with that there implement of his. Well, there he was, Chairman of the Miners' Benevolent Fund with powers to dish out the lucre to the families of any poor miners who left various of their extremities down in the pit. There was this rumor that he enjoyed many a fine mine-widder, but I doubt that's true, he wasn't the sort to dance on any man's grave. Though you know when that-there Sam Peeps was Secretary of the Navy to the old British tyrant Charles II he used to get his way with many a sea captain's bride who called there at the Navy office in Old London town to fetch her absent husband's pay. And ole Hugo was of a literary turn and had read Peeps' book setting down all these particulars, so if he did get his corner into a nice mine wife then he was but following the dictates of literature."

Usaph saw Gus hunching down on his side and glancing at the brassy sky with this wide childlike grin on his face. So, Usaph thought, why should I spoil things by scowling at this story? But the question of what ole Hugo Wheat did to miners' *widders* raised the question of what men might one day do to his *widder*.

"Well, sometime on about twenty years ago," Wheat pressed on, "my gran'daddy discovered that another member of the committee was using the funds to issue personal checks for his own purposes. With one of the checks, this feller had bought a racehorse, and with another a new kiln from Chicago for his china works, which were called the Monongahela Pottery Company. So we'll call him Mr. China for the purpose of this-here narrative and we'll call his wife Mrs. goddam China. It happened that old Hugo always had a leaning towards Mrs. China and that governed Hugo's actions in all that followed, for Hugo was a victim of the heart as they say in those yeller-back novels. He went to Mr. China and told him as a friend that a member of the committee had found the gap in the Society's books and that the best thing Mr. China could do was to clear out to Parkersburg on the Ohio and on to Cincinnati and raise the missing funds from the bankers and the merchants of that city, given that he was known to many Ohio merchants because of the quality of his goddam china-ware. Of course, he could never expect to be taken back into the bosom of that-there committee, but nothing would be said as long the money came back. So Mr. China took off on his racehorse at night and left ole Hugo free to stay in Clarksburg, yet riding as sweet a mount, if you can fathom that riddle, gentlemen. For Hugo was left with none other than Mrs. China and they took delight in each other in the morning and on them dry mountain afternoons in summer, and they were together according to their will in that first hot flush of night and after the dogs had gone to bed and in the first grey.

"Well, Mr. China was absent a good five weeks and didn't return till this time of the year, round on about the first rains. He comes riding up to his fine house at Nutter Fort and there's a horse in the rain there, gran'daddy Hugo's horse, and there ain't any niggers about to put it in the stable, because Mrs. China's sent all the house and stable niggers, about five of them, all to town on errands. And Mr. China is in the door yelling blood and murder before Mrs. China and ole Hugo know anything of him. It's a situation ole Hugo has been in before this and he has this here facility—a true lawyer's gift—to make everyone feel goddam at fault, including the goddam judge.

"He is as yet still wearing his britches and vest, though his boots are off, so as far as propriety goes he might as well be naked with his goddam weapon in his hand. Mrs. China, well Mrs. China is stark white as her husband's produce and lying bare-assed under the sheets. First gran'daddy grabs the big pitcher which the niggers had placed on the wash table for Mrs. China's afternoon toilet, and he carries it across the room near the door and pours it over himself, some of it falling on the carpet in his recklessness. Then he flings a few towels about the floor and opens the door and faces Mr. China. 'Will you be quiet there, goddamit, China?' he calls. 'Quiet, you serpent!' yells China and more in the same vein, and he gets all popeyed and comes up to Hugo as if he's going to hit him. So Hugo gets to it first and delivers a great blow to Mr. China and yells: 'You ungrateful cur! Do you realise what kind of a woman you have here as your spouse? Grief-stricken at the rumors that sweep this community—rumors which I hope, China, you are about to allay by replacing the money you took from the Benevolent Fund—she sends all the nigras away to town and leaps in the stream, crazy with the loss of your conjugal presence, demented with shame, China, demented with it, your shame, man! By a happy providence I came out here with a message from your works manager for Mrs. China and found her struggling in the mighty Monongahela. Off came my jacket and shirt, my heavy boots. Well might you, China, bless my prowess in the water and the strong goddam sinews I built up as a boy. I brought her back to you from the murky bottom of the great river, you sow's ass, China, and I bore her indoors and chafed her extremities with towels, as I hope a friend would do for my wife's extremities if ever she were in Mrs. China's position. And I put her into her warm bed where you will find her trembling, sir. I shall stay here now only long enough to gather up my coat, my shirt and my boots.' And gather them up he did and was gone, leaving Mrs. China— who was what they called a woman of spirit—to carry the act on."

Both Gus and Usaph were in now, and Usaph had forgotten the question of Ephie. For this was such a tale of villainy. And Wheat thought, even in the enthusiasm of his story-telling, "I'm binding you two boys to me by the magic of my narrative."

"A little later," Lafcadio Wheat went on, "Gran'daddy Hugo met Mr. China in Main Street, Clarksburg, and Mr. China was a little cool and said: 'P'raps you could tell me, Mr. Wheat, sir, how you transported my bride from the muddy banks of the Monongahela to her bedroom without dropping any water on the stairs?'" And Gran'daddy Hugo winked at him and said: 'Why, by about the same methods you use, China ole friend, to transmute the mites of mine-widders into racehorses or kilns. Come on, China, let's be friends. Your goddam wife and your goddam name are intact and just because of my good will.' 'Intact,' says China. 'My wife intact?' But he starts to laugh and they go and drink and go on being friends."

Usaph and Gus chortled and they could see that the way they received the story brightened Wheat even more. And the colonel bayed out his laughter, so the cannon could not drown it.

"He was," yelled Wheat, "the greatest hell-raiser in Harrison County and one day, gentlemen, I mean to write a book about that old man. For though my speech may be mountain-rude, my style, gentlemen, my style is pure Augustan."

— 7 —

THAT NIGHT, AT a meeting in one of those eternal little Virginia farmhouses down by the crossroads, Tom Jackson conferred around a kitchen table with Lee and Longstreet. Robert Lee praised Tom.

"Well, Tom, it seems from the reports I have here that today you held off Sigel's corps and Reno's and Milroy's and Reynolds' and Hooker's and Kearny's. Good men and bad, your boys held them off. Some 37,000 or so. With losses we know about. Well!"

But not much was decided. They would hold on to that godsend of a railroad cut, and sometime—whenever Jimmie Longstreet thought it was "militarily possible"—the troops under his command would attack John Pope's flank.

"That'd be by noon?" Jackson asked.

"Perhaps, perhaps," Longstreet muttered. Jackson reflected that God and Ambrose Hill and Popeye and Andy Lawton and himself had been doing what was militarily impossible for days. But Jimmie Longstreet still had to wait for possibilities to present themselves.

His camp that night stood in a clearing up behind the Stonewall Division. Here Jim Lewis his servant—who'd arrived that afternoon with Longstreet's wagons—had a good fire going and coffee on. Hotchkiss the mapmaker and Hunter Maguire were sitting by it, resting on a rubber sheet and sipping Jim's good coffee. Jim was good at all cooking. He could do duck *à l'orange* and *carré de porc roti*. Tonight all he'd been able to get together was some ham and cornbread, but he baked cornbread better than a farm wife of sixty summers.

Jim came up to the General's stirrup and helped him out of the saddle and gushed away as was his manner. "Why, it's a blessing to see you whole, General Jackson. I got to thinking with all that noise we could hear on our way down here this evening that no soul at all would be left standing."

Tom Jackson never passed up the chance to instruct blacks

and poor people in the ways of the Lord. "Our Heavenly Father," he said, "had his hand on me. And if he withdrew it, how could I complain, Jim? Can I have some of that coffee?"

Jim poured a cup with all that jolly black willingness that always made Tom Jackson uncomfortable. The General had never felt at ease with the institution of slavery. He was one of those Southerners who said they were fighting for the constitutional issues. His favorite way of talking of the conflict when he wrote letters or spoke of soldiers was, "our second war of independence." He didn't think much about slaves unless he was forced to and his thinking on them wasn't so very original. He guessed a time might come when they'd be sent back to their homelands in Africa. Tom Jackson wondered what Jim Lewis would do, either with freedom or an African homeland.

The General remembered the day when he was seventeen and he'd ridden over to Parkersburg on the Ohio with his friend Thad Moore. Uncle Cummins Jackson had sent them there because there was a lump of mill machinery waiting for collection. On the way home they passed the farm of a friend of Uncle Cummins's called Mr. Adams. Mr. Adams was burying one of his negroes, and the boys reined in to watch the little funeral procession. The farmer's five grown blacks, including the dead man's wife, carried the coffin across the road to a deep hole. It was a fine black coffin, such as you'd put together for someone you respected, but it always made Tom Jackson pause when he saw a black buried. It made you think that now that black man had the freedom of the kingdom of death, for surely he had at least that much, given the way darkies sang of death as the great river crossing. He remembered he shocked his friend Thad Moore that afternoon. The opinion came out of him and he couldn't stop it. "They ought to be free and have a chance," he'd said.

"Chance of what?" asked Thad. "What chance could they handle other than the chances they have already?"

"Joe Lightburn says for a start they ought to be taught to read so they can read the Bible." Joe Lightburn was a respected friend of Uncle Cummins. "I think they should be too."

Thad Moore had made one of those Southern rumbles in his throat. "I don't think you should make known them views, Tom. Why, they're regular Nat Turner views, those ones, and if they was carried out, we'd have to end up blacking our own boots."

"That's no big thing," Tom Jackson at seventeen had said. "I black mine only on Sundays and even then not in the winter months."

By this fire in northern Virginia years later, Tom Jackson was getting similar ideas from watching the way Jim Lewis poured and brought the coffee.

The General sat on a camp stool Jim had placed and sipped away. Tall young Dr. Maguire came up and stood at his side. Maguire began reporting on the casualty numbers and the health of officers Jackson knew who'd been wounded that day. He talked of Forno, the Louisiana general, and General Isaac Trimble. And then he said: "And there's young Billie Preston with a wound in the chest. The right lung is perforated. There's nothing to be done."

Billie Preston was one of those Lexington boys whose fathers had been professors with Jackson at the V.M.I. Professor Preston had married one of the Junkin girls of Lexington as Stonewall had himself. Then he'd gone into business with Stonewall—they'd bought some land in Randolph Street, Lexington, and a tract about eight miles distant in the Blue Ridge. As well, he'd been Jackson's chief aide for a time in the Valley. Now his seventeen-year-old boy was dying.

Jim Lewis, who as a house slave in Lexington had known all these boys—Sandie and Billie Preston and the others—sat and began to rock with grief and to wail when he heard the news. Stonewall stood still for a while but then turned like nothing so much as a judge on Maguire and grabbed his shoulder. Stonewall had that mountain-man kind of strength to him, and Maguire could feel it in the punishing force of Stonewall's fingers.

"Why did you leave him?" he asked Maguire.

"Why . . . he isn't aware any more who's with him and who isn't."

"Do you know this will kill his father? Kill him, sir!"

And then Tom Jackson walked away into the shadows. Maguire felt a little insulted. We're not back in peaceful Rockbridge County, he thought. It's not such a strange thing these days for young men to die.

Two minutes later Stonewall returned to the camp stool, straddled it, picked up the coffee mug from the ground and held it out to be filled again by Jim, who had by now also finished his thrashing and rocking.

Hunter Maguire said in a low voice: "We won today by the

hardest kind of fighting I've seen."

Jackson spoke gently. "Hunter," he said, "we won it by the grace of God."

Hunter shook his head. "That too," he muttered.

— 8 —

DORA WHIPPLE HAD gone to sleep that evening of her first day of captivity in a happier frame of mind than she had up to now enjoyed. You can teach yourself to tell the mere truth, she promised herself, you can teach yourself to refuse to answer some questions and to mystify the judges.

She woke when the morning train from Charlottesville hooted in the dawn of the next day. She was eating a breakfast of eggs and coffee when Mrs. Randolph, wife of the Confederate Secretary of War, a sweet-faced, brown-haired woman, was brought in the front door of the lockup by the old gray-haired colonel.

The old man did not know what to do. He could not very well lock up in a cell the wife of such an important man; so in the end he led Mrs. Whipple out into the outer office, and then left the two women alone.

Mrs. Randolph was wearing a light green dress and a pink hat, which was wise of her, since the day was starting out hot. She said, with a musical laugh: "I got to Orange as soon as I could, Dora. We'll have you drinking tea in the parlor of the Lewis House by this evening, my dear gal. I mean, this is ridiculous, isn't it?"

Dora Whipple's eyes flinched. She wouldn't lie to this good, intelligent friend. She could find therefore nothing to say.

"Isn't it ridiculous?" asked Mrs. Randolph, starting to frown.

"There was always the danger this would happen, Isabelle," Dora Whipple said. She could not look at Mrs. Randolph's eyes any more.

Mrs. Randolph thought a while, but then decided to chuckle bravely. "I mean, Dora, this *is* a joke, Isn't it so? You're

playing at being jailbirds; you're waiting for them to discover
their mistake so you can make them feel their own foolishness,
so you can cut them to pieces, the way . . . you have to admit
it . . . the way you often do with people, Dora, the well-known
Dora way. Tell me it's so!"

"You know I come from Boston," said Dora, half turning
away.

"What has that got to do with the business?"

"Isabelle, just listen to me. I love you like a sister, that's
no news to you. But your whole cause, Isabelle is . . . a disease.
And that's all."

Dora Whipple saw Mrs. Randolph's eyes widening. A statement like that terrified her. "Shush! Hush yourself there, Dora!
If you say that kind of thing, no one can help you."

"It's likely no one can, Isabelle."

Mrs. Randolph shook her head, wrapped up with the struggle of believing all this. "Dora," she said, "did you use our
dinner table to . . . ?"

Mrs. Whipple did not answer that.

"How could you do it to us, Dora? To decent men like
Randolph?"

Mrs. Whipple, having nothing to say still, plopped on the
edge of a chair and tried to control her tears.

"Don't worry, Dora," said Mrs. Randolph. "The loss of
Yates Whipple was too much of a shock for you. Even if you
go to jail, we'll look after you . . . your head's been turned,
poor creature . . ."

Dora looked up at her. "I'm not weeping for myself. I'm
weeping for the South. For your husband. For Buchanan, for
Davis. For the slaveholders. For the sod-busters. For the mad
cause!"

"I've never seen anyone weep for the South," Isabelle said.
And she began to shed tears too and sat down beside Dora
Whipple. And they held each other. "It don't matter, you
couldn't help yourself, Dora. Randolph and I will stand by
you, as I said. Or I will, even if Randolph won't."

The idea of the Randolphs standing by her was suddenly
more than she could tolerate. What was the sense in fighting
against the Confederacy if its champions insisted on standing
by you when you were caught? Mrs. Randolph's simple decency filled that cell like a terrible reproach.

"Isabelle, I don't want you to visit me again," Mrs. Whipple
said, mopping up the tears.

"But I've come all the way to Orange," Mrs. Randolph said, aghast.

"Under the idea that the arrest was a mistake, you came to Orange. Now you know it wasn't. *I* know it's different now. We can't be friends again, Isabelle; we can't be sisters." She thought about this a while. "No, I don't want you to visit me."

"We *can* still be friends," said Isabelle Randolph, her voice edged with a sort of panic that made Dora Whipple's need to get rid of her sharper still. "I forgive you, Dora. Your mind was turned as I say . . ."

Dora Whipple shook her head. "Get out! Please, Isabelle!"

"I'll bring you lunch," Isabelle promised frantically.

Dora Whipple couldn't take that. She reached towards Mrs. Randolph and slapped her face.

"Ugh!" said Mrs. Randolph.

"Get out when I tell you," said Dora. "Your charity means nothing any more. At least allow me my cell. Leave and don't come back!"

Mrs. Randolph backed to the door, still too forgiving, holding her face, her jaw open. It seemed that the pain of the blow got to her only after half a minute, for she became angry then, after having been understanding at such lengths. "I hope they punish you good, Dora! I can't understand how you could do this, it surpasses my understanding, ma'am."

She went out and dragged the heavy wooden door of the lockup sharply closed behind her. From outside she called: "And don't expect any more visits in prison from *me!*"

Mrs. Whipple felt so desolate then. The best of friends is gone, she thought. But at the same time she was frightened Mrs. Randolph would forgive her and appear again by lunchtime.

Isabelle Randolph did not. Later in the day the gray-haired colonel said the wife of the Secretary of War had caught the train back to Charlottesville.

"AGAIN," CALLED LAFCADIO WHEAT. "Again, boys. And it's fresh'uns for us."

It was the harshest morning of the summer. A sharp-as-needle sun sat high over Virginia, sat like a heathen god sure of itself. It didn't intend to move. That sort of morning is bad enough for farmers who sow and crop the corn. And it has even more malice on a morning when the Yankees are still trying for that railroad cut as they have been since first light.

The Yankee regimental colors over there on the fringes of the woods looked so fresh and untorn and such a fierce confident blue and gold that the Volunteers grew silent. Usaph saw this boy and that looking over his shoulder, making mental ciphers of the distance back to the shelter of the woods. Wheat noticed it too.

"I don't want no boys looking for lines of flight," he called. "You fellers ain't going to need no lines of flight."

But everyone was thinking, so many of them! So many!

The flags that had come up the slope towards the cut earlier this morning had had *Michigan The Beaver State* written all over them. These new ones said *Vermont* and underneath, the *Green Mountain Boys*. Oh God, a far place, Usaph thought. All them fresh blue boys from a fresh, far, green place.

The look of those well-dressed boys awed everyone and no one was talking along the railroad cut; or if they did it was in whispers. Even Wheat didn't talk straight out but in mutters: "If we have to get, Usaph, I want you to get the fastest of the lot of us and take the news to Colonel Baylor. Mind you, I don't want no premature getting. But you know what I mean."

When hollow case exploded in the air above the Vermonters there'd been these noises like an axe to a man's skull.

All at once some three or four or six Vermonters somewhere in the line would be heaped atop one another and there'd be a sudden show of raw meat and white limbs with the blue clothing ripped off them by the bang of the shell. But this officer who you couldn't see—he was striding behind the boys' shoulders—would call: "Remember ole Ethan Allen, you Green Mountain Boys. Steady and close up and remember Ethan Allen."

"Ain't he a talkative son of a bitch?" Wheat murmured. "Can't you see him, Usaph?"

"No sir, Colonel Wheat."

"He must be a stumpy whoreson. If you can get a sight on that there orator, Usaph, shoot the son of a bitch through the heart."

It was a season of grass fires. Flames might start of their own mysterious accord, and a shell came down in the sere crabgrass in front of the Vermonters and shattered there and started fire. The flames went fast along the slope towards the Green Mountain Boys.

The thing that tipped Cate's reason happened then. There was a Michigan soldier who'd been wounded on that slope an hour before. He began heaving on his arms to get himself out of the fire's way, but it caught his blue coat. And he must have had cartridges in his pockets the way soldiers often did, for as he screamed as frightful as anyone in history ever had, the rounds in his pockets went off and tore his side away.

Usaph looked away. He saw Walter, the fiddler's fancy boy, begin to weep and slide down the fill and curl up on his side in the rank grass.

Sean went down after him and began to kick him as if he was a troublesome stranger.

Meanwhile Cate had rolled on his back and started gasping. "Jesus Christ," he called, loudly addressing the high sun, "do you enjoy these things? Do you goddam enjoy them?"

Wheat overheard this but didn't seem to know who it was who had spoken. "Who was it blasphemed?" he yelled. He knew what ill fortune it was to blaspheme on the edge of a battle. "What son of a goddam sow blasphemed there?"

"God damn us all!" Cate screamed even louder. Now he stood up on top of the cut, the better to be shot at. His chin was back; he was still roaring at the sky. "God damn us all. It is my sin. My goddam crime . . ."

Usaph was flabbergasted to hear Cate talk that way. To use a word like *sin*. Did it mean the son of a bitch wasn't a total godless mocker? But if he believed in sin, what sin was he talking about?

Lucius Taber stood up beside Cate. He had one of the lumps

of granite that seemed to be scattered up and down the cut.
Holding it in his two hands he brought it in a slow but mighty
swing against the side of Cate's head, knocking Cate's forage
cap off. Then Cate and Lucius fell together down the embankment, as if Lucius had done himself as much damage as
he had to the conscript. But Lucius got up in the end and
crawled back into his place atop the cut. It was Decatur Cate
who didn't move. Usaph could see a patch of Cate's face and
it looked pale and there was blood from his temple.

"I hope the son of a bitch is finished," he muttered to
himself. But he knew it was a lie. Because you can't get the
dead back to question them. And there was that thing Cate had
said about sin and crime and damnation.

Colonel Wheat called out as if it were a battle order. "I
want no more goddam insults to the Almighty."

Bumpass's mouth was making water now. He wondered
why? Why under this sun?

Well, it was a frightful reason and it came to him. The
smell of meat was the cause. The grass fire burned the Union
dead and there'd be this stammer of sharp noise whenever the
flames got to a dead boy's cartridges. Usaph spat the guilty
saliva from his mouth but more took its place. Best to ignore
it.

Through the open places in the smoke Wheat and Gus and
Usaph could see the Vermont lines coming on. If they had
fancy boys who wanted to sit and weep, and Cates who wanted
to call defiance at Christ, they had somehow settled them. In
some places they formed columns to cut through corridors
amongst the blazing grass and then re-formed in line again.
Soon they were but three hundred paces off, a little scattered
about, but looking business-like.

Lafcadio Wheat, using his field-glasses, looked past them.
Beyond the distant woods were further hillsides where regiments were forming. He saw a nice brisk regiment lined up
on the edge of a wooded slope perhaps half a mile off. It would
back up the Green Mountain boys.

"Do they have no bottom to their goddam barrel?" he asked
himself. He called lazily that everyone should fire at will. The
first volley went out, Usaph fixing on a tall captain and firing
but missing. There seemed so little damage to the Vermonters
that they got excited and started to come on faster.

Fifty steps further along they got while Usaph loaded, but

now the fire had a harsher effect and they began to sit or fall over in some numbers.

You could make out their faces now. They started to run. There was a boy only a little way from the cut, running crouched, his lips set in a sort of wince of effort that made him look as if he were laughing. Usaph shot him in the top of the hip on the right side. He tottered on a bit and the grin got wider, but in the end he toppled over. When that had been done Usaph loaded yet again, now lying on his back and holding his musket between his knees. When he had the new round ready and peeped over the cut again, they were on the far side not the length of a farm parlor away, and they were standing awhile, letting their brothers catch them up so that together they could all jump into the cut and mix business with the enemies of their Republic. But as fast as they mustered there they were shot down. Too close. Too close. Some of them looked up at you as you lay atop the grading and shot at your face. Usaph and four others all aimed at the sergeant who was holding the Vermont flag, and when he fell, it was picked up by a boy with a moustache who was red in the face and waving it like he was in some sort of competition at a fair. He stood there like that for half a minute till Lucius Taber shot him twice, in the forehead and the eye. And then there were some three or four others who picked it up and were each shot. Usaph had seen this sort of flag madness once before. Once the man with the regimental colors was shot, the others wouldn't let the colors just lie, they would line up for a turn to hold them, and in turn they would be shot.

At last a boy of about fourteen who was a drummer picked it up.

He lasted a long time there because, hardly knowing they were going easy on him, the crazed, dazed Shenandoah Volunteers in the cut avoided shooting at him. He was moon-faced, that boy, and he didn't do anything with the flag, he just stood with its stump on the toe of his shoe and its staff in his right hand and with his left he had to hold both his drumsticks. And he blinked all the time. And he seemed apologetic about what he was doing.

Well, everyone knew without having to be told how it was with drummers. They were generally orphans. This one stood there blinking all the time for perhaps some three or four minutes. Each time Usaph loaded he'd see him standing there.

And then all at once he was sitting on the flag like a farm child sitting on a mat. He'd been shot in the foot. Maybe it was an act of mercy. Or an accident.

Sometimes those Vermonters would stagger forward into the cut in twos or threes, and one who did that, and stood dazed in the cut, was himself staggered up to by Lucius who cracked his skull with stone—maybe the same stone he'd used on Cate. It seemed Lucius had no cartridges left for his fine blue-surfaced Colt. So every time Usaph looked there was Lucius stumbling along the cut hitting the sons of the Union on the skull.

Then up through the slope and the grass fires came the reserve regiment Wheat had seen more than half an hour before. To the abstract military part of his brain it seemed a sort of military crime that the Yankee generals hadn't sent them along earlier. Lafcadio Wheat did some calculations in his mind and decided that his boys might have no more than seven or so rounds—excluding of course what could be taken from the dead. He grabbed Usaph by the shoulders. Usaph was alarmed by his popping mad eyes and by his hot breath which was tainted by some disorder of the belly Wheat had. "Find William Baylor up in the woods. Tell him—God, you know what to tell him, Usaph. We are low in all ways. All our powder nigh on shot away. Tell him I need his reserves at *this* point if he has any sons of bitches in reserve. Take the message, Usaph, and may the Lord preserve your ass!"

Usaph slid down the embankment on the said part of his body which Colonel Wheat had just called on the Deity to protect. He met Lucius Taber at the bottom, resting mutely between excursions into the cut. Lucius and the granite in his hand and a fixed frowning look on his dirty face. And Wheat, looking from above and anxious for the boy, saw that the young officer was about to punish Usaph as a deserter. "Lucius," he screamed. "*Lucius!* He's my runner, don't you mind? Let him goddam *run!*"

Well, there were grass fires all over the Confederate slope too that Usaph was running on, taking the colonel's message. Since the railroad cut traveled in a bow here, there was—just a little way off to his left—a place where Yankees had got through the cut and were trying, face to face, to put bayonets into the Irishmen of the 5th Virginia. And like apparitions, there amidst the hot tang of grass smoke, came two Vermonters right up to Usaph's side and front.

"You take him from that side, Albert," one of them said, not taking his eyes off Usaph. Usaph began to urinate and he saw their faces with all the sharpness of his sick terror. Albert was a soulful long-mouthed boy, but he must have been a tough one to have got this far. The other one, the one who was giving instructions, was a broader-faced pug-nosed tall man with soot all over his face and a drooping black moustache. Both of them had bayonets of triangular mold fixed on their muskets and meant to transfix Usaph from each flank.

Usaph had some seconds looking from one to the other before he understood that his own musket still carried a charge. Up to then he'd been in such a sickness of fear that he wasn't sure whether he would go down on his knees and vomit and wait the bayonet, or actually try to do something about these two. Now he started to calculate his chances.

Albert's bayonet flashed at his side; Usaph was sure it touched his jacket at the waist. The lunge made Albert stagger. "Stand still, Reb," he told Usaph. Usaph thought, if they knew about Ephie and about all my doubts, would they still try to pierce me through? The one with the moustache probed for the right side of Usaph's body. At the second Usaph fired straight at the man's belly, his musket was knocked away by the bayonet. There was an upwards discharge and Usaph's attacker took the ball in the side of his face. The wound appeared through, and was just about hidden by the cloud of powder his dirty musket blew at the Vermonter. The boy's eyes rolled upwards, he swiped at them with a hand as if trying to keep his sight. Then he dropped down.

Now Usaph really had to dance to get from Albert's bayonet. He danced once, and wondered how many more seconds of this awesome nonsense he could take. He knew Albert would get him. So he himself got a vast anger against his executioner from Vermont and he took his musket by the barrel and screamed, "Come on, you goddam Vermonter son of a bitch. You goddam horse-fucking Yankee whoreson."

Albert said nothing except he was whimpering with the effort of getting that French-style bayonet of his into Usaph.

Usaph considered it a sort of death dream when he saw Cate come empty-handed and bare-headed, stumbling up behind Albert and picking up the dropped musket and bayonet of

Albert's fallen friend. And running it into Albert's back with
such a dose of mad energy that the thing came through the
front of Albert's jacket. Mad as a mink, Usaph thought the
bayonet point sticking from Albert and the coughing and yelp-
ing noises Albert made were a sort of prefiguring of what was
just about to befall him. He went down on his knees, bowed
his head, spat his bitter breakfast on the yellow grass and
waited for the steel to enter him. It was a little time coming
and his crotch began to itch with the urine and all them crabs.
And he forgot that an itch wasn't worth worrying about on the
verge of eternity and he began to scratch and said, "God have
mercy," and looked up. Cate stood there with the musket in
his hands. There was all kinds of muck on it, on the bayonet
torn from Albert. Albert lay on his side, eyes fixed and nose
pinched up and making a little protesting noise that had no
meaning.

Usaph got straight up and left the site like a man getting
clear of a murder in a bar. Cate sat down by Albert and went
into a trance which Usaph knew well was part of the granite
on the head he'd had from Taber, part of the terrible thing he'd
just done to the fabric of the Union.

And all the rage Usaph felt now was rage against Cate for
going to those lengths to save *him*, Bumpass. What did these
goddam lengths mean? Usaph got nearly to the edge of the
Confederate woods before he turned and saw Cate again, still
there, and yelled at him, "Don't you expect me to be goddam
grateful. You goddam black Republican . . . !" But Cate did not
even look at him.

Then Usaph remembered he had a message for Billie Baylor,
the commander of the shrunken Stonewall Brigade. He dashed
on through the pine trees to find him.

— 10 —

THE DAY AUNT SARRIE vanished from her farm, leaving Ephie
in Montie's care, she had been on her way to see Captain
Stilwell.

Captain Stilwell was a kindly but patriotic man of nearly

seventy years of age. He had got his rank during the Indian wars over in the western counties in the '20s. Now he was recruiting-and-conscription officer for Bath County, Virginia, and he worked from a corner of his large dry-goods business in Warm Springs. In the past week he had served conscription notices on some one hundred or more feckless mountain boys who hadn't managed to hide in the hills or to outride him.

On the day of Aunt Sarrie's visit to Warm Springs, he had been lunching at the Springs Hotel with some of the other town worthies and was walking out of the dining room with them, smoking a rotten wartime cigar, when he saw a plain but live-eyed woman of about fifty years sitting in the lobby and looking about as good as she could hope to in a yellow dress and a small green hat. I know that woman, he thought. Why, that's Sarrie Muswell, looking not at all like a widder. Her eyes met his. He told his friends to excuse him and went out and bowed at her.

"Mrs. Muswell, you're looking a treat," he told her.

"Better than I feel," she said. "I've come all this way to Warm Springs to speak to you, Cap'n Stilwell."

"My dear lady, I'm sure flattered."

"Do you have time to sit down awhile?" she asked.

He agreed that he did. When he had settled himself and stubbed out his foul cigar, she began to talk.

"You know I have this nephew serving in that Shenandoah Regiment . . . ?"

"A renowned battalion, ma'am."

She nodded her head impatiently at his military politeness. "My nephew's wife happens to be staying at my place, for she hails from Strasburg, at least Usaph does. Now his wife—Ephie's her name—hails all the way from the coastal swamps of South Carolina. She's one of them authentic swamp lilies, is Ephie."

"Pretty, you mean?"

"Like a rose . . ." said Aunt Sarrie.

"But not of such a good background?"

"You said it, Cap'n Stilwell. Dragged up by a trashy paw—some sort of fisherman. A fine gal, mind you. Of the best intentions . . ."

Captain Stilwell had a soldier's ear for that kind of hint.

"You don't mean she's seeing a new man . . . ?"

"No, I don't mean exactly that, Cap'n Stilwell."

The old man actually blushed—Aunt Sarrie could see the

blood reddening his creased old neck. "Forgive me then, Mrs. Muswell."

She told him that any trouble, if it were to come, was yet ahead of sweet Ephie. But this portrait painter was working on her. Aunt Sarrie could tell he wouldn't leave without trying to take Ephie with him.

"Has the blackguard said so, ma'am?" gallant Captain Stilwell asked her.

"He has not. Not yet, I mean. But I am a worldly enough woman, Cap'n Stilwell. And I can tell."

Captain Stilwell looked at her. "But do you think Ephie would be tempted to go?"

"She ain't a worldly woman at all. She'd never met a man like Cate. She ain't never been to a city except once to change trains in Richmond. She thinks Cate's the cleverest man she's ever like to meet. Whereas he's jest your average spruiker." She frowned at her hands a little. "I don't want my nephew Usaph to lose his wife, Cap'n Stilwell. Specially not when she's in my hand. What I think is . . . I think this Cate ought to be in the army."

She stared at Stilwell. The old man smiled. "Why ain't he already?" he asked.

"He hails from Pennsylvania, he says."

"A Lincoln man?"

"He says he ain't in particular."

"I wonder if it's much use recruiting Lincoln men . . ."

"I think, sir, to be honest, that you ought to conscript this boy no matter what his politics might be. Marriage, sir, has its value and it's a higher value than any politics I can think of."

The old officer nodded for a while. "I can be at your place Friday, ma'am," said the old captain. "With a militia guard. Make sure someway he don't run off on us before then."

"He won't run off. While ever Ephie's there. Cap'n Stilwell, I want you to know how grateful I am."

She put her hand on top of his well-scrubbed old wrist. Well, it's a good thing to be treated as a gallant, he thought. Aunt Sarrie could see how happy she'd made him. A liveliness came into his eyes.

"Are you staying in this house, ma'am?" he asked.

She nodded. "I wouldn't have no chance of reaching home by dark."

She saw his adam's apple bob. "My room is 38," she told him.

"38," he whispered. "Obliged, ma'am. For that news."

Well, thought Aunt Sarrie, there's nothing wrong with hugging a nice ole man if it brings some good. "One thing," murmured Aunt Sarrie, her mind still working, "he has money of his own—I owe him $10 myself. It'd be a perversion of our intentions for the boy, Cap'n Stilwell, if he was able to buy himself a substitute."

The old captain smiled in his grandfatherly way. "I'll blacklist him, ma'am, before the event, I'll blacklist him, so no substitute-broker'll touch him. By hokey, dear Mrs. Muswell, I shan't give him time to look sidewise for a substitute." Then he coughed. "Ain't you anxious, ma'am, that something bad will happen during this brief absence from your home? With the miscreant, I mean, and your nephew's wife?"

"Don't worry, cap'n. I told my slave Montie to look out."

Aunt Sarrie *had* done that. The problem was Montie didn't exactly know what she meant. If she had told him to watch out and make sure the painter and Mrs. Bumpass didn't dance a reel, he'd have been in less doubt. But of course she couldn't have said any such thing to him.

That evening Montie knew this much: that the painter ate supper on his own, for Mrs. Ephie Bumpass had said she wasn't in need of food. It seemed a good enough thing to Montie that the painter was left on his own like that. And by ten at night when all the doors were closed and Mrs. Bumpass was safe in her room, and the painter had gone out to the barn, there seemed little much else to watch for. For Montie had reasonably enough thought that Aunt Sarrie meant, *watch the painter while he's in the house.*

From the barn that night, Cate could see a low light burning in Ephie's room. It seemed a hopeful sign to him, even though she hadn't been at supper. How could they have talked at supper in any case, with Bridie fluttering round them?

Part of the time while he waited he spent lying on his cot in the stall he occupied. And whenever he looked the light was still burning in her bedroom upstairs. I'll wait until a half-hour after midnight, he told himself; then I'll break in somehow. Love's burglar.

Ephie came just before midnight, by way of the front door so that Montie and Bridie could not see her from their bedroom at the back of the house. All Cate could say was, "You *came*." That made it seem more miraculous than if he'd had to get into the house somehow, and without alerting that big black plowman.

"You touch me, Mr. Cate," she said insistently, seeking his hands, pulling them into her bodice. And perhaps the whole Cate–Bumpass mess started there. Because Cate thought, she can't wait to be satisfied, she has desired me so many long hours. Whereas Ephie wanted him just to be quick, so that she could forget what she was about, so she'd have a little holiday from the arguments her brain suffered under. Likewise, when she opened his britches and clutched him, he thought it was all runaway desire, when half of it was runaway shame.

His little camp cot seemed to him wider than a Louis XIV, for they were so close they needed little room except to writhe. And when at last he put his hand between her thighs and found her moist, again unwisely he took it as straight-out homage for Decatur Cate. And she said : "No delay, Mr. Cate. Come in and no delay, oh dear God," and he made the same mistake about that.

Cate had never known such a woman—she made such frank cries that he felt bound to put his fingers over her lips. When he flowed away into her, she was straight away grasping him again, demanding life of him . . .

And when she felt the mass of him in her she thought, I can't bide a war, I must have *this*, this which Cate is here to give. By hokey, I'll go to California with him.

After they had coupled a second time, Cate noticed how quiet she was.

"You'll travel with me, won't you? Say you'll travel with me."

"Yes," she said, but it was like a statement of despair.

She found her way back to the house "by owl hoot," as the locals said. It was some time after two. If I go with him, she was thinking, it'll mean I won't have to stick here to confess things to Usaph, to be shamed in front of him.

When Aunt Sarrie got home the next day she found that Ephie was baking away in the kitchen. The kitchen table was covered with apple and boysenberry and blackberry pies. Aunt Sarrie had rarely seen so many pies outside a bakehouse.

"Why, Ephie, you preparing for a harvest party?" she asked.

"No," said Ephie, but did not smile. "Jest felt like baking."

Aunt Sarrie looked at her and inspected her in her movements. Ephie did not look at Aunt Sarrie, though. The older woman could tell from Ephie's manner and from this crazy number of pies that had been baked that something had happened. She could guess what too. She said gently: "You want to have a rest, gal?"

"I do," Ephie said, and started weeping. "Aunt Sarrie, I don't want to do no more sitting for Mr. Cate."

Cate came in to lunch, half bold, half wary, but found there was no one there to eat with.

"Mrs. Bumpass ill?" he asked Bridie.

"I wouldn't know that," said Bridie, and not too politely. She didn't know anything, though, she was just picking up her manners from her mistress.

All day Cate failed to sight Ephie and he was really in a sweat. "I need one more sitting from the lady," he told Aunt Sarrie at suppertime.

Aunt Sarrie chewed slowly and stared at him. Then she took and opened the purse she had, right there at the table, and counted out ten silver dollars. "Maybe you'll have to abandon that portrait, Mr. Cate."

He looked at her through lowered lids, hating her frankly. "I'll finish it overnight," he said.

"Maybe you ought to get some rest," she said, and smiled as if it were a private joke.

There was no doubt now. The hatred between him and that old widow was out on the table.

When he went to his bed that night, he took the canvas with him. On his pillow he found a note. "I sall go with you to Calliforn," it said. He put the paper close to his lips. "Tomorrow," he said. "Tomorrow."

The day began sweetly enough. He did not go near the house, but he propped the portrait on a chair where the morning sun would catch it, and as the last of it dried, it faced her room. It waited there on the chair like his morning gift. Then he began to pack. There were some of his sketch books and oils still in the parlor, but he could fetch them later in the day or, if Mrs. Muswell proved too hostile, he could leave them behind with a free heart.

In the early afternoon he failed to hear the small detachment of militia trudging up the path to the barn, and he was just fetching his mare from her stall when the old officer knocked on the barn door.

"Mr. Cate?" the old man asked.

Cate could somehow see the coming disaster in the old officer's old-fashioned braid. You didn't have a chance with those old boys. They had such a heart-and-gut interest in killing off the young.

"I am Cate," Cate said, feeling ill.

"I don't want to get the wrong man. Is it Decatur Cate?"

"Yes, sir."

"I am Cap'n Stilwell, recruiting-and-conscription official for Bath County. I give you notice that you are conscripted into the army of the Confederacy, young man. You got maybe half an hour to pack your things."

Cate put a look of amazement on his face and looked about, grimacing. "I've got a horse and dray, Mr. Stilwell. I can't very well pack them."

"You will of course ride them to the Staunton military depot, where you can sell them. You ain't likely to be needing a dray when you fight for Jackson, boy."

But Cate smiled, for he'd just remembered the substitute system, and he knew he could sure afford a substitute.

"I shan't need to do that, sir," he said. "I do of course have a substantial amount of money for my use. I shall buy someone to stand in for me."

"No you won't."

"I beg your pardon, sir."

"I don't tolerate the substitute system in Bath County," the old man said.

Cate chuckled at him indulgently. "It's provided for by Act of Congress. You don't have the power to disallow it."

The old man, with an extraordinary quickness, had all at once got a great revolver in his hand. "You will not find a substitute-broker to deal with you, boy. Nor will you find any local boy to take your money. Bath County is pretty well cleaned out of possible conscripts now in any case, son. Let me tell you, I'm an energetic man and I sure believe in my work. I ought to remind you too, son, that if you resist conscription I am powered to confiscate your property. Now, if you obey me, I'll sell your horse and dray for a good price and hold the money for you or send it to your regiment for collection, jest whatever you like. You'll find it more satisfactory, I believe, than forfeiting everything. Come now, son, you're wanted at Staunton military depot, and you ain't got much time to pack."

Cate looked at the four militia men who were waiting by the barn. The youngest seemed to be fifty. Escape must be a possibility, he thought. I'll tell him there are things of mine in the parlor, and then I'll escape out the back door and up into the woods. And then I'll send Ephie a message.

"There are things in the parlor I have to collect," Cate said.

"Rob, Hennie," called the old man, and two militia sergeants of more than fifty years apiece appeared in the door of the barn. They carried smooth-bore muskets. Loaded? Cate wondered.

These two marched him into the house, straight in the open door, and into the parlor. There were a few sketchbooks round and a tray of oils. The two militia men, as country people will, looked around at the walls and furnishings. Yes, Cate was sure, there was a chance here. As he picked up the tray from the sideboard he noticed something distracting though. It was a letter addressed thus: *To privet Bumpass, Guess Co., the Shenandoh Regiment, Stonewall's Divishun, neer Richmun.* Ephie had written that at least three days ago and had left it there. She could have given it to Aunt Sarrie to post in Warm Springs yesterday, except there was so much for her to think of these past few days she clearly forgot. For a reason Cate could not understand—maybe as a gesture of victory over Private Bumpass—he put the thing in his pocket, then turned and faced the two rustic sergeants. "Look," he said, and then hurled the tray of paints at them.

He edged between them and ran down the hallway. Through an open back door he could see the sky and the deep forests just a sprint beyond.

Then Montie stepped into that doorway—he'd been waiting on the back porch with Aunt Sarrie all that time. He took Cate in his arms and held him in a bear hug. There wasn't any breaking that fierce hold. Mrs. Muswell's strong man had him neat.

The militia men caught up. Cate saw Aunt Sarrie looking up at him from the kitchen garden. She had a bowl of runner beans in her hand. Now that his flight had been stopped, he wanted to get at her and strangle her.

"Let me go, you goddam black brute!" he screamed at Montie.

"I thought all you Pennsylvania folk loved the black man," said Mrs. Muswell.

"God rot your barren old womb, ma'am," Cate screamed.

At this insult to Southern womanhood, one of the militia men grabbed his hair and pulled his head backwards.

"And you, sir," said Aunt Sarrie, "you do your duty."

The militia and Montie dragged Cate down the hallway. "Mrs. Bumpass!" he yelled near the stairs. "Mrs. Bumpass!" But Ephie did not show herself. "I'll come back!" he called, holding on to the door-jamb of the front door. But no one answered.

As they wrestled him towards the wagon they'd brought with them, ignoring his own horse and dray, he watched her window. But there was nothing to see. They've made her prisoner, he concluded.

Another boy of saner mind might have got the right meaning from Ephie's failure to show herself. Might have taken the meaning that the girl had decided against him. But Cate was too deep in love. They've made her a prisoner, he went on believing.

— 11 —

THIRTY-SEVEN UNION regiments had struck the cut that noon. The body of Albert, who had tried to run his bayonet in Usaph, was one of the higher marks that tide had made.

Neat little Sean the fiddler, who hadn't a sort of obsessed guardian angel to guard his flanks the way Cate had guarded Usaph's, who had only Walter his boy-love to look out for him, *had* been bayoneted to death against the fill of that railroad cut. Sean lay on his side, his eyes open. Walter sat on in some species of trance, his back to Sean's. Lucius Taber couldn't get any answer out of him.

Danny Blalock looked down at Sean, at the open eyes and gritty face, the neat little mouth drawn back and the bones of the skull already pushing up through the flesh. Danny began to kick dirt over the serpent's nest of Sean's torn stomach. "You should be doing this," he told the boy. "You should be doing this, you goddam sodomite."

Walter didn't hear. He was staring mad. He would have to

be carried away, but there was little chance of that, Danny Blalock knew. Even the wounded would be lucky to get litters by dusk. The mad had no chance.

Hans Strahl's father had, in the summer of 1861, asked his son: "Vat ist about dis var? I don' see dis schweine Lincoln at my damt farm gate, do you dis damt Lincoln see troublink your momma or me?"

It was a fair argument. But Hans still wanted to go to the war, for the war meant his liberation from that little German colony near Newmarket. Until the war began, the Lutheran way of things had seemed a good enough way to him. Sure, you could court a girl only under the heavy eyes of aunts, generally the girl's. You sat heavy-suited and squeaky-booted in the parlor of a good German farm and old women listened to everything you said to the girl and then denounced you in church the following Sunday if there was something they didn't like.

Your only chance of something different was to get to town on market day and make an arrangement with one of them fast girls they had in Newmarket or Woodstock or Strasburg. Otherwise you courted nice girls like Emma Groener in front of an audience of her relatives, who weren't the most joyful folk you'd met, and you went home and dreamt of what might have happened if they'd ever left you alone for half an hour in one of them plain, no-nonsense parlors. But there wasn't sense in complaint. That was the way everyone Hans knew up to the summer of '61 had ever courted. And he didn't, up till then, think it such a bad thing to live and die that way.

The coming of war churned him up though. The Strahls owned no slaves. They were gently in favor of the Union, but only in so far as they felt closer to their brethren in Pennsylvania than they did to any big landholder of British descent down in the lowlands. But Hans could tell that this war was his chance to change himself, and to taste a wider life, and to get loose from those aunts and elders, and to speak to women without a crowd of spectators, and to be profane for a while and earthy and, in the end, to have a call on the gratitude of a bigger bunch of people than he would normally get noticed by, on Methodists and Presbyterians and other *englische* people in towns like Newmarket.

So he made an honest soldier. He was happy with what had happened to him. He had stories to tell his grandchildren. He had memories. In Winchester early in the year, when local girls were able to pick with whom they'd walk, an Irish girl called Molly Nagel walked with him and coupled with him away from witness in as wild a way as you could want. He learned to speak profanity too in English, so he would know when he went back to that little clutch of Germans what he was giving up by talking seemly.

He'd always guessed that these kinds of reasons were the reasons half the boys were here, and that there must be Danes or Germans or others over in that Yankee army who were working away for just about the same reasons. Of course he wasn't thinking about any of this today. He was generally aware of being in line in a cause a lot of clever people said was holy, and he had Americans both sides of him. He was not afraid any more and felt just about as good as he had three afternoons back, during the feast at Manassas Junction. He was sure the dysentery, which had plagued him these past three months, wasn't going to trouble him any more.

That afternoon James Longstreet decided it was "militarily possible" now to move his infantry in a great crescent-shaped line across the fields either side of the Gainesville turnpike. Jackson's boys were able to leave the cut at last and go ahead. Since the Shenandoah Volunteers were close to the place where Longstreet's line hinged on Jackson's, they found themselves stumbling forward behind a line of Hood's Texans.

All of them, Strahl too, had not untangled the sights and noises of the morning. Their minds were jumbled and dazed. The Texans, however, moved fast; they were a hundred paces ahead. Whenever they got to a fence, they'd dismantle it quickly, as if they didn't want their movements hindered by fences.

They passed a schoolhouse, white, with a little belfry, and its windows locked. Deep in its summer sleep. From here, through open views amongst the trees, you could see lines of Rebel soldiers and battle flags away off to the south in a great sickle. When the Texans saw that they started making their funny noises. Tired and numb as he was, even Strahl felt their excitement and in the midst of that Texas yelling shells began to lob in the neighborhood or burst in the air. One struck the school bell in a way that caused it to give a *comic* bong.

"Goddamit!" the Texans were hooting. "They's musical bastards, they is."

The Volunteers crossed the main pike in the wake of the Texans. Though some of them stumbled, they were drawn along by the magnetic drag of the frenzy of these strangers from the Confederacy's further corner. Hans Strahl could see a good stone fence ahead and a parsonage beyond it. From behind this fence Yankees rose and shot the Texans fair in the face, but the Texans overran the parsonage yard. Now everyone was running for the cannon, both the Texans and the Yankee fleers. Hans Strahl, stepping amongst the fallen around the parsonage, felt like little more than a witness.

The Yankee gunners were so frightened on their little hill that they had their cannon filled to the lip of the muzzle with those terrible bunches of balls called grape. The Texans who were struck fell down to make a sort of animal hedge in Hans's path.

It was the nature of the battle that though these heaps gave off screams, they meant as little to Hans as would the cries of migrating birds. The voices of those Napoleons and Parrotts on the hills were the only voices of any merit and drew on the Texans the way sirens draw sailors.

Later many boys wouldn't remember approaching the guns. All Usaph, for example, could remember was being amongst them suddenly, a cannon wheel by his shoulders. The cannon fired and the wheel jolted backwards, spinning him with it. The blur of wheel and the shock of the firing dropped him down on the ground with a bleeding nose.

It was poor Hans Strahl, stumbling innocent in blue smoke, who happened to be fair in line with the mouth of one of those cannons just when a charge of grape went off into his chest. The man who had pulled the lanyard was himself already dying, for a Texan had pierced him with a bayonet. As one ball of grape tore Hans's head off, others burst it into fragments and hanks of his dark hair were scattered wide. Both his arms were likewise torn away, ripped up and thrown wide. His entrails were scattered over the hillside, his left leg sundered into small lumps and his right thrown away to one side amongst Texans and strangers. Ash Judd, beside him, did not know where he had gone—to Ash, Hans Strahl's vanishing was as magical as the ole man of widow Lesage. Later Ash would go seeking him in the fields around the parsonage and up forward, as far as Chinn Hill.

Hans felt nothing but a fearful shock bigger than the known world. It is likely that the fact of his death seemed a small thing beside the size of that great tearing he suffered. Indeed, his mother would report seeing him around the farm for some years after that afternoon at Manassas and, being his mother, she could tell he was hanging around bewildered and in need of a simple explanation.

Whereas the Yankee who had pulled the lanyard had a deep and decent sleep.

While Usaph lay in his bloody-nosed swoon, the four-mile sickle of the Confederate army ran on over Chinn and Bald Hill and on to the Henry house and beyond it to the Stone Bridge over Bull Run. Cloud came up in the evening, and with it rain, and the Federal army set nervous pickets along the Centerville Road and kept dragging off north. And all that time Wheat's regiment stayed on their hill, guarding the captured cannon and putting the dead in three pits—one for the Union, one for the Confederacy, and one for corpses that carried no signs other than those of their humanity.

— 12 —

INTO A PLAIN decorated parlor in the White House in Washington that evening, two Union officers brought a brown dispatch case. One carried it, the other served as escort. They stopped in front of a long table topped with morocco leather. Fair under the round bulbs of a gas chandelier and beneath a portrait of Andrew Jackson, Old Hickory—by an irony, the last Southerner to have become President of the Union—sat Abraham Lincoln, looking a little ill and scurfy by gaslight.

This was not his accustomed office, but he'd been working here since a meeting of the cabinet broke up only an hour before. It was after ten o'clock now and, as the President's secretary, young John Hay, knew, the President had not yet eaten dinner.

The officers saluted, and one of them handed the dispatch case to John Hay. Hay undid the case, took out the dispatches and laid them on the morocco-top table. The President began to read them without any expression. "You might wait outside for a while," he suggested to the officers after a time.

John Hay knew how far down in the glooms his chief could go, but he didn't see anything to worry about in the way Abe got rid of these two clothes-horses from the War Department. When the door was closed behind them though, Abe's head began to loll as if he would be sick any second or just faint away. There was this half-whimper, half-groan from him. "Well, John," he said, "it's happened again."

He said nothing more for a while and John Hay didn't ask.

"We've bin whipped, I mean. You can read it all." He let the dispatches flutter out of his hands. "Johnny Pope says he's licked. He's scuttling back to the old lines round Centerville. Right where we were at the start of last winter, mind you."

John Hay himself wanted to slump down in a chair. The Union generals had wasted this summer. They had done more than waste it. John Hay had a normal respect for the office of the presidency but he didn't think this was a decent version of it—to sit and work in Washington and hope that the generals out there would show the average enterprise of a hardware store proprietor say. And to be always disappointed.

Abe Lincoln suffered from a strong disadvantage for a man who liked power—he felt, almost as a personal hurt, the length of the casualty lists and the individual agonies and losses that they spoke of. He said, "By heaven and earth, John, if I was one of those thousands of boys who went under this summer— by heaven and earth, John!—I'd want to know what for, I would! I'd want to know what *for*!"

The President's head went on lolling. "Do you want me to fetch Mr. Secretary Stanton, Mr. President?" John Hay asked.

"That I'll think about," Abe Lincoln told him. Abe lifted another paper, the way a professor lifts an especially bad examination essay. "McClellan has diarrhea, John, and Mr. Secretary Chase of the Treasury tells me we can't raise any more money and that he doesn't want to take that easy way out the Rebs took and print the stuff. I tell you, the bottom is out of the tub, John. The bottom is out of the tub."

He closed his eyes for a while. "Fetch General Meigs," he said in the end.

As John Hay went to find a messenger, he met General Meigs in the waiting room outside and was able to bring him straight in. "At least some things get done fast in this Republic," the President said, seeing the general.

Meigs was the Quartermaster General of the U.S., a sane

old professional dedicated to the Union and the constitution. So he was the sort of soldier who—unlike the McClellan bunch—didn't see the military as a holy brotherhood with rights to bully any civilian, even a President.

"Is it time to pack yet, Montie?" Lincoln asked.

"Pack, sir?"

"I mean, is it time to leave Washington? Is it time to choose a new capital? By hokey, the Bostonians would like that. What I'm getting at, Montie, is whether Pope can hold them at Centerville. Do we have to look forward to a siege?"

General Meigs smiled. "I don't think we have to pack tonight, anyhow," he said.

"What is the cause, Montie? How could anyone fail as thoroughly as Johnny Pope?"

The Quartermaster General shrugged. "I hear reliably that his staff work this past three days has been poor. And his intelligence poor. This afternoon of course he was gobbled up on the flank by an immense force that he scarcely knew was there."

The President nursed his lean jaws. "That's just about the same as going to a circus and failing to notice the damn elephant."

Two hours before the news came in from Manassas the President had talked to his cabinet about a document he and Hay had got together between them. It was the document that had been waiting to be written for months. It was a decree freeing the slaves of the Confederacy. He had already signed an Act ending slavery in the District of Columbia by the device of buying slaves from their owners for no more than $200 each and then freeing them. Already the War Department had revised the regulations compelling army or naval officers to return runaway slaves to their owners. And from Vienna, the U.S. Ambassador, John Motley, was saying that only one of three things would stave off recognition of the Confederacy by the European powers; there had to be a great conclusive win over the Confederacy; or else there had to be the capture of the cotton ports so that cotton could be released to Europe; or else there had to be a clear-cut emancipation of the slaves.

Well, things were a little more complicated than that. Even Secretary Seward, who'd been so keen on abolition all his life, could see that you couldn't have a clear-cut emancipation of slaves unless there was first a great compelling sort of victory. And with Johnny Pope whipped and McClellan in the privy

with runny bowels, there was no way you could suddenly
declare Confederate slaves free without looking ridiculous.

"Montie, tell me this," said the President. "No reflection
on you—but where do you think generals are manufactured?
And how come the Confederacy seems to have cornered the
market in them?"

— 13 —

THERE WAS A stillness in the valley of the Cowpasture, an
endless hot day sat over Aunt Sarrie's place and everyone
moved slowly at their eternal tasks: Aunt Sarrie upstairs making
beds with Bridie, Montie in the river pasture sowing corn for
that summer's second crop, Lisa crooning on the stoop and
Ephie in the kitchen at the churn. The gurgling and whumping
of that churn was just a background rhythm in Lisa's quiet
song.

Some counties away Ephie's spouse toted sharp-edged ammunition boxes, but Ephie thought little of him this afternoon;
not because she was not beset by him, but because she was
fighting away at an urge to retch. She kept her hands firm on
the churn handle, for she knew Aunt Sarrie had been looking
sideways at her, looking for signs to back up certain ideas
she'd got about Ephie's condition. So Ephie worked the churn
hard both to distract Aunt Sarrie from fretting about her and
also in the sweating hope that it might just clear her problem.
Why, she'd had a cousin who'd lost four of them at an early
time and only eventually managed to keep one till term. It had
made it seem like the longest child-carrying in history. Other
women used to joke with this cousin, "What you carrying in
there? A brown bear?"

What Ephie had been saying to herself, sometimes aloud,
each miserable night since Cate had left, was something like:
you ain't no decent wife, Ephie Bumpass. Sure, you were
playing at being one since you met good Usaph Bumpass but
you knew how it was but playing. You happen to be one of
them swamp whores Daddy Corry sometimes brought into the

house. You lay with a man jest because he could ply oil paints.

Oh, Ephie's shame was like a sickness. It cramped her belly when she tried to eat. She'd get to bed tired, but it would pepper her brain up and her legs would twitch like something frantic. She thought how, when he was caressing her, Cate had said, you'll come with me and travel the wild world, and how she'd thought Amen, how heady that would be, to travel with an artist and watch him do his work, watch him squint and frown and make lines and hues that no other creature on the earth could do. Whereas, and there was no denying it, one farmer could and did do pretty much what any other farmer could and did do. And thinking about this became part of the shame as well.

It seemed to Ephie the shame that followed on adultery with Cate was enough tax for a woman to pay without this extra thing that had befallen her.

All that hard work on the churn did for her this morning was make her want to puke. She stood up in a fever of sweat. Old Lisa's song gave her sickness a sort of rhythm. "Lisa, will you be quiet for a minute!" she called. But Lisa didn't hear. It was Aunt Sarrie and Bridie who heard, and Aunt Sarrie who answered from the top of the stairs.

"You calling there, Ephie?"

Ephie staggered into the hallway and turned and, so it seemed to her, could not stop turning. The stairwell was tipping up, she believed, and falling on her. She felt a hardness under her shoulder-blades and thought it was a wall, but then was surprised to find it was the floorboards. Bridie stood over her, working at her nose with the neck of an ammonia bottle. The fumes stung Ephie's brain, but swung the house back on to its proper foundations.

Aunt Sarrie said: "Bridie, now you go and get lemonade for poor Mrs. Bumpass. You'll find us in the parlor. And mind you knock before you bring it in."

When Aunt Sarrie got her back on her feet, Ephie didn't quite want to go into the parlor. The parlor meant Aunt Sarrie looked on all this as a solemn event and wanted to talk solemn with her. And there was in that parlor, beside the Bible and the daguerreotype of Aunt Sarrie's dead husband Lewis, and many other intimidating items, that accursed portrait on the wall.

Sarrie got her in there though and sat her in the velvet-upholstered seat and stood back, a righteous sensible woman in a gray dress. Her plainness seemed to Ephie to be a blessing, and Ephie wanted plainness like that more than brains or riches. "I know what it is, Ephie. I bin makin' little guesses these past two weeks what your state is, gal."

Ephie shook her bowed head. What could she say? "I only been making little guesses these past two weeks myself, for sweet Lord's sake, Aunt Sarrie," she whispered.

"Well you see, Ephie, I thought *it* had happened, you see. I thought it *had* or *would* happen, gal. I thought that artist feller and yourself had a fancy for each other. I take it it's the artist feller. You got no further surprises for me, have you, Ephie girl?"

Ephie had her eyes closed and shook her head yet again. It was so sweet to have it out now, and Aunt Sarrie spoke to her in a way she hadn't expected, like someone who was in a secret with her and who might herself have once or twice slept with men other than her daguerreotyped dead husband.

"We could put it out for fostering but that's cruel on a child . . . besides, with all the waggle-tongues and gossips we have in this county, there ain't no ways the news won't get round." Aunt Sarrie sighed. "Usaph shouldn't have the hurt of that. It would follow him till he was an ole man. So . . ."

Bridie knocked and came in with the lemonade, putting it down in silence, and Aunt Sarrie kept a special silence, as if Bridie was in on the news too but it was against the rules to say so. So Ephie began to blush deep in front of the slave lady Bridie, who left the room while they were still, all three of them, locked up in that knowing silence.

"That's it," said Aunt Sarrie then. "We got to go and see Grannie Ambler over to Williamsville."

"Who's this Grannie Ambler?"

Aunt Sarrie set her mouth on strong, no-nonsense lines. "Well, I believe you don't want your Usaph to see you grow big with another fellow's child come Christmas. Grannie Ambler helps people in your situation."

"Helps? Does it hurt?"

"Tolerable," said Aunt Sarrie. "But woman is a creature made for some pain. And you must be brave, Ephie."

Ephie knew it was settled then. When she wept, she didn't know if it was fear or gratitude that sparked the tears.

— 14 —

JED HOTCHKISS, THE MAPMAKER, had a mess of maps to get
ready by dawn and a poor place to do it in. He was working
at the kitchen table of a farmhouse up near the Chantilly estate,
just twenty miles west of Lincoln's nervous capital. It was cold
and the rain clamored on the farm roof. He knew this was
September 1 and that the year had begun to turn now and that
maybe a muddy fall and a fierce winter were just ahead.

The surface of the table he worked on was all holystoned.
The farmer's wife had spent so much effort on it that it had
great hollows in it and wide cracks. There was a good table
in the front room but it had the corpse of an important Yankee
laid out on it. So Jed had to make do with a surface that just
about followed the contours of the country he was making
maps of.

By him he had inks and pens and pencils, rulers and com-
passes and protractors, sheets of drawing paper, rough diagrams of northern Virginia with triangulations pencilled in all
over them, and notebooks full of figures.

At the end of the table sat his assistant, a young engineer
from Augusta County, making a general map of western Maryland from a number of sources—old farmers' almanacs and
year books and an old-fashioned volume called *A General
Description of the State of Maryland*.

Jed himself was drawing a map of the Aldie and Ball's
Bluff regions. One of his sources was a map he'd made himself
as a younger man. One college vacation he'd set out to map
the entire Commonwealth of Virginia just for the fun such an
exercise would give him. While he worked now Jed listened
to that English scribbler Searcy, who was sitting by the banked-
down fire with very little to do except talk. Searcy was arguing
away in his seesaw British voice about prices.

Searcy was in a strange mood. The sense that he was fatally
locked to this foreign war frightened him. He had always been
an observer before, it was a role that suited his unattached

soul. He'd never felt a particular war would get him. He felt it now. The image of pixie-faced Mrs. Whipple tonight only made him all the surer that *this* war wouldn't let him off free as all the others had.

As well as that he was grieving, though he didn't tell Jed that. It was now two days since Pope was routed at Manassas—and began his retreat. This afternoon, in the low muddy fields round Chantilly, Stonewall's wing had been halted by terrible rain, and as well as that by a firm stand over a two-mile front by U.S. generals Porter and Kearny. What upset Searcy was that one of the best men in the Union was laid out on the good table in the front parlor, a captured corpse.

Searcy had been covering up all this worry and loss by arguing—as had been said—about currency and prices with Jed and the boy engineer from Augusta County. That boy seemed to have no trouble talking and at the same time drawing firm, exact lines.

"My paw," he was saying as he worked away on that map of western Maryland which Stonewall wanted by breakfast-time tomorrow, "works in the War Department in Richmond. When he got the job last year at $110 a month, I thought— whoo-ee! My mammy and pappy is rich! They rented a house right there on Marshall Street, jest a stroll from the Capitol, for $50 a month and lived like a king and a queen with the rest. Alas, alack..."

"I know, I know," said Searcy, as if he were gloomily pleased about it. "You can't rent an attic in Richmond for $50 a month any more."

"Are you telling *me* that?" the young engineer asked. "Per-digious prices prevail in Richmond, Mr. Searcy. Perdigious prices. For an instance $3 for a pound of candles..."

"$8, I believe," said Searcy, still seeming to Jed to hang onto the words with a perverse joy, "for a pound of tea."

"Goddam! Whisky $10 a quart. Butter a goddam luxury at $2.50 a pound. It's all that goddam paper money..."

All that goddam paper money. Searcy remembered a time just after the start of the war, before the conflict claimed him and took him over. At that stage the center of the Confederacy was a little whitewashed Greek-style building on a modest hill in Montgomery, Alabama. Here he had interviewed the Con-federacy's Secretary of the Treasury, a long-faced, very sober man called Chris Memminger. Searcy found it pretty easy to sum Memminger up. He'd had a modest law practice in Sa-

vannah. You could tell just by looking at his suit that he was
a thrifty man, and cautious. But the nature of the war that was
just starting would soon turn him into a gambler. Memminger
confessed that there hadn't been enough money in the Treasury
Department to buy him a desk—he'd had to get one on his own
private bank draft.

"I recall a time," said Searcy aloud, "when there wasn't in
the entire Confederacy one sheet of banknote paper to print
money on. Well, things have changed. Things have changed."

Jed whistled, shook his head and went on drawing. He knew
nothing about economics. But he didn't like to hear Englishmen
running down Confederate notes.

Why, earlier in the evening a gang of ten Rebel soldiers
had tried to break their way into this very kitchen. Jed had
shooed them out at gunpoint. Ten hollow-faced boys who
hadn't had rations since yesterday morning, or so they said.
Ten boys in rotten butternut jackets and shredded britches. Two
of them barefoot. It seemed to Jed that the English government
could put shoes on the feet of those boys, bread in their bellies
and value into the Confederate dollar just by the simple act of
recognizing the South. And that for an Englishman to take
delight in the fact that the Confederate dollar lacked value was
altogether too rich. However, Jed didn't say anything. He was
busy enough.

Yet Searcy seemed to pick up his unspoken ideas and to
get piqued by them.

"I know exactly what you're doing, Major Hotchkiss,"
Searcy called out. "You're making maps of Loudoun and Jefferson Counties, paying special care to mark in the fords on
the Potomac, and our young friend here is putting together a
map of western Maryland. I know all that. And Jackson means
to rampage all over Maryland, and go straight on into the
North. But what has he got to pay for it all with except Treasury
notes? Memminger prints banknotes as if they were so many
harmless pages out of the Bible. But there's no hard money,
Major Hotchkiss. All the collateral that the South has is their
hope of winning the war."

"Maybe that's enough," said Jed simply.

Searcy laughed. "There's something to be admired about
your people."

Jed didn't like the way it was said. Searcy used those in-
dulgent tones that are reserved usually for talking about fools

and hicks. "I'm finding it hard to work," he told Searcy all at once. "I don't understand any of this bank talk. I only know that Stonewall wants more maps by morning than I'm likely to have finished. Would you mind leaving, sir, or at least going to sleep?"

Searcy shook his head and sort of laughed and got up.

"I think your *paw* should understand," said Searcy to the younger mapmaker, "that things won't get better in Richmond. For paper money is like the hounds and the good things, tea and coffee and candles, are like the fox. When you have too many hounds chasing too few foxes, no one has much sport."

"Please!" said Jed. "Please, Mr. Searcy!"

So Searcy went out into the hallway, leaving the mapmakers alone.

"Goddam, he talks some, don't he?" he heard the young engineer mutter before he'd closed the door properly.

Searcy kept on down the dark hall with nothing but a little radiance from the fanlight above the front door to help him. "Oh what a world!" he whimpered as he collided with an overcoat.

In the front parlor Major General Phil Kearny, U.S., lay between four burned-down tapers in a box on a cloth on a cedar table. Searcy came to a stop beside the table and inspected the man inside the coffin. Even laid out, Kearny looked tall, and his dark sensitive face was as Searcy had remembered it. Just four hours past Phil had been raging through the rain looking for a Yankee brigade to send against Ambrose Hill's division. Instead he'd found a string of Confederate skirmishers behind a rail fence. Their fire had torn his back open and cut most of his right hand off as he turned to warn his aides to flee.

Two hours ago the body had been borne here in an ambulance, and the farmer got in black women to undress Phil Kearny, to sew up the back and wash the body and put it again in its uniform. A glove now lay over the remnants of Kearny's right hand.

Searcy had been traveling with the French General Le Tellier in the hot north Italian summer in 1859 when he first met Phil Kearny. The English journalist had the beginnings of what turned out to be typhus, and General Le Tellier had kindly let him travel in his carriage. Carriage! Searcy couldn't imagine Tom Jackson traveling in a carriage. The carriage, like the rest of the French army, was making for Milan, a city that lay wide open to it. In the midst of all the traffic, there was a cavalry officer giving orders in bad New Jersey French: "*A bas! A bas! A droit, vacheur! Mon dieu, à droit!*"

When he had the columns and wagons moving again, this same officer leaned in the carriage window, reported to General Le Tellier and found the fevered Englishman there. That was the start of the friendship. Searcy went through his fevers and his convalescence in a vast cool room in a palazzo in Milan. Phil Kearny used to come round with fruit and brandy. That had been another world. A world of Popes and French dragoons in uniforms dreamed up from grand opera, and generals who weren't much different, really, from ordinary men. He wished he were back there now, in a war between the French and the Piedmontese on the one hand and the Austrians on the other. He wished he were back in a war that meant damn all to him.

Searcy put his finger out and touched the little red cord that was tied to the top button of the dead man's jacket. It was the Legion of Honor. There weren't any other Americans who had it. "Why did you come home, Phil?" he asked the large serene face. "Why in God's name?"

Later in the night Union officers would come under a flag of truce to collect the body. So now Searcy took some papers from his own pocket, and into the side pocket of Kearny's jacket, he pushed a report on what he knew of Confederate strength and intentions. Phil was the best means for sending a message. Even if Mrs. Whipple had by now been contacted by Federal agents and was again a depot in the line of information that passed northwards, Searcy could not reach her in her Orange hospital for at least three days. After the past four or five days Searcy had got a low idea of the skill of Union intelligence officers. But surely *someone* would go through the corpse's pockets before they buried it.

In the notes he had put in Kearny's pocket was a sentence underlined three times. It was not in Horace Searcy's nature to underline things. But you had to make the main facts stick out somehow. "Lee therefore," he had written, "cannot take more than an army of 60,000 into Maryland."

He feared they wouldn't believe that. That they would sooner hear McClellan's Colonel Pinkerton insist that the Confederacy had a quarter of a million young men. For only that explained why it was growing so hard for the Union to win its battles.

About the time Searcy placed his dispatch in the pocket of

dead Phil Kearny, Robert E. Lee was writing a letter to James Longstreet. He wasn't actually writing it in his own hand, for both his hands were bandaged. His adjutant did the writing for him.

A few nights back Lee had been waiting in the rain, standing by his horse Traveller, expecting a reconnaissance report from Jeb Stuart. A couple of cavalrymen came up yelling that there were Union horseman all round. In stretching for Traveller's bridle, Robert Lee tripped on the long rubber cavalryman's overall he was wearing and lurched sideways. His hands went out to break the fall. A bone was broken in the right hand and the other one was sprained. Since then, hands bound and taped, he'd travelled round the area by horse ambulance.

"Dear James," he was dictating now. "I agree with you there are only two things we can do now. We can pull back to Richmond and wait for the Yankees and hope to beat them again in detail as happened in June. I know you favor that. The benefit of that is that we have short lines of supply that can easily be protected. But I wonder what would happen if the Yankees get hold of the Virginia Central Railroad. That, James, would put the squeeze on us.

"You say our boys lack everything. They lack meat, you say. They lack leather. Well, perhaps they will find everything in Maryland. You say McClellan can get some 90,000 against us without even concentrating on it. I say, James, with respect, all the more reason for keeping moving."

As Robert Lee dictated he moved his bandaged hands around like a man playing an imaginary piano.

"I intend to go to Maryland, James. I intend to open up the Valley as my line of supply. I know what you're thinking. Harper's Ferry is smack in the middle of this line of supply. They say there are perhaps 12,000 Yankees there. It is my belief that all we need to do to have them surrender or drift away is to drive a wedge between them and Washington.

"Think of this, James. All our representatives in all the European capitals say we are close to being recognized. Do you think those European countries will recognize us if we pull back to Richmond? You know the answer to that one, James. And there is this as well. In two months the North will have Congressional elections. We can affect those elections if we enter Maryland and stay there. Northerners will vote Democrat in the hope of Congress ending the war.

"Mr. Davis told me once at dinner that we don't need to win the war. Like the American colonies some ninety years back we need only to avoid losing it. There is some truth in that. But our one chance of avoiding the losing of it is there in Maryland. It's when we break the Baltimore and Ohio Railroad, James. It's when we go further and pull down the Susquehanna Bridge at Harrisburg, Pennsylvania, and leave Abe with just one line of communication east to west, and that through the Great Lakes. And, doing that, we can win it all, James.

"The orders will be for the army to cross the Potomac at a place called White's Ford, just near Ball's Bluff. The river is half a mile wide there. The bottom is pebbly. A depth of two to three feet. Tom Jackson has prepared maps..."

— 15 —

RAMBLING ROSE WAS in bloom on Granny Ambler's fence. As Aunt Sarrie's trap pulled up by the gate, Ephie saw a little plump woman sitting on a rocker under an oak in the garden.

"That Granny Ambler?" Ephie muttered.

"That's her," said Aunt Sarrie.

The garden was well kept and the house whitewashed. It didn't look at all like a witchy place, and that at least took the edge off some of Ephie's discomfort.

"Hey, Granny Ambler, you sleeping there?" Aunt Sarrie called as familiar as if they'd been girls together.

The little plump woman shook herself, struggled out of her chair and came towards the gate with her arms wide. "Why, it's young Sarrie. Why ain't you been to see me since that last time?"

And she thrust her front teeth forward and gave a rabbit-like giggle.

"That potion you provided, Granny, it didn't ever land myself and Muswell with a child."

Granny Ambler shrugged and looked solemn. "Man proposes," she whispered, "God disposes." Then she raised her voice. "And Granny Ambler does the best she can by her friends. But who's that rose by your side there, little Sarrie?"

Aunt Sarrie made the introductions in a quiet cheerful voice, like this was just a social call. Then she dropped her voice, though there was no one around in this wooded lane on the edge of the village of Millboro; there was damn near no one round in the whole village of Millboro itself. "I think we should talk in your parlor, Granny, if you'd be kind enough to give us an invite in."

Granny said she was very happy to. They dismounted and she bustled them up the pathway, over her stoop, into the house. The parlor was an average farm parlor, the furnishings just a little more old-fashioned than those in Aunt Sarrie's place. A little old man almost lost in a big beard glared from a daguerreotype over the fireplace. Against one wall were shelves on which stood unlabelled jars and bottles. The smell of the place was strange and dry and herbal, but that was to be expected.

The two older women settled themselves deeply in chairs on the one side of the room. Ephie found another by the window and sat stiffly on its edge. It had been agreed between Aunt Sarrie and Ephie that Ephie should be the one to outline the problem. She was, after all, a grown girl.

It was as if Granny knew what they were there for, however, for she sat directing her chubby rabbit grin towards Ephie and ignoring Aunt Sarrie.

"I'm with child," said Ephie. She had meant the words to come out deliberate. They came out as they were—a shameful secret.

"It's common enough," Granny Ambler murmured. Now Ephie wished Aunt Sarrie would take over. But Aunt Sarrie sat pat.

"I've a husband off with Jackson someplace," Ephie continued.

"Oh yes, oh yes," said Granny Ambler, nodding her head, but not in a judging way, more as if Ephie had been describing the conditions under which she'd caught measles. "Well of course your husband who's off with Jackson—he's got enough grief on *that* account alone, ain't that so?"

"It's so," said Ephie.

Granny Ambler thought a while.

"How long since you bedded down with this other feller?"

"Other feller?"

Granny grinned a little. "That other feller that's been and gone."

"Six . . . seven weeks," Ephie murmured.

The old lady struggled up—her legs were very short—and approached a line of drawers. Opening one, she took out what looked like a sachet.

She brought it and dropped it in Ephie's hand. It made the little, dry, husky sound a sachet does when it's dropped in a hand. "Take that in your coffee for three days to come. It's bitter'n a bad end, so use plenty sugar."

"What is it?"

"Why it's ergot. Don't you mind if it makes your limbs jump some!"

Ephie went home hopeful, but just round the corner of her mind she wished she could keep the child. She day-dreamed, anyhow, that it was Usaph's and could be kept.

Three days, as prescribed by Granny Ambler, Ephie took the ergot in her coffee. It brought her much discomfort. Her arms and legs crept, her belly clenched. But three weeks went by, and there was no result.

By now the idea of the child was less endearing than it had been. She was getting anxious. It was Ephie who suggested Aunt Sarrie return with her to the old lady.

Granny Ambler shook her head like some great surgeon. "It's known to be a potent specific and it's most times enough."

"What happens now?" asked Aunt Sarrie.

"You should get out of your drawers, gal," the old lady told Ephie.

Ephie stared at her.

"Take off them nice drawers you got on," said Granny, more commanding.

Aunt Sarrie nodded at Ephie. So Ephie turned away, towards the open window. It didn't matter, there was nothing but blank Virginian forest out there. She rucked her dress up and dragged her camisoles off, placing them on the edge of a sofa by the window.

Granny Ambler was already lighting a candle on a small

round table in mid-room. "We don't need light," said Aunt Sarrie warily. "Why, it's mid-morning."

The old sorceress ignored her, fetched a blanket from a cupboard and spread it across the sofa. "You should lie on that, Mrs. Bumpass."

"But why?"

The old lady surveyed her, looking more than ever like a well-meaning mama rabbit. "There are other means, gal. Other means than that-there ergot."

"Should I wait out there in the kitchen?" Aunt Sarrie wanted to know. You could tell she would have preferred to be absent now.

"No, no," Ephie said quickly.

Granny Ambler had picked up from somewhere a very thin skewer maybe a foot in length. As soon as she saw it, Ephie knew what was to happen—Granny Ambler meant to put that thing in her. It brought bile into Ephie's mouth to think of the wound it would make in the faceless mass inside her and maybe in her own vitals as well.

On the sofa therefore Ephie stirred and shivered as the old lady let the candle-flame play over the steel.

"You can spend months jumping off chairs and taking them there hot baths, and all it will do is maybe make a runt of the baby. Quick methods is best."

For some seconds Ephie was stiff and agog, staring at the needle. Then she remembered to appeal to Aunt Sarrie and turned her eyes to that lady. "She's right, girl," Aunt Sarrie nodded. "There ain't no way it can be avoided."

At some signal from the old herbalist, Aunt Sarrie clamped Ephie's shoulders to the sofa. She was no weak one, was Aunt Sarrie. Granny Ambler spoke on, very soothing—or so it was intended to be; it did nothing to soothe Ephie. "You jest have to be still. Elsewise you'll hurt yourself."

Ephie had decided now she'd fight them both, she'd rather a wound by accident than to have Granny calmly lunging into her nether parts. She just didn't want the steel! So she tried to sit up.

"No chance!" she yelled. "I ain't having that thing in me!"

Aunt Sarrie clamped her shoulders fiercer than ever and the little old herbalist clearly had some strength to force the girl's legs apart. Ephie was however a young and healthy country girl, well-shouldered, and now she began to writhe and kick in earnest. She got the old lady high up in the stomach. Granny paled and let the needle fall, and Aunt Sarrie was so shocked to see this ungrateful kick that her hold on Ephie loosened a second.

Ephie slipped sideways now, up over the back of the sofa, towards the half-opened window. Pushing through it, she fell into rose bushes, but did not feel the thorns. Struggling upwards, she'd already begun to wail, and still wailing, got through the gate and took the road back through Millboro, leaving her camisole drawers as a sort of bounty in Granny Ambler's strange parlor.

She was crossing the Cowpasture bridge, her face red but her tears choked down now, when Aunt Sarrie caught up to her in the trap. "Get in, girl," said Aunt Sarrie, in an exasperated voice, but low, just in case some citizen of Millboro was observing her from one of the higher windows of that white little town.

Ephie just stood, staring at her, as if to say: "Yes, but can you be trusted?"

"Get in, you young fool. We're going home. Poor ole Granny will have to rest the remainder of this day."

So Ephie let herself climb into the trap. When they were well down the road, Aunt Sarrie said: "You'll have to have it done, now or later. Sure, some gals get ill by means like these. But that's part of the whole business, ain't it? Part of the business of coupling with strangers."

Aunt Sarrie did not speak to her again for two weeks, but just waited for her to say, yes, I want to go back to Granny Ambler yet again. At meals Aunt Sarrie would talk with Bridie the slave, leaving Ephie out, and Ephie sometimes thought, to hell with it, and would speak to Bridie herself.

But Aunt Sarrie was not a vengeful person. At the end of the second week she appeared at Ephie's door late one afternoon with a plate of pie and a cup of coffee. Ephie wanted the old woman to pass her a kindly cup and plate, but not if it meant the steel needle. "It don't make no difference," she muttered, "I ain't going back to that Ambler woman."

"You can still have the pie if you want. And the coffee."

"As long as it don't mean I agree to go back to the hag."

"I said so already. But goddam, Ephie, I hope you're doing some jumps off tables, gal!"

Ephie wasn't doing any though, and Aunt Sarrie knew it. She shook her head. "We'll get that little Yankee of yours fostered out. . . . I know the people who run that Methodist place in Staunton."

Ephie worked well that summer, did not go out to any social events, not even the ones to which Aunt Sarrie took Bridie. The girl did not know what she hoped for from that child she carried or what she wished for the child itself. But she could see it was right what Aunt Sarrie had said. The little creature would need to be fostered out in secrecy.

But in a household of two good slaves and in that still corner of Bath County, secrecy was possible.

— 16 —

As THEY LED her in through the schoolhouse door, Mrs. Whipple saw that her counsel, Major Pember, was already seated at his table. As one of the elderly soldiers helped her to her chair by the elbow, Pember rose and bowed to her. She nodded back. She watched the shafts of sunlight that fell across the floor from the high windows and dreamed she was a child, sitting in this classroom, taking her ideas of good and evil from a teacher.

"Ma'am, sit down," her counsel invited her.

She took the chair on his left side and put her hands on the table. There were no bonds on her wrists. Somehow she wished there were, wished she had been treated a whole lot rougher than she had been up to now. "Ma'am, I believe the good news from Manassas . . . good news for us . . . the Confederacy, I mean . . . might make the judges more rosy. More lenient, I mean . . ."

She looked at him and smiled. Inwardly she was still plagued by that eternal nausea. "Sir," she said like an apology, "I have given you a rough time."

Pember smiled. "Lawyers are meant for that, ma'am." He lowered his voice further still. "Surely, surely, Mrs. Whipple, you won't feel bound to make any sort of full confession. Surely you'll plead your sex, the loss of your husband, the influence of this Mr. Pleasance . . ."

Mrs. Whipple raised her chin. "We've been through that before, sir." She looked about her. Across the room, close to the teacher's rostrum, a man of maybe 35 years stood. He wore a uniform with artillery patches on it, but one of his arms was missing at the shoulder. "That the prosecutor?" she asked.

"It is."

"What sort of man is he?"

"A little jaunty for my taste, ma'am. A good talker. Pushy. He might even manage to turn the judges our way, ma'am."

She stared at the one-armed prosecutor. He did not look back.

"There's something I want you to do," she told Major Pember. "I have a friend who will not know I've been arrested. If I swore to you that the letter I wrote him is harmless, would you see it is delivered?"

Major Pember frowned.

"Just answer me straight," she advised him.

"Mrs. Whipple, how could I do it? You've spent the last week confiding to me that Confederates have consciences that are crippled, ma'am. Forgive me, ma'am, but maybe you consider we deserve to be lied to. You're asking too much."

Mrs. Whipple turned her face away and stared at the elms beyond the schoolhouse windows. "Very well," she said. "I shall find someone else to do it."

At ten a.m. the three judges of the court entered. They had all come up from Charlottesville in the night train, and they looked pale, as if they hadn't slept well. There were two old men—a brigadier and a colonel. The third was a junior colonel at least thirty years younger than the others. He walked with a stick. A deformed prosecutor, Dora Whipple thought, a deformed judge. And two old men. Two young men with cause to hate me, two old ones to hector and browbeat me.

But she felt calmer now she'd seen their faces.

The president of the court, the ancient general of brigade, read a paper in a muttery flat voice which said she was charged with willfully passing information designed for the aid and comfort of the enemies of the Confederate States of America. When he had finished reading, he blew his nose in a grandfatherly way and nodded to the prosecutor. He had made an atmosphere in court that was drowsy and easy, like say, the atmosphere in a realty office in a small town. The prosecutor tried to change all that.

He got up, stuck out his chest, arranged his empty sleeve

with his remaining hand, and began to speak. "Mr. President and members of the court, the evidence indicates that Mrs. Whipple has willingly consorted with an enemy of these states, a man who has already paid the ultimate penalty for treason. I shall use my best efforts to show that this lady willfully passed information to our enemies by means of her association with that person. As I do so, I shall be aware that the members of the court may feel disposed to go gently on the prisoner on account she represents a sex given to unpredictable and flighty behavior, that she belongs to a gender known for its susceptibility to be influenced unduly by the personalities of others, particularly by the personalities of males. Let me therefore suggest with respect right now that these considerations should not enter the minds of the court. Consider the means by which the information she passed was gained. It was culled cold-bloodedly from the mouths of the delirious, the maimed, the dying, whom she had undertaken to *nurse*. While her hand might have sponged the brow, fed the broth and staunched the bleeding, her tongue questioned and her ears listened. Her connection with the late Pleasance and with other persons presently under arrest indicates that she was willing—no—not willing, gentlemen, but anxious—that the numbers of Confederate dead, dying, wounded and fevered should increase. Only a very cool and very satanic mind could behave in such a two-handed manner, gentlemen, a manner so remote from the normal delicacy and gentility of female behavior..."

Dora Whipple found that to block out the prosecutor's oratory, she fell back not on thoughts of Horace Searcy but on the remembrance of Major Yates Whipple. She remembered him as concretely as if he were standing in court today. A gingery man, solid, of only average height. Already getting a paunch when the battle at Ball's Bluff had finished his life. How we would have grown old! she thought. Him a plump and happy and ginger little man, me his loving scrap of a wife. He knew whether I had the delicacy of a woman or not. Yates Whipple knew and knows and would willingly cry out against this one-armed stranger if he were in court now.

At last the prosecutor got to his peroration. "I do not delight to see anyone suffer fierce penalties, and women less than others," he said. "But the extent of Mrs. Whipple's guilt will be shown in this special court-martial. I am prepared to say, right now in front of this court, in front of the defendant, that I can see but one final penalty for this traitorous woman—and that penalty, the penalty already suffered by her associate Pleasance."

Mrs. Whipple, distracted by the pleasing thought of Yates Whipple, did not even bother taking in that last sentence. She heard the prosecutor call his first witness, a peace officer for Henrico County. This man said that when Pleasance was arrested a notebook had been found on him. In it a list of names and a series of dates and times beside them. One of the names belonged to a clerk in the War Department who had already confessed to passing on documents to Mr. Pleasance. Yet another man listed in Pleasance's book, a schoolteacher from Petersburg, confessed also to buying War Department memoranda from a local officer and giving them to the same Pleasance. And so on. Mrs. Whipple heard the instances pile up, but her strange indifference did not leave her.

The prosecutor asked the peace officer if Mrs. Whipple's name was present in the notebook in the same terms as those in which the name of the other two gentlemen were?

"Yes," said the peace officer. "In the exact same terms. And the others were listed as agents. Therefore, so was Mrs. Whipple."

It was Pember's turn to question the peace officer. He asked were there other names in Mr. Pleasance's book that had nothing to do with spying?

"Well, there were the names of tradesmen, you know. Plumbers and such."

"Were there the names of any officers?"

"There were. Names he'd noted down—the staff of this general or that. He noted down."

"And have you arrested those officers because their names are in the book?"

"Their names appeared in exact different way."

"Is that so? I've looked at Pleasance's book, sir. Is it not true that on the same page as Mrs. Whipple's name there is the name of a drainer Mr. Pleasance wanted to employ for digging a ditch. And that as well as that there's the name of General Magruder's chief of artillery?"

"There's the name of the drainer at the bottom of the page and a note that says *N.B. Major Henderson Magruder's C.O.A.*, but at the top of the page is the name of Mrs. Whipple and dates and times set out just the way the name smack under hers is—and the name smack under hers is that of a schoolteacher from Petersburg."

Poor Pember could tell the thing was going badly. "My question," he said pedantically, "is whether Mrs. Whipple's name appeared on the same page as that of General Magruder's chief of artillery."

"When you put it in terms like that . . ."

"I do put it in terms like that, sir."

"Then that much is true. Her name's on the same page. For what that means."

Major Pember thanked him.

Mrs. Whipple kept on being inattentive through all this. All that was being said seemed to have little to do with her. It was like someone else's ritual—the prosecutor's ritual, the judge's. All she could do was wait till the end and see what they intended for her.

When she looked up again, she saw with something like a shock that Canty had entered the schoolhouse door. The prosecutor called his name. He came forward in his worn uniform. He looked better brushed than she'd ever seen him before. Yes, she thought, he would dress up well to come and do me a disfavor. Oh well . . .

He trod up the length of the court steadily, but his livid face showed he'd been fortifying himself to give his evidence.

The prosecutor asked him what Mrs. Whipple's hospital work was like. "Efficient," he said, just like a man struggling to be fair. But of course, Canty hadn't come here to run her nursing down.

"Did Mrs. Whipple receive any visits from people you wouldn't normally expect her to associate with?"

"She did, sir. One of her visitors was an Englishman, a newspaper man, a lord or something. Searcy was his name."

"The Honorable Horace Searcy?"

"Yessir."

The prosecutor turned to the judges and explained to them that the Honorable Horace Searcy was a correspondent for *The Times* of London. He turned again to Canty. "The time the Honorable Searcy visited Mrs. Whipple, how long did he stay?"

"He came early afternoon. And stayed till after supper. I know that because the day he came Orderly Harris showed him out, and Orderly Harris did not come on duty that day till six p.m."

"And was this the one occasion you know of that the lady met this Searcy?"

Major Pember got up bravely and said mixing with an Englishman was surely no crime. The prosecutor asked the judges to tolerate his line of enquiry until the meaning of it emerged. The judges nodded.

"Yes," Canty said, "I had the feeling this meeting with Mr. Searcy might not be for the best reasons. So I set Orderly Harris to watching Mrs. Whipple. The night of the day Searcy visited my hospital, Mrs. Whipple went to the Lewis House where Searcy was staying. She was wearing a veil like she was trying to hide her face."

Mrs. Whipple's Major Pember stood up yet again. "Please, gentlemen, natural delicacy prevents us . . ."

Mrs. Dora Whipple herself hardly cared about Canty's slur on her. She knew she should have, but somehow couldn't manage it. She feared for Searcy a little, however. Yet they wouldn't dare touch Searcy, she thought. If they did, he might have been arrested already. The idea there was someone close to her they couldn't touch was a great comfort.

Anyhow, the prosecutor said he'd finished his questioning of Surgeon Canty. Major Pember took over. He set out to make Canty look unreliable, he asked the surgeon whether he had any idea why Mrs. Whipple spoke to Mr. Searcy.

"Maybe I didn't have much idea in the afternoon," said Canty, grinning broadly and trying to involve the judges in his humor, "unless it was to set up the meeting of the evening."

"Sir, in any other surroundings you could not get away with such an insinuation. Do you realize that?"

"Maybe."

"Did you therefore know that the purpose of their meetings had any criminal intent to it?"

"Well, we can all guess, sir," said Canty, just falling short of winking at the president of the court.

"Even if you guessed right, sir, in your snide hints, it would not make the defendant subject to the judgment of this tribunal. I take some pleasure, therefore, sir, in finishing with you for the purposes of this court."

Major Pember, sitting again, seemed pretty pleased with himself, and his pleasure lasted some thirty seconds, till the next witness appeared and was questioned. This one happened to be an intelligence officer from Longstreet's command. The prosecutor asked the intelligence officer what he could tell the court regarding Searcy. The officer said he had to tell the court in confidence that Searcy had at least attempted to get information to the North. The officer himself (so he said) had searched the body of captured General Phil Kearny, U.S., before it was shipped North for burial and had found in its pockets notes written by Searcy concerning the disposition and numbers of Lee's army. The president seemed to be agitated for the first time during the trial. He began tugging at his whiskers and asked: "Why haven't you people arrested this Searcy?"

"Well," said the intelligence officer, "he is being watched. But the whole affair is a mite delicate, sir. His father is powerful with the British government. . . ."

"We care too much concerning the British government," the president barked, and the intelligence officer shrugged.

Poor Major Pember, more shaken now, asked the officer if he had any proof that Searcy and Mrs. Whipple knew each other for any reason that had to do with the passing of intelligence.

"No," said the intelligence officer. "But I've got to say this: it seems to me *that* is a fair presumption."

Dora, blushing inwardly perhaps, weeping somewhere in her chest, but not giving the court the benefit of seeing her lower her eyes, noticed that when Major Pember sat down again he no longer looked at her with little encouraging lifts of his eyebrows.

So she ended in front of the prosecutor herself. She answered his questions in a level voice, and the interrogation went along at a clipped pace, without hesitations. She was determined not go give him the chance to be pompous.

First he asked her, had she got information about regimental and divisional movements from patients in Chimborazo?

She said: "Yes, sir, but it was often inaccurate."

"And did you pass this information to Pleasance?"

"Yes, sir, after trying to separate out the unreliable material."

"And did you pass to Mr. Pleasance information obtained from the English correspondent, the Honorable Horace Searcy?"

"On one occasion only. Yes, sir."

And so it went. She made no explanations. She knew explanations weren't any use, would be to these men a worse insult than blunt honest answers.

"And what was the nature of the information Mr. Searcy passed to you?"

"The Union generals show an unwillingness to believe that the resources of the Confederacy are stretched and that the

Confederate States have problems in gathering more than 70,000 men in any one zone of war. Mr. Searcy's information regarded the size of the army in Virginia, the size and disposition of the various corps."

She glanced across at her own lawyer, who was cringing at all these free admissions she was making. The president of the court, who'd been patting his whiskers during the earlier evidence of the intelligence officer, was fairly hauling on them now. "Ma'am, do I hear you right?" he asked. "What was your purpose in passing on these figures and so forth?"

"You know the purpose, sir, fully as I do. It was in the hope that the Union generals would behave with more purpose than they have up to now displayed."

You are certainly destroying yourself, Dora Whipple, she thought, but there's nothing you can do with yourself to stop it.

After she returned to her seat, even the prosecutor made a chastened speech. He accused her of no foul intentions. He just said again the judges had no choice. Everyone in court, apart from Dora Whipple, seemed to be suffused with a great sadness. Even when the president began to speak, Dora heard him with composure.

"Ma'am, this court believes that you have done fine work amongst the sick and wounded. Did you not see any contradiction between *that* work and those politics of yours?"

She sighed, because she had to give the old answer, the one she'd given already to Searcy.

"Sir, I simply believe this rebellion can end but one way, and that the greatest mercy is to attempt to end it quick."

The president said, almost apologetically, "We all on this bench believe *that*, ma'am, that it can end but one way. In the triumph of the Confederacy. I don't suppose you happen to mean that?"

"Sir, my heart cries out for the boys in Chimborazo. And in this town, sir. But I know that the fact that my heart cries out is in no way evidence."

At some stage they made her stand, her counsel standing beside her. Poor Major Pember had gone pale, and the president of the court and the other two judges sat there looking like victims.

"This court," said the president, in a voice you had to lean forward a little to hear, "finds you guilty of high treason against the Confederate States. The statutory penalty for a civilian is

death by hanging. This court therefore has no choice but to
allocate a date, namely next Tuesday, September 18, at nine
o'clock in the morning, as the date of your execution. We do,
however—in view of your sex—recommend you to the mercy
of the President of these States. I just don't know, ma'am,
what hope you should put in our recommendation. The court
admires your demeanor, ma'am, but notes you have condemned yourself with very little help from the prosecution.
May God have mercy on you, ma'am."

Dora Whipple simply sat. There was nothing more that they
could do to her, there was no leverage they could use on her.
She had even taken the solemnity out of the judges and the
starch out of the prosecutor. A terrible fierce calm grew within
her. So they'll hang me? Well, that means I shall be with Yates
Whipple soon.

She found though that, when her counsel helped her up
towards the door of the school where her guard stood, her legs
would not take her weight. Major Pember whispered in her
ear: "They've made it Tuesday so the President will have time
to act. I am sure, ma'am, he'll decide for mercy. Please don't
distress yourself, dear lady. . . ."

It was just what he had been saying all along.

"Let go of me," she said. He looked confused. *"Let go of
me!"*

He took his arm from beneath her elbow and she stood
alone, persuading her legs to hold firm. At last she took a
tentative step and found she did not fall. So she proceeded
down the steps of the schoolhouse. *Well, they'll hang me.*

Already the outside world looked to her like someone else's
county which you visit for just a few days.

— 17 —

IT WAS SOME CROSSING! It was the sort of thing that caught you
up the way that banquet in Manassas had, that banquet Bolly
died of. You got the feeling that it was no use having personal
opinions about going into Maryland, there was a sort of great

opinion working in that mass of men. It pushed along some North Carolina boys, who didn't think it quite right to cross into the North, just as sure as it pushed someone like Usaph, who approved of it all anyhow. And Cate it pushed too—Cate in a daze—pushed him along as sure as it pushed Wheat.

It was a Biblical morning, and Maryland shone beyond the water like the bountiful country it was. On the Maryland bank of the river stood a village. Oaks grew out over the water on both sides and wore in their branches the flowers of the trumpet vine. The white flowers and crimson berries of trailing arbutus shone on the far bank, the army's path was over and amongst the wildflowers which grew everywhere—lobelia, tobacco plant and goldenrod and lupin and May apple—all scarlet and blue on both the banks. And partridge and ruffed grouse rose up protesting out of the crabgrass.

Cavalry came down there to White's Ford at dawn and squinted awhile at the far bank, which was high, before crossing. When they did cross, the first thing they found, beyond that high bank and across the fields, was the Chesapeake and Ohio Canal. Half a dozen barge men and farmers had tied up their barges there for the night. Three of these barges had melons on them, and the horsemen bought melons from a farmer-bargee who took their Confederate dollars deferentially, even though he felt a little cheated and would rather have got his melons down to the markets of Washington without hindrance. Whatever he felt, this was the first time ever that Confederate money had spoken in the North. The farmer was ignorant of that historic fact.

After the cavalry a band came through White's Ford, playing "Dixie" in the mild mountain air, and behind them a boy carrying the flag of Virginia, the great blue flag with the maiden slap bang in the center trampling on the tyrant. And then the first infantry regiment went down into the river. The 10th Virginia. At the bank, its soldiers broke their ranks and stripped their britches off amongst the wildflowers or rolled the legs high, and they took off their shoes and strung them round their necks and bundled up their powder in their blankets, and carried all they owned on their heads like so many negro washerwomen, and waded in. The water was so good they would have stayed and swum if it had been any other river. The band waded too, holding their instruments high, drummers toting the drums on their heads. But as soon as they'd battled up the high slope on the far side, then they formed up again and took a stance in the meadow there and began in on "Maryland, My Maryland."

> "The despot's heel is on thy shore,
> Maryland, my Maryland!
> This torch is at they temple door,
> Maryland, my Maryland!
> Avenge the patriotic gore
> That flecked the streets of Baltimore,
> And be the battle queen of yore,
> Maryland! My Maryland!"

Tom Jackson came on right behind the 10th Virginia. He was riding a big cream-colored horse, for Sorrel had bolted off in the Leesburg area, lured away by the bluegrass pastures. Jim Lewis the slave had stayed back there to find him. With Jackson rode his usual retinue, including foul-mouthed old John Harman, the quartermaster.

The 10th Virginia ahead and everyone behind were singing and hollering when they saw Stonewall. And Stonewall did a pretty grandiose thing for once. He splashed two-thirds of the way across, and then parked his big cream horse and his staff right there in the water, and he dragged his dirty old forage cap off and sat bareheaded under the genial sun.

Now there were more bands and regiments crossing, and the tune of "Maryland" fought the tune of "Dixie," and "Dixie" fought the "Bonnie Blue Flag." And everything fought the Rebel yell, that resonant howl which was like the baying of some mean animal that meant to eat flesh.

While all this noise went on, the staff thought their thoughts. Kyd felt all the flush of a boy coming home. He'd been born in Shepherdstown on the south bank of the river, but grew up on Ferry Hill over the river. When the army was properly across he'd ride upriver to see his mother and father and sister; he would liberate them and taste their admiration. Because he'd been a student and a militia private when he last saw home and now he was coming back as Stonewall's adjutant and friend. If that wouldn't make a man's parents sit up and glow a little, he wondered what would.

The sight of the Potomac's steep and tangled banks worked powerfully on Kyd today. The last time he'd been in this area was a clear night last year when he'd led a little patrol down to the river. With field-glasses he got a view of his father's house on Ferry Hill burning. The flames broke from the windows of the gallery where his father and mother would sit at evening drinking a cocktail and looking south over the hills of Virginia.

Later Kyd's younger brother crept over the Potomac to join the Confederacy, and from him Kyd learned that the burning of the gallery had happened at the end of a party held by some Yankee subalterns there. It was the result of stupidity not malice. The barn had burned later for the same cause. Most of the house could still be occupied. His father and mother and sister were prisoners in the house though—Yankee privates were allowed to go into the rooms of the womenfolk and root through bureaus looking for jewelery; for some brutal reason a Yankee sergeant had attacked petite Miss Douglas's feather bed with a bayonet and torn it apart. All the fences right up to the door of the Ferry Hill mansion had been torn down for campfires, the wheatfields had been turned into artillery parks, the lawn was decorated with rifled Parrotts, and rifle pits stood in front of the Greek revival doors. All the corn and fodder and hay on the property had been forfeit to the United States.

Sitting mounted with Tom Jackson in midstream, Kyd relished the quiet ferocity that rose in him now.

Bulky and profane, Major Harman felt satisfied because the bottom of this ford was pebbles, and firm. It would take wagons.

Surgeon Maguire amused himself identifying the plants that grew all over the embankments of the river. He was pleased to see the lobelia tobacco plant with its chunky red flower growing in wild numbers. A tincture could be made up from that plant which Maguire considered the best expectorant and tonic for sufferers from chest disorders and pneumonia. And if the campaigning in the North that was beginning today should drag on until late autumn, there'd be lots of chest disorders. One of the things Maguire liked about the lobelia tincture was that it had that smell about it, like real tobacco, and that made it easier to get down soldiers' throats. It tasted good and, unlike real tobacco juice, didn't burn going down.

The Shenandoah Volunteers crossed before nine o'clock; Cate in a daze, most others singing and making noises. And in Usaph, such a certainty that this was the act that would end it all, this barefoot crossing which all the millions and the malice of the North had not in the end prevented!

By then Stonewall had got out of the river and you could see him and the staff atop the far embankment, their position marked by a large Confederate flag just about as big as a country ballroom. Sandie was talking low there in his general's ear.

"Lawton says no more than 250," Sandie was saying.

"Folly," said Tom Jackson. "Folly."

"Lawton says there's no use punishing them. You'd never get a court-martial to sentence men like that."

"Surely justice can be universal," said Tom Jackson. "Surely they are deserters in the truest sense."

"I suppose it's that we can't spare the men to go after them."

Some hundreds of North Carolina boys had deserted in the night and Tom Jackson would certainly punish them if he could reach them. North Carolina people often played this game of being the sanest and most regretful of Rebels and therefore the most morally impeccable. The governor of that state, Zebulon Vance, struck these moral airs whenever he made a speech, and regularly attacked Jefferson Davis for trying to control the troops of North Carolina and employ them this way or that without taking account of their fine spiritual fiber or of the opinions of the said Mr. Vance.

Last night, around Big Spring, the North Carolina regiments, unlike regiments from any of the other states, held formal meetings, with their colonels actually present, to discuss the question whether a North Carolina boy had a right to invade Maryland. The 7th North Carolina had had a meeting, the 21st and 24th, the 28th and 33rd. Right on the question of whether their enlistment covered such a thing as crossing into Maryland.

"The meetings were orderly," Sandie went on reporting, "according to what I've been told. Most of them were hot in favor of crossing...."

Jackson was shaking his head at the arrogance of such gatherings and of the 250 Tarheel deserters. Maybe it was the morning, but he began to make quite a speech by his standards. "This crazy argument about whether the South is fighting a war of defense or offense, Sandie! It's all words. It's debating society stuff. It doesn't have any meaning. If any of them are captured I want the Adjutant-General to treat them with full severity. I consider their actions worse than an act of cowardice; God forgives the coward, Sandie, on the perfectly good grounds that the coward cannot help himself. He does not forgive the proud. Satan did not fall through cowardice. He fell, Sandie, through a brand of Tarheel pride. Prepare a letter for my signature."

"I think," Sandie said, swallowing to get the words out, "if any of them *were* sentenced to death, the Confederate Congress might overturn the decision. There aren't many votes in . . . in executions."

But Jackson just put those scorching eyes on Sandie for a while and said no more, for he wouldn't be drawn into bad-mouthing Congress.

"I want Ambrose Hill's division watched closest of all," he muttered. "They're the worst stragglers."

"There's a cavalry guard marching behind them, stopping boys from dropping out."

"So be it."

Well, even loyal Sandie Pendleton didn't know if it was the truth that Ambrose Hill's division were worse than anyone else. But he'd seen Stonewall and Ambrose have another falling out. It had been yesterday morning in the meadows round Big Spring. One of Hills' brigades was late starting out from those lovely fields full of late lupins. It had been allowed to wander off to a run of sweet water down amongst the quaking aspens and to fill its canteens. Stonewall had heard about this, who else from but Sandie and Kyd? So he'd decided to march beside Hill's lead brigade.

This brigade was commanded by a Brigadier Ed Thomas, who was soon to be the meat in the sandwich. Poor Thomas had Jackson on his shoulder, and 200 yards ahead Ambrose rode, leading his division as he should, pretending Jackson wasn't anywhere around. Then, at the end of the first hour's march, when there were standing orders for a ten-minute rest, Hill kept his boys striding right on. Jackson spurred the little way he had to catch up to Thomas and told him to halt. Then Ambrose galloped back and asked him: "Who told you to stop, Brigadier Thomas?"

All Ed Thomas could say was: "I halted because General Jackson ordered me to do so."

Ambrose lost all his aristocratic coolness when he heard that. He stood up in his stirrups, dashed his horse towards Stonewall, pulled out his sword and offered it hilt first to this dullwit from the mountains. "If you take command of my troops in my presence, sir," he said, "you might just as well take my sword too."

Stonewall didn't let anyone get away with big gestures like that. "Put your sword away and consider yourself under arrest," he told Ambrose.

So one of Ambrose's stragglers today would be Ambrose himself, for he would enter Maryland this morning in the traditional place of an officer under arrest, that is, right at the rear of his command.

Some of the local landowners and businessmen from Frederick rode out on good horses and found the General on that embankment. They said fulsome things like: "It is our pleasure, sir, to welcome the liberators of Maryland."

But they told him that most of this part of Maryland was Union. Even this very county, Frederick County, was divided. The town of Frederick itself was by and large Confederate but there were lots of Germans round about who were hot for the Union, and some people that were just pro-Union out of the perversity of their politics. "I think I speak for most of my fellow townsmen," one of them said, pretty grandly, "in telling you that the town of Frederick is all yours."

Another said, "And I think we can get you, sir, a better mount than that-there artillery nag of yours." And Jackson patted the big cream horse and laughed and said he wouldn't turn back any such offer.

Tom Jackson was still there on the north bank at noon. The army was passing him and spreading out into the fields of Frederick County. It was as fine a day in early September as you could wish for. The sun was high, the temperature—according to Hotchkiss, who kept thermometers with him—stood at 76° Fahrenheit. That was just when a crowd of wagons rolled down into the river. They were the light wagons and ambulances of the Stonewall division, followed by those of Dan Hill's division and of Ambrose's. There must have been 600 or more of them, creeping up through the town of White's Ford and edging down to the river. The trouble was they were so slow getting across. The mules got delighted this warm day to be in the cool water and halted with the ripples tickling their bellies. Some drivers steered their wagons past the first ones that halted, only to have their own mules stall before they were two parts across. It happened almost without anyone noticing, that the whole river was jammed with wagons, wagoners were yelling, the mules were drinking and grinning in a contemplative manner, and the wagons on the Virginia side were halted and had nowhere to go.

Old John Harman saw all this from the Maryland bank. "Goddamit!" he yelled. "They'll never move that mess. Half them wagoneers are goddam Dunkers." The Dunkers were a peaceable German church strong in the Shenandoah Valley. They did not believe in warfare and so had been conscripted as wagoneers. More important to the matter at hand, they held against the uttering of oaths.

John Harman operated under no such religious handicap. He spurred his horse down into the water, not taking the road that was cut into the embankment, but riding the beast down the slope on its hindquarters. All that jolting only put the quartermaster into an even sharper frame of mind. He rode into the mass of wagons and kicked mules and yelped at them. He spoke at them in a great baritone voice that Kyd could hear above all the other voices of wagoneers, above both the voices of the gentle Dunker drivers and of the more profane.

"Way-hay, you hinnies," he screamed, "you comic beasts, you sons of whores and callithumpians, you no good eunuchs, you childless sons of bitches. Way-hay-hay! Goddam your granite brains, God blast your eyes, get out of that water there! Way-hay-hay! Is this a water resort and are you goddam Christians, you Monday morning whimsy of the Creator? Up, you goddam hinnies, up, you draft mules, go, you eunuchs, you goddam jests! Go on and way-hay and God blast your sterile flanks . . ." and so on.

Any mule Harman got close to began to haul again, and others, seeing that the train was starting to move, came to believe that the bathing was over and began to pull as well and to compete with others. Soon the wagons of Jackson's corps were grinding up the road to Frederick. Touching his hat coyly, expecting to be chastised for his cussing, Harman rode back to the General. "The ford's clear now, General," he announced. "Lookee, there's only one language that will make mules understand on a hot day that they must get out of the water."

Tom Jackson coughed. "Why, thank you, Major Harman," he said. He didn't seem to be very interested any more in the train. He was pointing across the fields. "See that thirty acres or so of corn," he said. "I'd be right obliged if you bought that from the farmer concerned."

"Easy done, sir."

"Corn to the men and the stalks to the horses. I want you to buy up fence rails too, so a day's ration can be cooked."

Harman nodded, made a note in a notebook and tapped the saddlebag at his pommel that contained the promissory note forms he was authorized to issue when buying supplies. He thought it was crazy to buy fence rails and not just take them the way the Union did. To John Harman's mind, the Confederacy couldn't afford to spend money on a commodity that was just lying round the countryside fit for picking.

The place Tom Jackson camped was called Best's Grove, just south of the town, a sweet clearing amongst oaks and maples and sycamores, renowned round Frederick as a place for lovers and picnickers. At Best's Grove at mid-afternoon a crowd of the businessmen who had visited Jackson that morning brought a gray mare and made a present of it. Watching the handover, Kyd thought this horse looked even more like an artillery nag than the one it was replacing. There seemed to be something about Tom Jackson. Elegant horses evaded him.

"Try him for size, General," the businessmen were calling. They were plump and wore good cloth. The war hadn't touched them much or raised the price of Northern tailoring beyond the reach of ordinary men. Beside them, Stonewall looked dusty and his clothes awful shabby. Shabby as he was, he hauled himself up into the light saddle the great mare was bearing. "Take her for a canter, Stonewall, sir," the businessmen called in their hail-fellow way.

Stonewall pressed her with his knees and she took two steps, but baulked dead. So he put a spur to her. At that she reared up, some few hundred-weight or more of gray mare, and fell backward, taking Stonewall with her and clamping his left leg under her ribs. The businessmen came fussing up to the fallen General and the mare on top of him. But it was Kyd and the others of the staff who got that gift horse up off Stonewall's leg.

The leg seemed whole, but Stonewall couldn't stand on it. He'd hit the back of his head as well and lay stunned right there in the middle of the grove for half an hour. Maguire tried to force brandy on him but he'd shake his head. He'd never touched liquor since a wild night he'd had as a cadet with other cadets in Washington years ago. They'd had a top floor room in Brown's Hotel on Pennsylvania Avenue, and at one o'clock in the breathless morning, under the spur of liquor, they'd locked their door, stripped off, climbed to the roof and began singing "Benny Havens."

"Come, fill your glasses, fellows, and stand up in a row,
To singing sentimentally, we're going for to go;
In the army there's sobriety, promotion's very slow,
So we'll sing our reminiscences of Benny Havens Oh!
Oh! Benny Havens, Oh! Oh! Benny Havens, Oh!
So we'll sing our reminiscences of Benny Havens, Oh!"

Those were days when nothing broke the night serenity of Washington after the hour of nine p.m. After old Mrs. Brown threatened to call the police the cadets had climbed down and passed out on the floor of their room. Afterwards Stonewall always said he'd had to give up liquor for life because he'd liked the taste too much.

So now, though needing stimulants, he wouldn't touch Maguire's brandy. At last an ambulance came up and they lifted Tom Jackson on to it.

"It'll have to be Daniel, Sandie," he muttered through his pale lips. "Daniel will look after the corps."

It would have had to be Ambrose, who was under arrest, except that Lee had happily assigned Stonewall's brother-in-law, Daniel Hill, to General Jackson's corps. Daniel was a North Carolina Hill. Tom Jackson liked him a sight better than he liked the Hills of Virginia. So Daniel Hill was named in command, and Maguire gave Tom Jackson laudanum for the pain in his leg.

— 18 —

So MUCH FOR gifts from Frederick town.

But the people of Frederick offered services as well. Mrs. Julia Fishburn and her niece Jess appeared by the paling fence of the field where the Shenandoah Volunteers had spread their blankets and cooked their corn and the last of their Manassas coffee. Mrs. Fishburn was a dark little woman, well made, and Jess was a little lanky but with a sweet sort of cowlike face. Mrs. Fishburn leaned on the fence, her head just showing above it. The first soldiers she saw on peeping over were handsome Ash Judd and Danny Blalock, who were lying flat out on the crabgrass with their belts undone.

"Welcome to Frederick County, boys," called Mrs. Fishburn. But although her voice was rich and full, her words were sort of private. As soon as Ash heard them he knew what manner of woman she was.

"Well," he said, sitting up and grinning that slack grin. "Well, I always did hear how fine were the ladies of Maryland!"

"Ain't these Southern gen'lmen jest gallant as hell, Jess?" Mrs. Fishburn asked her niece.

Danny started laughing, a little nervous. He looked round to see where Lucius and Captain Hanks were.

"My honey," said Ash, coming up closer to the fence and not knowing quite which of the women he was talking to, since he had such a fancy for both of them, "I had exactly you in mind when I took it into my head to come visiting at the North."

"Do you think," said Mrs. Fishburn, darting her eyes about and winking towards Virginia, "that some of your friends would care to meet my niece Jessica and your humble servant?"

"Praise the Lord, I know they jest would," hooted Ash. "That's so, ain't it, Danny?"

"Indeed," said Danny, laying his eyes on the angular niece.

"Of course," said Mrs. Fishburn, "my niece and I have had a hard time of it, being like trueborn Virginia ladies of proper-minded Southern sentiment and living as it were—in exile. Mind you, we seek Lincoln money, you must understand that, gen'lmen, since it is our fate to go on living under that tyrant."

"Why that ain't·so, ma'am. You and your niece're now liberated. And liberated you'll stay..."

"Still," said Mrs. Fishburn, "Jess and I feel we must insist on Lincoln dollars."

"It happens we have a little Union money," said Danny. He couldn't stop himself lifting his hand to the fall of blond hair on Jessica's cheek.

So Ash and Danny climbed the fence, and Mrs. Fishburn made Ash welcome and Dan clung to Jessica, with nothing to separate the two couples, and nothing but further sedgebroom and the paling fence to screen off Ashabel's and Danny's bare-asses from the view of other regiments in other fields. And when they had finished, Ash full of gaiety and Danny sort of pensive, they raised between them some three and a quarter U.S. dollars in coin, and climbed the fence again to tell others—Gus and Cate and Usaph and all those—that fancy women had come to camp.

Then a whole string of boys came up to the fence and peeped over at Mrs. Fishburn and her niece, who sat there amongst the broom with their blouses a little unbuttoned. Once more, boys began to climb the fence, but then straddled the rails deciding peaceably who should go first; and thus a waiting line of soldiers grew.

Usaph stood a while considering the question of the women being there. Knowing they *were* there, just beyond the snake fence, his need of them wasn't a thing he could readily argue with.

It had nothing to do with pleasure—you knew if you knew anything there wouldn't be much pleasure. It was more akin to the need of the blood to flow and of the breath to wash in and out.

But fighting his wish to climb the fence was a great rage against both women. As much as he wanted to have one of them, he also in equal measure wanted to drive them away, maybe with a length of knotted rope. For Mrs. Fishburn and her niece seemed to be telling Usaph something about the nature of women he didn't much want to hear, not at this time of his doubts about Ephie. So you think Ephie is a loose girl under the skin, do you, Bumpass? That's what he asked himself, and he wondered if he *did* think that way, after all.

Still he didn't move. He must have waited there ten minutes, debating with himself, and he was still arguing privately about it when he saw Cate begin to climb the railings. That made him move. He couldn't bear that, somehow. To see Cate scaling a fence to get a woman! It seemed all right for him, Bumpass, to fret about Ephie's true character. That was just about a husbandly right. But the slinking way Cate mounted the barrier, Usaph believed, showed what he thought of girls, that they were each just another harlot, and Ephie was included in that.

Usaph ran after Cate, who was astride the fence now, one leg on Mrs. Fishburn's side of things, one on Usaph's, and grabbed him by the ankle. "Is this the stamp of women you like to mix with, you son of a bitch?" he yelled. "Is whores the order of your goddam day, Cate? You filthy black Republican son of a bitch?"

Cate didn't want to be delayed on that fence in front of some fifty boys. He was as ashamed as anyone of his need of Mrs. Fishburn and Jessica and he wanted to make his visit to them damn quick and inconspicuous. He began to kick, but Usaph hung on now with both arms.

"Release me, goddamit, Bumpass," Cate said, near blind with shame, grinding his teeth.

"Come down there," Usaph kept screaming. "I'll cut your goddam water off, you goddam turd of Lincoln!" And if Usaph could have got his hand in his britches' pocket and still hung on to his old enemy, he would have fetched out his clasp knife and began a wild job of unmanning Cate, not being too careful how wildly he plied the blade.

Other boys began dragging Usaph off. Ashabel Judd, sated and therefore rational, was yelling, "Easy Saph. You'll attract them goddam officers. Easy, boy! What manner of goddam behavior . . . ?"

Gus Ramseur could see from the half an eye he had on them that lawyer Hanks and that crazy Lucius had noticed the huddle and the brawling and were now stepping out across the meadow to inspect. He began to give Usaph brotherly little secret punches in the kidneys. "Goddamit, Usaph. They'll send them there sweet things back to town!" And he knew he needed the skinny one so bad he would have signed away a year's pay to her.

Gus did not know that Wheat also had noticed the fracas and was coming across the field on a different bearing.

Lucius arrived first though and started kicking at Usaph and trying to knock him away from Cate with a punch to the shoulder. That swept the last of Usaph's reason away. He sprang up and shaped his arms as if he meant to put young Lucius flat out on that pasture. "Don't you touch me, Mr. Toffeenose!" he yelled. It was lucky for everyone, for Usaph and Lieutenant Taber and especially for Mrs. Fishburn, that Colonel Wheat got there just then.

"By hokey, Mr. Decatur Cate," he called at the artist, who was still stuck atop of the fence. "It gratifies your ole colonel to see how willing you are at last to come to close grips with the people of Maryland." He hit Usaph as Lucius had done, on the shoulder, but Usaph didn't mind it, even though it struck bone. "Don't you go getting so goddam fantastical, Bumpass.

What are you doing, boy? You taking an interest in that there conscript's morals?"

Usaph had no answer to that.

"And I hope I didn't see aright, but I can't believe that was you making some gesture of defiance to Mr. Taber. I think in case it was though, you'd better cook an evening meal for Mr. Taber this very dusk and take it to him with humble regrets."

Hanks raised his voice. "There seems to be some low women beyond the fence there, Colonel Wheat."

"Goddamit, there is? By hokey, don't that jest always lead to this stamp of nonsense we jest seen Corporal Bumpass indulge in?"

Beyond the fence Mrs. Fishburn and Jess were quivering and lying low in the broom.

"It's the chance of disease," Hanks said, frowning, an honest man who did not like being thought a killjoy. "It seems to me that this army's had its fill of disease without . . ." and he nodded towards the fence.

Wheat blinked his big parrot eyes. "We must discuss this thing, Captain Hanks," he said, drawing Hanks away out of the hearing of the boys. Everyone was in their place still, the line of boys in its exact order and place. No one was willing to give up that line until it should be broken by Wheat's order. Even Cate was still up on the fence and looking pensive. "Come down off there, goddamit, Cate," called Ash Judd. "You resemble a goddam dazed rooster."

When Hanks and he were out of the hearing of soldiers, Wheat said, "As to the disease of Venus, captain, they say a sovereign goddam cure is lead. And half these poor boys will likely take the lead cure soon enough. You get my drift, Hanks?"

"You mean they'll be shot, I take it, Colonel? All the more reason, sir, they should go to their God uncorrupted."

Wheat didn't raise his voice. He lowered it and talked more secret still. "Do you think there's a God that will damn them boys for jumping a fence? *Them boys*, that have suffered such fear, Captain Hanks, and walked such goddam distances and ate worse than a goddam callithumpian monk in his cell? Are you about to tell me that? If so then I agree we must take some action. I want yourself and that goddam young fool Taber to get yourselves off to town, to the town of Frederick jest one mile up the road, and extend a welcome to the clergymen of the town to visit this here encampment at their convenience.

I am right glad, sir, you are possessed by a sense of urgency. And I suggest you and Lucius set out at once."

Hanks stood still awhile and frowned and said not one willing word, but he knew he had to do it. He fetched Lucius and they set off for Frederick on foot. Meantime, Wheat approached the fence and the intact line of soldiers. He was snarling, and they thought that their small joy in Mrs. Fishburn and Jess was over.

"You understand the word of my officers is your goddam law?"

Various of them said, "Yessir, colonel." He was telling them that, just because he'd sent Hanks to town, it didn't mean Hanks was lacking in power over them. "Yessir, Colonel Wheat," they chorused, almost pleading.

Wheat let his features settle right down. "I take it," he said in a hissing voice, "someone from town is trading you boys plug tobacco or some such from the far side of that fence."

"That's about it, colonel," called Ashabel Judd. Mrs. Fishburn and her niece Jess didn't say a word though Usaph thought he could hear a hissing and a stuttering that might have been Jess with the giggles.

"Well," said Wheat, "I think there's a few things local traders have to bear in mind. A prime consideration is that a colonel of a regiment would be likely to arrest any trader that failed to give satisfaction."

Some of the boys began to laugh and nudge each other. Cate seemed far off, up on the fence, pondering some point of ancient history maybe. Laughing, Gus Ramseur nudged Usaph to try to jolly him into laughing. But Usaph stayed most solemn of all. He still had a mind to cut Cate's genitals off.

"Another thing," Wheat continued, "is that any trader is bound under pain of military goddam arrest to take our excellent Confederate note money and coinage on the grounds that we're staying sometime in this fair state. Other than that, I think our dealing with them should follow a peaceful goddam pattern. I hereby wish you well, boys, in your commerce."

He turned away and went off to visit a friend of his who was the colonel of one of the Virginia regiments in Ambrose Hill's division. On the way he found a huckster selling whisky and bought a bottle for four dollars, which was a damn good price by the standards of Southern whisky.

Back in the meadow Usaph kept in that black state of mind, but after an hour of brooding, composed his face and went and climbed the fence himself. He found Mrs. Fishburn looked a little tired under the eyes, and some of the width had gone out of that smile she'd first flashed on Ash Judd. But her skirts were still up and her nice dimpled knees shone under the clear sky.

Usaph rode her hard and with his eyes mostly skywards.

"Easy, honey!" she had to tell him. "This ain't the Chesapeake Gold Cup and I ain't no filly..."

But in her trade she must have been used to boys punishing their womenfolk through her own poor flesh.

$$— 19 —$$

SEARCY HAD COME all the way. He camped now in a small tent in the parkland called Best's Grove. It was a sizable glade—large tents and ambulances were pitched and parked close together.

Longstreet, Lee and Jackson were all camped here, within call of each other, all three of them lame or injured. Jackson kept to his ambulance, his leg still a mess of bruises, but any rumor that his head hadn't cleared seemed to be unproved, for he kept a string of staff officers rushing and galloping all over the landscape. Lee still had his hand bandaged and couldn't write, but he sat in the open at a table and dictated swathes of orders to Colonel Chilton, his adjutant.

As for James Longstreet, he could just move at the hobble. His heels had got blistered badly and then gone morbid, all because of a new pair of boots he'd got that had chafed him. General Longstreet entered the North wearing nothing more glorious than cutaway carpet slippers.

From Best's Grove, Searcy rode to town a few times to see how the people of Frederick were behaving in the presence of the Confederate army. If Frederick was any example of the way Maryland welcomed the Southern liberators, Lee was in for a deal of disappointment. Half the shops were shuttered. Few locals were in the streets buying goods. Some of the houses were shut up as if a public calamity had taken place.

You would see people in the street, neat women and well-dressed middle-aged men. They would watch with polite interest as detachments marched past. Most men of military age were right out of sight. People sat up on the balconies of Main Street but didn't show much enthusiasm. There were few flags, few waving handkerchiefs. The citizens of Frederick seemed to look at the ragged passing soldiers in a way that said, yes, but how long can you stay in this county, you poor tattered nomads?

It was through living patiently in Best's Grove and observing the generals there that by Tuesday Horace Searcy began to suspect that with luck he might be able to send the North the most important spy intelligence of the war.

Actually it started at breakfast-time Monday. There was a very young officer on Robert Lee's staff called Angus. Angus was a lover of British culture. He liked to corner Searcy frequently and talk to him about how wonderful Keats was and what a novelist was Charles Dickens.

On that Monday morning, Angus and Searcy ate a breakfast of bacon and drank their coffee together. They held their meal in a little clump of woodsy boulders, away from the trestle tables, lent by the Corporation of Frederick, where most of the staff officers ate.

"Anything happening?" Searcy asked the boy. He always did. Angus was *a source*, as newspapermen said even then. Searcy yawned and cut at his bacon while he asked, but the yawn was a fake. He had noticed last night that the lamps had burned to a late hour in Lee's tent, and Longstreet and Jackson had limped in and out and staff officers had wandered around, talking low, with maps and estimates in their hands. Lee's lamps had still been alight at three a.m. when Searcy had fallen asleep. So, "Anything happening?" Searcy asked.

Well, Angus had that vanity some people have, the vanity of being in the know. He said: "There's some revision going on, Searcy ole boy."

"Revision?"

"Ole Robert" (Angus meant Lee) "ole Robert—he always thought that once we got into Maryland, the Yankee garrison at Harpers Ferry would clear out as a matter of course, *a matter of course*, Searcy ole boy."

"And . . . ?"

"Well, they're still there."

Good for them, thought Searcy. Can it be? A display of

resolute behavior from the side of right? A bit of blessed stubbornness? "Awkward for you chaps," he said lightly.

"Well it seems the War Department in Washington might've ordered them to stick. But as you say, Searcy, damn awkward. There they are, stuck in the mouth of the Valley like a cork in a bottle..."

"And of course, Lee... ole Robert... can't get his supply line running up the Valley and into Maryland while ever they remain."

"Exactly," said Angus. "Exactly, Searcy."

"And would I be right to guess, old chap," Searcy asked, "that your chieftain is looking for someone to go and drive the cork out of the bottle?"

"No fool you, Searcy ole boy."

"But that means dividing the army again, doesn't it?"

"Not such a terrible thing," said Angus, yawning. "General Lee knows he can depend on ole McClellan to be slow and wary as a Christian bride."

"Of course."

That was the first item of value Searcy was given, the word that Lee meant to send part of his army away to the Ferry. The Lord Christ himself could not get away with dividing an army in the face of the enemy three times over. Lee had already tried his luck with that ploy twice. It excited Searcy that he might now try it a fatal third time. If he does that, thought Searcy, there is hope for Mrs. Dora Whipple and one wandering soul called Searcy.

So he sat still and watched everything that was happening in Best's Grove all day. He propped himself on a rock in the fine September sun and wrote in his notebook.

In the early afternoon he saw Longstreet make another hobbling visit to Lee's tent. The Confederate generals didn't snooze after lunch, no matter if they did have blisters and broken bones. Longstreet was in the tent for about two hours.

When he came out again, Angus visited the British journalist and had another long talk to him. The rumor was Lee had asked James Longstreet to go down and take Harpers Ferry. And Longstreet had said no, the men needed rest, and anyway he didn't think it was militarily wise.

"You can bet," Angus told Searcy, "Lee will ask Jackson to do the job. Jackson's bruised leg is taking his weight now and he can ride. You can bet he'll be asked to go, and go he will."

But nothing happened overnight. Jackson, limping just a little, didn't visit Robert E. Lee's tent till early Tuesday morning. Searcy was up early like everyone else and again was eating breakfast with Angus. And there was Stonewall thumping along through the thin ground mist.

"Stonewall was keen as mustard as soon as ole Robert mentioned it," Angus told Searcy later. "He's a tiger, that Stonewall! One of the boys who was there told me he looked Lee fair in the eye and said to him, I've got friends in the Harpers Ferry area I've neglected too long. Meaning certain Union generals, you know. And ole Robert took up the joke and said, Sure, Tom, but there are some friends you've got there that won't be so very pleased to see you. He's got a fine turn with words, ole Robert. An orator and a writer, Searcy ole boy!"

Searcy just sat on in the sun again, sketching and writing. It was harder for him to keep himself calm than it had been yesterday. If there were going to be orders that would split the army in bits, he was sitting some fifty steps away from the spot where the disposition of those bits was being planned. He—of all the friends of the Union—had the honor and the burden of finding out what they would be. He knew he could be killed trying to do that. There was at least this. Little lovely Mrs. Whipple would honor his martyrdom. But he didn't really want to be a martyr.

Angus saw him taking a dose of brandy about three o'clock in the afternoon. He knew it wasn't like Searcy to be drinking so early in the day—so early for a Britisher that is. "Feeling the strain, ole chap?" Angus called in his friendly but fake British accent. Searcy surely was feeling it. He looked at Angus. He had this urge to take him aside and tell him to go home. The boy couldn't have been more than eighteen years. I am planning the death of all you stand for, you poor child.

Searcy was tempted to tell him.

Then it was as if Angus handed him the whole future history of North America on a plate. "You need a ride, ole man, and it's fine weather for it. Look here, I have to stand by to take orders to Daniel Hill's division."

"Orders?"

"Movement orders of course, my friend. You know what orders. Why don't you come for a ride with me seeing you look so confounded peaked?"

Searcy looked at the boy really hard now. The way he talked was a sort of pitiful Virginia imitation of a horsy young member of the British gentry. It seemed unfair to plot against someone like that. Will I have to kill him? Or will he kill me? And can I fool him? And how can you fool staff couriers? They had to hand the orders to the general they were sent to or to the general's adjutant. Then they had to bring back the empty envelope to General Lee as a sign they'd delivered the orders properly. If Angus didn't come back with the envelope with Daniel Hill's name on it or if it disappeared, the tough Confederate cavalry would be all over Frederick County searching for it, which was the same as saying they'd be searching for the Honorable Horace Searcy as well. He got cold in the legs when he thought what they might do to him in their crazy old-fashioned righteousness.

And then, as if the whole thing came to Searcy direct from the god of Reason and Freedom and Decency, it struck him how he might get away with it.

That Tuesday, early, Colonel Wheat was also planning a ride. He brushed down his coat and told Gus to fetch his horse from the place it was informally stabled, namely in the corner of the field. He saw how Usaph and Gus watched him, sort of begging with their eyes to be taken into Frederick, but he felt today like being alone. To have a good look at a town, a nice white town with its nice glass-fronted shops, could sometimes be a private need which must be privately satisfied. This is so especially if you had sat up half the night suffering from the sudden thought that, by hokey, it was very likely that Frederick could be the last town you'd ever encounter.

Colonel Wheat followed the same path Tom Jackson had on his way to church a few nights back. From the garden of one of the big white houses a blackbird sang to him. It was a fine morning.

The town was quiet, but he found Hemming's Emporium open. There wasn't in its windows much that an army could want: a few winter hats for women, some books—sermons and novels fresh from Boston, New York or London, China tea in small decorative tins, button-up shoes, patent lamps, china that was too delicate for camp use.

He went inside. Ah, it was nice, that clothy smell you get when there are rolls of fabric round about.

A man about sixty in a shiny suit came up to him and offered to help. "I'm jest looking with admiration at your stock, sir," said Wheat.

"I'm afraid we're rather low on stock at the moment, sir," said the man in an off-putting way.

"My friend," Wheat told him warmly, "if you transported this here store to one of the major cities of the South, it would be considered a branch of the goddam Cornucopia."

"Please feel free," the old man muttered, as unwelcoming as he could make it. Flying a flag for ole Abe, thought Wheat.

Wheat looked around and, first off, saw a woman. A pale girl of maybe 28 years old, wearing a green dress and a shawl. She had green eyes and a tilted nose and rich lips and good lines, goddamit it, good lines! A middle-aged black woman was standing by her to carry her parcels. The shop clerk, herself a young woman, was displaying rolls of chintz to this lady, and the lady was reacting to it with these delicate movements of the lips and subtle creasings of the bridge of the nose, as if she was responding not to curtain material, but to a profound song or a metaphysical question.

Wheat told himself, I want to be with that girl sharper than I've wanted anything this past year.

He looked at goods and squinted in jars. "That's ginseng root," the old man told him once. "From China."

"Why, thank you for your kindly information," Wheat told him.

Wheat found the book section by the door and pulled down a book, any book he could use as a cover to observe the woman from. Married, yes, you could tell that. Her husband would be some merchant or lawyer. A little skimped for money maybe, since the green dress wasn't so new. But what a lucky son of a bitch he'd be at evening tide.

The Diary of an Austrian Secretary of Legation, Wheat read with half an eye on the title-page of the book and the other one and a half on the girl. *At the Court of Moscow in the Reign of Peter the Great. Together with a Narration of the Dangerous Rebellion of the Strelitz*, etc. Translated by Count McDonnell, London, Bradbury & Evans, 11 Bouverie Street, 1861. Goddam Bradbury & Evans and to hell with Austrian Secretaries of Legation! They had never seen this-here girl and so were beneath pity. But the transaction of that curtain cloth was taking her such a long time.

"Do you have any cheroots, ole man?" he called to the shop clerk.

"No, sir, we're clean out," said the man, as if he was delighted to be out of stock. "We hope there'll be some by train if the train is let through from Baltimore."

"Why I think it will be unless it's got goddam Abe Lincoln aboard."

"I hope so," said the old man in a choked voice.

"Mr. Browning!" said a voice behind him. It was a sort of rich county girl's voice, more West Virginia than Baltimore. Wheat wasn't going to begin to complain about that. "Give the poor man a cheroot. I'd want someone to give my Dudley a cheroot."

The old man stared past Wheat at the girl who had finished with the cloth and had come up behind them.

Wheat watched the girl. Her green eyes were on him. Her eyes were so wide and piercing he wondered if she were short-sighted. She had that look astigmatic people often have of seeing through to the soul of things even when they're day-dreaming.

The old man produced two cheroots from behind a counter and wrapped them neatly in paper. "You have to understand, sir," he announced, just a little more nicely than he'd been speaking up to now, "that we have to try to keep on to the last of our stock for our regular customers."

"With some luck and a little valor," said Wheat, bowing, "I might jest become a regular in Frederick."

The lady gave a little mocking laugh. As the old man handed Wheat the little parcel she said: "I hope you'll consider this a gift from the small body of Union sympathizers in Frederick."

It was said so neat and friendly that he bowed again. She left the shop with her black lady. Like a true Republican, she carried one of her parcels, while her slave or servant carried the others.

Wheat followed her out into the street. She made for an old surrey that was some twenty paces down the street. Though it wasn't the most fashionable carriage you could have seen, it was good enough to have attracted a couple of Georgian privates, who were kind of sniffing around it. They sidled off when they saw Wheat.

"Ma'am," he called. She turned. Oh God! His hands sweated like a goddam ploughboy's. "I feel that to a lady who offered me such kindness I should make some return. I am willing to escort you to your home. I am a colonel, ma'am, by name Lafcadio Wheat, and I can offer you protection from that set of unruly fellers you'll run up against even in an army of gentlemen, ma'am."

The woman shook her head. "I came to town this morning, sir, through myriads of your young men and wasn't once troubled," she said. Wheat thought the combination of an educated word like *myriads* with her country intonation made a dazzling mixture. He itched to touch her hair right there, while standing on the pavement.

"You didn't likely meet any of those Louisiana Cajuns, ma'am, or those hoodlums from the Brazos who go by the name of Texicans..." To stay close to her for a while he was willing to bad-mouth the entire population of the Confederacy. "Please, I have to insist on it. I shall be your guardian as you journey home."

She argued, she shook her head and he shook his. "I'm a colonel, ma'am. You can't argue with colonels."

"Very well," she said. She wasn't very friendly about it any more. She drove away, handling the reins herself, her house nigger by her side, and Wheat making his horse step dainty, keeping close to her right wheel and enjoying a view of the right quarter of her face and body. A woman on a porch at the north end of Main called out: "Making friends of the Army of the South, are we, Mrs. Creel?" And there was laughter from another female voice on that same porch. The girl did not answer, and they were just about clear of the town before she spoke to Wheat.

"You don't know the humiliation you put me to, sir. My husband is absent, serving as a captain in the Delaware Infantry."

"The army of the Union, ma'am?"

"Yes. I am by no means very popular in the town of Frederick."

Wheat leaned right forward as far as he could over his horse's ears. "Ma'am, you are powerful popular with me," he whispered so that even her black woman—perhaps—couldn't hear.

"Sir, do you think that's a proper remark," the girl said low and angry, and stared up the country road northwards.

"Forgive me, ma'am. I am the one regimental colonel left in my brigade and that fact maybe makes me a little forward. I believe I was kept safe by a merciful Deity jest so that I could set eyes on you today. I know I would not be forgiven if I jest set eyes and said, thank you, Lord! And then went my way."

The girl saw that he said this without a smile and was serious about the duty he had, which was to stick by the wheel of her surrey. That scared her a little but it excited her too, and Wheat himself could see as much. "Are you adding blasphemy to your rudeness?" she asked, but she didn't sound as firm and sure as she would have wanted to.

"If I am, missy," he said, "then the Lord take in His hand us two poor pilgrims."

She began to shake her head and bunch her lips. She looked out at the encampment of the enemy, the poor skinny enemy cracking lice in the fields and boiling up their cornmush amongst the little naked tepees of stacked rifles. "What do you want me to tell you?" she asked him.

"I won't go away," he whispered, "until you let me rest my poor head on your heart."

"Goddam you, sir!" she said, very roughly, enough to scare Wheat. But then she laughed and it wasn't a welcoming laugh. "You'll go away because I tell you so," she said.

"What does the man in the Bible say, ma'am? I am a centurion, accustomed to being obeyed? You'll have to find a general if you want a whisker of a chance of orderin' me away."

They turned off the main Emmitsburg Road and passed through apple trees on which the summer's last apples hung heavy. Then they came to a white frame house, something that wasn't quite farmhouse but was surely not a residence of the gentry. The girl's old horse pulled the surrey in through the gate and the girl called over her shoulder: "I thank you for your escort. I take it you don't intend to force your way into my house?"

"I was hoping for an invitation, missy."

"You can go whistle for an invitation."

"I won't go away," he told her levelly, "without one."

A young black boy of maybe fourteen years took the horse out of its traces for her. She went right indoors without looking at Wheat. The colonel sat his horse for a while by the gate, but by noon it was so warm that he moved beneath a sycamore by the side of the road, and he got down and sat against the trunk. He wished now he had a book, that book about the Austrian legation, any book. I'm being a goddam fool, but I'm proud of it, he told himself.

He fell asleep for a while about one, and then towards two a few Arkansas boys came along, and he gave them a dollar to take a letter to Captain Hanks. "Dear Hanks, can be found if needed at the Creel house..." For he owed a knowledge of her name to the old man in the store, and to the insult that woman had shouted from her porch. "... a mile north of town and half a mile or so to the left past apple orchards. Slightly indisposed. But can be fetched from her if needed. Lafcadio G. Wheat, Lieutenant-Colonel, C.S.A."

Sometime past three, the middle-aged black woman appeared at the fence with a jug of lemonade. "Did your mistress send you with this, dearie?" Wheat asked. "Nassah, Mrs. Creel would noways like to see me doing this. But I knows what it is to be dry." About five the black boy who worked there turned out the gate and headed home. The shadow of the sycamore reached way east then and Wheat felt lost in it and, from a window of the house, looked young and pious. Then the black lady turned up again.

"Miz Creel tells me you should come in and take sherry with her, sah."

"I'm obliged to Mrs. Creel," he said.

He was led into the front parlor and left there alone. There was a picture of the Austrian Alps on the wall. After a little while the girl called Mrs. Creel came in. She looked a little pale and her hair just a little astray, as if she'd come straight from working in the kitchen without making use of brush or comb.

"What did you say your name was?" she asked, like someone settling down to business.

"Lafcadio Gawain Alfonse Wheat," said Wheat.

There was a little tremble in her voice as she passed him and as she put her hand on the neck of a crystal sherry decanter. "I watched you from the window," she said. "You are a firm-minded man, sir. Take sherry with me. Dudley Creel used always take sherry with me at this time. Then will you please... will you please go."

As soon as she said that she began to weep. The need to be embraced was sharp in her. He went up to her and held her and soon they were so close, breast to breast and tongue to tongue, that he felt he wasn't a solid being any more and might run downhill like rainwater into the pores of the rejoicing earth.

— 20 —

BY THAT EVENING General Lee's adjutant Colonel Chilton had
written out a number of copies of the new orders that would
split the army into pieces. He worked at a camp-table in the
open at Best's Grove and by the time he got to the last copy,
he needed light to continue by.

Each copy was headed *Special Orders No. 191*. It contained
ten numbered paragraphs. The first paragraph forbade any men
or officers to visit Frederick that night. Colonel Wheat, in Mrs.
Creel's bed, was out of bounds but ignorant of it. The second
paragraph suggested what route sick soldiers or any others
unable to march should take back over the Potomac to get back
towards Culpeper. The other eight paragraphs were the solid
meat.

A copy would go to every general who was specifically
mentioned in the orders. It would, Searcy knew, be placed in
an envelope marked with the name of the general it was intended for.

From his nervous position on the far side of the Grove, the
Honorable Horace Searcy watched Adjutant Chilton working
there at the table in his relaxed American way, while grooms
and lieutenants lazed on the ground round about and chewed
tobacco or smoked corncobs, and occasionally cavalry men
sauntered by leading their horses. Half a dozen or more envelopes lay haphazard about on the little table, ready to be
inscribed with the names of Longstreet, Tom Jackson, Daniel
Hill, and anyone else they were meant to go to. Ready to be
stuffed full of the most valuable papers in America.

If Searcy were interested in money he could demand and
get $3m. U.S. in bullion for one of those envelopes. Secretary
Stanton would consider that a mild price and might even ask
if Searcy wanted to sell so low.

It wasn't that Searcy didn't need the money either. The pay
from *The Times* was abominable—£150 sterling a year, which
was as much as they paid anyone. He made maybe an extra
£50 a year from royalties on his books about the Crimea and

the Italian War of 1859. His father gave him an annual allowance of £150. A whole £100 of that went to keep the girl who'd had a child by him three years before. The little girl child. He envisaged her in a cottage garden in South London, pointing at butterflies. He wanted so much to see her just once before he took this risk he was envisaging. He did not have the same urge to see her mother. He did not love her mother.

While he was here in America he had to keep a town house going in Green Park near Piccadilly. It contained a manservant and a cook, and he had told many of his Oxford friends that they were always free to use it when they were in town. That cost £100 a year to run, even in his absence. If tonight went badly, the manservant and the cook would be out of work, though they wouldn't get the news for a while.

Altogether he was left with a little over £150 a year to live off—travel, restaurants, club subscriptions and gifts to women all came out of that. It wasn't enough to lead a really full life in London. It was just as well he had always been attracted to battlefields. At least they made few demands on the pocket.

Soon Chilton was handing out envelopes to the young couriers. Angus came striding across the clearing towards Searcy.

"Got your horse saddled, ole chap?"

Searcy sent an ostler to do it. When the horse was brought to him, he slung a saddlebag over its shoulders.

"Say, ole chap, you don't need any saddlebag. We're visiting D. H. Hill's headquarters. Not Portland, Maine."

"Some comfort," said Searcy, looking cunning and patting the saddlebag as if to hint there was a bottle of whisky in there.

The bag did hold whisky. He had excused himself from the Grove for half an hour this afternoon, ridden at the pelt into town, used his superior British ways to get a Frederick shopkeeper to find him a bottle. And from the same shopkeeper he'd bought the hatpin. There was this long ornamental hatpin in the saddlebag with what could well pass as a lump of jade on the end of it. Searcy could see the storekeeper presuming that this Britisher was having luck with some Frederick lady and that was why the hatpin was being bought. The shopkeeper thought that gifts of hatpins must be some sort of British custom.

Before the couriers rode out, a black man brought Angus and Searcy plates of bacon and beans. Searcy found it hard to eat his. He feared he would retch up the beans.

Ten minutes later he and young Angus were riding through

the shuttered town. It looked finally shuttered now, as if it knew the army and all its needs were going to vanish overnight, as if it were now money-counting time and time to take thought about what attitudes to strike whenever the Union army should arrive, as it would surely soon do, pursuing Lee.

Beyond town, they turned east and were amongst cornfields and orchards and the eternal white frame farmhouses. That was the startling thing about America, Searcy thought, it was so big it went on for ever, and the towns kept repeating each other eternally, and every country road you saw was immensely beautiful but immensely the same.

On that stretch trees came down over the road and made it very dark. The fireflies of the summer of 1862 had nearly all done with their breeding and flashed away no more in the branches of oaks. But sometimes you could see campfires. Angus nudged his horse into a run and Searcy nudged his own to keep up. He'd left his saddlebag unlatched and, on this dark length of the road and almost at the gallop, was able to reach in with his right hand and find the hatpin. He spurred his horse till its head came up within Angus's sight, and Angus grinned and hunched further forward like a jockey. Searcy hoped sincerely the boy would not die of whatever injuries his horse was about to do him.

The journalist had the hatpin held overhand and close to his own knee, carrying it as a minute and secret weapon. Next he drove it into the croup of Angus's mount. Two or three inches in and then out again before the muscle and the agonized clenching of the horse's hindquarters held it there. He did it so deftly he reminded himself of those wild Indian Army horsemen who could lean at right angles to their saddles at the gallop and behead a goat in passing, instantly and without apparent pain to anyone.

There was apparent pain, however, in this case. Angus's horse baulked on its front legs and threw its back madly into the air. One of its rear hoofs struck Searcy's horse a blow on the thigh which would before long turn to an abscess.

When it had finished plunging, Angus's horse reared unevenly on its hind legs and started striking at Angus, who was lying on the ground now on his side. Slowly, like a sleeper, the courier drew his legs up out of reach of the striking hoofs. At a risk to himself, Searcy urged his own horse close in, grabbed the other mount's reins and dragged it away from

Angus. He still did some rearing and plunging, that horse, but settled down at last. Searcy tethered him to the low branch of a hickory tree and went and knelt by Angus. The boy's forehead was bleeding.

"Searcy, ole chap," said Angus, "my wrist is done in, I think."

The left wrist *was* bent back on itself, palm up, and a bulge of misplaced bone showed on the surface of the flesh. Angus turned on his side and retched in the dust and fainted. Searcy lifted him and carried him to the edge of the orchard, laying him down at the base of an apple tree. Angus knew nothing of it when Searcy took the envelope away from him. Standing up, Searcy was able to get some moonlight on the document. The envelope was addressed to D. H. Hill, as Angus had said. The pages inside were written on printed Confederate stationery. Searcy was grateful for that. It would cause Union generals to take them as authentic.

He began to read the meat of the thing. "Holy God in heaven!" he muttered now and then throughout the eight paragraphs. For Lee meant to divide his army not just in two, and not just in three, but in four.

Searcy whistled and did a lot of head-shaking there in the dim orchard, on the question of how this war would have gone if Lee had just stayed on in Arlington last year with the army of the Union.

Once Searcy had done with reading the pages, he put *Special Orders No. 191* in his breast pocket and the envelope with D. H. Hill's name on it in the side pocket of his coat.

"Come on, Angus, ole chap," he said, mimicking Angus but almost tenderly. The young officer woke at his name. "Searcy, goddamit, my arm's afire."

"We're getting you to a surgeon, ole chap."

Beyond the orchard and across a pasture thickly sown with human excreta, Searcy, toting Angus, staggered into the encampment of a South Carolina regiment. "Boys," he called. The word sounded strange the way he said it. It sounded creaky even to himself.

This regiment came from up country in South Carolina and their accent was so broad and loopy Searcy had as much trouble understanding them as they did him. They crowded round the delirious Angus, admiring his injuries and his staff clothes, which were pretty splendid compared with their rags. "Lookee, his chicken guts" they said, pointing at his braid. And: "I'd say you'd travel three counties before you'd set eyes on a bust wrist as fine as thetyer one."

After a while their captain came up, a dark, bearded young man. No more than 22 years, very likely not even that. Searcy took him aside by the thin fibrous arm of his jacket. "You know, sir, where the generals are over in Best's Grove."

"Generals?" the boy asked as if it were news to him the Confederate Army had any.

"General Lee in Best's Grove."

"Oh yeh. I heard that one," said the boy, just like Searcy had tried to tell him a profane joke he'd already heard.

Searcy took the envelope from his pocket. "This gentleman rode orders to General Hill and on the way back had the accident you can see so clearly. The envelope has to be returned to General Lee's adjutant so that the staff know that the orders have been delivered."

"That's procedure, I believe," said the young captain.

"Now I have an appointment with my friend General Ambrose Hill, otherwise I'd return the envelope myself. Could one of your boys take it back. Right back to Lee's adjutant, Chilton."

The boy wasn't quite as simple-minded as Searcy had hoped. He wanted to know who Searcy was and why he'd been riding with Angus, and Searcy had to produce that impressive letter from Longstreet asking all officers to help this British journalist. Once he'd done that, the boy got friendly again. "Forgive me, sir," he said to Searcy, "but when a gentleman looms up talking so outlandish and carrying envelopes with generals' names on and all, then it behoves me to ask what's up and what's down."

"On the way to my friend General Hill," said Searcy, "I'll find a surgeon for poor Angus there."

"Don't fuss yourself, sir," drawled the captain. "There's a passable surgeon jest across the field there. And I mean to send a boy down to the road to fetch this poor feller's nag."

So, no later than 9:30 in the evening, Searcy found himself with the freedom of the night and with those amazing orders in his breast pocket. He went on back through the foul meadow and the orchard and got his horse. He believed it would be some hours before Daniel Hill decided there were orders he should have got and hadn't. He was hopeful that at Best's Grove Colonel Chilton would accept the envelope as a sign of delivery and, most likely, crumple it up together with the other envelopes returned by all the other couriers and throw them in the fire.

Searcy got his horse and rode a little further east. After twenty minutes, he turned off the road and sought out some deep shadow amongst trees. He waited there till midnight. In that time he could have learned the orders off by heart and destroyed the copy he had on him. But he wanted to hand the pages themselves to the Union as they'd come from Lee's office, written with Lee's ink on Lee's paper, so that no one— not even McClellan—could argue them away as, perhaps, false or forged.

Searcy had four tries that night at escaping eastwards, in the direction of Baltimore. First he probed down the road where Angus's horse had thrown its tantrum. He met cavalry who turned him back politely. He cut across the meadows to a road further south and was turned back after traveling down it a little. Next he passed along from farm meadow to farm meadow, using the gates, but even then ran into cavalry vedettes.

It was hard for him to pretend to be a Maryland farmer or anything other than he was. He put on this act of being lost, a British bumbler, and he always produced that letter of Longstreet's and they always firmly turned him back, and gave him a lot of friendly directions on how to find his way to the main encampments.

"Sir," one of them told him, "ole Mac's cavalry's jest ten miles up the road in goddam Newmarket, Maryland."

Searcy made the last attempt at the first glint of dawn. He moved through woods to the south, but as had happened before, horsemen rode out from the foilage and closed round him. This time they sent him back with two couriers to guide him.

One of these was a talkative young man from the Kentucky-Tennessee border. He had a loud laugh too that kept on setting the birds twittering wherever he passed in that first light. He asked Searcy about farming in England, how big was your average British farm, and where the farmer hired his labor from without slaves to help out. Searcy answered with only half a mind on what he was saying. *Special Orders No. 191* weighed in his breast pocket like two pounds of soil. "Goddamit, but don't you look all whey-faced, Mr. Searcy," the chatty one said. "You look like you could sleep a goddam week."

As they came out on the road towards Frederick, they could

see ahead, closer to the center of the army, lots of dust rising
even this early, and they could hear shouts and the creak of
axles. They paused to watch some 600 Tarheels march out of
a field, led by the flag of their State. Searcy's escort said they
were Daniel Hill's young'uns. He'd spent all the spring bivouacked with those gentlemen. His cavalry squadron had been
their flank guard, no less. And that-there body of men was not
one regiment but the leftovers of a brigade. There'd been a lot
of falling by the wayside, the young horseman told Searcy.

"Did you say those are Daniel Hill's chaps?" Searcy asked.

"Sure I did."

So D. H. Hill had got his movement orders from somewhere.
And that would seem to mean Chilton and maybe Lee knew
of the theft. And that soon, maybe within two minutes, the
headquarters cavalry will be along this road, looking for me.

The field the Tarheels had left was a pleasant one, sloping
slowly up to woods. A stream cut round its far margin and then
bubbled along under a little stone bridge further down the road.
It came to Searcy at once that when the Union army came to
Frederick, a portion of it must surely camp in this sweet field.
The first brigade commander who saw it and its freshet would
want it for his men. The Union army being twice in number
what the Confederate was, there would be some competition
for a field like this!

"I say," said Searcy. "I'm taken short, old man. I must ask
you to let me make use of that field."

The horseman nodded; "Willie and me, we could likely
benefit from a squat ourselves."

The rail fence round the field was still intact, as it would
not be once the Union troops arrived. Searcy and the two boys
tethered their horses there. Searcy opened his bag and took out
some soap and a long envelope of heavy weave. "Like a cigar,
you gentlemen?" he asked, dredging a handful up out of the
saddlebag.

"Why, obliged!" they both said and each took one. He
transferred the other three to his pockets as if he meant to
smoke as he crossed the field. They moved through the fence,
the cavalry men unbuttoning and unbelting as they went and
squatting after no more than twenty paces. Searcy went as far
in as he could, till he reached a family of sizable shade trees
just at the point where the field took a sharper slope up to the
woods. The horsemen seemed to think it was natural for a

British gentleman to want a little more privacy than ordinary men and to walk further off to excrete.

Beyond the shade tree, Searcy dropped his own trousers. He noticed that his member barely existed after this fearful and frustrating night he'd spent. Since it knew there was the risk of a bullet, it behaved like some sort of sensible tortoise. As Searcy laughed at it, it grew by a few millimeters. His bowels came in a gush. God help me, he thought. Too much bacon fat, too many beans, too many flapjacks.

While he was hunched there, with his back to the tree and the trunk between himself and the others, he took out *Special Orders No. 191*, placed the three cigars he had left squarely in its pages, wrapped them up in it and placed them in the envelope. It happened to be an envelope from Stiles Bros. Stationers of St. James's, and was said to be ideal for military staff work and for explorers and foreign correspondents. Stiles Bros. claimed that it was waterproof and that there was a sealskin lining inside to keep contents dry. It didn't feel to Searcy that it had a sealskin lining, but it would not be like Stiles Bros. to say it had if it hadn't. He placed the whole package, the cigars wrapped in the orders and the orders packed in the envelope, half in under some weed but in clear sight. Then he cleaned himself up and went to the stream and washed.

When he got back to the fence the two young horsemen were already waiting there, puffing away on the cigars he'd given them.

"Grand goddam weed this is, sir," said the chatty one.

"Indeed," said Searcy, smiling for the first time that morning.

And as they rode away, he knew now he had some chance of not being killed. The orders were off his hands. No one would be sure about him even if they suspected something. And they could not, without being sure, shoot or torture an English gentleman.

— 21 —

IT HAD BEEN towards midnight when Hanks sent Usaph and
Gus to seek out the Creel house and tell the colonel that orders
had come and he was needed. They'd found the place by recognizing Wheat's horse which was still drowsing under the
tree by the gate. When they knocked, an old black lady came
and took their message and went and fetched Wheat. Wheat
didn't seem happy at first to see them. He was in his shirt and
britches and his boots looked somehow like they'd been pulled
on in a hurry. But the grievance he felt was directed at Hanks.
He was thinking, Hanks should have been the goddam preacher
and dear dead Diggie the lawyer.

He ordered Gus and Usaph to go and wait under the sycamore with the horse.

Gus seemed happy enough about that. When Hanks had
first ordered them to go and fetch Wheat, the music teacher
had been a little sullen about spending his evening seeking out
a particular house on a particular back road. But it hadn't been
a hard search and now Gus leaned against the fence and said:
"Nice little place."

It was Usaph who was feeling a sort of bilious unease. "It's
someone's place," he said. "Someone's wife or someone's
widder."

"Oh Lord, Usaph," Gus said softly. "You do talk a deal
about wives and widows."

"I wasn't aware," said Usaph. "I wasn't aware I talked so
damn much on them-there topics."

At last they saw the door open again and Wheat came out
fully clothed from the darkness of the house into the clear
night. But he seemed to baulk and turn back, and from the
hallway right out on to the porch rushed a woman in a long
loose gown. She hung on to him. She was tall. Wheat hardly
had to bend to clamp his mouth on hers. Then they whispered
a little and she went inside, and the door closed with a slow,
regretful crunch.

Even though they came from the Valley, where men were a lot more truly equal, one to another, than they were down in the tidewater, Gus and Usaph would have been most comfortable if Wheat had come down the path, swung himself into the saddle and pretended that his orderly and his runner had seen nothing. If he'd done that they could have just looked at him out of the corner of their eyes, making their separate judgements about him, whether he was to be admired or condemned. Instead of that, Wheat felt bound to explain everything.

"That lady," he told them, not even getting into his saddle, leading his horse away instead, staying on their level, "that lady, boys, is . . . a lady. What you jest beheld, boys, I want you to know . . . maybe Usaph understands these things, being wed—what you jest beheld is nothing but generosity." Wheat coughed. He was finding these words harder to form than was usual with him. "The quality of mercy is not strained, is how the poet puts it, and that means that this generosity I speak of is a virtue, and all tightness, boys, and strictness, and for a man never to be passions's goddam slave—all that is a curse. And people who are tight and strict, boys, might as well be bankers, or find some such other abominable way of putting in the golden days that are the portion of a man on this earth. Do you understand that, boys?"

Gus said he did. "Of course, of course," said Gus, wanting to put an end to the conversation.

Usaph thought, if the colonel can talk frank to me, I can talk frank back.

"Is the lady some man's wife?" Usaph's voice was so taut the colonel looked at him. There was a sort of gentle hurt in the colonel's eyes.

"Usaph," he murmured, "I believe she was."

Gus caught Usaph's eye and made a disapproving mouth and frowned at him, and they continued back through Frederick in silence. When they got back to the encampment, and stood amongst all the prone sleeping figures, and when they'd said goodnight and Gus had started to move away, Wheat detained Usaph by the elbow.

"You oughtn't to judge me, son."

"No sir, colonel," said Usaph in the same tight voice as before.

"Goddamit, Usaph, it's time you loosened up your thoughts a little. I did not touch that lady's affections, boy, they are stuck as ever on her absent husband. Only the flesh wavers, Usaph, not the goddam heart."

Usaph dragged his arm loose. Wheat said: "You worried about your own wife, is that it, son? If so . . ."

"If so?" Usaph called out in a hard challenging voice.

Wheat bared his head and shook it.

"Don't judge me, boy," he asked again. It sounded like genuine begging.

That morning, by five o'clock, the Confederate army left Frederick by various roads. Tom Jackson's corps walked away westwards by Mill and Patrick Streets.

Stonewall himself came through town by his own route. He could ride now and went with a few of his staff and an escort of horsemen, Blue Ridge boys called the Black Horse Cavalry. From Best's Grove he rode to the Presbyterian manse, where an old friend from Lexington lived called the Reverend Doctor John Ross. But it was too early for the Rosses in their side street. Not even the house blacks were up. So, without getting joy from friends, Tom Jackson wrote a note and then rode on into Mill Street and joined the main stream of the march. Like Wheat, he dozed his way out of town.

Years later a poet called John Greenleaf Whittier wrote a poem that said that, on the way out of Frederick, Tom Jackson had seen a Union flag flying from an attic and had ordered his infantry to fire on it, and that an old woman called Barbara Frietchie, being of German blood and pro-Union, grabbed it before it fell, leaned out of the window with it, and:

> "'Shoot, if you must, this old gray head,
> But spare your country's flag,' she said."

At which Stonewall is supposed to have been shamed and

> "'Who touches a hair of yon gray head
> Dies like a dog! March on!' he said."

But Barbara Frietchie lived that morning in Patrick Street near the Town Creek Bridge, and Tom Jackson did not leave town that way. Humbler men did: Usaph Bumpass, Gus Ramseur, Lafcadio Wheat. But their thoughts were not broken into by any gray-haired Unionist. In fact, since she was more than

ninety years old and the hour was so ungodly early, maybe
Barbara was still between her sheets as the Confederacy in all
its tatters followed its path out of town.

Searcy travelled at something like his ease beside Lee's
headquarters wagons. After leaving *Special Orders No. 191*
in that meadow, he'd felt so lightened, so free, that he rode
right back to Best's Grove. The grove was full of officers
eating their breakfasts standing up, tents were being pulled
down, horses were snuffling and stamping, pricked by the
electricity of hope and urgency in the soldiers all around.

And no one took any notice of him. One of Angus's young
friends met him by accident in all that rushing around the
grove.

"Mr. Searcy sir. What is it that has befallen Angus? Rumor
is he split his head."

"He broke his wrist. Jolly bad luck, I say."

"It sure is, sir. With all that's likely to happen."

And that was all. Adjutant Chilton had packed up his portable table and his pens and his inks and was in a hurry to move,
and no one, no one in that great passionate corps of officers
wanted to question or punish the Honorable Horace Searcy.

When he knew that, Searcy leaned his forehead against his
horse's saddle and wept silently and ached for Mrs. Whipple.
Then, because no other course offered, because the army would
not let him escape it, he took a long mouthful of brandy and
mounted his horse when the order came for the headquarters
staff to do it. And rode away with them.

The following Saturday morning, Union Colonel Silas Colgrove of the 27th Indiana saw the fine sloping field where
Searcy's envelope was hidden and moved his men into it about
noon. They stacked their muskets and lay on the grass. The
marks of old cooking fires were here and there but the Indiana
boys wondered if these fires had been set by Confederates,
since there weren't any relics around, no bones or tobacco
wrappers or candy papers or old shoes or other army detritus.
For the men of the 27th Indiana didn't have any more idea than
McClellan did himself how hard up their enemy was.

A well-liked young soldier called Private Barton W. Mitchell went behind a tree to make water and saw the fat envelope
and picked it up. Inside were the cigars and Bart thought them
quite a prize. They were the sort you bought in the best hotels.

He rushed out in his generous way and showed them to his friend, First Sergeant John McKnight Bloss. Bloss was a generous enough man and said Bart should have two out of the three found cigars. But Bart solved it by cutting the third clean in two.

They did not light them at once, for they did not know what fatigues they might be ordered to do this afternoon that would spoil the savor of the cigars. They decided to leave them till evening, to smoke by their fires in front of other boys who'd be jealous as hell and think they were real worldlings.

After he'd put away his one and a half fine cigars, Barton Mitchell began reading the papers inside the envelope. He thought someone was joking. The first page said: "To Major General D. H. Hill, Commanding Division. Special Orders No. 191. From Headquarters, Army of Northern Virginia near Frederick, Maryland." Bart Mitchell turned the page and read the signature. "R. H. Chilton, Ass. Adj-General."

"What's that-there, Barton?" asked Sergeant Bloss.

"Just some stuff," Barton Mitchell told him, reading away. The pages said stuff such as that Jackson's wing was to move beyond Middletown, cross the Potomac and "by Friday evening the 12th take possession of the Baltimore and Ohio Railroad, capture such of them as may be at Martinsburg, Virginia, and intercept such as may try to escape from Harpers Ferry." It didn't say who the "them" was, but that was clear enough.

The pages said in addition that John G. Walker's division of Longstreet's wing was to come down on Harpers Ferry from the other direction. It said that General McLaws with two divisions was to close in the same unfortunate town from the Maryland side. It said too that Longstreet was to clear out of Frederick and stick at Boonsboro and that D. H. Hill was to stay behind and form a rearguard.

Well, Bart Mitchell was a literate soldier. The armies of North and South in the failing summer of 1862 knew more of generalship than did the poor peasant privates of the armies of Prussia or Austria or England. Bart could readily understand that if these pages were anyway correct, then Lee's army was going to go four or five ways at once, all split up. Except all this read more like a Northern pipedream than like something that was likely to happen.

"Jest look at this here, Johnny," he told Bloss, and handed the pages to him.

Bloss had this natty self-importance a sergeant should

maybe have. He read the pages and said: "Come on, Bart."
He carried them, as if he'd done all the finding of them, to
Captain Kopp of Company E. Kopp read them, looked at the
two soldiers, dismissed the private and kept the sergeant with
him, and went to show them to Colonel Colgrove.

Colgrove, willing to be thought a fool, took them along the
road to the farmhouse where General Alpheus Williams had
made his headquarters. It happened that the adjutant in General
Williams's front office was Colonel S. E. Pittman, an old West
Point friend of Colonel Chilton in whose firm handwriting
Special Orders No. 191 were written. So a despatch rider took
the pages straight to McClellan's headquarters, further still up
the road. It wasn't a bad performance by the standards of the
Army of the Potomac. In an hour from the time Private Bart
Mitchell found the envelope behind the tree, George B.
McClellan was reading the Confederate document.

McClellan called a meeting of his staff and some of his
generals and marched into the drawing room of the big house
on the Liberty Town Road where it was held waving the papers
at the gathering of gold-braided men. "Here's a paper," he told
them, "which if I can't whip Bobby Lee with it, I'll willingly
go home. Tomorrow we'll pitch into his center, and if you folk
will only do two good hard days' marching, I'll have Lee in
a position he'll find it hard to get out of."

When some of the gentlemen there knew what was in the
orders, they thought McClellan shouldn't propose to pitch into
Lee's center tomorrow, he should start off to do it right now,
this Saturday afternoon.

George McClellan rode to Frederick then and met businessmen at the Liberty House. He began by making arrangements with them about supplying the army with farm produce
and flour. Then, even though he didn't know what their policies
were, he thanked them for staying loyal to the Union while
the Confederates were in town. At the end of the meeting, two
or three came up to talk to him and he started to get garrulous,
with them, as was his way. After a while he told them he had
Lee sorted out and by the ears, that he had Lee's inside orders
and that he knew Lee's army was in fragments.

One of the three he spoke to was Confederate by sympathy
and left town that afternoon and rode for hours up over the low
spine of the Catoctin Mountains, through Middletown until,
late at night, he ran into Jeb Stuart's Confederate pickets.

Just before dawn on Sunday Lee, sleeping fitfully in the

bedroom of a good house a little north of Boonsboro, was woken by Colonel Chilton. Lee levered himself crookedly up in the bed, for his hands and wrists were still paining and he could not put weight on them.

Chilton said: "There's a corn merchant from Frederick out there who says McClellan's got a copy of your orders."

"That's easy for a corn merchant to say," said Robert E. Lee. "How would he know what that general has and hasn't?"

"McClellan told a bunch of Frederick merchants. According to this corn-dealer, ole Mac waved a copy of your orders and said 'I've got these orders written in Lee's own hand' . . ."

"But they were in your hand, Chilton."

"Exactly, sir." Chilton winced. "I don't think we can afford to ignore the idea that they *were* an original copy, sir. In my hand. And ole Mac said they were in your hand just to make a splash."

"That man is, I think I can safely say," said Lee, "a fool. He could have had any old document in his hand, he could have been lying."

"I wish I could believe it, sir. You see this corn-jobber says further that McClellan called out, 'I got'em, gentlemen. They've sent Jackson off to the Ferry and Longstreet over to Boonsboro. And all I've got to do to get right in between them is knock Dan Hill out of the way.'"

"No one," Lee murmured after a silence, "could speak like that. Unless they had some idea of what was in 191."

Most men would have panicked now, in that instant, but the commander-in-chief just sat there staring at the plaster on his right hand and yawning a little.

"Do you want to speak to this corn-jobber?"

"Indeed." He tried to pick up a watch with the hand in which the bones were broken.

"It's 4:30, sir."

"I'll be with him in five minutes."

"Yessir."

"And, Chilton . . . are you satisfied this man is not a Union plant?"

"I'm watching him close. But he does have two boys in Early's brigade."

"I want you to start making enquiries then. About 191, I mean. Did you get all the envelopes back?"

"I did, general." Chilton seemed a little hurt by the suggestion.

"Begin by questioning your staff. And the staff couriers."

"Yessir. As bad luck would have it, one of them's gone back to Virginia with a nasty broken wrist."

Lee said: "Do what you can."

"Of course," said Chilton, "I can't make enquiries with the various generals until the army reassembles again. But I'm sure they treated 191 with care. Jimmie Longstreet, I believe, chewed his copy up and swallowed it."

This tickled Lee. "Did it help with his diarrhea?" he asked.

Chilton left and Lee sat on his bed, considering whether his army should go home to Virginia before the fragments were gobbled in five easy pieces.

BOOK FOUR

— 1 —

HIGH UP ABOVE the steep-streeted town of Harpers Ferry, Usaph
lay at dawn in a misty forest. At his side, Gus stirred and sat.
Cate and Judd and Daniel Blalock, schoolmaster, were stirring
too. The frosty vapors of this mountain place hung between
the pine trees with that sort of false stillness things and people
can have when you feel that until the second you looked at
them they were moving about and working on some plot against
you, and that as soon as you look away, they'll start again.

The bladder can be a stronger influence than that kind of
mad suspicion and Usaph got up, went through the trees across
somewhat slanting ground and urinated near the place where
Brynam's black guns stood, their barrels darkened with moisture this morning. The battery was only four guns these days.
Their gun-crews had sighted them the afternoon before, when
the town and the Union defence lines down below had stood
so sharp-defined in the sabbath light. So they could fire blind
if they had to, sending cannister and grape and case shell down
through the cloud.

They had wanted to start firing the afternoon before, but
the rumor was Stonewall was giving the Union general a chance
to move the folk of Harpers Ferry out of town. There was the
rumor too that the idea was to offer the Yankees the chance
of giving in. Others said that Stonewall, being a good Pres-

byterian, hated to call a battle on a Sunday, seeing that he'd done just that so often in the past.

Usaph had this terrible hunger for a good farm breakfast; he could taste the eggs that were not to be had here on this mountain. That phantom flavor of breakfast eggs wasn't half so sharp though as his puzzlement over Colonel Wheat. He found he'd forgiven Wheat because Wheat, though a colonel and a member of the Virginia Bar, was so anxious to be forgiven. He had forgiven the adulterer! It was a dangerous thing to do; it raised questions, he didn't like it. But it had just happened. He hoped it wouldn't happen with goddam Cate.

Boys got their wet and smouldery fires going on the site of last night's fires and heated up their handful of cornmush and their coffee. Even Wheat had little more than that to eat this morning, and the starey-eyed crazes seemed to be on him, so he began telling tales once again of his gran'daddy Wheat, as if that would stem his hunger. "Breakfast awaits you down in Harpers Ferry, sir," boys told each other, trying to sound like British butlers they'd seen in plays performed by touring companies. For they thought they'd be in Harpers Ferry in time for a fair breakfast.

Cate? Cate had ague. The shivers. He sat up in his wet blanket as he'd sat up all night, hard for breath and quivering away. He had no friends of the sort to bring him coffee even if they'd had plenty. All the conscript friends he'd had were killed or ill or deserted. Earlier on in his military career, someone like Judd might have become his friend through getting all dazzled by his line of talk. But Cate didn't have much of a line of talk any more. Since crossing the Potomac into Maryland he'd got sullen. He'd got sullener still after that incident when Usaph grabbed his ankle while he straddled the fence beyond which lay those whores from the town of Frederick. And when Stonewall led the Shenandoah Volunteers back over the Potomac at Williamsport last Thursday, back into Virginia itself with the bands playing "Carry Me Back to Ole Virginny" as lusty as a week before they'd played "Maryland, My Maryland," Cate hadn't made a whisper of a speech about it all being comic or ironic or any of that stuff.

While eating a gritty ball of cornmeal, Usaph watched Cate. Hans Strahl vanishing in the air worried Usaph, but it worried him too that Cate stuck on. It was almost as if the painter was dragging along just to get a word from him, from Usaph Bumpass. Amongst all the noise of the march and the bivouac, the silence between them was stretched now thin as a spiderweb. Usaph's detestation of the man had waxed sharper than ever since Cate delivered him from those Union bayonets.

The place where they sat this morning eating their mush and their ashy little balls of cornmeal was called Bolivar Heights. Way below, beyond the town, the grand Shenandoah, daughter of a thousand mountain streams, ran boiling up across heaps of shingle against its equal partner the Potomac. Even up here you could hear, though you couldn't see, the boiling business of the two rivers. And as Usaph lolled there, frowning and hearing Wheat's ancestral story, he kept watching Cate and feeling a little panic. If I don't give him a kindly word to break his fever, he thought, who will? Yet I'm damned if I will. I forgave goddam Wheat, and that's enough.

Wheat's story that morning threw light on the whole business of how the Wheats came to this sweet land in the first instance. It also had a more moral ring than the tale about Mrs. China. Gran'daddy Wheat, in his young days a sugar refiner in the English town of Bristol, had got into cash problems and so had forged a bill for £1500, in the name of someone else, against Lubbock's Bank in London. Gran'daddy Wheat got to London with his young wife, cashed the bill for somewhat less than its nominal price, and bought a ticket to Norfolk Virginia, on a ship called the *Wellesley*. Then he'd said goodbye to his wife, and boarded his ship. The young Mrs. Wheat headed back for Somerset and, on the Bristol Road, met a constable and gran'daddy Wheat's partner galloping towards London to catch the forger. Since she was sure the ship was already out in the Channel going westwards for Virginia, she told them all the details of gran'daddy Wheat's escape. Her husband, she said, would send for her later. She crowed at them a treat.

"Where's Somerset?" Usaph asked, a little sullen. "Where's this Bristol?"

"Far from here, Usaph boy," said Wheat. And Usaph would have had to own up, *that* was part of the appeal of the story.

According to Wheat, the two men went on to London and found that the *Wellesley* had been delayed for some reason—something to do with tides. They hired a boat and hailed the captain, saying who they were and that they wanted to know in the name of the King no less if gran'daddy Wheat was aboard. Gran'daddy Wheat came up on the quarterdeck wearing a cloak over his head and offered the captain the bulk of his money if he'd weigh anchor right away for Virginia.

Now this made a fine story, but even at this point, when the destiny of gran'daddy Wheat hung on whether the captain would clear harbor, Usaph couldn't stop watching Cate.

"So the captain agreed to my gran'daddy's offer," said the colonel. "It was some risk, for if gran'daddy's partner and that constable could beat the ship downriver to the marine station, they could get off from the bank with troops, and that would sure end gran'daddy's flight and likely his life as well. For this was 1820 and they hanged men who forged bills as big as that. Just as night came on, when they was at the mouth of that famed River Thames, the captain and gran'daddy saw a pinnace full of goddam redcoats bobbing about in the tide, but far enough astern for the captain to pretend he hadn't seen them. And that's how gran'daddy got his start in a new life, landing without a cent on the docks of Newport News. And he was always aware of his good fortune and said that he could jest as easily have become a dishonored corpse as an honored citizen of Harrison County. And it wasn't that he got away free with his little trick with that bill he wrote. His wife stayed on in Bristol with the partner and died there of the goddam typhus. And that was when gran'daddy married Mrs. Ettie Pleasant, a rich young widder of Doddridge County and the grandmother of your humble friend."

Throughout this whole fine tale, as well as being plagued by the presence of Cate, Usaph could see Captain Hanks standing wrapped in a blanket, and Lucius Taber, leaning up against a wet pine tree, staring at Wheat, and both of them disapproving of the commonness of the colonel in sharing round stories of his ancestors like this, and both of them wondering if Wheat was fit for command.

Usaph got so troubled and distracted by the sight of them that he got up from his place without thinking of it and edged away from Wheat, and found himself walking through moist pine needles towards Cate and standing over him. The first words were like forcing cores out of a boil.

"You ailing, Cate?" Usaph asked. And then he felt stupid for asking. Anyone could see, Cate *was* ailing.

Anyhow, Cate said nothing.

"If you're ailing, Cate," said Usaph, keeping his voice flat so that there was neither brotherliness nor hate in it, "you should maybe stay on round here. Rest yourself up in some farmhouse here. Look at them brogues of yours. Stitching all gone. Yeah, I'd say you might stay on. Hereabouts..."

Cate still said nothing, but his shivering got worse. Usaph turned from him. He tried to move without his movement saying one thing or the other, hatred or forgiveness.

"I don't mean to leave off," said Cate behind him. He said it like a drunkard talking about the bottle. Like he was really saying, *it don't mean to leave me off.*

"Well, you have to suit yourself, Cate. But there ain't no one to look after you on the road."

Again Cate had nothing to say. The lonesomest man in the whole goddam Army of Northern Virginia.

"You got coffee?" Usaph asked then in spite of himself.

He could tell by the nature of Cate's silence that he didn't have.

"Goddam you," Usaph said, like not having coffee was some sort of crime. "I'll go get you some."

He went and fetched a little of Lafcadio Wheat's coffee. The colonel didn't object. He was listening rapt to Gus's story of how the Ramseurs turned up in the New World. When Usaph gave Cate the coffee, the conscript put his quivering hands round it and his nose down to the steam. "That's a comfort," he muttered.

"Cate, did you maybe see something of young Hans Strahl the other day. Did you maybe see him walk away, out of line?"

Cate shook his head.

"Then where did he go?" Usaph asked, as if it was up to Cate to know these things.

"Maybe he got sick and went behind a tree."

"He wasn't goddam sick. I seen him at noon and he wasn't a hair of sick."

"Maybe he just sidled off."

"What? Him? Hans Strahl goes? And goddam Cate stays? Is this what you tell me?"

"I stay, Bumpass," said Cate, and Usaph couldn't make out whether he was joking or bitter, "because I got this view of history. I see that you and me, Bumpass, in all our present discomfort, are dead in the heart of history, like currants in a cake." He laughed a little, secretly. "Did you ever in your life hear, Bumpass, of an old battle called Cannae. Long ago and far away, boy. A general from North Africa called Hannibal got all round the Romans about lunchtime and scarce a poor suffering son of a bitch of them lived through the afternoon. History, Bumpass, history is a building whose goddam mortar is the blood of the young. History is a river, Bumpass, in which you and I are the fish. Have you caught a river perch, Bumpass, and when he lay panting wondered if he'd had a happy morning before you hauled him ashore? Did you wonder what his passions were, if he'd been near lady fish that day, what the poor son of a bitch had had for breakfast? Neither does God or history enquire such things of us, Bumpass. Yet without us, God and history would not be a river. That's the puzzle, Bumpass, that keeps us here."

"Take care, Cate. Blasphemy ain't easily forgiven jest on account of you having a fever when you utter it."

"Now the Yankees, Bumpass, down beneath that cloud are nameless as the 50,000 young Romans that Hannibal chewed up one afternoon. And you and I, we're faceless as the boys of Hannibal's infantry, as his goddam Celtic cavalry. But we have here, among us, a grand Presbyterian Hannibal, a goddam Confederate behemoth who'll likely consume them thousands down there under the cloud before shop opening time. And you ask me, Bumpass, to give up observing the manners and tricks and ways of this behemoth, to give up my part in them . . . my place in the goddam river, Bumpass. You want me to go for a rest on a farm?"

Usaph was so mad he kicked the bark of the trees nearest to sick Cate. "You tell me, Cate, you're travelling around with us jest to see the circus? Goddamit, Cate, you ain't even decent. Jest listen to me, Mr. Clever. I ain't going to carry your goddam musket or anything else of your truck. You understand that?"

There was noise now in the forest, shouting, the thud of the lids of limber chests opening, the chink, chink of artillery horses stamping and sniffing the excitement of the gunners. As Usaph reached Gus and opened his mouth to speak, the most tremendous banging he had ever heard began. Confederate fire went down on the invisible village from four sides. From over on the other mountain top that showed above the cloud the blast and the flashes reached Usaph. Across the other side of the Shenandoah, John Walker's artillery screamed on Loudoun Heights, and just over there beyond the place where the two rivers met, on top of the straight-up cliffs of Maryland, Lafayette McLaws had his guns working. Down on the lower ground, on both sides of the bank of the Shenandoah and to the south of town, Ambrose Hill's boys were firing fair up the valley at the Yankee lines and at the sweet town itself.

Gus and Usaph stared at each other. Gus looked amazed. How would he fit a noise like that into music?

Down there by the Potomac, behind the long brick buildings of the old arsenal, there was a flutter of white on a flag-pole. Tom Jackson saw it through his field-glasses.

"Tell me, Captain Pendleton. Can you spot a patch of white down there past the old superintendent's house?"

Sandie squinted. His war, like the general's, had started here. He knew the little town well and could name all its old buildings. But although the cloud had cleared away, there was such a taint of purple powder smoke washing across the town and away over the Potomac on the wind from the south that it was hard to see much. Way over on the cliffs on the far side of the Shenandoah, a few batteries of Johnny Walker's force stopped firing—they had seen the show of white too. But then they started up again.

Tom Jackson stood on a hill within sight of the river and the town. But Ambrose Hill's boys were closest of all to the village, and Tom Jackson was just about thinking of sending someone to ask Ambrose if he'd seen something, when Kyd Douglas came riding along, returning from that very same gentleman.

Ambrose was back in command, but just for battles. The rest of the time he was under arrest. Kyd thought Ambrose's boys had done fine work down there by the river; the Federal guns that faced them from behind mounds of dirt were just about silent now. But when Kyd spoke to him, Ambrose was sort of clipped and hostile like he *abominated* Tom Jackson and all his friends, not just plain disliked them.

Anyhow Kyd was back at Stonewall's hill now, back amongst friends. "That's a white flag they're showing, General," he was calling. "I don't know whether it's official or just a scared boy. But you can see it clear from down by the river. Canvas. A square. Cut maybe out of a tent."

Stonewall closed one eye and thought awhile. He could see there was scarcely more than two Federal guns flashing away down there.

"Would you care to visit Harpers Ferry yourself, Mr. Douglas?"

"*Visit* Harpers Ferry, General?"

"I would like you to ask the Federal commander what he means to do?"

Then Tom Jackson closed his eyes chastely like a parson in a bar. Kyd Douglas wanted to shake him. Rejoice, he wanted to say. Jump up and down and whistle and strike your thigh. 13,000 Yankees are about to be yielded up to you!

But Tom Jackson wasn't about to whistle or slap his thigh.

"I . . . I don't have a flag of truce," said Kyd. His big white handkerchief was soiled and he was such a natty young man, he didn't want to ride into a conquered town waving it.

Sandie Pendleton, subduing a smile that had come to his lips, offered his. It was an immaculate white kerchief which, if you unfolded it, was just about as big as a battle flag. Kyd took it, fetched an officer of the Black Horse troop to ride down the hill and along Shenandoah Street with him and to wave the handkerchief. As he turned his horse away, he heard Stonewall.

Stonewall Jackson was full of a wild impatience now, an impatience just about as hectic as Kyd's. But he knew men didn't exist to give way to such passions.

Sitting there waiting, he asked the Lord to curb his, Tom Jackson's, pride. The pride that made phrases like "brilliant manoeuvres" rise in his mind when he thought of what had been done around Harpers Ferry these past few days.

Hard prayer can be as distracting to a man as solid vanity is, and he woke up all at once with a shock to the fact that all firing had stopped. Through his glasses he could see white flags all over the township now. From the balcony of an hotel on Shenandoah Street, above the river's high bank and beyond some stilled and sullen Union cannon, sheets were being waved, and tablecloths, the whole linen supply of the establishment.

Stonewall spurred his big new mare—the one who'd given him his bad leg—downhill on to the road towards the ferry. Hunter and Hotchkiss and Sandie tagged after, and the cavalry escort.

— 2 —

SEARCY, HALF HAPPY but his nerves strung out tight, sat on a rocky embankment just to the south of the village of Sharpsburg writing in his journal that Monday morning.

He tried to write in an objective style, as if he had no stake in the outcome of whatever happened here on these low ridges, in these country lanes amongst the low hills. As if it was just another country skirmish that was shaping, he wrote slowly, squinting around at the foreign landscape. Anyone approaching him—and there were two men approaching him, even though he didn't know it—would have noticed how relaxed he looked, a man doing a small, unimportant task on a humid day at the end of the summer.

Inwardly, of course, he knew that these pleasant hills behind a stream called Antietam Creek had been chosen by whatever forces act in these matters, as the venue for one of this earth's crucial fights—just as the same forces, half a century before, had picked out the environs of a Belgian village named Waterloo as the place where Wellington could stop the tyrant Napoleon.

None of this crept into Searcy's notes.

"Lee has chosen a fair place to make his stand," he wrote. "He is on a low ridge facing a creek called Antietam Creek. (This is pronounced by the locals with the accent on the 'tie'— that is, An*tie*tam.) Behind him, looping like a snake, some of its body only a mile back, two miles back in other cases, the Potomac flows. Beyond the Potomac is Virginia. Just behind the ridge, on its back slope, sits the little town of Sharpsburg, much much smaller than Frederick. Even whiter, more dreamy, the great American rural slumber. Population—I would guess— 500 souls. Green fields all round. Corn in big acreages. This arrival of the Army of Northern Virginia is the biggest thing that has happened here, so a local told me, since the wars against the French and the Indians in the days when the British and the Americans, friends then, had a fort here . . ."

He always liked to sit on rocks to write. Later, long after the war, people who were asked to describe their memories of him, always remembered that. The sun was thin today. There'd been some mists earlier. Now and then he looked off to the east. If you looked hard at the forest a few miles beyond the Antietam, you could see the blue of Federal cavalry. You could see the dust clouds that meant infantry. The Army of Light were arriving and making their bivouacs. And all these staff officers whom Searcy had met at breakfast were talking about ole Mac's unexpected spunk.

But if there was one man Searcy despised it was McClellan. He had an image in his mind of the handsome square face and the lush, fashionable whiskers. Searcy wanted to get at him and shake till those whiskers flapped. He imagined meeting the general when the war was over and tongue-lashing him. "While I, sir, risked my skin, you dawdled around Maryland and made decisions only in office hours . . ." That sort of thing.

McClellan could and should have come over the Antietam last night and at least flanked, if not *surrounded* Lee's minute force. Searcy remembered how Secretary Stanton once murmured: "The trouble with McClellan is if he had a million men he'd swear the enemy had two million, and then he'd sit down in the mud and scream for three."

"I estimate," Searcy went on writing, "that here, around Sharpsburg and along the ridge, Lee has some fourteen brigades. The remaining 25 are still off in the Harpers Ferry area. It means that until Jackson and the others return, Lee and Longstreet have some 11,000 men to hold this line. McClellan, I would guess, has some 40,000 troops in reach of Sharpsburg this very morning."

What was it about the bugger that he couldn't roll on and on? Why was he the sort of general whose favorite exercise was to make camp and set sentries?

Still none of this bitterness entered his notes. "Lee will hold on here because he *is* here—he is in the North, he is on the flank of Washington. If he can stay here and put McClellan into disorder, he has won the whole game . . ."

As well as his general chagrin against McClellan, there was a sort of secondary pique working in Searcy—this one against the Union Intelligence Service. Intelligence Service? Colonel Allan Pinkerton led it, the renowned sleuth of railroad robberies. Obviously he didn't know enough about military work to go through the pockets of dead generals returned to you by the other side. If he had, Mac couldn't hold off like this, not even him. He'd know how short of men Lee was, he would have no excuse but to swamp him.

Searcy, thinking these savage, frightened thoughts, didn't notice the two Confederate officers who were approaching him along a deep-set country lane. One of these approaching officers was a man of about forty. The other was a lieutenant in his early twenties. Their faces were in set lines; that Southern affability wasn't there.

"Mr. Searcy," the older one said, "General Lee wants us to escort you to your horse."

Searcy didn't know what that meant, but he knew it must mean something worse than it said. He knew it by the lines on the faces of these men.

"I'm afraid I don't understand you, sir," he said, as haughty as he could manage.

Searcy recognized the younger man. A boy from Fredericksburg. No fool either. His hand was on his revolver. "We are authorized to take you at gunpoint," he said. "It would be better if things weren't done that way, sir. If there's a fracas and rumors get around about your activities, then we couldn't protect you from the wrath of the troops."

Searcy's hand, the one holding the pencil, began to tremble. He stopped it by fixing his mind on it. "Let me put my things away," he said. He packed his papers and writing gear in his satchel and stood up and managed to stare full face at the officers. "Of course," he said, very cold now, "I will demand in the most strict terms an explanation of all this."

The elder officer just nodded downhill. Go that way, the nod said.

"I realize I am a guest," said Searcy, balking. "I realize I am here on sufferance. But I will not be ordered around at gunpoint or under any other conditions without being told why. Tidewater gentlemen are not the only people on this continent with rights."

He was surprised how firm that sounded, whereas what he very nearly wanted to do was sit down on the grass and weep and confess, and find out if they meant to execute him or had other torments in mind.

"All right, Mr. Searcy," the elder officer said. "Shall I say this? Certain notes were found in the pockets of a dead Union officer who was being sent North for burial. It wasn't easy, I can tell you, sir, to find out whose they were—we looked at the handwriting of many officers. It didn't come to anyone till later, sir, to take a look at yours. We've done that now. The writing on the notes that were taken out of the dead general's pocket was *your* writing, Mr. Searcy. We didn't find that out soon enough to stop you taking your little ride with Mr. Angus."

"Listen to me!" Searcy said, choosing to snarl a little. "I am a neutral and a representative of the press and my belongings are immune from search..."

The older officer wasn't very impressed with that sort of thing. "Our colleague Angus," he said, "was tossed from his horse and we all thought, sir, it was after he'd delivered his papers to Dan Hill. You were damn lucky we went on thinking it, Searcy, ole boy. You see Colonel Chilton sent a copy of 191 to Dan Hill and another one to Tom Jackson. But ole Tom wrote out a copy for Dan, because Dan was under *his* orders and he didn't know Dan was meant to get one anyhow from headquarters. So Dan Hill *did* get a copy of 191 and didn't have to complain to General Lee that he didn't know what to do next—which would have made General Lee pretty damn suspicious, sir, pretty damn reasonable suspicious indeed."

"What a tale of fiction," said Searcy, though his hands had started trembling again.

The older officer narrowed his eyes. "I think," he said in a quiet voice, "the gods or the fates, or whoever looks after people like you, have done a good job of it so far, have gone, sir, to a lot more damn trouble than they ought."

Searcy pursued the haughty act. He felt it was all he could do. "We are all under the same rules of fate and destiny," he said loftily.

The young officer said: "We got a letter from Angus this morning, sir. From Waterford in Virginia. Marked *Urgent*. It seems Angus's head is clear now and he knows for certain he didn't deliver any message. He's distressed as well as that, on account of his horse has shown signs of blood poisoning, and he wonders could it be anything connected with a small wound that's been noticed on his horse's hip and has now ballooned up into quite a tumor. This morning, my friend and I have been through your saddlebags, Mr. Searcy, the ones you left in the encampment. That's something we don't usually like doing to any Christian. We find, sir, a hatpin." The young man was really outraged now, at the idea of such malice against good horseflesh. "March, sir, I warn you."

So Searcy did, still managing to look like an aristocrat on his way to an unjust execution, but wondering fretfully all the time if they were really taking him off for just that purpose— to put a bullet in his head in some clearing in the woods. His palms were sweating. If I am shot, it will surely create an incident. It will put a headstone on any British urge to recognize the Confederacy. Therefore I'll come to be considered a martyr. Mrs. Whipple will be reverent when she speaks my name. None of this comforted Searcy as they hustled him on down towards the Hagerstown–Sharpsburg Road.

He felt it was below his dignity to threaten them but when they led him into woods, he couldn't help himself. "I take it you realize that if any harm came to me," he said in an uninterested sort of voice, "Britain would demand a heavy price. I hope you understand how heavy."

The younger officer, the lawyer, hissed through his lips, almost like the start of a laugh. It was as if he admired Searcy's sass.

They came through the woods and out into the broad day again and Searcy felt better. A Confederate sergeant was standing by his, Searcy's, horse just there at the edge of the little town. The horse was facing south. Its saddlebags were in place and the sergeant held it as if he were holding it for an important man who had a journey to make.

The elder officer said: "We've taken nothing but your weapons. The Colt pistol and the Derringer. We've left you your knife. A week from tomorrow a vessel called the *Calliope* leaves Hampton Roads for Cork. Here is a letter of introduction to the captain." The officer handed him an envelope. "If you do not sail on it, peace-officers and provost-marshals throughout the Confederacy will be warned to apprehend you, dead or alive. A reward will be posted."

"And if I insist on staying on?" asked Searcy.

"You'll get a military trial, sir," said the elder.

"Your humble servant will be the prosecutor," the young lawyer said. "I shall demand the noose for you."

The elder officer patted the saddle of Searcy's horse. "I suggest you cross the Potomac just over here and make for

Centerville," he said. "Then you've got railroad all your benighted way."

Searcy climbed on to his horse.

"I shall make my complaints to the Secretary of State, Mr. Benjamin, in Richmond."

The two officers looked at each other and shook their heads. "Don't visit Benjamin, Mr. Searcy."

"And why not?"

"You'll only make a fool of yourself." The two officers consulted each other again before the young one went on. "Just for one thing, Mrs. Whipple, an associate of yours, has been charged with treason by a military court in Orange."

Searcy's belly seemed to shrink to berry-size and he thought, from the tingling in his hands and feet, he might faint.

The older officer said. "She's been sentenced to die by hanging come Tuesday. Allowing a week for any appeals to be made. Or maybe even a pardon to come through."

"You are lying, sir," Searcy yelled.

"I would not lie about the life of a lady," the officer yelled back. Then, in a softer voice: "Mrs. Whipple did not have the protection that comes with being British and belonging to the press . . ."

Searcy said: "That's right, sir, the greatest newspaper in the world. If this is true, I shall condemn you all so roundly in *The Times* that no one will touch your godless cause, gentlemen, no one will dare. The Sultan of Turkey won't give you the damned time of day."

"You do that, Mr. Searcy," said the younger officer. "And bring the Sultan greetings from all those boys who'll perish by Thursday."

He gave Searcy's horse such a swat across the tail that the thing behaved almost as madly as Angus's had the night Searcy drove the hatpin into it. The journalist kept his saddle, though, as the creature galloped south, and after half a mile he eased back to a canter, and took thought. If you have eighty miles to travel, it's quicker to canter. The worst thing is to work a horse so hard its heart bursts between towns and you have to carry a saddle for miles. It was therefore not fruitful to think of poor Mrs. Whipple's panic of soul as she sat in detention. Maybe she suffered no panic of soul. Maybe her friend—the wife of the Secretary of War and all those others—were visiting her or working for her pardon.

Confederate soldiers in the fields watched him with dull eyes. Tears for them and for Mrs. Whipple and for his own escape ran down his face, his hands on the reins began their trembling again. Only two miles to Shepherdstown, Virginia, and in Shepherdstown he could ask about the best roads, and that act of asking would settle him down.

He wasn't going to travel by Centerville, as the older officer suggested. He could get to Orange and still make it to that ship—the *Calliope*?—in time. He would board the *Calliope* with a sweet travelling companion!

Drying his face, he saw Dunker people, Sharpsburg families, up ahead on the road, making for Shepherdstown too, escaping the battle which could not now be begged off.

— 3 —

THOSE DUNKER FAMILIES Searcy had seen came from farms round about. That morning they'd decided it was time to take shelter at last.

The Dunkers were a German church keen on all the Ten Commandments and especially the one about brotherly love and honoring the lives of other humans. Their religion did not even allow them to take differences to court. In this reign of Christ, they thought, there shouldn't be need of courts. It was savage and strange therefore that the Confederates were making a line amongst the fields and behind the fences of peace-lovers like the Dunkers.

Up till last Sunday the war had kept a fit distance from them. They'd heard the sound of cannon from the direction of South Mountain, but they'd still read their Sunday services. Their little church stood on a small rise close up by the Hagerstown pike. Since they didn't believe in vanities it was a simple building. No steeple on it. After the service the Millers and the Poffenbergers and the others had all gone to supper at the Mummas' house and the noise from the east began to die as dark came. Though they couldn't know it, it had already become certain, even while they ate their sabbath meal, that their meadows would be the battleground.

The Dunker farms were mainly on the north side of Sharpsburg. Until Monday morning the Confederates of Lee and Longstreet seemed to be strung out towards the south side of the little town. But by mid-afternoon cavalry began to turn up all round the little white church and cannon appeared on a hill called Nicodemus Heights on Johannus Hoffman's farm. An infantry brigade stacked rifles by Miller's big cornfield and sent off a line of skirmishers towards the north. There were Confederate infantry and guns at Mumma's farm and on the other side of the pike, all round Poffenberger's place. Overnight other Confederates arrived and by morning the Dunkers knew the war was taking their fields away from them and would use their farms for its abominable rites.

So they closed the doors of their farmhouses—there were no locks since they considered that locking things up was an insult to human-kind—and packed up their wagons. Along the Potomac were caves they could shelter in till the godlessness passed. They shared the road to the river with many of the townsfolk of Sharpsburg. A shopkeeper and his wife and daughters crept along in their good surrey behind Poffenberger's wagon. The shopkeeper called: "Sharpsburg's a hundred years old, Brother Poffenberger, and ain't this the very first time any Christian has been forced to leave it!"

Farmer Miller had his eye on the detachments of young boys straggling up the road towards the town he himself was leaving. They would get over to the side, these young men, to let the wagons of the Brotherhood past. Some of them would call, "Goin' to market, daddy?" and such, but they were mostly quiet. He felt right sad for them.

He was sad too about his thirty acres of corn in that big field by the Hagerstown pike. He guessed it would be trampled or stolen by one army or another or crudely harvested by cannon before he could ever get back to it. He'd felt since the sabbath that that crop was doomed but it was too late by Monday morning to start getting it in. Newspapers said generals were meant to pay for corn they consumed or trod down, but Miller—though he read newspapers—knew it was against God's law to take money off a general, especially if young men had suffered amongst the corn. As angry and sharp as he felt about his thirty acres of corn, he felt worse about the cropping of the young men that would happen. Of the young Georgians who'd camped by his corn on Sunday evening and had told him: "Yessiree, we mean to stand, Mr. Miller. Did you think we was going back to Virginia without getting a better look at that-there McClellan . . . ?"

The Shenandoah Volunteers, limping into Sharpsburg towards noon, saw these men in their black coats and wide, round-crown hats sitting up on the boards of their drays. Saw the wives and daughters with their hands in their laps and their faces hidden deep in wide-brimmed bonnets. And the young Dunker boys looking at the soldiers with that horror and that interest a country boy always has, be he one of the Brethren or not, when he sees soldiers marching.

Stubble-chinned Ash Judd called out some of the normal teasing remarks: "Going back to join the quartermaster corps, are you then, Mr. Dunker?" For Judd was in good heart. While they marched back towards Maryland, he'd got his usual sight of the old man on a fence in a village called Leetown. The old man, as he often did, had a clay pipe in his mouth, and his eyes had that usual look, as if they were just about to wink at Ash, but that the old man didn't want to give the secret away to that extent.

Usaph didn't feel near as genial as Ash did. He had the usual belly-aches from eating two days' rations cooked in too much bacon grease. To add to his grief, he was carrying Cate's musket as well. Goddam Cate had kept slithering and shivering along with the regiment, keeping up somehow, and first a conscript had offered to take the goddam thing for Cate, and Usaph felt bound somehow to rest the conscript now and then. Deep in his belly, it made him itch and squirm for being so stupid. That feeling didn't help the pains he had already.

But the Shenandoah Volunteers, with pop-eyed Colonel Wheat at its head mounted on his mare, with Captain Hanks and Lieutenant Taber striding behind, and Daniel Blalock, schoolmaster of the Valley, carrying the flag with the insignia of Virginia on it, and with all the scrawny boys in its poor-formed ranks, now numbered just 83 souls. Amongst so few, Cate, a lean streak of misery, chattering and shivering in a blanket, stood out and couldn't be turned away from. That was how it seemed to Usaph, anyhow.

In spite of feeling foolish, Usaph and everyone else had this feeling as well that things were getting close to their end.

Wheat had said at breakfast that morning, while they were resting at Shepherdstown: "It seems to me that we've whipped Pope and now our indicated task is to whip McClellan. And when that is done, then there's no one else on God's sweet earth left for us to whip." And then Danny Blalock had spoken up in that sort of quiet excitement that was in everyone and said something they just about all believed. "They won't fight the way they did round Groveton and Manassas. Why, they spent all their courage there. You can't tell me they've got any more to spend."

So this noon, even Gus was humming now and then. A straightout tune, "Mister, Here's Your Mule," he was humming away at, just for the straight enjoyment of it.

And Usaph had said: "Gus, damn me if you ain't singin' a straightout tune."

And Gus had grinned. "Damn me if you ain't carrying Cate's Springfield."

"No town to pay much mind to," said Ash Judd as they went through Sharpsburg. Main Street lacked shops and was all quiet shuttered houses. An officer at the corner of Main and Jefferson pointed them north up the Hagerstown Pike. In the churchyard of the white Dunker church they fell out. The Stonewall Brigade. 300 boys. They stacked their arms. Usaph added Cate's to the stack. The church was closed up, its blinds drawn, just as if the Lord Christ was sleeping. Usaph fell on the ground without spreading his blanket and slept for a while in the September sun. He had a dream in which he was in an office. Jesus Christ sat behind the desk and he and Ephie stood before it. Ephie wept, and the Lord tried to explain something to Usaph on her behalf, something she had done that Jesus had forgiven but which Usaph felt offended by. In his sleep, Usaph knew what that something was. But when he woke there was nothing left of it except the flavor of grief.

— 4 —

WHEAT WAS A profane and adulterous man. It hadn't escaped Usaph that to be his runner might not be a pleasant thing if the Lord all at once singled Lafcadio Wheat out for special vengeance.

Though the runner for someone as important as a Virginia colonel didn't need to do picket duty, Usaph was glad to take a few messages up to the picket line that night, just to avoid the colonel's speeches and stories. It wasn't that they weren't fine stories and eloquent speeches. It was just that they came on so ceaseless and without stint. Besides, Wheat had taken to winking at Usaph and calling him "the Reverend Bumpass." The way he did it was half-mocking and half-begging and Usaph didn't like it.

So Usaph was happy to leave Wheat's campfire and move north down the Hagerstown pike, a fine straight pike amongst the smoky meadows of Maryland.

The pickets stood along the north end of the wood, just a little way from the Dunker church. Some of them were chatting low and chawing and huddling by the railing fence on the turnpike. Others were across the road by a big cornfield. Lucius Taber had charge of the fifteen or so Shenandoah boys who stood in this picket line. It had come on drizzly as Usaph delivered his letter to Lucius. Lucius stood by a stone fence looking north, reading the letter in little bursts and then raising his eyes again. The Yankees had crossed way up the Antietam stream and were off in the wood there, at least a good half-mile away. But sometimes you felt you could just about hear their whispering. It was like a shuffle of leaves, their conversation.

Usaph thought he could feel a joyfulness up here amongst the dripping leaves. There was a sort of breathiness in the way boys whispered, as if they couldn't wait till morning. It wasn't like that back where the rest of the regiment were trying to sleep against fences and in murky little ravines along the road.

But the excitement was here, and as sweet as it was to taste, it made Usaph ill at ease.

Ash Judd, one of the pickets, was resting against a walnut tree. As Usaph turned back from talking to Lucius, Ash called to him.

"Saph! Saph!" He pointed north with his thumb, as if the north was not dark but was lit up. "Tell me what you can see there, Saph?"

"I can't see nothing," said Usaph.

"There you go!" Ash whistled, very pleased. "You see, they don't have no fires, Usaph, ole friend. Their goddam generals are pretending we don't know where they are and so no fires're permitted the poor sons of bitches." And Ash whistled low and shook his head. To him it just showed what happened to Northern people all the time as a punishment for electing Lincoln and all them other Republican hoodlums. "They're up there chawing on dried coffee grounds and shivering to theirselves."

"You ain't much better off yourself there, Ash."

"Ain't I? Goddam, why, I had a conscript bring me a mug of coffee up from that-there cornfield right there, and it was goddam nectar, Saphie, goddam nectar." And Ash grinned up at Usaph like one man grinning up at another amongst the comforts of the lobby of the Virginia House in Richmond.

"Tell me this," Ash said then; "is ole Wheat still telling Gus back there them stretchers regarding his gran'daddy?"

"When I left him, yeh, Ash. He was still telling away."

"I wonder what tales of *their* gran'daddies them Union colonels're telling the Yankee boys to keep 'em warm tonight?"

Far away, where the Union pickets must be, there was quite a clatter and yelling all at once. You couldn't tell what words were said, but it sure sounded like loud oaths. "Some goddam conscript of theirs must've tripped over a nag," said Ash.

Going back to the shed by the pike where Wheat was sheltering from the drizzle, Usaph left behind all the temporary optimism young Ashabel Judd had given him. He felt clammy and scarcely knew whether it was drizzle or fever. The moon was thin when it came out over beyond the pike, and in the low pastures near the Antietam stream mists were forming. One more day, he promised himself. Just one more day of conflict. "Oh, Ephie, oh, Ephie," he said out loud, without knowing he was doing it.

"Be quiet there, boy," said someone from the darkness.

— 5 —

THAT MORNING DORA WHIPPLE received three sets of visitors in her cell. The last of the night's rain was dripping from the eaves when the first one arrived. It was her counsel. She could tell from his dismal face what he had come for.

"There's no mercy," she stated, looking up from her chair by the table where she was composing a long painful letter to Mrs. Isabelle Randolph.

"There is none," he said. "My poor Mrs. Whipple."

She nodded like someone who had just found out that the storekeeper has run out of coffee. She was amazed herself at how tranquil she could be. She saw that her attitude was confusing poor honest Pember. "My dear sir," she said, "it's a matter of what is inevitable, that's all." She chewed the end of her pen a little. "Thank you for all you did. But a crime is a crime, sir." She looked down on her letter as if re-reading it and placed a deft comma in one of the sentences. "Tell me, who is doing it?"

"They are bringing the navy executioner from Norfolk, ma'am. He's said to be the . . . the best. By that I mean, ma'am, the least . . . *painful*."

They shook hands and he left. He said he would have stayed but . . . he had been ordered back to Richmond by his superior officers. She wondered if that was true.

She'd just about finished eating her breakfast when she looked up and saw standing in her doorway in silence her second visitor, a bulky man with a brown beard and wearing the uniform of a chief petty officer in the Confederate navy. She looked him fair in the eye, as was her manner, and he did not flinch away. He looked like all the others she'd been seeing lately—a serious, kindly man.

"Ma'am," he said.

"Sir, can I help you?"

He shook his head. After some seconds he nodded to her

and left. She rang her little hand bell and one of those elderly guards came.

"Corporal!" she barked. "I don't want any visitor . . . *any visitor* . . . being brought in here without my being told. Do you understand?"

He said he did.

But later still, when he had gone off duty, she heard quite a crowd of people being let into the lockup. Oh my God, she thought, undertakers and all that rabble!

"Friends of yours, ma'am," the guard called as he turned the key in her lock. She went on writing even while these visitors were entering.

"Mrs. Whipple," she heard in a voice that shook her ear and resounded through her body. She looked up and it was Searcy. He placed his forefinger on his lips while the turnkey locked up and went away.

"I paid for four passes to see you," he told her. "You see, help is feasible, and it has arrived." He spread his arms.

She looked at those who'd come in with him. There was first of all a minister of religion, and then a middle-aged couple standing together, probably husband and wife. They all waited there, looking at her with the usual solemnity, the look she was getting used to.

"It is not easy getting passes," Searcy said with a wide smile. "But seeing you is worth every trouble. Mrs. Whipple?" He smiled and took her hand and pressed it against his lips.

"I am in good heart, Mr. Searcy," she said, smiling remotely. "It is such a wonder to see you. I have a letter for you . . . I was trying to get someone to deliver it . . ." She frowned. "I hope you take no risk, coming here."

"They would not dare touch me, Mrs. Whipple. In half an hour, I assure you, they will not dare touch you."

"Oh, they won't touch me anyhow, Mr. Searcy. They won't touch me where I reside, I'm very happy to say." And she tapped her chest, above her breasts, to indicate the place she resided so safely.

"They will not touch you, my dear lady," said Searcy exultantly, "because you will be my wife. The protection of my name and of my family will hang over you. This, Mrs. Whipple, is the Reverend Archer, and this Mr. and Mrs. Brownley. They are of like mind to us. Mr. Archer will marry us now, Mr. and Mrs. Brownley will be our witnesses. I shall drop our legal wedding certificate on President Davis's desk by this evening at the latest. He will then know that if he proceeds with harming you he will become a pariah in Europe—"

"Amen," said the Reverend Archer.

"—that his name shall be synonymous with Bluebeard's and Genghis Khan's. If he did not even care about that, he cannot afford it in the political sense, madam. Therefore, I think I can say with humility, my dear Dora, that I've come to save you."

She inspected him for a while. He's coming on a little strong, she thought. She closed her eyes and sat down again. While she loved him for going to this trouble, she was amazed how little bearing it had, how little it meant.

She waved her hand in a negative way. "Please, I am honored by all your trouble..."

Searcy went pale. Everyone is going pale, she thought. Everyone but me.

"You'll surely do this, Mrs. Whipple?" Searcy asked.

"You know I can't settle the matter this way," she said.

"My dear lady, the preservation of one's life," the Reverend Archer said, "is the first issue of all..."

"I can't let myself escape by these means," she said. She resented this preacher horning in between Searcy and herself. "Searcy, you know how it is. You can tell. The conflict which finished my dear husband is meant to finish me as well. Simple as that."

"This is too much fatalism, ma'am," said the Reverend Archer, like an amateur theologian.

"Dora," Searcy whispered, "I am begging you...for my sake..."

She was beginning to feel desperate. She said again: "I cannot escape by these means, Searcy. You understand that. I could not live on as anyone's proper wife under these terms. Our union, Searcy—which honest to heaven I'd want under any other conditions—would be poisoned by this stratagem we're using here. You can see it, Searcy. I know you can."

"Mrs. Whipple," the Reverend Archer pressed on, "your conscience is too delicate, ma'am. There is no shame in saving one's life by reasonable means."

My God, he talks like a damn mathematician, in here when I should be on my own with Searcy. She began to shake her head. "I've been Yates Whipple's widow so long—it seems to me so long anyhow, even though it's only been a year.

Don't you see, Searcy, I want to die as Whipple's widow?
That's the appropriate thing. Don't you see?"

Searcy grasped her by the shoulders. She pitied him for the
sweat he was in. "Dora! Please, Dora!"

His cheeks were getting so muddy from his tears that you
would have thought he'd been crying even before he came in
here, that he'd been weeping since dawn. "I can so easily save
you. You...you can so easily save me. We'd live so well in
Devon, Mrs. Whipple, a world away from Union and Confederate. Please, Dora!"

Mrs. Whipple couldn't understand how he could talk like
that. He sounded like a dilettante, an idle admirer of the Union.

"You can forget the slaves? You can forget them as easy
as that?"

"Yes. For you, yes. How much will *you* remember them
if you hang?"

The eyes of Searcy and his parson and the two witnesses
were fixed on her. They were all at once a greater combined
torment for her than her judges had been.

"You're causing me pain!" she told Searcy.

"No. I'd never cause you pain."

She shook her head in a frenzy. "Let me alone. Let me
alone!" She glared at them, especially the Reverend Archer
who seemed to her to be the most unyielding of the quartet
and to have fouled this meeting between Searcy and herself
with all his cold moral talk. "Don't persecute me, please. I
can't do, Searcy, what I can't do."

Searcy kept on weeping, but he did not bully her any more.
"Our passes are good for a return visit this afternoon, my dear
Dora," he said.

"Come back yourself, Searcy. Come back to sit with me
and talk. But please don't bring any strangers. Please, please."

Searcy nodded to the Reverend Archer and the Brownleys
to go. They stumbled out, Archer not quite brave enough to
argue with Searcy. When they had gone, Searcy held her for
a while. He could feel the reverberations of her heart against
her ribs, the way he had the first time he ever had hold of her.

"Be still, be still, my little bird," he told her. "The town
is full of guards, all those middle-aged men are standing double
watches. There's no escape that way. The only escape..."

"You promised not to talk about it, Searcy. Hold me, just
that."

He obeyed her, but within a minute could tell, just by holding her, that it was useless, and that the turnkey was in any case waiting for him to leave. Going out, he promised again to be back later.

He found Archer and Mr. and Mrs. Brownley waiting disconsolately outside the lockup door.

"I shall try again this afternoon, good people. Perhaps if it's convenient you could wait within call."

"Of course," said Archer. "Of course, we must."

But when they came back in the afternoon, they found an old grey-haired colonel at the lockup door. He said Mrs. Whipple had a letter for Searcy and did not want to see them again. Searcy waved the parson and witnesses off, staggered away to the shadow of one of the elms and opened the letter.

> I would be your wife if the world let me. I respect you, Searcy, and feel great affection for you, but I cannot see you again without pain to us both. I know, somehow, that you will remember me as a woman, not as something akin to one of those Russian icons or Christian martyrs.
> Yours,
> D. W.

— 6 —

"WHY AIN'T YOU got shoes on your feet?" Usaph yelled at the drummer. He had to yell because the noise had been going on since three o'clock in the morning.

The drummer boy blinked and didn't answer, but just looked down at his young horny feet. Goddam, he was young. Fifteen at best. Little bullet head. Mouth always just a little opened. He was Wheat's newest interest, this boy. He'd slept last night huddled up at the colonel's feet like a dog.

"Shoes?" asked Gus. "Tell my friend Usaph why you got no shoes."

"Had a pair but they got took," said the boy drummer. "By a feller looked something like you."

"I ain't got your shoes, boy," Usaph assured him.

"So you say," said the drummer. He yawned. Wheat had had him playing drum rolls half the goddam night. A drummer was getting to be something of a military novelty. The Shenandoah Volunteers had last had their own drummer way down there near Richmond, all that time ago, at high summer.

This drummer had therefore been rattling away with his sticks in the misty grey as daylight came. The drum rattle got boys up from their wet blankets in the edges of the forest. Boys who'd slept uneasy and with their cartridges inside their jackets, near up against their heart warmth to keep the powder dry. And as they rose, they were muttering now about the open secret of Wheat being mad.

"What's your name, boy?" Wheat had asked the boy on finding him last night.

"Rufe."

"What's your other?"

"Got none."

"My. What's your daddy's other name, then?"

"Ain't got no daddy, colonel."

"Do tell! You the virgin birth, is that so?"

Rufe didn't say anything. He didn't understand.

"Where you from then?"

"Everywheres."

"Goddamit, Rufe, ain't you jest the universal American child!"

"I did some living on the rivers, colonel," said Rufe, like an old man with lots of phases to his life.

"The river goddam Jordan, Rufe?"

"The Mississip. The Arkansas. Working the rafts. One time a cap'n told me my pappy came from Arkansas. Don't know if that's true."

Anyhow, Wheat now had this orphan child to make drum rolls in the first misty light. Rufe's rat-tat-tating not only woke the boys but directed them to their places by the high worm fences just beside the pike. Though they squinted up the road towards Pennsylvania, they could see nothing. Hearing was different. They could hear cannon speaking to each other up there in the rural murk.

Kyd passed by on the pike, going north towards the Confederate cannon on Nicodemus Heights. These roads and gentle hills round about were the hills of Kyd's boyhood. He had travelled up this pike with his father on the way to Harrisburg and Philadelphia where Douglas senior seemed always to have dealings. Down the laneways of this countryside, the Douglases had hunted or picnicked or visited friends or relatives. Stonewall knew all this and had given Kyd, at four o'clock in the morning, his orders for the day. "I want you to go right now and find out where all our cannon are placed. And I want you to consider what roads can best be used for drawing off disabled guns and for supplying ammunition. Next I want you to advise all battery commanders on these specific points. That's all you have to do all day, Kyd."

Kyd had thought that maybe that was a joke of some kind, but he couldn't tell, for there was no flicker along Stonewall's heavy-bearded lips.

So Kyd was on his way, and when he heard Rufe's artistry with the drumsticks, he urged his horse a little more and thought almost joyfully: "Today is the most dangerous day I'll spend in my life."

Usaph waited by Wheat's side behind their fence and watched the first-rate pike running moist-topped north through this rich country. Maybe because it was so misty and he could not see far, things appeared to him the way they had to farmers Miller and Poffenberger. That battle lay like an abominable beast resting across the laneways, fields and woods of Washington County. Since the small hours it had been stirring, making careless grunts and growls. But when the mist rose off the Hagerstown pike off Antietam creek to the front and the Potomac at the back then the beast bestirred itself fair and proper, took its feet and uttered a roar that farmer and Mrs. Poffenberger and family could hear even from the caves along the Potomac.

Next thing Usaph knew, after the rising of the mist and the roar of the beast, was that all the skirmishers who had been up the road during the night came running back through the wet stands of trees to the fences where Wheat's regiment stood, with Rufe still drumming for them but no one being able to hear him. Lucius ran back with his revolver in his hand. Mad Ash Judd hooted as he came to show this was going to be some picnic. Even from his place in the line, Usaph could see that it was going to develop like every other battle, only in greater quantity. He got an image in his mind of the stone fences of his first fight at Kernstown. The Yankees who had charged the fences that day were plenteous, but even as you fired at them, you knew they came in but finite numbers. Usaph got this sudden spurt of anger, for Kernstown had been no fitting class-room for what was happening this morning. Such lines of blue came out of the woods, to the north and assailed your vision, that you thought it was a sudden disease of the eyeballs.

Coming on in four lines across the fields, they now and then stopped a second and fired. Usaph saw three Confederate skirmishers all climbing the snake fences along the pike at once, crossing the road to get into the woods behind. All three of them were shot in the one second, one of them putting his hand up behind his ear in a fly-swatting way before he slumped there across the railings with the other two. They hung like ragged and drying animal hides.

Rufe kept rattling away at his drums, competing with the great blocks of cannon sound. Half the boys loaded and passed muskets to the other half, who discharged them at the enemy. The only voice you could hear was Wheat's and even he was cut back to the ordinary and normal things colonels uttered. Stuff like, "Steady, steady," and "Mark your target, boys."

And then the cannon really got to it. Confederate cannon on Nicodemus Heights started tearing into the Yankees from sideways and Union cannon from up the road started ripping the trees up behind Usaph. Something awful was happening to the Georgians over in Miller's cornfield, and in the little torn snatches of time between bangs you heard a human shriek-ing there, and the air above the cornfield, you saw between blinking, flew with bits of farmer Miller's corn crop and with limbs, naked and clothed, and with haversacks and heads and hands.

This, Usaph believed, was an amazing thing to see. But it did not horrify him, even though he had average feeling for his fellows. There was something in him that stopped him being horrified as the heads and armless trunks of Georgia's children rose from the corn. The cornfield was a good 200 paces off, and something cool in his belly whispered to him that 200 paces was as good as a county.

He began to cough. Others were coughing too. The morning was coming on overcast and the stained powder smoke did not blow anywhere on a breeze as it did on an average day. It sat low on the pike and got into Usaph's pipes. He got more wrapped up in the condition of his throat than in the terrible whacking of balls against tree trunks and fence rails. A lump of fence rail about as long as a rule flew up and slashed Wheat's cheek, but he just felt the place and cursed.

Almost in the same act, he turned, cupped his mouth and yelled to Usaph: "Get on back to Grigsby. Tell him that in my calm goddam opinion, Usaph, this line of fence jest can't be held." He said the Georgians on the flank were going to hell in numbers, that ammunition was already at least half spent and so on.

He squeezed Usaph's elbow, as if to say: "Don't think of my oddities, boy, jest do this work proper."

Usaph turned. He knew Grigsby, commanding the Stonewall Brigade, was posted by a stone fence below the little Dunker church. He headed down the fence by the turnpike. A shell fired from over the Antietam and meant for the piteous Georgians in the cornfield lit some twenty yards to his right, where Captain Hanks was standing, tore the captain open before Usaph's numb eyes and split the bodies of half a dozen boys round about.

Later Usaph could not quite remember the journey back to the Dunker church, could not even remember speaking the message about what great quantities of Yankees were coming on, and about the way Union cannon were ripping up those Georgians in the cornfields who were Grigsby's flank, and about Wheat's estimate of remaining powder and balls. He did remember that even that early the open grounds below the Dunker church were sort of sown with lines of wounded lain down on the trampled grass.

He had just turned back towards Wheat when he saw some of his own friends scuttling towards him, retreating fast as they could towards the church, vaulting fences between fields. The first he saw was Rufe, the young drummer, and Rufe was running hard, carrying his drum under his left arm like a boy carrying the pigskin in a football match, and his drumsticks like a relay baton, in his right hand. Sprinting barefoot and no, not like a footballer or an athlete, more like a farm boy in a novelty race at some fair.

Then Usaph could see Wheat and Gus and Lucius and all the others walking back across the field, coming straight for the Dunker church, and Gus and Ash dodging behind trees to fire off a quick, useless, dutybound round.

And from across the road a few Georgians were fleeing from that cornfield, their clothes a mess of oily muck; and such a scream arising now from that cornfield that it was like a goddam vent of hell.

Usaph turned back again and got in behind the stone fence by the church. Again a great volley took boys in the back as they were fence-climbing. If you had time and sight enough to look, you could see all the fences of Washington County, Maryland, filling up with lolling corpses.

As Decatur Cate climbed up that stone fence by the Dunker church, finding the big flat stones pretty slippery in spite of his long hands, he got the sting of a ball in his upper leg. It went straight through the meat and, by the time he fell on the far side, not far from where Lucius was now standing, he already knew somehow no bone had been broken. "Get up, Cate," yelled Lucius. And though Cate could not hear him, lip reading was enough. He rose and faced the immense lines of the blue regiments 300 paces off. Dear Christ, he thought. This is just Cannae all over and there is no chance now, God and history really are going to swallow Decatur Cate. He blinked at the storm of balls hissing and emanating from those regiments. Shells fell and burst behind his back amongst the lines of wounded around the church. And when you bit your cartridge and glanced up, you saw this or that boy look at you all at once in a pleading stunned way and then decide there was no charity left in the world and drop down dead. And only when he'd drop would you see the wound. Oh yes, Cate decided with the workaday despair of the damned, we're going to die right together here. Sublime Ephie can be some sort of double widow and go uncomforted. And so he just stood there and gave himself up to the darkest forces of history.

While matters were thus going to hell at the church, two or three meadows back, maybe somewhere between a quarter and a half a mile, General Hood's Texans had fires lit. In spite of all the noise, they were cooking their breakfasts, a meat ration they hadn't got till about dawn. It was their first meal for three days. When it was just starting to get nice and rare, and whatever juice was in the meat was starting to drip in the fires, Sandie Pendleton rode into their meadow and told General Hood that they were to break their arms-stacks and save the Dunker church.

Hood gave his orders. Adjutants lined the boys up. They were damn angry. They waved their arms and spat a lot. In spite of the noise, they uttered outlandish curses.

When they came over the crest by that church and ran down to the fence where the leftovers of the Stonewall stood, they were screaming with an anger as elemental as that of the cannon. Wounded boys, leaned up against the fence, looked up at them wide-eyed, as if they weren't reinforcements but some final satanic enemy.

It turned out pretty bloody for the Union boys as well. Confederate cannon in the woods and on Nicodemus Heights and from the Dunker churchyard did them harm. And the Texans, just about out of the control of their general, started to climb the fence and rush the close enemy.

Grigsby told Wheat and anyone else that was by that fence to follow on behind them.

Wheat had Rufe by the elbow. "Goddamit, Rufe, you ain't meant to go running like that. Why, your proper place is by me, son. You got your drum there, boy? I see you have! Then Wheat untied the dirty yellow sash from round his waist and tied one end of it round the belt of Rufe's britches, so that he could lead Rufe along like a pet. "Where I go, Rufe, you go. Now you sound the advance on that pigskin drum of yours, Rufe."

Somehow, connected like that, the colonel and Rufe got over the stone fence and so did the sixty or so Volunteers who were left or who found fence-climbing within their powers.

They dragged on across a field and got to the fence by the pike. Here you had to choose gaps to climb the thing, for it was all hung with doubled corpses. So they rushed over the pike and found they were all at once in farmer Miller's bloody cornfield.

Walking just about as easy as ever in spite of the puncture in the meat of his leg, Cate went with them. He would have been too stupid with the noise and the event to know why. To him as to Usaph and Gus and maybe even to Wheat, the morning was now too savage to be thought of as a real morning. To all of them it became a morning in a foul dream. The verges of the cornfield were heaped with mounds of poor flesh, and fences with their crops of dead had been shattered by cannon. And timber and grey cloth and blue cloth and human remnants lay in heaps that must be climbed. Ahead the Texans had chased those Yankees clean out of the corn, but as you stepped into the crop you could hear all these hidden groaning and pleas for mothers and water and for the God whose sky was cut off by the cropped tops of the stooks. Usaph trod on a mat of Christian boys, all of them defaced this way and that by cannister and shell pieces. He was too close to them now to get away from the fact that they were *there*. But after a step or two he did not look, there was no sense in picking a path. He could see Rufe ahead at the end of his leash of silk. And Rufe kept drumming but would turn his head aside to retch and gag.

When he came out of the north end of the corn, the air seemed thicker with balls, yet every one of them seemed meant for someone else and not for Usaph Bumpass. The whole earth of Maryland was sown with the young in blue and butternut, and their seed was dead inside them. And Usaph felt with a despair he could taste on his tongue that there'd never be fatherhood again until boy children, now living in safe towns, grew up.

Poor Ash Judd, with *his* magic seed still living within him, caught up with the Texans and climbed with them yet another snake fence. He saw woods fair ahead. There were such storms of balls emanating from those woods that Ash could just about see them in the air, just like insects. Carrying his musket across his body, Ash took one of them in his arm. He felt all the tendons around the bone up near his shoulder tearing and writhing but, through tears, understood somehow they did so to save that precious bone itself. You'll live on whole, he told himself. The Texans were starting to drop all round him, going down yelling and cursing, as noisy as they'd been all along. Ash was intent to inspect the hole in his jacket. So fast he couldn't tell which came first, a bullet tore his groin and another his upper leg. Still no bones; he told himself. If there hadn't been such noise he might have yelled across the field. "Still no bones!"

Next, one in the face, just beside the corner of the jawbone. Ashabel Judd fell forward, not feeling the impact with the ground. During the fragment of a second in which he toppled down, the phrase *Prince of Lies* repeated itself in his head. His face ended up nose first into the warm crown of his dropped hat. It was a new Union cavalry hat he'd got at Manassas and it had no holes other than the one or two little sweat holes in the side. These his blood clogged too readily. The further flow of blood from his face filled his hat and painlessly drowned him. In this self-same way a lot of boys would drown that morning in landlocked Washington County.

— 7 —

THERE WAS A PATTERN, and Usaph and Gus and Wheat and his drummer got caught up in it. They staggered back through the corn yet again and sheltered behind another fragment of fence, and fired yet, oh yet again, at the oncoming sons of the Union.

Usaph noticed in a quiet second that Wheat stood frowning, side-on to the fence and the enemy, a man conferring with himself. He had a handful of Virginians near him—there was Danny and Cate as well as Usaph and Gus—and even as they took aim they kept looking at him as if he was about to provide a magic deliverance.

Wheat couldn't tell where the rest of the Stonewall was. Maybe there wasn't any rest. He stood fingering the wound on his face that the fence splinter had made. Rufe his drummer waited by panting and dull-eyed at the end of Wheat's sash. His sticks were idle in his hand.

It was then the strangest thing of Usaph's whole day happened. It didn't seem at all crazy at the time, in fact it convinced every one of them, Usaph counted in, that Wheat was one of the great men of the time. But those who saw it and lived through the day would remember it later with some horror.

"Where's your colonel, son?" Wheat asked a Texan lieutenant passing by along the fence.

"There's no colonel, sir. He got shot in the head jest awhile back."

Wheat frowned, still fingering the injury to his face. All along the fence the Texans were strung out, firing at their own will, rudderless.

Usaph looked at Wheat. The colonel grinned back at him, as if he was saying: "And are you still worried by the small joy I had in Frederick, Reverend Bumpass?" Still grinning away, Wheat dipped a finger into the wound on his face and began ornamenting his features with his own gore, making scarlet marks on his dirty skin.

"Put on the war paint, boys!" he began to scream. "Put on the war paint!" He began to stride up and down amongst the Virginians, amongst Blalock and Cate and the others and down along the line of Texans who were loading and firing, the loaders cussing the firers and yelling at them to fire faster, and the firers screaming curses about the slowness of the loaders. And as he walked with his painted face he dragged Rufe with him. "Put on the war paint!" he said. And his blood showed up on his powder-blackened face, and so did his broad, fixed grin. "Put on the war paint!"

It seemed to appeal to the Texans. They paused in their loading and yelled, and rubbed the torn edges of the cardboard cartridges over their dirty faces making marks, and began whooping with their mouths open. The whoops spread down the fence.

Usaph walked with Wheat, as he was meant to, striding beside the dragged-along Rufe, and keeping pace with Gus. "Give 'em the whoop!" Wheat screamed and the Texans started whooping even more. They were some tribe, those Texicans! Usaph saw Gus streaking his face. Gus? Gus, the great man of music? Usaph had already broken a cartridge and was decorating his own visage with powder. Then he saw Cate engaged in the same work. Cate? Why?

Cate himself didn't know, but he was laughing to himself and daubing away.

Soon, Usaph knew, they'd all get up over the fence and howl through the cornfield. He could scarce wait for it. For Wheat had turned them all into a vengeance, a force of nature. They would be terrible to face, maybe even Cate, a Union lover—he'd be frightful for the Yankees to face.

"Sound the charge there, Rufe!" Wheat yelled at the drummer child.

Rufe did it. Whether they heard him or not, they all raged up over the fence, all painted with blood and powder and all unholy mad. Some Wisconsin boys they sent hurtling back through the corn. Union soldiers they overtook surrendered to them and were shot or sent back towards the church. No one paused to disarm these prisoners.

Beyond the corn, Wheat and his Virginia handful and all

those Texicans ran into a New York Irish regiment that advanced in battle order across a bare field. Usaph saw two women there, walking beside their men, looking like laundresses. Sergeants' wives or women. Right there in the lines. There was this harsh swapping of fire. Then Wheat ran charging at them, and some two hundred Irishmen and both their laundresses surrendered and were pointed towards the rear.

Wheat's line went through another little wood and surprised a green U.S. regiment waiting in a lane. The Union boys were dressing their lines there by the edge of a lane, dressing by their right and shuffling busily, when they looked up and saw wild hairy beasts with painted faces roaring out of the trees.

Beyond the lane the ground got rocky, you could see granite poking up out of the earth, and in saner times you might pity the farmer whose field it was. Amongst this rocky earth stood a farmhouse with faded white walls. Those green boys of Lincoln's scuttled back to this farmhouse, some of them, panicked to the limit, trying to hide amongst the black back walls of a burned-out barn, others forming a line by the farmhouse back door, and others around a pump and a small shed in the farmyard.

By now Daniel Blalock and Lucius were out in front with a few screaming Texans. With those few they lived through a volley and scattered the boys near the farmhouse door and ran into the farm kitchen, almost as if the core of the house had to be taken and occupied.

Usaph and Wheat arrived at the side of the house in time to see the Yankees running off, and a man in a good grey suit, no doubt the farmer, stumbling after them, trying to rally them as if he was an officer. A Union farmer, this one. No Dunker. For Wheat's mad Indian rush had brought them beyond the Dunker farms.

Usaph stood round in the farmyard with Wheat and Cate and Rufe and Gus, and everyone was panting away. "Did you see them, boys?" Wheat groaned. "Did you see their poor childish faces?" Usaph decided to try the pump, for his tinplate canteen was empty. He found the handle had been removed from the apparatus. He groaned and even wept for a few seconds, leaning against the *Made in Pittsburgh* metal, railing at the meanness of the farmer.

But before he had time to grieve at length over the loss of the pump handle, a regiment flying a Connecticut flag, tough boys, appeared out of the farmer's lower meadow. They clustered behind a stone wall and fired. Lucius, at the farm window, was shot in the throat. He went to his knees, hawking, and Danny Blalock held his elbow. While he died not knowing he was dying, he thought, all right, this is war enough. Spring semester, I'm going back to Euripides.

Danny Blalock understood all at once that the Yankees were a bottomless barrel. Say you drove off that Union brigade that was coming on now three lines deep, then they would loose on you another. He knew from reading the right journals, all about the industries and populations of Yankeedom, and what he had seen today bore it all out. He took up someone's Springfield from the floor, found it was loaded, fired it, and then decided to leave. While he was considering this idea that had about it an aspect of novelty, the Connecticut people came on another fifty paces. He had noticed a cellar door in the floor of the kitchen. Opening it he went down there into the cool and dark. He wedged himself in by some barrels. Blinking, he saw that there were three Texans there already. One of them, the oldest, a man of maybe forty, put his fingers to his lips in a shooshing motion. All three Texicans were armed and had their muskets pointing up over the barrels at the door of the cellar. "They kin come in but oncet a time," said the Texican.

But the Connecticut boys did not want to fight for a cellar. Once in the farmhouse, they just slipped the bolt on the kitchen side of the cellar door, and that meant Danny and the Texicans would not get out until midnight. They would, however, get out whole.

Meantime, in the farmyard by the pump, Usaph saw now that the bedevilment that had brought them here, the madness of painting their bodies with blood and powder, now locked them here. They could not run like normal uncrazed beings; they were stuck.

Usaph saw four or maybe five wounds appear in the chest of Colonel Lafcadio Wheat. Wheat, who'd wanted to grow up to be someone's scandalous gran'daddy, had suffered these injuries all in the same second, for the Connecticut riflemen could see he was a colonel, could spot the tarnished oak leaf on his collar.

It was natural that Wheat, seeing Usaph and the drummer Rufe staring at him so childlike and terrified, would want to make a speech to tell them to be of good heart. But sadly he had no breath for it. He noticed as he fell that the sash that linked him to Rufe had somehow been split, very likely by a bullet, and Rufe looked down on him like a child orphaned twice over. Wheat drew up one knee, tried to smile up at poor Rufe. But it came to his face as a snarl.

Wheat had read correctly the fears of Usaph and Rufe. Usaph felt more afraid and bereft than he'd ever felt before. Poor Wheat was fluttering his eyes and waving his right hand at Usaph, and Usaph got the idea that Wheat wanted to tell him something that would save him, some bit of advice the colonel had himself until now forgotten to pass on.

But when Usaph bent low he saw that Wheat's belly was a spring of gore, and all that sassy and oratorical blood ran forth on a tide, and the britches were drenched. Wheat's voice was so low that there was no chance of hearing unless you could lip read. "Wife," he seemed to say, and Usaph thought, in judgement, "Well might you say so." Usaph worked his head closer and felt peevish. A colonel was meant to give hard advice. Maybe they were right, all them goddam critics who said Wheat had gone off in the head.

"Tell them . . . Clarksburg," said Wheat. Usaph began to weep. He almost wanted to hit the colonel. Where are all your goddam words gone now I need a few of them? "What are we to do?" yelled Usaph.

"Not the knife," said Wheat, very loudly.

Usaph looked about. He saw Cate and Gus surrendering to the soldiers of the Union, and Rufe still standing there in a mute way which could be interpreted as surrender. There was lots of yelling, some crying. But the noises were fading some. None the less, no one had any words to say to each other, neither the Connecticut boys as they made Cate and Gus captive nor Cate and Gus themselves. They looked well enough, those Yankee boys, they even had their goddam great-coats strapped to their shoulders like boys who meant to go a long way this autumn. It all began to look to Usaph like a goddam tableau— he saw Gus and Cate as two ragged and all at once strange-looking Rebels with their hands up, and the Yankees almost neat as toys out of a box, and their Springfields and their bayonets pointed straight at Gus as if he wasn't the earth's greatest goddam music man.

Someone's cannon was sighted right then on the farmyard. It was perhaps a cannon of the Confederacy on Nicodemus

Heights, beyond the Pike, which wanted to stop the advance
of the New Englanders towards Miller's cornfield. Or else it
was one of Lincoln's pieces trying to nip off the rush of the
Texicans. Because smoke lay so low over the farmyard, the
man who ordered the gun to fire had little play for the exercise
of any knowledge of Greek, Latin, Optics, Ethics or Mathematics he might have picked up in college. That is, he was
firing as blind as any ordinary man would.

Later, when Usaph was suffering the results of the shell,
even in his pain and bewilderment, it came to him that the
thing had been fired from a rifled piece manufactured, you
could bet, in the North; that it was hollowcase shell, about
twenty pounds. The little of its noise he heard before it struck-
led him to believe this. For it made a shrieking of the kind
shells from rifled pieces, the lead of their bases fluted from
their journey up the tooled barrel, made in their passage through
the air. He believed later, from the effect of the thing, that it
carried one of them percussion fuses in its nose. Percussion
fuses were more likely to work when fired from rifled pieces
instead of from the old smooth-bores.

Anyhow, it landed by the pump and pieces of Pittsburg iron
from that device flew all ways, together with fragments of the
shell-case itself. Usaph was of course lifted and then slapped
flat on the earth, and when the dirt stopped plopping was deaf
and could see but in a blur. He did however notice that a rolled
overcoat had been blown on to the roof of the farm. There
were also naked limbs up there, and the top half of a man still
wearing a jacket. The boyish figure of Rufe had been thrown
all the way to the porch and was bent in two.

Next with his hazed sight, Usaph saw Gus was on his back,
his britches torn at the knees, his belly split and all his inward
parts strewn out. Gus lay in a posture Usaph had seen, without
looking too close, with other boys slain by artillery. Head back
on its crown, eyes open, mouth parted as if to yell, arms bent
at the elbows and the fingers spread and hooked like those of
a spruiker making a point. Gus, the most original man Usaph
knew, had taken up without complaining or making any apologies this posture that wasn't goddam original at all.

Usaph opened his own mouth, but the terror and concern
he tried to let out didn't make any sound. How could they have
done this to Gus so easy, in just the winking of an eye? The
news of it, the noise of the shell was—he didn't doubt an

instant—like to end the war. You could bet they had heard the noise in Richmond and Washington, and by now they must be starting to repent of it.

Usaph had been blown a little way and was sitting in a sort of sump by the barn. This little dip of earth was full of chicken feathers, for the farmer must have lately dressed his chickens here. Or likely the farmer's wife and daughters. The daughters of the man who broke the pump handle! What a goddam awful father he must be!

Usaph noticed that the left arm had been ripped away from his jacket. The muscle of the upper arm was sort of hanging down in a flap, dangling by a piece of gristle. Usaph's eyesight was double and kept on clouding and stinging, worst when he tried to look down on this wound. He would get a double version of the damage at the one time, a double version of the gluey tendons and the bone in there.

When his hearing came back in a rush he was frightened of what it might tell him. He felt a hell of a lot safer while he suffered that ringing deafness. Close by him he could hear someone chattering away now. It was a Yankee with his coat ripped off who lay in the sump with him. This Yankee seemed a mess from the waist down. It was a matter of debate whether he'd ever beget children. Just the same he was yammering away to himself, this boy of whom battle had made a steer.

Usaph got the feeling he'd had earlier with Wheat, that maybe he should listen to this man, that maybe there was good advice to be got. So he lifted his own damaged bicep up and held it in its place with his right hand—and that brought him some ease—then he blinked and his eyesight firmed all at once, though not as good as it had been before the shell, and then he looked at his companion and got a milky image of him.

It was Cate.

That goddam Cate had got a pair of blue britches in Manassas and worn them since. And with the one good shoe, gift of Usaph Bumpass, that was left on his remaining foot, he looked as lean and well set-up a Yankee as anyone ever drew a picture of.

Cate was speaking at tedious length about that goddam Punic general called Hannibal. All over the farmyard were Yankees, making a line by the farmyard fence, congratulating each other. Over by the porch some of them were arguing about how to fix the flag to the roof. You could hear as well a hundred separate pleadings and whimpers and callings of names and, worst of all, the farmer arguing with an officer. "How much more of this is a man's goddam property meant to take? My perfect Pittsburg pump is broke off at the base. What oh what!"

Sometimes he would feel dizzy or time would lurch the way it does for drunks. For example, he was beside Cate without remembering the struggle to get there across that space of chicken feathers. He inspected the wound across Cate's groin, something lodged there, something harsh—hardwood or shard of shell or a piece of pump—lodged across the crotch and the upper leg, fixed, a deep part of Cate now. Whoever eased it out would release all Cate's blood and that would end things. Cate had been punished even more severe than that though. All down the legs were wounds and crushed places. The left foot was blown or broken off at the ankle.

Usaph was not so dizzied or double-sighted that he could not conclude Cate was doomed. It was the first time he'd ever really believed Cate might be taken away, that he wasn't eternal like rain or the devil. He stank like the pit as Usaph leaned over him—the stuff in his wound had pierced all his bowels as well. Usaph had to stop himself growing boastful. No one's ever like to desire you again, Mister Artist, he came close to saying.

It was no shame to ask Cate questions now, for God or someone had chosen Usaph above Cate, chosen Usaph to be kind of whole and chosen to crush Cate's manroot and loins. And all that made it right to ask.

"Cate, you son of a bitch? Tell me this. Did you ever misuse my Ephie, did you ever, you black goddam Republican? Did you ever *have* her?"

Cate blinked madly. "Oh, Bumpass, unless I've slept it is yet morning. Shops are not even open in Washington, Bumpass. But look what it's like round here already."

He began weeping.

"Stop it, Cate," said Usaph—he would have hit Cate, apart from that he needed his right hand to hold his left arm together. "None of that college boy horseshit, I warn you. Not a word— do you hear?—of that son of a bitch Hannibal."

"This, Bumpass," Cate persisted, "this earth, Bumpass, that will drink our bodies . . ."

"Not my body, Cate. Not mine."

"We are already done for, Bumpass. It is not a matter of

men and women, and of whether A had B. It is beyond that
for us, dear friend. We are the manure of Washington County,
Bumpass. Like I told you."

He even reached a hand out towards Usaph's shoulder.

"Not me, not me, Cate. Not manure, goddam it! Not done
for. Not me."

He wasn't going to take this goddam college boy argument
of Cate's, that things were so bad that he didn't need to know
about Ephie. As if the whole golden world had come to an end.
Maybe it had, but there was still Ephie, and the blood of Usaph
over which Ephie reigned, in which Ephie was still a fever,
had not left Usaph and wasn't going to; he felt certain of it,
he felt arrogant certain. He felt a meaner bastard than ever he'd
been when whole.

So, still holding his left arm together, he reared up and
struck Cate's chest with his right elbow. The jolt of that elbow
on Cate's ribs somehow all went to his own wound and Usaph
was overtaken by great giddiness and the wish to puke.

Still dizzied, he felt hands dragging at his shoulders.
"Friends, be content," said the voice that went with the hands.

There were two tall blue litter-bearers there and they began
to lift Cate out of his sump, being careful to support his buttocks
so as not to start the groin wound pouring. They laid him flat
on a canvas litter, the bearers thinking by the blue cloth that
showed through the blood and feathers that Cate was Union.
Usaph felt wildly joyful. They were about to carry the bastard
away from him. They were about to carry Cate away to his
own country.

"Bumpass, Bumpass," Cate raved, but Usaph did not look
at him and the bearers thought it was just those delusions of
the brain that go with wounds.

Usaph could not understand where these prim brave bearers
had come from, who didn't cuss or treat the wounded man as
an enemy delaying and burdening them in a dangerous place.
Later he would decide they were two of those Quakers the
Northern states had just started calling up. If so they may not
have been in the army more than ten days. But the Lord knew
what he was doing, inducting them. The Lord wanted Cate,
who had given Usaph a season of torment, to be plucked out
of Usaph's flesh like the thorn he was and would ever be.

Anyhow, both these Quakers had little haversacks full of
dressings and such, and one looked to the stump of Cate's

ankle while the other, a blonde man of maybe thirty years,
spoke to Usaph. "Brother, there's no way we can carry you,
so you must walk to a field post. I'll dress your wounds so
everyone will know you're a wounded Southerner and no danger to anyone."

He opened the flap of Usaph's arm and while Usaph threatened to faint spoke of how good Providence had been to him,
how a blade of shell-casing had sliced the arm but touched
neither the shoulder nor the bones of the limb, and how by a
miracle an item called the brachial artery had not been punctured. Usaph sometimes tried to pull away. He feared getting
into the hands of surgeons. "But we are not surgeons," said
the litter-bearer, understanding fully. From his haversack he
took a bottle of fluid about the size of a whisky bottle. It was
more or less the right color for whisky and Usaph thought he
would be offered a drink. Supporting the flap of flesh and
tendon in his left hand though, the litter-bearer uncorked this
bottle with his teeth and poured the liquor all over the wound.
It seemed to Usaph that his whole body had been set alight,
that his brain was going up in a vapor. Bellowing, he choked
and swooned away.

He did not wake till there was a mighty noise. Cate and the
littermen were not to be seen. His arm was tied firm in bandages
and pulsing away. Yankees were running everywhere. One
bleeding from the mouth flopped on the earth by the sump and,
while dying, looked Usaph full in the eye, as if he expected
suggestions from Usaph the way Usaph had earlier expected
them from Wheat. Later, Usaph would remember, at times
when he was considering the question of what kind of beast
man was, that he had felt cozy there and safe in that little dip.

Then yet again the farmyard was full of yah-hooing Confederates. "We's come to stay," one of them yodelled at the
sky. Tarheels.

Usaph got up about then. Everyone ignored him. He could
walk, he decided, if he kept his mind to it and locked the knee
joints. He walked straight out the farm gate like a man going
on a stroll. What was out there set him shuddering. He could
see some of the flattened stooks of Miller's cornfield beyond
the woods, and the line of the Hagerstown Pike, and the wood
beyond the pike as far as the little white church of the Dunkers,
and everywhere was this mat of young flesh and meat, sometimes mounded where a Texan had fallen on a New Hampshire

boy and a Connecticutter had fallen in his turn on the Texan and a Tarheel had gone down writhing atop the Connecticutter. And the mounds stirred and protested as the still living tried to crawl out from beneath. And everywhere the three Deities of God, Mother and Water were being called on amongst the strewn pieces of youths. And at the call of water Usaph remembered his own profound thirst but had nothing to drink and took again instead to cussing that farmer who'd broken the handle off the pump. Trembling as he went, he took a country lane down towards the pike. He was shuddering away. He believed that America had been changed. That instead of fields of corn the fields of the dead seed of the young men ran away for ever, even to the Gulf of Mexico, maybe, which he had never seen. In the fields all around him the wounded that had their legs still, and the fearful as well, staggered about. By the side of the lane a plump Irish girl, laundress or whore, knelt by a dead Yankee keening.

"Oh it will be remembered," she sang,
"How cursed General Meagher fell drunk from his
horse as battle began,
But still sent my love to be pierced through.
My lovely boy is dead,
The shroud is on his head.
And he is gone
Who knew the sun. My lovely Sergeant O'Shea."

It was such a ghosty sound and it gusted quivering Usaph along the lane as if he were the victim of a wind or a season. He drew level with a hobbling Rebel whose face was wounded and he was carrying a live grunting pig. Where he had got it from and what his exact hopes were for it were beyond guessing. Fruit of the battle.

THOUGH IT WAS only ten-thirty in the morning, it was yet already the worst day America had seen. Three U.S. corps had come in against Jackson's end of the Army of Northern Virginia. First Hooker's and then Mansfield's and then Sumner's. General Abner Doubleday of Hooker's corps, founder of baseball, saw more good pitching arms shattered and blown off in the fields along the Hagerstown pike than in a lifetime of instructing college boys in Cooperstown, New York. Hooker was shaken. Joe Mansfield, white-whiskered and an old regular and fighter of Indians and Mexicans, was shot in the stomach. Sumner was dazed and trembling.

Tom Jackson spent the morning visiting batteries but saying little, just frowning in his saddle and considering amongst all that noise the reports Sandie and Kyd and others brought in. General David Jones was out concussed by an explosion, one report said. There wasn't a colonel left in the Stonewall Division, said another. Andie Lawton had a wound in the shoulder. General Billy Starke was dead. As for units, there were some 600 men left standing in the whole Stonewall Division. Douglass's Georgian Brigade had lost two-thirds of its boys. Hay's had lost three-quarters. Maybe six out of ten of the Texans had been shot.

Tom Jackson wasn't amazed or trembling. All statistics came from the hand of a hard but fatherly God. He told his staff to watch for stragglers. At ten o'clock near the place where the Smoketown road met the pike he himself found a straggler with a light face wound carrying a pig in his arms and therefore sent him back.

Surgeon Maguire had come to talk to Tom Jackson around 9:45. At that stage Stonewall was standing by an artillery battery near the Dunker church. The noise was beyond all telling. Maguire gave Tom Jackson some peaches he'd picked from a tree in passing on his way across from Shepherdstown. While Hunter talked in his ear, Stonewall split the peaches in long fingers and ate them hungrily, getting the nectar in his whiskers. All through the woods on the left of the church there was this crackling and hissing, and Maguire could see Yankees through the Miller cornfield and the woods beyond.

"Over there," yelled Maguire, pointing to the masses of Union soldiers. "They look like hordes."

"Indeed," said Tom Jackson evenly, mashing the peach flesh.

Maguire said, "I admit I'm disturbed by what I've heard, sir. The Shepherdstown Road is crammed with stragglers. Some of them officers. They all say the business is going bad, sir."

Tom Jackson didn't like his surgeon being hysterical like this. "Stragglers will always tell you the business is going bad, Doctor Maguire."

"I'm wondering if the wounded as a group shouldn't be evacuated south from Shepherdstown straight away."

"Down the Valley?"

"That's right."

"Maybe," said Stonewall, still ripping into the peaches, and as if it didn't have anything to do with him.

Hunter Maguire decided to make a speech. "Look, General, we have six churches in Shepherdstown—the Episcopal, Methodist, Presbyterian, Catholic and the rest. Already they're all full. There are men laid out on the steps of the altar. I saw an armless boy propped in the pulpit of the Lutheran church." Maguire could feel the edge of panic that was in his own voice now. He expunged it. He could tell how little Stonewall appreciated edges of panic.

"You should take over the schoolhouses," Tom Jackson muttered, looking all the while up the pike and at the cornfield.

"We have," Maguire said, more deliberate now and calmer. 'The Oddfellows' Hall as well. The Freemasons'. Surgeons are working in the Town Council room. We're also using farmhouses, barns, corn cribs..."

"Corn cribs," said Stonewall dreamily, as if he was reminded of boyhood.

"Livery stables too," said Maguire.

"Well, Doctor Maguire, you must relieve the pressure as you see fit." Tom Jackson worked with his tongue at the peach skin lodged between his lower front teeth. "I'd dislike it an amount though if you let all this influence your thoughts." He gestured towards the northeast, towards the cornfield again, towards the sunken laneway over there where Daniel Hill was so short of fire that he was shooting a private's musket himself. '*They*," he said, "*they* have just about done their worst.''

God knows how he believed that. But at about 10:30 that day the Yankee infantry dragged back into the woods, far up the pike, that they'd started from that morning. When that happened, Jackson and young Junkin and Hotchkiss and Sandie rode up the pike themselves a little way. The cannon on both sides of the road were still blazing, and all the fences were hung with scarecrow corpses and, against the embankments, young boys lay with their heads back and their lips parted.

After some quarter of a mile, Tom Jackson's party came to what at first seemed a thick line of dead against the bank at the side of the pike. It proved to be instead a Tarheel brigade sheltering there. Their reason for sheltering was clear enough. There seemed to be a Yankee battery sighted on them—its guns stood in place way over beyond a farmhouse. Tom Jackson had got glimpses of that farmhouse in its stony yard all morning. It was about as far as anyone in his army had got. He could see through his glasses that there were corpses on its roof. It was from beyond that roof that the Yankee battery was firing now. Fragments of shell clattered down on the pike. Sandie and Hotchkiss and young Junkin sat their horses and waited to be killed by such fragments; but they were not touched. Once they had dismounted, they felt less naked.

A colonel rushed up to them as they stood under the embankment bowing their heads a little before the rain of metal. This colonel said his name was Matt Ransome. These boys here were his regiment. The 33rd North Carolina. They'd tried to get to the farmhouse and the battery on the rise beyond it, but they suspected there was still an immense force over there.

That was a question Tom Jackson was interested in. Hotchkiss knew what the General was thinking and couldn't help being a little shocked by it. Tom Jackson, after fighting off three attacks at a price the Confederacy could bare afford, was thinking now of counter-attack. Of rolling up McClellan's right flank in the Stonewall manner. If he tried that, few of these Tarheels of Colonel Ransome's would be complete men by noon.

Up on the embankment stood a big hickory. It seemed to Stonewall that a man ought to be able to see beyond the farm and even beyond the hill and the Yankee battery from the branches of that hickory. A man should be able to see what McClellan had in reserve over there.

He called for a volunteer to climb the hickory. "Everyone knows from when they were young," he said for those that could hear, "the hickory's one of the best climbing trees you can find."

A dozen boys started forward. They all wanted to be able to tell their grandchildren, thought Hotchkiss, that once they climbed a tree for Stonewall. The first who got to him was a lanky boy without any shoes. He said his name was Private William Hood. He had that easy rustic way and the sort of slack rustic grin you'd expect. He was up in the high branches inside half a minute.

"Can you see any troops beyond?" Jackson called up at him. Jackson himself had climbed the bank and was leaning his hip against one of the long lower branches.

"Whoo-ee," said the Tarheel. "There be oceans of 'em, General."

"Count the flags you see," Jackson said, not really happy with such an inexact report.

Private Hook started counting. "They be 1, 2, 3 . . ."

Just as well he can count, thought Hotchkiss. Bullets began to travel towards the hickory now, making a sharp rustle as they passed through the foliage. There were some sharpshooters firing at William Hood. *Chunk!* went a ball into the ancient wood of the hickory. Jackson didn't seem to notice.

". . . 7, 8, 9 . . ."

Hotchkiss saw that a dead boy hanging on the fence beyond the hickory and in a rough line with Jackson jerked as a bullet hit the unfeeling flesh. But Jackson had this Presbyterian belief that God would take him when the time was fit. Until then sharpshooters could just about go on wasting their ammunition.

". . . 19, 20, 21."

About the time Hood got to 30, a shell exploded above the apex of the tree. It did not stop Hood counting or Jackson listening. When Hood got to 39, the General held his hand up.

"That will do. Come down, sir."

Hook got down even quicker than he'd got up. Well, he has his historical anecdote, Hotchkiss thought.

A sort of whimsical light came into Jackson's eye. He turned to talk to Colonel Ransome. "Why ever did you try to take a battery that's supported by 39 regiments?" he asked.

The figure filled him with a divine contempt for McClellan. 39 flags! And he let them stand by. That's how (under God) we'll win it. By a whisker. By moving regiments around to whatever stretch of fence or pike or lane they're needed at. While McClellan permitted himself—and the Lord permitted McClellan to permit himself—to leave whole corps, perfectly good ones, standing around in the fitful sunlight of mid-morning.

There was a sunken laneway running near Mumma's burned-out farmhouse. It was beyond Miller's cornfield and ran sort of north-south, leading towards the township of Sharpsburg itself. Dan Hill had charge of its defense, but under Tom Jackson's orders. Jackson rushed some of the units, who'd got intact through the fight at the church and in the cornfield, across to the laneway to help Dan Hill's division. They found that thoroughfare filled to its lips with the dead and the wailing; yet it was held.

At the same time the Yankees moved against the laneway, a Union general called Burnside was meant to cross the Antietam by a stone bridge at the south of the hamlet and take the Rebels from that end. He did not get around to trying it till mid-afternoon, and then again the Confederacy—in the shape of its northern Virginia forces—survived by a hair, namely because Ambrose Hill's boys arrived back from Harpers Ferry at the exact right hour, about 4:30.

Weeks later, Searcy would read accounts of the fight in both Northern and Southern newspapers he managed to obtain. Already the North were into the habit of calling the day Antietam, for they had been engaged so much with that obscure country stream, with crossing it, pivoting on its banks. The South had begun to call the event Sharpsburg, for their line, their argument, their future had been anchored on the little town.

These accounts and any others he would ever read would always sicken Searcy. Why, knowing everything, hadn't McClellan managed to trap the beast, the Secession itself, the Serpent of Slavery between Antietam Creek and the big river that morning and so ended it all? It was a question he would bore people with for some years to come. It was the old question of how such incompetence could go hand in hand with a good cause.

Usaph had already left Sharpsburg. By noon he was on the Shepherdstown road and spent the afternoon and the whimpering night in a stables on the edge of that town.

Some orderlies moved through the stables with pails of water and dippers, and when Usaph had drunk deeply he slept. It was almost like he was devouring wedges of sleep; but like sour plums in a cake there was always a dream at the core of the sleep and it would wake him. Yet the day lurched on into the night, and he huddled in a corner behind an old harrow in the hope of not being bothered by surgeons.

In the morning he crossed the river at a place called Boteler's Ford, the water pulling at his knees and wearying him. There were many others crossing too, soldier-farmers who'd done what they could and now were going home. On the Virginia bank, an elderly provost officer with gentle eyes was trying to halt this drift. As Usaph came out of the river he heard him say to an infantryman: "Where's your furlough, son?"

"This is my goddam furlough," said the boy softly and raised his rifle and pointed it at the officer's chest. The officer could see the boy meant to shoot if he were stopped and so let him go through. That old officer knew the price wasn't worth it.

Usaph's sleeveless arm, tightly dressed in the Quaker dressing, was now *his* furlough. The bandages were hard brown like bark from all the stiffened blood and to anyone who saw it, it looked a frightful wound. So he was let through.

The wound was not just his furlough, it was his ticket, too. For Lee and the army left Maryland not fifteen hours after Usaph, and as the ambulance and ordnance wagons of the withdrawing force caught him up, he would be given rides, and when not in army wagons, farmers and people in carriages would often ask him to ride with them. And so he made his way down the Valley. And people fed him on account of that mess on his upper arm.

Whereas mere stragglers stole or starved.

— 9 —

IT WAS MURKY in Orange that last evening. Rain had settled in again at the hour when Mrs. Whipple got her last caller of the day. Young Surgeon Curtis, the head surgeon in the Orange Girls' Seminary, stood in the doorway. He was carrying a basket covered with a cloth.

"Dear Mrs. Whipple," he said. "I've brought you your dinner."

She liked the look of Dr. Curtis tonight. He had none of that solemnity most of her visitors had, the solemnity of people visiting the already dead. Perhaps it was his experiences in the military hospital that gave him such an easy manner at the door of death cells. The depression that had come on her after Scarcy's visit was lifted, and she smiled at the young surgeon.

"You are very welcome, sir. Do you think you can persuade the turnkey to let you in?"

The turnkey obeyed her wish without being asked. Once in the cell Dr. Curtis bowed to her. "I have wine, ma'am, light, dry, white. It is North Carolina wine, but good enough to eat fried chicken with."

The bottle sat in a bucket of ice which filled one corner of the basket. In the other corners were flourbread rolls, fried chicken and gravy, roast potatoes and green peas. By the standards of the Confederacy it was an expensive meal, and the surgeon must have commanded most of the resources of the Lewis House to get a meal like it together.

Chatting, they unpacked, then they sat and began to eat, not before having an argument about who would use the one chair.

While they ate, she asked questions concerning patients she knew. Some had died. Well, it isn't such a big issue to die. Others had got better and been put into detachments moving northwards. They would likely come back more grievously wounded or ill than they had been in the first place. That was the irony of the conflict.

Then she said: "I don't want to talk at length about this. But have you seen a hanging?"

"Once."

"What is your frank . . . *frank*, mind you . . . opinion of the sufferings of the hanged person?"

He looked at her direct, as if he could tell it was no use being coy. "I've spoken to this hangman," he said. "And I think I can assure you, ma'am, as a surgeon, that you will suffer nothing. The world, ma'am, is amazed at your courage, if not your politics. I can assure you, you won't be made to suffer."

"It wouldn't have mattered," she said simply. "I will see Yates Whipple again."

"Mr. Searcy," he said and coughed, "sends his warmest affection and hopes you would reconsider his offer . . . there is still time to contact Richmond by telegraph."

She lifted her hand. "Don't say it!" She thought a while. "Tell him I am as you see me. That I am settled in my mind, in other words."

"I'll tell him," he said. Then his face lit up. "Did you hear what the Marylanders did to Canty? They locked him in the privy at the Lewis House. Bound his hands, gagged him. There was a line of people, ma'am, if you don't mind my being indelicate, hammering at the door, and Canty not even able to answer them except for a grunt."

Mrs. Whipple clapped her hands and laughed. "He must have sounded like some case of dysentery."

"He *is* some case of dysentery, ma'am. Never mind, his brain will soon burst with all that booze."

"You are a good man, Surgeon Curtis," she said.

He closed his eyes and lowered his head, taking the compliment. "And you among the best of women, ma'am." Then he spoiled it a little by saying what they all did. "I don't know who is right, ma'am. But whoever is right, whoever prevails you will always be remembered. And if we are defeated . . ." He shook his head, "our name will be dirt for having done this to you."

"Not your name, sir," she said. "Your name won't be dirt."

"My name," he nodded; "my name with all the others."

The chicken was eaten and only half a glass of wine was left when the turnkey brought them coffee. Mrs. Whipple, already euphoric, found that an immense sleepiness overtook her as she drank the coffee.

"I'm not accustomed to wine, sir."

"Perhaps you should lie down, ma'am."

"In the presence of a gentleman?"

"Far from a gentleman, ma'am, a surgeon." He grinned. He helped her to her cot. She fell heavily down on it and went almost immediately into a profound sleep. Strange she didn't suspect, Curtis thought. She should have suspected, given her familiarity with hospitals. He felt her brow and her pulse. Then he called to the outer office and they let in a nurse to sit by Mrs. Whipple all night.

"She'll not be very aware in the morning," Surgeon Curtis told the nurse. "In fact she should not even be properly conscious. It will take you and one of the guards to get her to the scaffold. Hold her firmly all the way."

The nurse said she would.

"When she's cut down, be sure her body is as thoroughly cleaned and arranged as she has a right to expect."

Mrs. Whipple was snoring. The surgeon shook his head and gathered up the feast to take the basket and dishes, the glasses and the bottles back to the Lewis House. After he had delivered them to the kitchen there, he went into the lounge, where he found Searcy sitting in a corner, a hand over his mouth, his eyes lowered.

"Sir, there were two grains of morphia in her coffee," the surgeon told Searcy. "She will not suffer, no matter if the hangman makes mistakes."

Searcy began to sob, so loudly that people in the lobby began looking in at him through the doors. "I think of what the rope will do to her sweet little body," he said.

Curtis murmured: "Sir, there's no profit in that." He glared at the spectators in the lobby and frightened them off. "Be as brave as Mrs. Whipple is," he muttered. "I think we should have some brandy, sir."

— 10 —

THE IDEA THAT the Army of Northern Virginia should leave
Maryland came up clear on the afternoon of the day following
the fight. Stonewall and James Longstreet and Lee kept getting
reports of latecomers reaching Sharpsburg, a dribble of slow
and lame who were at last arriving. Stonewall rode up the pike
again with one of the artillery chiefs and they considered the
question whether they could with their fifty guns break up that
northern end of McClellan's army. Even Jackson decided it
couldn't be done, not with what was left and with a few thousand foot-blistered and weary stragglers. Across the creek of
Antietam, two new Union divisions arrived that day and took
up their positions on the low hills. Others still would be coming
up from Washington. Whereas Lee could expect nothing, nothing ever until today's fourteen-year-olds in Virginia and Alabama and the Carolinas grew up.

At two o'clock on Thursday afternoon, Lee made up his
mind. The army should depart Maryland that night, leaving
their campfires burning. Jeb Stuart's cavalry would screen the
exodus and the reserve artillery of Sandie Pendleton's father
would be placed on the banks of the Potomac to stop the river-
crossers being molested.

At the hour Lee made his decision Usaph was getting his
first ride in a wagon. His wrist in a linen sling he had made
himself, he lolled in a fever on the tailboard of an ambulance
bound for Leetown, Virginia, where surgeons were waiting.
He meant to slip off that tailboard and dart away before any
surgeon could get a sight of him. At first when he had waved
at the driver, the man said there was no room for him, but had
softened, reined in, inspected his load and found two dead boys
in the straw-filled inside of the vehicle. He laid them by the
road under a blanket for cavalry to bury.

Riding, Usaph did not listen to the mutterings from the
interior of the conveyance. He like Lee was in a state of decision. His decision was to reach the Valley pike by tomorrow

noon and to sleep in Winchester tomorrow night. He needed nothing to eat, he told himself. His canteen which was still at his left side unpunctured was full of the waters of the Potomac. He thought of nothing except the hundred miles and more he had to travel to Ephie. His decision to travel was locked up hard and dry as a stone in his brain.

There was a third American harried by decision that particular Thursday afternoon. Abe Lincoln. Because he could just about get away now with calling the fight along the Antietam a victory, he had the chance to issue that edict about the slaves without looking ridiculous. In his office in the White House he first read over the reports of the engagement that had come in from McClellan. In a covering letter, McClellan had written: "Even Lee admits he's been beaten."

"I wonder who in tarnation he admitted that to?" Mr. Lincoln asked John Hay. Neither of them respected George McClellan, but he had given the document they had prepared months before about freeing the slaves its only legitimacy. So they set to work revising it. They'd been careful not to make it wordy, so that it now sounded like a statement of a reluctant duty. They knew the opposition in cabinet would come from Montgomery Blair, the Postmaster General, native of Missouri. He'd rattled the old sword about how the border states, Maryland, Missouri and Kentucky, wouldn't stand for it. "You remind me of a man out west," Lincoln had said in cabinet one day to Montgomery Blair. He was always telling cabinet members they reminded him of a "man out west," by which he meant Illinois. "He's got two oxen in yoke, and they're pulling a wagon he's got loaded up with hay. And one of the oxen just dies, like that, in the yoke. And hours later the man's friend comes along that road and sees the man sitting on the stock-still wagon with one live oxen and one dead. And the friend says, Why don't you take that dead one out of its chains and then just continue the journey. And the man on the wagon says, The load is too heavy for just one ox. So for all I know, Mr. Blair, that man might be on that road still."

Well, the dead oxen was the institution of slavery in the border states, Kentucky, Missouri and Maryland. The live one was the impulse to free black people, an impulse so strong in so many parts of the Union. That impulse alone was strong enough now to drag the loaded wagon.

The document, as Mr. Lincoln and John Hay revised it that

afternoon, said that if the Confederacy didn't cease its rebellion by New Year's Day, all slaves in the rebellious states would be considered free. In Southern areas occupied by the Army of the North, their freedom would become immediately real on that grand New Year's Day, the Day of Jubilo. Slaves elsewhere would need to wait until their counties were liberated or until the Rebels gave in.

Abe Lincoln knew how this document would get them thinking in the Foreign Office in London. In one corner of his brain he knew too that there was a general on the Mississippi, a more or less successful one and that made him a rare breed. Ulysses Grant. Grant kept writing to the President that the work of slaves was the core strength of the South. This was because he'd had to punch his way through levees and along canals all dug by slaves. If slaves should find out Abe Lincoln considered them free, they wouldn't work so well as diggers of tough fortifications and all the rest.

When the draft was ready, Hay had confidential copies written out and sent all over Washington to the houses of the Lincoln cabinet. Abe sat at his desk reading a copy of his favorite humorist's latest book—*Artemus Ward; His Book*— just recently published and selling like cakes. He was reading this belly-thumper of a chapter called "Outraj'ous Behavior in Utika." It was about some citizens of Utica, New York, who smashed up a visiting wax show of The Last Supper because they didn't hold with Judas visiting their town. Abe decided that when the cabinet met next Monday, he would read them a bit of Ward to loosen them up before they made their comments on the text of emancipation.

— 11 —

ON THE AFTERNOON of September 24 that year, the black woman Bridie who belonged to Aunt Sarrie and knew nothing about the intentions Mr. Abe Lincoln had for her, went out on the porch to fetch in a mat she'd been sunning out there. The valley was full of that blue autumn shadowiness, but she could see clear enough a ragged man standing still at the gate. The man wore his wrist in a foul linen sling and stood there wavering a little on his legs but with his feet fixed in place.

Bridie thought of shooing him off on her own authority but then wondered if she should maybe speak to one of them white ladies.

There was no speaking to Mrs. Ephie Bumpass. Mrs. Bumpass was up in her room having more of the vapors. Just ten days back she had lost her child. Miscarried as Aunt Sarrie called it. Bridie had had to bear away the stillborn little lump and Montie, her husband, dug for it a decent but nameless little pit. That had been done on Aunt Sarrie's orders. Ephie had been too ill and in too sore distress to know what was happening. Though Bridie and Montie knew whose child it was, Aunt Sarrie didn't even have to warn them about keeping their tongues still about it.

Since that misfortune—or whatever else you'd call it—Mrs. Ephie Bumpass had been low at heart and wistful and full of shame. She felt that the women of the house were judging her. Well, that was true. Bridie judged her. Hard. But Bridie also knew that Aunt Sarrie, the real power, had decided to forget all about it, for ever, the way the forgiving Lord pretends that the sinner's sin doesn't exist once that sinner just turns a second to the Lord Jesus.

Anyhow, seeing the scarecrow at the gate, Bridie went to seek Aunt Sarrie for instructions. Aunt Sarrie was in the back garden among her beanpoles shelling green peas. She put down the bowl as soon as Bridie told her and went through the house to the porch, treading softly in case Ephie was asleep.

Out of the same consideration, she did not call to the man from the porch itself, she went halfway down the path. From there she could tell the man was quivering about the shoulders in a way that reminded her . . . yes, of a man quietly weeping.

It was a slow business for her to get to the conclusion that this was a wounded soldier and that those were military tatters. It was slower still to get to the fact that it was Usaph. First there was the unkempt whiskers to see past, then the dirt, then the lousy clothes. Fragments of the gunpowder with which Usaph had adorned himself at the urgings of the late Lafcadio Wheat still stuck in the seams of his skin. His hair, light-brown when he left home, had gone black with clotted mud and maybe even blood. He was leaner than his aunt had ever seen him. He had the pinched face of the very ill.

When it dawned, she ran up to him. But the mystery of how he'd got this way stopped her a yard short. She could smell him too. He smelt of urine and bowel dirt and the foul sweat of an entire summer. She could see the tears making mud on his filthy cheeks. The mess of black bandage on his left arm shocked her.

"Aunt Sarrie," he said, and it sounded as if the words caused him pain. "You got coffee at all?"

She started shedding tears too and she touched his right arm, but he looked such a mess that she forebore to caress him in case it hurt him too bad. She was already accustomed to his stench.

"Yeah, darling Usaph," she said in a small voice. "I got coffee. Come." She led him up to the house by the right hand. As they passed Bridie, Bridie recognized him. She began to wail. "Oh I never seen a nigger look so bad! Oh I never!"

In the front parlor Aunt Sarrie steered him for the sofa. "Lice," he said. He nodded his head, indicating the length of his body. "Lice."

"If lice get at the sofa, why I'll burn it, Usaph. To hell with the sofa! Bridie, get him maybe buttermilk. And brew coffee."

From her bed Ephie heard the noise of some small domestic emergency and came out of her room and stood at the head of the stairs.

"Aunt Sarrie!" she called.

Aunt Sarrie came to the foot of the stairs, looked up all solemn at Ephie.

"Mrs. Bumpass," she said, almost like someone passing sentence, "your husband has come. He's in something approaching a state. You'll find him in the parlor."

Bridie's husband Montie came in from the barn and began wailing like his wife at the sight of this poor man. Ephie too, coming in, was blinded by the stench of Usaph, but part from remorse and part from love and pity, forced a head down on his lousy thighs, crooning: "Oh, Usaph, my darling husband, my poor man." From the back landing ole Liza, Usaph's slave, already in her mind if not in her body passed over into the land beyond Jordan, increased the volume of her ancient song as if she somehow knew.

So in that parlor, the three women and the slave man took

Usaph's clothes off—it was Montie's job to burn them—and sponged him with warm water and gave him drink and wrapped him naked in blankets. The wound they dared not touch, but sent Montie over to Goshen with an urgent note for a Doctor Benson who lived there.

This doctor got back after dark with Montie. He cut the wood-hard bandages away that the Quakers had put on Usaph, and whistled as he looked at the swollen wound, and then lanced it to let the pus out, and said it seemed fit. He gave Usaph a draught of laudanum that put him to sleep for twelve hours.

"Feed him," the doctor told Ephie.

"Oh yes, I sure will, sir," said Ephie.

Ephie sat up all night and sometimes, when they were sure that Usaph's sleep was deep and his breath deep and steady, she would go to the kitchen to have a cup of coffee with Aunt Sarrie, who could not have slept tonight anyhow.

"Well, your husband's home, gal," Aunt Sarrie said.

"And I praise God, I do, ma'am. It's more than I ever merited."

"You don't say that. You been a stupid gal by my lights, but don't go looking for punishment. I think that you make a good woman, Ephie, all taken in. But you're a beautiful and kind of lusty gal, not that that's any excuse. But it makes things harder."

Ephie was blushing but so happy to hear Aunt Sarrie forgiving her her transgressions. Now she wanted Usaph to have her, oh so badly, but we must wait for the muck to drain and the flesh to heal. But it's hard, Lord, hard. She dug her fingers through her dress into the flesh above her left knee. It was just a little way to give vent to both her happiness and her desire.

Of course, the happiness she felt wasn't quite the whole hog of happiness. Usaph had either to be told of the baby or to have it kept secret from him. And Ephie's urge was to tell him.

Before she could say so, Aunt Sarrie forestalled her.

"I can see it in you though, you silly gal, that you have this itch to let him know of the child you carried. Well, you know by now that itches ain't there to be attended to too willingly. You are to forget that child, I tell you. You're not to start indulging your queer idea of what is truthful by mentioning anything of that child to Usaph. Mister Lincoln done his best, gal, to kill the poor boy. Don't you join in that damned effort. You understand me?"

He woke up weeping. Ephie was sitting by him. It was the third night she'd sat by him.

"What troubles you, my love?" Ephie whispered.

"I don't know where they're buried," said Usaph. For he had dreamed something confused, that the bodies of Gus and Wheat and Judd and that strange little drummer Rufe had not been justly treated.

His dream had foundation; for when the Yankee burial parties moved into the farmyard they threw Rebel bodies down that well from which the pump had been blown off. The farmer had argued about it with the Yankee officer, but since the well was already fouled, he decided he might be as wise to fill it up with dead Rebels for a contract price, and seal it over with stones, and then dig another well just up the hill a little. So he went to Union General Hooker and got a contract price of $1 per head for each Confederate corpse he slung down his well.

Into that pit then went Texans and Wheat and the drowned Ash Judd and Gus Ramseur for whose music the world would now wait, and Rufe the Arkansas drummer. And from that mute place they called out in Usaph's sleep. But as he got better and more distant from them, their cries and his own diminished.

There was still the problem of his connection with the army. Ole Cap'n Stilwell, the conscription official for Bath County, came round to Aunt Sarrie's to take his name so that his place of residence and the nature of his wound could be conveyed to the War Office in Richmond.

"You need building up, boy," said Cap'n Stilwell. "I think we should keep you here till spring."

Ephie smiled in gratitude. But Usaph looked at his hands and his face turned red, as if he had decided never to go back, as if somehow the old officer's kindness was an insult.

He had the sweetest and most wistful Christmas of his life that year and the balm of Ephie's body made him weep as he lay beside her, and his last doubts of her were diminished by that, and he was already on the way to forgetting Cate for ever (if that was possible).

In the spring he went back to the army, which was upon the Rappahannock round Fredericksburg, the town where the Confederates under their old General Lee had had a great Christmas victory over the Army of the Potomac under their new general Burnside. Danny Blalock, having got out of his cellar, was up at Fredericksburg and had become an officer. He found a place for Usaph to sleep in a little winter-dwelling dug into the earth and roofed with canvas and boughs. It was cosy enough by the standards of the Army of Northern Virginia, but within a month, Usaph caught pneumonia and was sent to Chimborazo Hospital in Richmond. His lungs would remain wheezy the rest of his life.

In May of 1863 he was discharged and caught the train to Staunton, where Ephie met him and danced him to a good hotel. There they ate and drank as well as you could in an embattled nation.

They had four children in the end. All of them got to adulthood. One of the boys became a lawyer, the other a farmer, and there were two girls.

Usaph died of a lung condition in 1873 when his eldest child, his daughter, was eleven.

Ephie married again three years later to a man called Bridges, a Democratic Senator in the State House of Virginia, who saw her at a political social one evening in Staunton and loved her beyond all cure. Bridges ended life as a U.S. Congressman in 1903, but Ephie lived till 1922, and every year on the anniversary of Usaph's death put a notice about him in the *Richmond Enquirer*, how he never got over the damage he suffered doing his duty, and how loved he was.

Of the other survivors of that summer, Danny Blalock died at Gettysburg, a major by then. In a Pennsylvania hospital, Cate mended stubbornly. His father had got him exempted from imprisonment on the condition that he took an oath of loyalty to the Union. This he did with a full heart. His wounds had however castrated him and this, and the lack of a foot, made him a bitter young man. He left Philadelphia for Paris in 1866 on the pretext that he was going to study art, and lived there off an allowance from his father, with a series of woman companions, for five years. In 1870 he completed a two-volume novel which he published himself in Paris. The French compositors made a mess of it when they set the type.

In 1871, the day after his 23-year-old French companion left his apartment in Montparnasse, he shot himself. Neither Usaph nor Ephie ever heard of what had happened to him.

The Honorable Horace Searcy caught the *Calliope* after first dispatching a scalding account of the Dora Whipple affair to *The Times*. In 1863 he wrote a narrative of his journeys in the

South and admitted in it his connection with Secretary Stanton. He attended and spoke at British meetings in support of the Union cause and the emancipation of the slaves.

Although to the average American he seemed a characteristic stiff Briton, he had never enjoyed his destiny as the younger son of an English peer. In 1867 he emigrated to Canada, made money in railroad and mineral stocks, bought into iron in northern Michigan. He did not marry until 1882, by which time he was a Liberal member of the Canadian Parliament.

He had a statue of Mrs. Whipple built in the market place of Langport, the town in Somerset which Dora Whipple's forebears had left to settle in Boston. He lived long, and as he got richer, wrote less and less.

On May 2, 1863, while Usaph was still in Chimborazo with lung trouble, Tom Jackson was wounded in the arm by a Confederate horseman on the evening of one of his best days. He had led his corps fair round General Hooker's flank at Chancellorsville. The rout of the Yankees was complete by dusk, and then one of his own cavalrymen shattered his arm by accident. Hunter Maguire took the arm off in the parlor of the Chandlers' house in Chancellorsville, but pleural pneumonia set in. Maguire applied heated cups to the right side and administered antimony and opium. Stonewall's wife, Anna Morrison, came up from North Carolina to nurse him. On her way to the Chandlers' she saw soldiers digging by the side of the road. She realized they were exhuming a coffin. When she asked them they told her it was the body of General Paxton, an old Lexington friend of hers, shot dead just a week past and now being dug up to be shipped home to Rockbridge County. The sight struck Mrs. Jackson with a terrible fear.

Amongst her husband's last spoken sentences were these, uttered in delirium: "Order A. P. Hill to take the right flank. Major Pendleton, go see if there is higher ground between Chancellorsville and the river. Where *is* Pendleton? Tell him to push on those columns!"

But his last words of all before dying on the afternoon of May 10 were: "Let us cross over the river and rest under the shade of the trees."

Bibliographical Note

In telling this narrative, the author received invaluable assistance from a number of works, but especially:

Stonewall Jackson, volumes 1 and 2, by Lenoir Chambers (1959)

The Blue and the Grey, volumes 1 and 2, edited by Henry Steele Commager (1973)

The Confederate Reader, edited by Richard B. Harwell (1957)

My Diary North and South, volumes 1 and 2, by W. H. Russell (1863)

I Rode with Stonewall by Henry Kyd Douglas (1940)

A Southern Woman's Story by Phoebe Yates Pember (1959)

The four volumes of Bruce Catton's *Centennial History of the Civil War*

The Life of Johnny Reb by Bell I. Wiley (1943), and by the same author,

The Plain People of the Confederacy (1944) and *Southern Negroes, 1861–5* (1938)

May all these authors, the living and the dead, flourish in reputation.

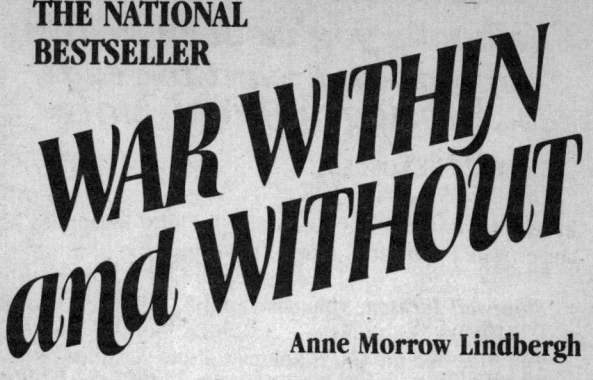

Bestsellers from Berkley
The books you've been hearing about—and want to read

__**THE FIRST DEADLY SIN**	04692-3—$2.95
Lawrence Sanders	
__**MOMMIE DEAREST**	05242-0—$3.25
Christina Crawford	
__**NURSE**	04685-0—$2.75
Peggy Anderson	
__**THE HEALERS**	04451-3—$2.75
Gerald Green	
__**WHISPERS**	04707-5—$2.95
Dean R. Koontz	
__**PROMISES**	04843-8—$2.95
Charlotte Vale Allen	
__**THE TENTH COMMANDMENT**	05001-7—$3.50
Lawrence Sanders	
__**WINNING BY NEGOTIATION**	05094-7—$2.95
Tessa Albert Warschaw	
__**PRINCE OF THE CITY**	04450-5—$2.95
Robert Daley	
__**VITAMINS & YOU**	05074-2—$2.95
Robert J. Benowicz	
__**SHADOWLAND**	05056-4—$3.50
Peter Straub	
__**THE DEMONOLOGIST**	05291-5—$2.95
Gerald Brittle	

Available at your local bookstore or return this form to:

Berkley Book Mailing Service
P.O. Box 690
Rockville Centre, NY 11570

Please send me the above titles. I am enclosing $_____
(Please add 50¢ per copy to cover postage and handling). Send check or money order—no cash or C.O.D.'s. Allow six weeks for delivery.

NAME_____

ADDRESS_____

CITY_____STATE/ZIP_____ 1D

More Bestsellers from Berkley
The books you've been hearing about and want to read

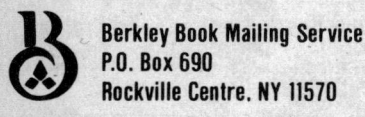

MS READ-a-thon— a simple way to start youngsters reading

Boys and girls between 6 and 14 can join the MS READ-a-thon and help find a cure for Multiple Sclerosis by reading books. And they get two rewards — the enjoyment of reading, and the great feeling that comes from helping others.

Parents and educators: For complete information call your local MS chapter. Or mail the coupon below.

Kids can help, too!